Fantasy: The Best of 2002

ABOUT THE EDITORS

ROBERT SILVERBERG's many novels include *The Man in the Maze*, *The Alien Years*, and *Up the Line*; the most recent volume in the Majipoor Cycle, *The King of Dreams*; the bestselling Lord Valentine trilogy; and the classics *Dying Inside* and *A Time of Changes*. He has been nominated for the Nebula and Hugo awards more times than any other writer; he is a five-time winner of the Nebula and a five-time winner of the Hugo.

KAREN HABER is the critically acclaimed editor of *Meditations on Middle Earth*, the Hugo Award-nominated collection of essays examining the works of J.R.R. Tolkien, and the forthcoming *Exploring The Matrix*. She also created *The Mutant Season* series of novels, and co-wrote the bestselling *The Science of the X-Men*. She is a respected journalist and an accomplished fiction writer. Her short fiction has appeared in *The Magazine of Fantasy and Science Fiction*, *Full Spectrum 2*, and *Women of Darkness*.

THE ROBERT SILVERBERG COLLECTION

Sailing to Byzantium

Science Fiction 101:

Robert Silverberg's Worlds of Wonder

Cronos • Nightwings

Dying Inside • Up the Line

The Man in the Maze

ALSO AVAILABLE

Science Fiction: The Best of 2001

Fantasy: The Best of 2001

Science Fiction: The Best of 2002

Robert Silverberg & Karen Haber, Editors

CONTENTS

Introduction

Here is the second in an annual series of collections of the best fantasy short stories of the year—the latest contributions, ingenious and inventive, to this most ancient of all manifestations of the human mind at play.

Fantasy is the oldest branch of imaginative literature, as old as the human imagination itself. It is not at all hard to believe that the same artistic impulse that produced the extraordinary cave paintings of Altamira, Lascaux, and Chauvet, fifteen and twenty and even thirty thousand years ago, also produced astounding tales of gods and demons, of talismans and spells, of dragons and werewolves, of wondrous lands beyond the horizon—tales that fur-clad shamans recited to fascinated audiences around the campfires of Ice Age Europe. So, too, in torrid Africa, in the China of prehistory, in ancient India, in the Americas; everywhere in the world, in fact, on and on back through time for thousands or even hundreds of thousands of years. Surely there have been storytellers as long as there have been beings in this world that could be spoken of as "human"—and those storytellers have in particular devoted their skills and energies and talents, throughout our long evolutionary path, to the creation of extraordinary marvels and wonders.

The tales the Cro-Magnon storytellers told their spellbound audiences on those frosty nights in ancient France are lost forever. But surely there were strong components of the fantastic in them. The evidence of the oldest stories that *have* survived argue in favor of that. If fantasy can be defined as literature that depicts the world beyond that of mundane reality, and mankind's struggle to assert dominance over that world, then the most ancient story that has come down to us—the Sumerian tale of the hero Gilgamesh, which dates from about 2500 B.C.—is fantasy, for its theme is Gilgamesh's quest for eternal life.

Homer's *Odyssey*, with its shapeshifters and sorceresses, its Cyclopses and many-headed monsters, is fantasy. The savage creature Grendel of *Beowulf*, the Midgard Serpent and the dragon Fafnir of the Norse Eddas, the immortality-craving Dr. Faustus of medieval German literature, the myriad enchanters of *The Thousand and One Nights*, and many more strange and wonderful beings all testify to the endless fertility of humankind's fantasizing imagination.

In modern times fantasy has moved from being a component of the human mythmaking process to a significant form of popular entertainment. The wry tales of Lord Dunsany, the grand epics of E.R. Eddison and H. Rider Haggard, the archaizing sagas of J.R.R. Tolkien, the sophisticated novels of James Branch Cabell, and the furious adventure stories of Robert E. Howard demonstrate the reach and range of fantasy in the past century and a quarter. In the middle years of the twentieth century fantasy underwent a further evolution during the all-too-short lifetime of *Unknown Worlds*, edited by John W. Campbell, in which such well-known science-fiction writers as L. Sprague de Camp, Theodore Sturgeon, Alfred Bester, Robert A. Heinlein, and Jack Williamson applied the rigorous speculative techniques of s-f to

INTRODUCTION

fantasy's wildly playful wizards, elves, and demons. And in today's publishing world it has established itself in a vastly successful commercial form that manifests itself as immense multi-volume series that carefully follow expected narrative formulas.

The present anthology is intended to show that reach and range as it is demonstrated nowadays in the shorter forms of fiction. You will find very little that is formulaic here, although we have not ignored any of fantasy's great traditions. There are stories set in the familiar quasi-medieval worlds to which modern readers are accustomed, and others rooted in the authentic myth-constructs of high antiquity, and several that depend for their power on the juxtaposition of fantastic situations and terribly contemporary aspects of modern life on Earth, stories that would have fit very readily into John Campbell's *Unknown Worlds*. There are even two stories that examine the concept of angels from the standpoint of science fiction. (It is our belief that science fiction, rather than being a genre apart, is simply one of the many branches of fantasy literature—and surely a pair of s-f stories about angels go a long way to support that argument!)

These eleven stories—which we think are the best short fantasies published in 2002—are reassuring proof of fantasy's eternal power even in this technological age.

—Robert Silverberg
—Karen Haber

"Our Friend Electricity"
Ron Wolfe

I loved Tori. Tori loved Coney Island. The moral is such an old one, maybe you know it already.

Don't take any wooden nickels.

-1-

Our first time at Coney, I guessed Tori liked slumming. Anything Tori liked was fine with me. Especially when we got there, it was fine with me. The place did something for her, made her the ballerina of the boardwalk.

Every wisp of a breeze, every movement she made that day played in her summer dress the color of white sand. She whirled and her hair streamed in waves of blonde, bright as glass in the morning sun. She breathed in the salt air as it mingled with the smells of cotton candy and seaweed and spoilage, and her eyes were like fireworks of green and gold sparks.

"See, we *are* having fun, Brad," she said. "Didn't I tell you? Run, silly, catch me!" I ran, and I caught.

Coney's old parachute drop haunted the beach like a dim metal ghost in the salt haze. The roller coaster was broken. The Wonder Wheel turned its sad, slow revolutions as if it were grinding time to a fine dust. But then, I looked at Tori. She loved it, every bit of it.

We ate "Hygrade Frankfurters" from a stand with painted pictures of sausages and pizza and ice cream cones that looked like freak show attractions, and Tori loved it.

We saw women with white and yellow snakes and tattoos, and men with nipple rings; and some hunched figure in a filthy ski parka; and a straw-haired girl in a nothing bikini, just standing there, hands clasped between her breasts in the way she must have learned singing in church; and the Latina woman with the tragic face, the wet eyes, trying to win a goldfish in a ring-toss game.

Cheers and organ music reached us from the new baseball stadium. I imagined a different crowd there: families, boys with baseball heroes, girls with the clean look of suburban shopping malls. Tori wouldn't go there.

"It's awful," she said the only time she even glanced toward the stadium, where the Brooklyn Cyclones were winning.

The score didn't matter. I don't know baseball. The Cyclones won just being there, Brooklyn's first professional baseball team since the Dodgers left forty-five years ago. They meant change.

"I want the old—the real Coney Island. Don't you?" Tori said, pulling me toward a shooting gallery. I didn't need the reminder of guns.

Old and real is where the fun is all worn out, and marked down, and sold broken with sharp edges to people who can't have anything better. But Tori loved it, and so all I saw was Tori.

"Did you know? I have a talent, Brad. A super secret, psychic talent," she said, making the "s" sounds in "super secret psychic" a conspiratorial whisper.

"You could fool me," I said. We'd met yesterday.

"You tell me the name of the last girl you cared about even a little. I'll tell you how much she really meant to you."

My tongue caught.

"Please?"

"Tori, it was a long time—"

"Just her first name. What could a name hurt? You'll be surprised how good I am."

"Anna," I said.

Tori took a soft breath, as if breathing in "Anna," who had taught me how to thumb wrestle and to sort my laundry colors, and whose cheeks had blushed when she laughed.

"It wasn't all that serious," Tori said, "but, oh!—she broke your heart. They all break your heart."

I swallowed and tried to smile as if she'd told a joke, and then did smile, I think, at the flattery that beautiful women trampled through my life—a parade of heartbreakers. I needed Tori's healing touch, yes, almost a mother's touch, tracing my face, as if to check me for a fever.

"It's just a game, Brad, silly," she said. "You try it. Ask me."

"I will. Later," I lied.

We aimed squirt guns into the red-rimmed mouths of plastic clowns, each of us trying to be the first to pop a balloon. Tori brushed my left arm. Crowding me to the right was some withered brown mummy who had shed his ancient wrappings for a pair of red-striped Speedos, and then a kid who looked like he might kill somebody if he lost.

My pistol was sad to the touch. Nearly all the once-shiny black paint had worn off the grip, and the metal beneath was a dull blue-gray, the color of a bad sky. But Tori aimed well, and her laugh was so high and sweet, I swear even the old guy and the kid threw the contest. They wanted her to win like I did. They wanted to see, like I did, what winning would do for her smile. We all got the prize that day.

And then, I asked her.

"His name?" She worked the teddy bear she'd won like a puppet, making the bear's head nod as if in greeting to me. "Skip," she said. "The bear's name is Skip, too."

Skip, I thought, and I'm no more psychic than a sidewalk, but something came to me. I swore I'd never play this game again.

"Skip had money," I said, "lots of money, and he knew how to throw it around."

"Could be," Tori said, and she made the bear say it, too, "He might have been rich. *I'm a rich, rich bear. But I was a long, long time ago.* How did you know?"

"Skip…," I said. "Skipper, skipper of a yacht, makes him rich Skipper."

"The gentleman wins the bear," Tori said, tucking Skip under my right arm, and then taking my left arm herself, a cool touch of possession.

She taught me how to promenade the boardwalk.

Casey would waltz
With a strawberry blonde,
And the band played on

-2-

We met cute. Doesn't everybody?

I'd been browsing through the sale shelves and boxes in front of the Strand bookstore, 12th and Broadway, that Friday evening. I was working my

4

way from the one-dollar books to the forty-eight-centers.

It was down there among the most sadly forsaken—the ones you had to stoop to, literally—that I found the first book I'd ever candied and cudgeled through publication years ago as Brad Vogler, Boy Editor. It was a science-fiction paperback called *Crimson Cosmos*.

Then: "Yeww!" she said, our moment of introduction.

My line of sight rose from the book's clotted red cover to a surprise glimpse down the neckline of Tori's white shell top (lacy white bra, front catch; first sight of the pendant she always wore, a white disk in a silver mounting), and all in a rush: neck-lips-eyes. Ice blue eyes in this light.

She didn't see me at all; she was leaning toward me, staring at the book cover. I felt like I'd been caught with a dead frog in my hand, just when a barefoot boy finds out nothing matters but girls.

"Are you buying that?" she said.

No, I yearned to answer, but I couldn't.

I remembered how it felt to write the letter of acceptance for that book, the first I'd ever bought. My letter told a fifty-five-year-old newspaper sports reporter in Denton, Texas, that he had sold his novel, his first. I believed I had discovered the next Robert Heinlein, if not the next Norman Mailer, and he thought he had uncovered the next John Campbell.

It turned out that all we had found in each other was another paperback book with stock art for the cover: blood oozing down like a sloppy coat of Sherwin Williams, and a couple of flat yellow eyes staring out of the red. But the author had gathered nerve and got married on the strength of that sale, and rounded out his belated brood with two girls adopted from China. He still wrote—high school football scores and "Merry Christmas" in the family photo card he sent me every year. And I couldn't say no, so I said something crazy.

"I've read it, but I'll buy it for you."

"Really?" she said, or maybe, "Really!" or "Realllly…." or Latin or dolphin talk. I just knew I was being sized up.

I paid with a five-dollar bill. Forgot the change. Some eons of floating time later, I woke up having coffee with her, our fingers almost touching across the little table. Talking. Still talking over empty cups.

She liked white in the summer, red in the winter; oatmeal sprinkled with Red Hots, and she didn't like earrings. Mostly, she asked about me.

I felt so right with her, I didn't try to sound interesting. Maybe I came off coherent.

Listening, Tori withdrew a silver case from her white purse, and a card from the case. The case was inscribed with initials in script, TCS. The card had nothing but her name on it, as if I'd ever forget Tori Christine Slayton.

She added her phone number to the card with a silver pen, slid it to me, and our hands brushed and lingered, mine slightly over hers.

"Can I call you tomorrow?" I said.

"No. Meet me tomorrow."

"Anywhere."

"Brad, silly—" A bit of a smile crossed Tori's face, quick as a butterfly. Then, mock-serious, she said, "You mean that? *Anywhere*? All right, I dare you."

She took back the card, turned it over to plain white

and wrote something tiny on the back. She folded the card twice, so I couldn't see what she'd written, and placed it in my hand, folding my fingers over the hard-edged little package with a squeeze.

"No fair peeking," Tori said. "Read it tomorrow morning. Meet me there. We'll have fun, I promise."

I went strictly by the rules, afraid of breaking the magic spell if I didn't. In the morning, I read the card and caught the subway, a line I'd never ridden before, to a place I'd never been before. But I'd heard of it. Everybody's heard of Coney Island.

Tori was waiting for me in front of the Headless Woman sideshow. ("Still alive. See her living body without a head. Alive!")

And that was our first time at Coney.

I'll be with you
When the roses bloom again

-3-

Roses. I sent her white roses on Monday. She called; I called; she called. We had lunch on Wednesday, a quick bite.

She had a small antiques shop on the Upper West Side—high end, American Federal furniture and some Victorian, she said. She was antiques, and me?—in a way I hadn't told her yet, I was collectibles. The comparison was close enough to make me uncomfortable.

We arranged to meet again Friday after work in front of the Strand. "Dress up for me, won't you?" Tori said. It seemed to be a hint.

Thursday, I laid out the best of my two summer

suits, the white one that made me wonder how Tom Wolfe kept his so clean.

Friday, I had the night planned as well as I could. So much about her made thoughts drift away. Her perfume: I fancied it was made of champagne and cinnamon. The way she said my name, the way she played with it, making it sound like an ice cream flavor. The way people watched us, talking when they thought we couldn't hear.

"...*Vogue*, I'm sure of it." "...stare at her, at least close your mouth...." "...Grace Kelly...."

Those same eyes, finding me, blinked and narrowed with itchy guesses. *He* must be...her brother. Her boss. *He* must be rich, but he sure doesn't look it.

I clean up all right, fair shape for a desk job, and thirty-seven isn't so old. But Tori is twenty-five, twenty-six, close to that, and nobody ever took me to be such great company until she did.

I had this idea of a movie at the Angelika, and then dinner in the Village, candles and spumoni. I was full of love songs, old ones that I must have half-heard sometime and filed away, just in case I ever felt like grinning like a street loon.

Ida, sweet as apple
Ci-hi-hi-der

-4-

Tori had warned me she might be late; she expected some buyers who liked to haggle at the last minute.

Waiting, I made up stories about Brad the Mad. Every now and then, Brad the Mad escaped from the insane asylum, but the police knew where to find him. Whenever he broke loose, Brad the Mad dressed up in a white suit and stood in front of the Strand Bookstore, waiting for the woman who was only a delusion.

Tori arrived moments before I conjured up police sirens. She looked laser bright. Somehow, she'd guessed I would wear white, her color, and her dress was a whipped-cream white linen with a silver chain around the waist, silver bracelets, ornately of antique design; white silk scarf, heels. The moon-white pendant was ivory. It was faintly carved: "*Elephas*...."

"I guess you like the look," Tori said. I'd been staring.

I rushed into my dinner-and-a-movie plan as if the combination might amaze her.

"Could we do the movie another time?" she said. "I've missed you, Brad. I just want your attention."

The candles and spumoni part held up, and I caught a break on the waiter. He was gay, and he left us alone.

"So," Tori said, "Mr. Important Book Editor, you still haven't told me enough about your job."

I wished I were a handsome photo on a dust jacket, riding princely over an author's bio full of lies. He flipped crêpes, he topped trees.

"English major from Lincoln, Nebraska, seeks literary career," I said, trying not to shrug. "Braves the big city, finds job as editor with fly-by-night science-fiction and mystery publisher...."

"*Crimson Cosmos*," Tori said. She lifted her wineglass, a toast. Her fingernails showed silver edges.

"You've read it?" I said.

"No, but it's my favorite book." And that smile again, fire and innocence.

"The meteoric rise continues," I said, "a career arc

9

that takes our hero from rockets and murders, to cookbooks, and then grade school science texts—"

She questioned with an eyebrow. "You know what I like about you?" Tori said. "You have smart eyes. You haven't found your niche yet, but you will."

"—*Our Friend Electricity*, thank you, please hold your applause. And now, I'm at Recollections Publishing. I do price guides for nostalgic baby-boomers."

"Like?—"

"*Jungle Fever: A Collector's Guide to Tiki*."

"Oh, no!"

"Tiki music, tiki dolls, even snow globes. I don't get it, but there were GIs coming home after World War Two, already feeling nostalgic about the South Pacific. And now, their kids are collecting old tiki stuff all over again. But I don't feel nostalgia for much of anything." I caught the mistake. "But I like antiques."

Tori laughed. "Oh, Brad, silly, you do not. I don't blame you. Antiques aren't nostalgia, antiques are investment. You can love an antique and not like it in the least."

I splashed the last of our bottle, a French Chardonnay that Tori had chosen, into our glasses, and raised mine.

"To the brand new," I said, already planning a second bottle I couldn't afford to keep the table and the company.

Her expression drifted, blanked for a moment. Her eyes seemed to mist, but it might have been a trick of the candlelight.

"I have to go," Tori said, half rising. My face must have slid into my lap like slush.

"Oh my, I said that all wrong, didn't I?" She reached across the table to touch my nose, a playful flick. Her finger softly traced a smile across my lips. "Brad, silly. Let me try it again. We should go."

And now, she had neon inside her, excitement that flickered and caught with the words, "Coney Island! We could, still."

My dumb grin seemed to encourage her.

"Tonight. We had such fun the last time, Brad, let's do it, let's go. Now. Can we?"

I may have yammered something about the subways being bad at night. But Tori had the answer: She had a car. She knew ways to Coney Island, and we could be there in no time.

We whisked down the street to her car, if that's what you'd call it, parked at the curb between a red Mustang and some blocky sort of coupe.

Tori's car was a low, sculpted swoop of black metal and polished wood. Street lights played laser tag over the hood. Then, metal gave way to the cherry coach, made tight like an admiral's skiff. It was open-topped, brass-and copper-trimmed, upholstered in leather, and the wheels were wire-rim. The Great Gatsby could have wrestled for the keys to Tori's car with Deckard from *Blade Runner*.

I set foot on the running board. The car welcomed me like a butler with muscle. The seat had been tailored to me.

"It's a Panhard and Levassor Sport," Tori said, pulling into the street. "1914. Like it?"

"What's it doing outside the museum?"

She drove fast, as I should have guessed she would, and she knew the streets, how to work the lanes, how to keep moving.

I must have looked pale as my suit.

"It's some of the original chassis, but then a lot of

11

restoration," Tori said. "Not a faithful restoration at all, though. The engine is something else, and it has protections built into it that aren't even close to the market, some that probably aren't legal. Watch your fingers."

The car seemed to repel other traffic. Even Pakistani cab drivers were afraid to come near it, scared of scratching it.

"Don't worry. It's not mine," Tori said. "I borrowed it from one of my customers—part of the deal for an eighteenth-century bedroom set he just had to have. I meet some interesting people."

Next thing I knew, we were sailing over the Brooklyn Bridge, the wind whipping Tori's hair like white fire; and then onto the Queens Expressway. We hit 70, 75, 80. Tori's white scarf streamed, it pulled loose, and I turned to see it go soaring like a ghost into the night. I reached as if I should have caught it, Tori laughing, and me laughing; and I pulled off my necktie and let that go, too.

Mermaid Avenue welcomed us with its offers of salt-water taffy, beer, and body-piercing, pawn shops, gun shops. Dim lights shone in old windows above the striped and rusted awnings.

A gaunt woman stopped to watch us from the sidewalk. Her hair was dyed orange, and she wore a black plastic trash bag twisted elegantly across her shoulders like a feather boa. To her, we were the aliens. I was Bug-eyed Brad from Planet Starbucks.

Bug-eyed Brad scans the ruins for life as he knows it, life that bags the trash, that fixes broken windows. But he is the stranger in a strange land of knives and needles. He expects to be eaten.

"...Giuliani saying he wants to make Coney Island 'something very special again,' can you believe it?" Tori said. "It's special the way it is. Special the way it was. Oh, look!—"

We passed the remains of a shabby little candy store. Inside, the shelving and fixtures had been pushed to the center, giving the painters room to work. Already, it had the promise of something the mayor would approve.

But Tori had seen something else, and we turned toward the crawling lights of the old amusement park.

Coney Island was a different world in the dark, too bright and too shadowed. It left me straining to recognize anything I'd seen before. A mist of raindrops fell and passed, cleansing no part of the night.

Tori parked facing the roller coaster. High over us, the big letters read "Cyclone" in a way that chilled me like a cold smile: The letters looked eaten away, so many bulbs were dead. But Tori loved it, and I was high from the car ride. We ran like Mouseketeers into Disneyland.

The roller coaster was shut down again, or still, but Tori coaxed me onto the Wonder Wheel.

"You can see *everything* from the top," she promised.

At the top, our metal cage groaned and swung over a nightscape more speckled than lit with yellow bulbs and red neon. The rides below us looked tiny and meaningless. We faced toward a jumbled rim that appeared to be housing projects, mostly dark. But the air smelled fresh.

"Feel better up here?" Tori said, holding my arm,

leaning tightly against me. I nodded. "I knew you would," she said.

Her pendant seemed almost to glow. An elephant was carved into the ivory, the creature's trunk lifted, and the words read, *"Elephas non timet."*

Tori smiled as if pleased that I'd noticed. She scooped the pendant lightly in her fingers, holding it toward me. "'The elephant does not fear,'" she said. "It's an ancient saying. The elephant's trunk raised that way means good luck. Long life. Wisdom."

"It looks old."

"Not so very, around 1900. A century is nothing to an elephant."

"So!—all this, and she's an elephant expert, too. What else?"

"May be you'll find out," Tori said, as the Ferris wheel descended us into the smells of hot grease and machine oil.

We took the funhouse ride into its hell of plywood demons and painted flames, and Tori loved it. We joined a drunken clot of teenagers on a whirligig called the Calypso. I came off with a spattered stripe of something blue and sticky across my left sleeve.

"Here, this way, this way!" Tori said, pulling me. "Let's see how good you are at Skee-Ball."

The Skee-Ball setup was between a couple other games that had their metal shutters pulled down, scrawled with spray-painted gang signs. We had Skee-Ball to ourselves, just us and the sour yellow glow that spilled over the row of games, and the attendant. He slumped on a dangerously tilted stool at the entrance, head fallen to his chest, asleep or dead.

I fished a quarter to drop in the slot that was nicked and dented from all the wasted coins that had gone through it. Nine balls clacked down the chute. Tori bounced on her toes like a little girl trying to see the top of her birthday cake, and I tried to catch the mood.

We took turns. She rolled a ball, and then I did, and I learned how she played: Anything I scored above a ten was good for a baby hug. The score was eight balls and three little hugs, and I knew how it might feel to hold her.

Tori poised the last ball. She glanced at the pink prize tickets that had curled out of the battered machine as we scored. I dreaded waking the attendant to redeem them.

"Here's the prize I want," she said, turning the hard wooden ball in her hands like it was made of phantom quartz, like it was telling her secrets.

"You'd have to steal it," I said.

"Maybe you'd steal it for me."

She gave me the ball, wrapping my hesitant fingers around it, and cupping her cool hands over mine. "It's old, it's very old," she said. "I think it's old as the park. I think it remembers all the hands that have touched it, just like we're doing. Hundreds, thousands, lives and lives and lives, and every touch leaves something. Every touch tells something."

I may have flinched. Tori's grip tightened. Her breath came warm, close to my face.

"What do you love about a book, Brad? That it can hold lives? Well, so can this, only real ones."

She let go, and I saw the ball; it was the decrepit brown of age and skin oil, nicked, scratched, dented flat in a couple places.

"...*he* doesn't care," Tori said, eying the big-bellied attendant. He had a Yankees ball cap pulled low. His

dark glasses suggested he had been asleep since daylight. He had on a red T-shirt, and a baggy clown's
pair of farm overalls with the ragged legs cut off to
make shorts.

"Just hold the ball close against your leg, away from
him, and we'll walk away. Please, Brad?"

I hadn't stolen since college. Petty shoplifting had
been a brief, edgy craze in my sophomore year. You'd
ask the check-out clerk what time it was, and in the
moment it took her to look at the wall clock behind
her, you'd snitch a pack of Dentyne. You'd buy a roll
of waxed paper, and she'd never notice that you'd
dropped two slim jars of olives down the cardboard
tube. You'd try for the cigarettes, even though you
didn't smoke—

I was good, and I was caught. A dumb thrill nearly
cost my degree. Now, I freak when I've bought
something that accidentally sets off the store alarm.

But we passed the attendant. "Shhhhh!" Tori hushed
too loudly. He never stirred.

We were outside the Skee-Ball game.

We were steps away; we were gone.

I gave the ball a tiny flick. It smacked my hand like
a soft kiss. I don't know what roused him.

The attendant roared a curse behind us. "Oh my,
oh my, that bad boy's mad!..." Tori warned lightly,
as if in answer to an amusing dare. She kicked off her
high heels to run. I had no choice.

We tore, dodging fat men and slow men and blue
jeans, belly buttons, baby carriages, we ran kicking
trash, our hands clasped. Her excitement shot me like
a current, jolting the fear out of me.

This was like another ride to Tori, like the Calypso
only faster. But something gripped me. Caught me at
the neck. The attendant locked a thick arm around

me, holding me back, dragging me down. I lost Tori. He smelled of whiskey and vomit. My knees hit the asphalt, and he was on top of me.

He moved to pin my arms and shoulders. I knew this position from grade school: I was going to take a beating in the face. No teacher was going to pull him off me. He drizzled me with sweat and saliva, trying to capture my right arm. My fist clenched the ball.

I swung at him, catching him hard on the temple with a crack that I only hoped was the ball breaking. But the ball didn't break. He fell beside me, rolling, howling.

I pulled to my feet. He made it to his hands and knees, head down, as if he suddenly had decided to study bugs on the ground. With his left hand, he clasped his head. Blood welled between his fingers. A slow drop. A drop, a drop. A stain.

For a moment, it seemed that blood was falling all around me. A real rain had begun. Tori shook me, and she caught my hand again, led me and ran with me through the rain and the yells that cracked like thunder, and nobody stopped us.

Once we hit the expressway, she slowed below the limit. She let the rain wash me. She swerved off to a gas station, where she pulled up the car's top. She brought me a Coke.

"See, we *are* having fun, Brad," she said, drenched and muddied and altogether the most beautiful blessing I'd ever imagined.

I found something in my hand. The ball. The damned, wonderful ball. I tossed it to her. She was a good catch, too.

"Yours, I believe," I said.

Wait till the sun shines, Nellie,
And the clouds go drifting by

-5-

We drove to my apartment in the East Village, listening to cool jazz on the Panhard and Levassor's Bose FM stereo. A parking space was waiting for us. It was that kind of night.

"I have something for you, too," Tori said. She snapped open the glove box, withdrawing some object she kept hidden.

I saw yet another Tori then, one hesitant with a gift, afraid to go through with it, anxious that I wouldn't like it. What she might have done that I wouldn't like, if a street fight didn't count as a problem, I had no wild idea.

"Here—" She showed me the copy of *Crimson Cosmos* I'd bought her. A smooth bit of cardboard peeked out of the pages. A bookmark.

"Pick a card," Tori said, "any card...."

Withdrawn, it was a Rolodex card. On it, I read the name of a Fifth Avenue publishing house, the first to which I'd applied for a job in New York, and the one to which I still submitted an updated resume every year. The man's name on the card, I could no more approach than the planet Venus. Below the name was a number.

"He's been one of my best clients for years," Tori said. "I've told him about you. He wants you to call."

My wet thumb smudged the ink on the card, only confirming it was real.

"But don't call him, Brad. Make him call you. That way, you have the advantage. And he *will* call."

I stared at her. She made a cross-eyed face that scattered my dumbfoundedness.

"You were right about Skip," Tori said. "He was rich, and he taught me about winning. So, Brad, silly, are you going to invite a lady in from the rain, or what?"

-6-

I used to collect bad writing to share with friends, mostly other bottom-feeders in genre book and magazine fiction. Six or eight of us had a regular beer night at Tad's Tap on Bleecker Street. We called it the Pen and Pitcher Club.

"Her globes suspended from her like bells on a Christmas tree, I mean the fair-sized round kind."

Collector's price guides don't produce keepers like that. I quit showing up at Tad's for being a bore. A few others made the climb to better jobs and bigger publishers. Finally, only the washouts kept the faith.

The author of "Her globes suspended..." may have been the best of us, after all. He had the fool's nerve to stick his pan in the stream, hoping for gold, and he dredged up mud. But it looked like gold to him.

And here I am, Tori, dipping my rusty pan into that same flow that can't convey the touch of sunlight, or the smell of chocolate, or the taste of tears, hoping for something that gleams.

-7-

We dripped and squeaked our way up the two flights of stairs to my apartment. As my key clicked the lock, I suddenly wished the door wouldn't open.

My first apartment in New York was in the meat-packing district. I left my shoes inside the door to keep from tracking livestock blood. My second was next to a coke dealer whose clientele wasn't much on apologies for having pounded the wrong door.

This one, I'd considered a spectacular move up: three rooms, or four if you count the living room and kitchen as separate because of a shelf divider. The neighbors were reasonably quiet. The previous tenant had been entrenched there since the '60s, and must have sat a lot. The lime shag carpet was good as new.

One day, I blinked the carpet to oblivion, just quit seeing it—

Until my door swung open, and I snapped on the light to hit Tori with a sock of green that would have flattened St. Paddy.

But the carpet made no impression. "Where's Skip?" she said. *"Remember me? Where am I?"*

The toy bear. Skip was in the bedroom closet, top shelf, stuffed far in the back.

I found him quickly, though, and placed him on the dresser. Tori arranged him with the Skee-Ball between his legs. Wet-haired Tori was in my bedroom, wriggling her toes in the shag.

"Let me get you a towel," I offered.

"I'd like to use the room," she said. "I need a little more repair than a towel."

I showed her, like there was some trick to finding the bathroom, and she closed the door. I heard her open the little cupboard where I kept my mismatched towels; heard, then, the familiar creak, cry and rattle from the hot water faucet over the tub. Rustling sounds. I stood there, as she must have expected I would.

"I knew you'd have books," Tori said through the door. "You have wonderful bookcases."

"They're oak. They're what I splurge on."

Sound of the faucets turned off. Sound of body in water.

"Umm, this feels good," she said. "You should do this, too."

I glanced back to the bedroom—the neckties that hung off the doorknob, the scatter of socks and magazines in the corner, the whole disarray. I began to scoop and hide.

The bathroom door slipped open with a wisp of steam.

The dullest part of me expected to see her step out dressed and dried and ready to leave. The rest of my awful imagination conjured up, I don't know, some Botticelli Venus-in-the-hallway with discreet hands.

Instead, she stood gift-wrapped in my best white towel, still sparkling with droplets of water, as if I had this coming—as if I knew what to do with it.

"You might try kissing me," Tori said.

I moved to her, my hands finding her warm shoulders, hers finding my face, my neck, my back. The towel fell between us.

We transformed my empire's five steps between bath and bed into another promenade: the lady wearing nothing but her pendant, and her dizzy escort with the ragged knees. Tori made the ceiling light go away. We closed to kiss.

The shag carpet worked its magic on us. A stinging blue snap of static electricity sparked between our lips.

"Our friend electricity," Tori said, rubbing her mouth.

"Our friend electricity," I said, pressing mine to the sore spot on hers.

Our friend electricity joined us and melted us. We soothed. We dared. We tumbled.

Bodies and bed sheets, her hands and her kisses, we danced to the brink of a thousand little deaths. She led me on; she held me back, only to rush again. In a gasp, she called me Skip.

I tried to pretend I hadn't heard. But hard eyes shone on the dresser: Skip watching me. I tried to hide my anger, but it found a way to show.

Skip!

"Brad, I'm sorry...."

Skip!

"Brad, you're hurting...."

Skip!

"Brad! Brad! Brad, silly...Brad...."

She clung to me, bound to my whim and forgiveness, but I was the one then who couldn't let go. I followed her into a soft, singing rhythm, a lullaby whisper.

"He was a long time ago—ohh!—"

In the wee small hours of later, I woke to find Tori sobbing. I kissed her neck. I kissed a warm tear. "I don't care...," I said. "He doesn't matter."

"It isn't him, it isn't you," she said. "It's nothing. It's me."

"Tori—"

"They all break your heart."

I touched her nose, copying Tori's little gesture from the restaurant. "If the girl thinks my poor heart is broken right now, the girl's not too bright."

"Just hold me."

Before had been only a taste of her. When I slept again, it was the deep fall of the feasted, and it was knowing that no Annas could ever break my heart again.

I slept on the currents of Tori's breath. Above me, her eyes were the sky. "Tell me what it's like to dream about Lincoln, Nebraska," she said. I guess we talked more.

In the morning, Tori was gone. I remembered her voice like music through a heavy wall, the rhythm but not the words, not the sense of it. Not then.

She'd taken Skip and the Skee-Ball. In their place, she'd left a name card folded twice.

I didn't have to read it.

-8-

"Mr. Vogler, this is Sara in library reference. I found the expression you asked about, and it means what you thought. But it's short for an even older saying—one that dates back to Pliny the Elder, the Roman author. Also, it became the motto of the Malatesta family, the tyrants of Rimini, Italy, in the Middle Ages. They believed it justified the criminal behavior that kept their family in power. *Elephas indus culices non timet.* 'The Indian elephant does not fear the mosquito.' It means, in context, 'does not fear to crush the insect.'"

So, Mr. Vogler, Mr. Important Book Editor, you with the hollow eyes in the mirror, tell me all about yourself.

Sit down and—no? All right, then, pace your cage in circles, but tell me. You like: The color blue, pancakes at midnight, and all you really want is to hold this little card so tightly that the ink bleeds into your fingertips; that's how much you want to hold her, any part of her.

You don't like: Needles, strep throat, Coney Island. Old, happy-creepy Coney Island. Wrecked and rotted Coney island. Tori loves Coney Island.

See these books? This shelf? All these books about New York? You've never read one. You knew these books would tell you all the ways you don't belong,

Which of these books throws the best, do you think? Way to go, sport! Hit the wall, win the lady a bear. Coney Island, pp. 139–141.

"...by 1904, home to three dazzling parks: Steeplechase with its mechanical horse race; Luna with its elephants, acrobats and a million incandescent lights; and Dreamland, for which the lovely waltz...."

Tell me what it's like to dream about Lincoln, Nebraska, and I'll tell you what it's like to dream of Luna.

"...200,000 people a day. They came for the beach, the parks, the fun rides, the crowd. The biggest attraction of all was electricity."

Our friend electricity.

"...time when a single bulb might have seemed a miracle or a terrible omen of change, Coney Island's electrical glow carried thirty miles out to sea."

Our friend electricity. What is it, really? Hm? Brad? Don't you wonder?

Hey, I just about wrote the book, remember? "Electricity is the flow of electrons—"

Brad, silly. Electricity is light. Light waves.

(Tori's sweet, soft hair, brushing my lidded eyes.)

Elephas non timet, Brad.

(Her lips to my ear.)

Want to ride the waves?

24

It was noon when I began searching for her on the subway platform over Surf Avenue. I stood there, grinning for a moment, as if she might come to meet me, carrying a picnic basket with a calico cloth.

A block west, I joined the boardwalk throng. I let the crowd sweep me to the aquarium, and jostle me back to Astroland, the amusement park, and Sideshows by the Sea. The Human Blockhead had nothing to show me.

I looked for her at Nathan's Famous, where the street corner reeked of wieners and mustard. Two policemen were eating hot dogs, holding their dripping dogs at a distance like medical specimens to keep from staining their blue uniforms. Head down, I hid in the crowd.

Damned and Delighted: A Collectors' Guide to Mermaid Avenue.

Clean people tried to avoid me. They eyed me the way I had stared at losers on the boardwalk. I found a restroom and checked myself in the tin mirror. Uncombed. Unshaven. I looked drunk. I did what I could with cold water.

By evening, I knew where I'd find her, where I'd known all along. Look for mermaids in the drowning depths. Thunder snarled as if to remind me of blood and rain, and the possibility that I might have killed a man—that the next policeman I saw might be carrying a sketch of me.

Tori stood just under the Skee-Ball sign, wearing the same white dress she had worn our first time at Coney Island. Her ivory pendant gleamed white. To her side, a new attendant watched the games —watched her. He was a shirtless beanpole with his eyes opened wide like a chicken's. Tori's left hand braced tauntingly against her hip. Her right hand flipped some tiny thing I couldn't see.

She came to me with a crystal smile, a face of such delight, I felt the sting of tears.

"I won," she said, kissing the back of her closed right hand. "Take me on the roller coaster, and you can have the prize."

The Cyclone was running. I don't know how we got there. We waited turn after turn, because Tori wanted the first car.

Finally, the train banged to a stop in front of us, and we climbed on. My hands clenched the safety bar. Tori squeezed against me, tight and warm.

"You don't like roller coasters," she said, a teasing tone that dropped to something else, something like sadness. "You don't like any of this, I know. I'm sorry."

She looked away from me. I felt her tremble as the car jolted forward. It ground its *racheta-rakkata* way up the first climb.

"Here—" Tori said, coaxing my hand loose from the bar. "What I promised you, the prize I won."

I looked at the object she'd given me. It was a rough wooden disk, with the image of an Indian's head stamped on one side. Around the head, the letters read: "Don't take any wooden nickels." A spatter of rain struck the coin.

"For luck," she said, and her tongue traced my lips. Her body, close against me, told me secrets; she had nothing else under the dress. She kissed me, hard, as we took the fall.

The coaster shook us like a mean dog. It shuddered its timbers, throwing us side to side. Once, it swooped a curve and gave us the same view as from the top of the Wonder Wheel, only better. Someone seemed to have knocked down the buildings like so many blocks. We could see the ocean.

Climb. Fall. Curve. Tori shrieked, and the nickel bit into my hand.

Climb. Fall. My face stretched back. Curve. I had a sense of shooting past a maze of towers, faces in the windows.

The last fall eased into the platform, the end of the ride. But we didn't stop. I saw the crowd, the ride attendants, as smears of surprise.

Climb. Fall. Curve. We screamed over the course again. Darkness triggered the lights, and the "Cyclone" sign crackled on. Tori locked close to me.

"They'll stop us," I said. "They have ways—" She didn't hear me.

Climb. The park washed in light. No one tried to stop us. They had no ways at all.

Fall. The towers again, become a giant's garden of lights. We cut through silver curtains of drizzly rain that whipped and stung our faces, and yet, in some crazy way, made us laugh.

Curve. We soared over the towers. Ant masses of people swarmed far beneath us. The white lights turned my eyes to burning water.

Climb. Fall. Twist. Fracture. Red. Black. Fire. Crystal. Rainbow.

Falling.

In the air, falling.

Casey would waltz
With a strawberry blonde
And the band played on.

He'd glide cross the floor
With the girl he adored
And the band played on.

Calliope music swirled through my head. I was spinning, up and down, and spinning. I clutched a spiraled pole to keep from losing balance.

His brain was so loaded,
It nearly exploded.
The poor girl would shake
With alarm

Tori! "It's all right, Brad." Tori! "I'm here." Tori! "Look at me. Look at me. Brad, silly. Please, while you can."

I tried, but the whole world kept revolving. Horses, lions, bears, swans, ran circles around me.

He'd ne'er leave the girl
With the strawberry curls—

I'd been wrong about the roller coaster. Terribly wrong. We were on a carousel.

Mine was the sterling white stallion, and Tori had mastered a gryphon with a golden head, riding perfectly sidesaddle. But Tori was different.

Her hair was combed up, arranged into heavy waves under a white hat with a silk bow. Her white dress had full sleeves with lace cuffs and flounced shoulders. The satin skirt swam past her feet. The square-shaped neckline, trimmed with brocade roses, showcased her pendant. But the ivory had fallen out of it, leaving just the silver.

A question shaped my mouth, but no words fit the question.

Tori said, "This is what it's like to dream of Luna."

She reached; I took her hand. The carousel toyed with us.

"What was it you said, Brad? 'The girl's not too bright.' She finally learned the secret. She took ninety-seven times to get it right. And you know what? Right feels like dying."

The carousel slowed. I lost her touch. Riders scrambled on and off, bodies and motion between us. I stumbled to the ground, calling for her.

"Tori!...." The crowd swallowed my voice, as it had my last sight of her.

Say this for madness. When madness is all around you, then madness is what you've got. You go with madness.

I accepted my new world of lighted towers, fairy-tale minarets rimmed with stars, Arabian spires circled with lights. I threw myself into a foreign crowd of women who dressed like Tori in long skirts, and some who bound themselves into breathless S-shapes, their waists cinched to nothing; boys in shorts, girls in ruffles, men wearing straw hats and bowlers, stiff collars, bow ties, suspenders, vests, watch chains, canes.

My clothes were something like that. They were like wearing my brother's clothes that I'd never have bought for myself, familiar and wrong all at once. But I seemed to fit with the crowd.

I pushed through knots of laughing strangers, searching for Tori. Someone slapped me on the back, as if I were part of a joke. I called her name, and another voice blended with mine. We sang rounds.

"Tori!"

"Lemonade! Peanuts!"

My throat caught. Sweat streamed my face. No one

else seemed to feel as hot as I did. I brought concern to other faces; I may have looked sick. The air wasn't helping.

The salt smell hadn't changed, but it mingled with human and livestock scents that assaulted me, like a circus locker room.

I wandered beneath acrobats, past tumblers and jugglers. Camels and elephants thumped by. Bands played, and midgets frolicked.

Lighted signs grandly promised "THE STREETS OF FIRE!" "TRIP TO THE MOON!" "THE LAUGHING SHOW!" "FIRE AND FLAMES!" "WHIRL THE WHIRL!" "INFANT INCUBATORS!" "LUNA PARK'S WORLD-FAMOUS SHOOT THE CHUTES!"

The crowd pulled me to watch the wrestlers, the bareback riders. Then, like crows, we were off all at once, rushing to the next attraction, gaining heads and legs along the way. We jammed, we stalled, we hurried on. I strained to hear those voices around me that seemed to understand the excitement.

"...were going to hang her, you know." "Hang? They couldn't. Would take a chain...." "...this, instead...." "...thunder and flash, do you think, when they give it to her?"

I pulled a man's sleeve to engage him. "I don't like it, sir, and I won't watch it," he said. His jaw set, and he bulled his way against the rush, but he lost.

We poured into an arena that smelled of dirt and animals, stronger than ever. We overflowed the tiers of seats, molding ourselves into a human wall around the open space.

"It's time, they're coming...." "...murdering elephant, three men she's killed." "They'll make a pretty light of her."

"OUR FRIEND ELECTRICITY"

Across the arena, a gray shape lumbered into recognition. The elephant walked passively toward the center, led by two men: one in a red uniform with gold trim and a high cap; the other, a shorter man in a brown tweed suit and derby.

The elephant's massive head came up as if she suddenly had broken the concentration of a deep thought. Her legs froze.

The man in the red uniform said something to her. I sensed it was not a command, but a comfort. His smile belonged in a hospital. He gently touched. He stroked the huge elephant's leathery trunk.

The crowd hushed. "Now, Topsy, now, now, old Topsy girl...," he said, but she backed away with a start that brought people to their feet, as if to run.

"I can't do this to her, Mr. Dundy," the man said to his tweed-suited companion. "I won't let her be—"

"You w-will if you work for m-me," Mr. Dundy ordered, his stammer like nicks in the blade of his voice.

"No, sir, I won't."

The man in the red uniform stood a moment, as if he might defiantly sweep the elephant into his arms like a baby and run with her. What he did, finally, was walk away. In the crowd, some jeered at him.

Mr. Dundy wiped his face with a sharply pressed white handkerchief that he stuffed back into his lapel pocket. He motioned, and a crew of other men took the elephant keeper's place. No shiny red suits masked their business. They had sticks with nails and hooks, and they prodded and baited the elephant into the center of the arena, all the while keeping their distance from her, wounding her in the nip-and-run way of small predators. They roped her to wooden stakes.

And now, yet other men set to work on her, much to the crowd's approval.

"...Thomas Edison's own...." "...in from New Jersey...." "...wires, see what they're doing, they're making what they call connections...."

Thomas Edison's men attached heavy copper wires and electrodes to chains around the elephant's right front and left rear feet, and scrambled away from her.

And now, all eyes were back to Mr. Dundy. He had taken his place barely apart from the crowd, just far enough into the arena to stand out, but safely away from the elephant. Two women stood next to him tightly, possessively. He had the swagger of a rock star. His left arm wrapped a brunette with pouty, apple-red lips. His right arm—

"Tori!" Her name exploded from my throat, but she didn't hear me.

I fought the wall of backs and shoulders that kept me away from her, edging, squeezing, forcing my way into the arena. Rough hands shoved me forward. I fell through a gap in the wall, landing sideways. Something snapped in my side; I felt a tiny, sudden loss of breath, and feared I'd broken a rib. But I gathered my feet beneath me in practically the same motion.

Thinking better, I would have run the circumference of the arena until it led me to Tori. I wasn't thinking that way. I headed straight across the opening, becoming part of the show. Band music struck up as if to accompany my act.

All around the cobbler's bench,
The monkey chased the weasel

In the center, I stopped, helpless. The elephant's gaze held me. I could have touched her. I did.

From a distance, she looked weathered and hard as stone. But her skin was warm, and my hand brushed silky soft hair that was nearly invisible.

"Topsy...."

Her massive front legs bent with a clatter of chains. She knelt as if to offer me a ride. Her eyes held vast secrets.

The crowd cheered. Mr. Dundy laughed his approval. He strode out to meet me, both women in tow.

"First thing we t-tried on her, we soaked her carrots in c-cyanide," he said. "She never f-felt a thing. Why, I'd just about decided she had no f-feelings at all. But y-you have a way with her."

He wanted to shake hands, but I stood there, numb, arms to my sides, looking at Tori. She give me not the slightest sign of recognition.

He saw my obsession. "Lillian," he addressed her, "do you k-know this man?"

She looked me up and down, but not like when I'd offered to buy her *Crimson Cosmos*. No play, no surprises. Her expression dismissed me.

"Tori, what's wrong?" I tried to take her hand.

"You are!" she said, peeling my fingers off her as if they were leeches. Her mouth pulled down to an expression she'd never worn before. "You're as wrong as I ever seen."

Mr. Dundy reclaimed her, and as he did, a dozen other men materialized from out of the crowd—dirtied workmen, some of them, and big men with clean, pressed suits and clenched hands.

"I'm a friend of hers," I said, as if somebody had to believe me.

"A f-friend, are you?" he said. "Well, here, f-friend. Take this, and g-get yourself lost."

He flipped something high into the air, where it caught the light, spinning, flashing gold. I caught it with a cold slap into my palm: a gold coin.

"Take...*this!*" Mr. Dundy cried in sudden recovery of his laughing mood. He hands emerged from his pants pockets with clutches of gold coins that he threw into the crowd, whirling as he let go. He made himself a fountain, spraying gold.

People *oooh*'ed, and cheered, and feet left the ground, and hands reached high. Bodies collided. Fistfights erupted. Screams. People fell to hands and knees, scrabbling after coins on the ground.

Then, laughter wove and threaded through the riot, somehow congealing into a chant, until it seemed that everyone took it up in one voice. The two women played cheerleader.

The earth may quake
And banks may break
But Skip Dundy
Pays in gold!

Whoops and laughter echoed off the bedazzled towers, until the noise startled Topsy. The elephant roused to her feet. She backed as if to turn and run, straining the ropes that tethered her legs to the ground. One of the heaviest stakes inched free.

Mr. Dundy and his women retreated. His derby jarred loose. His hairpiece slipped. He pulled the big handkerchief from his pocket again, waving it high over his head. The band broke out a drum roll, and the crowd picked up a different cry.

"Bad Topsy!" "Bad Topsy!"

Topsy lifted her enormous head to trumpet her rage and defiance. I ran from her, too. Mr. Dundy whipped the handkerchief down. The park's lights dimmed and flickered.

Billows of white smoke exploded from the elephant's feet. She stiffened in a series of shivers and twitches that tickled most of the crowd. Topsy seemed to imagine her death was only a funny feeling she could shake off.

Near me, a woman fainted. Someone cursed; someone cried.

In the end, it was like seeing a grand old building implode: that same confusion of wonder and terror, a thrill in the destruction of something huge and irreplaceable.

Topsy was dead on her feet, smoke coiling around her. Then, she seemed to lift. Absurdly, I thought of robot jets firing under her feet, blasting her high into the sheltering night.

She never reached the stars, though. She fell to her right side, her legs locked straight, as if she'd never lived at all. I felt the impact through my feet, and in the pit of my stomach like the sound of a cannon, and in my heart.

The elephant's liquid brown eyes rolled up. The current still surged through her. Her feet charred.

"C-cut the electricity!" Mr. Dundy ordered, but too late. Power hummed through the air. Blue fire crackled and arced around the fallen elephant. It snaked into the crowd. People fell back as if toppled by armies of invisible demons swinging sledge hammers.

The fire enveloped Tori.

A tendril of blue lightning snaked from Tori's eyes, connecting with mine, and I knew. I understood. I shared with her the jungle heat, the rain, the serenity, the sense of time as something soft and slow, like the rain.

And Luna Park went black.

-10-

I have to tell you. This isn't the place, but you need to know. If I were editing this manuscript, I would mark an "X" here and write in the margin: "author intrusion," meaning the author has barged in like a gatecrasher, spoiling the story. But this can't wait. You'll know why.

There are mermaids in the electric ocean of time. If you glance up from your reading right now, you might see one. She could be that close.

Something in her smile, something in her eyes, makes you trust her. The deeper she takes you, the more you feel safe with her. When you trust her completely, you're already into the drowning depths.

But that's not what she wants, and that's not why she drowned all those others before you.

How many? Pick a number, any number, say—ninety-six. She cared all she could for them, and a mermaid's slightest care is more than a king's richest dream. But she didn't care enough to save them with her mermaid magic. They were all wooden nickels.

You, though, you're the one. Maybe not to another soul in the universe, but you have this one great thing going for you: You're the one she's tried so hard to find.

She drowned ninety-six, and then you came along. Or she would have drowned 960, until you came along; or 960 million, looking for you.

Numbers mean nothing to her.

But you do.

Luna Park fell to darkness as completely as, moments before, it had been incredibly illuminated. The cries were like those of primitives in the grip of a solar eclipse.

Dizziness took me, but I knew it would be fatal to fall. I would be under panicked feet. Hands clutched at me, feeling for someone familiar, for husband or mother, and shoving the stranger away.

I caught a glint of silver light, of moonglow reflected from something familiar, the silver rim of Tori's hollow pendant—waiting for its remembrance of Topsy.

"Brad…" Her breath cooled my face. "Brad, silly." She held me. "I have something for you."

I dimly saw her touch a finger to the corner of her eye. She lifted a tear that she touched to my lips, and followed the taste with a kiss, and the blue fire poured into me. And the jungle, and the rain, and the river, and the ocean.

A fly in the water stirs ripples, tiny waves; and the elephant rides. Something shifted. The ground slid beneath me.

"I don't have the words—" Tori said.

"You don't need any."

The elephant's brain is twice the size of a person's. No one knows how much of the universe fits in an elephant's mind, or what becomes of the universe when the elephant dies. But I learned enough when the current ran through me.

I learned mermaids don't wander. They orbit. They swim in elliptical orbits that take them farther and farther away from where they started—from where they belong. They always return, though. They have to.

But once upon a time, there was a mermaid who swam out too far in the ocean—so far, she couldn't get back. She drifted, lost. She hid among people so well, no one knew she was a mermaid. But she began to have bad effects on them.

She belonged in the past, and the past infected her. She made other people long for the past, too. They cherished old pieces of times that never belonged to them, when they should have been thinking of now and tomorrow.

She needed something more than her mermaid magic to get back, and it took her ninety-seven times to find it—to find me.

"Ride the waves, Brad," she said. I kissed her for all I was worth.

I don't know when Luna's lights came back. But I know this:

When people ran home that night to say what wonders they had seen at Luna Park, it wouldn't be the lights, or the Shoot the Chutes, or that poor, dead Topsy creature they told about. It would be us.

But as the park's electrical power took hold again, Tori changed. She stood away from me. She had Lillian's mean mouth for a moment, but she smiled then, still my Tori.

I seemed to be climbing, higher and higher into a blue rain, away from her. *Racheta-rakkata.*

She faded, a white figure lost in the light.

What am I, Tori? Ninety-six, and then me, and we all loved you, Tori, and so what? Did I love you the most? The least? The fastest? The blindest? What made me any different?

I never heard the answer, but I read it. Her last gift to a reader. Her face blurred as I left her. Her image doubled, tripled, as if I were seeing her through rippled glass. I read the answer from her lips.

Oh Brad silly I love you
silly I love you
love you
you
you
you
you
you
you
Climb.
Fall.
Curve.

-12-

One night, the old Pen and Pitcher Club voted the worst cliche in science fiction. *The rose in his hand* swept the field. A man goes to sleep; he dreams of a rose; he wakes up with a rose in his hand.

The Cyclone ground to a stop. I got off alone. Nobody cared.

I shambled through the amusement park, side aching, vaguely aware of something digging at my hand. And then, I remembered: Skip's gold coin.

And then, I remembered: Tori's wooden nickel.

I'd come again, always again, to the Skee-Ball emporium. The attendant who'd fought me had taken his place again on the stool. His head slumped to his chest, and he looked almost the same as before, just as dead. The only difference was the bandage under his Yankees cap.

Closer, I saw it wasn't a hospital bandage around his head. It was a rag that he might have tied himself. The spot where I'd hit him was mottled the rust color of dried blood, and the rag was greasy from whatever ointment he'd smeared on.

A TEACHER'S GUIDE to
Our Friend Electricity

—Make an ACTIVITY BOX. Include a Skee-Ball, a gold coin and a wooden nickel. Challenge your class to discover how these things explain the workings of time.

—FIELD TRIP: Visit a nearby carnival or amusement park. Do the rides look safe?

—Quiz ANSWERS:

1: (A) 6,600 volts to kill an elephant; 2,000 for a man.

2: (B) TRUE. Thought is electric.

3: (C) NONE OF THE ABOVE. So far as we know, lightning strikes without a thought.

If he breathed, I couldn't see it. People can die from the delayed effects of a concussion.

I rolled the object in my hand. Wood is warm, metal is cold. But everything felt cold that night.

Without looking, I slid the coin onto the glass prize counter beside him, and I walked away.

What's a Skee-Ball worth, anyway?

The city no longer frightened me for being old. One day, I finished the books I'd been afraid to read.

Topsy was a bad elephant, but she had her reasons. The last man she killed had fed her a lighted cigarette.

Skip died of pneumonia by some accounts, but others say it was a hat pin stabbed through his heart by a jilted lover.

Nostalgia isn't selling anymore. People want brand new. New books, new politics, new streets, new meanings, new medicines, new lives. New Coney Island.

But Tori was right about me changing jobs. The last book I candied and cudgeled through publication here made it to the *New York Times* list. The publisher said he'd called me on the recommendation of a man I'd barely known in the Pen and Pitcher Club.

There!—I felt the tug, that little slide again, that tells me I don't have to stay here. I have just enough of Tori's mermaid magic in me to go out in the ocean and swim to...I don't know where. But what if I couldn't get back? What if I had to love someone new in order to get back?

I see her a million times a day, in sunlight on blonde hair, in a certain smile, in every white dress, in everything silver.

Sleeping, I search for my Tori through Luna, and Steeplechase, and Dreamland, for which the lovely waltz was written. *Meet me in Dreamland, sweet dreamy Dreamland.* But the old songs are out of my head.

I have a talent. A super secret psychic talent. You

tell me the name of the last one you cared about even a little. I'll tell you how much that meant to you.

It broke your heart.

They all break your heart.

—*For Jan, life's exception*

"King Rainjoy's Tears"
Chris Willrich

A king of Swanisle delights in rue
And his name's a smirking groan.
Laughgloom, Bloodgrin, Stormproud we
knew
Before Rainjoy took the throne.
> *—Rainjoy's Curse*

It was sunset in Serpenttooth when Persimmon Gaunt hunted the man who put oceans in bottles.

The town crouched upon an islet off Swanisle's west coast, and scarlet light lashed it from that distant (but not unreachable) place where the sunset boiled the sea. The light produced a striking effect, for the people of Serpenttooth were the desperate and outcast, and they built with what they found, and what they found were the bones of sea serpents. And at day's end it seemed the gigantic, disassembled beasts struggled again toward life, for a pale, bloody sheen coated the town's archways, balustrades, and rooftops. Come evening the illusion ceased, and the bones gave stark reflection to the moon.

But the abductor meant to be gone before moonrise.

From the main town she ascended a cliffside pathway of teeth sharp as arrowheads, large as steppingstones. The teeth ended at a vast, collapsed skull, reinforced with earth, wood, and thatch, bedecked with potted plants. There was a door, a squarish fragment of cranium on hinges, with a jagged eyeslit testifying to some ancient trauma.

Shivering in the briny sea-wind, Gaunt looked over her shoulder at the ruddy sunset rooftops. She did not see the hoped-for figure of a friend, leaping among the gables. "Your last chance to help, Imago," she murmured. She sighed, turned, and knocked.

Blue eyes, dimly glowing, peered through the eyeslit. "Eh?" wheezed a harsh voice. Gaunt imagined in it the complaints of seagulls, the slap of breakers.

"Persimmon Gaunt," she answered. "A poet."

"A bard?" The voice snorted. "The king exiled those witch-women, ten years gone."

"I am not a bard! My tools are stylus and wax, paper and quill, not voice and memory. I have the distinction of being banished by the bards, before the king banished them."

Gaunt could be charming, particularly in such a setting: her specialty in verse was morbidity, the frail railing of life against merciless time. Serpenttooth suited her. More, she suited Serpenttooth, her fluttering auburn hair a wild contrast to her pale, angular face, the right cheek tattooed with a rose ensnared by a spiderweb.

But these charms failed. "What do you want, *poet*?"

"I am looking for the maker."

"Maker of *what*?"

"Of this."

She lifted a small, corked bottle. Within nestled an intricate, miniature sailing ship fashioned of bone. Its white sails curved in an imaginary wind; its banners were frozen in the midst of rippling. Yet the ship was not the extraordinary thing. There was water below it, not bone or glass, and the water moved: not the twitching of droplets but the roiling of a shrunken corner of the sea. It danced and flickered, and the ship heaved to and fro, riding the tiny surge.

Gaunt waved the bottle in various directions, but the ship cared nothing for gravity, forever hugging its tiny sea.

"Exquisite," Gaunt murmured, and not for the first time.

"A trinket," sniffed the other.

"Trinket? For four years these 'trinkets' have been the stuff of legend along the coast! And yet their fame does not travel further. Most who own such bottles—sailors, fishermen, pirates, and all their wives, lovers, and children—will not sell at any price. It's said these folk have all lost something dear to the sea."

"Nothing to do with me."

"There is more." Gaunt unstoppered the bottle. "Listen. Hear the sound of the sea. Hear the deep loneliness, and the deep romance. To know it is to know mischievous waves, and alluring shores. To brush raw fingertips against riches and fame. To wrap scarred arms around hunger and harm. To know the warm fantasy of a home long abandoned, and the cold acceptance of a five fathom grave."

And there was a susurrant murmur from the bottle which held all these things, and more which Gaunt, too chill already, would not say. There came a long answering sigh from behind the door. It blended with the murmur, and Gaunt could not distinguish them.

Weakly, the voice said, "Nothing to do with me. Go."

"I cannot. When an...associate of mine procured this item, he found the private memoirs of the owner. We know who you are, Master Salt."

A pause. "You are base thieves."

Gaunt smiled. "Imago would insist he is a *refined* thief, I'm sure. And our victim was a dying lord who had no further use for the bottle."

"What do you want?"

"I bring you greetings," Gaunt said, "from your own maker."

There was silence. The door opened on creaking hinges. A figure stepped aside, and Gaunt entered.

The room resembled a captain's cabin, though it filled a sea serpent's skull, not a vessel's stern. Two oval, bone-framed windows overlooked the ruddy sunset sea. Underneath, shutters covered twin ventilation passages to the skull's nostrils. Nearby, a spyglass rested atop a bookcase of nautical texts. But the other dozen bookcases cradled dozens of ships-in-bottles, each bearing its own churning, miniature sea. Half-constructed vessels listed upon a vast table, pieces scattered like wreckage.

Gaunt plunked her bottle upon the table, ship sailing forever ceilingward.

Master Salt bent over it. "The *Darkfast Dreamweaver*. Fitting. Named for a great philosopher-thief of Ebontide." A smile sliced his face.

He was built like a sea barrel, yet possessed delicately shimmering blue skin. His bald head resembled a robin's egg gleaming with dew. "Her crew captured the hatchling of a Serpent of the Sunset. Quite a story. But they overfed the child, to keep it from thrashing. It outgrew its bonds, fed well indeed."

He nodded at the shelves. "Lost ships, all of them. I see their profiles in my dreams. Hear their names on the morning wind."

"They are astonishing. The king will be enthralled."

"Him," muttered Salt. "He neglected me, my sisters. Left us eight years in our tower, because we dared remind him he had a soul. We resolved to seek our own lives."

Gaunt said, "Now your exile is ended."

"Not exile. Escape."

"Surely you cannot abandon him," Gaunt persisted, "being what you are."

"If you know what I am, poet, you should fear me. Inhuman myself, I read the sorrow behind human eyes."

His gaze locked hers. Gaunt shivered as though a westerly wind scoured her face, but could not look away.

Salt squinted, then smirked. "You say *I* abandon? I see what you've left behind. You forsook the bards for the written word. And now you even neglect your art...for the love of a thief."

Master Salt's eyes changed. One moment they glowed a pale blue; then they resembled blue-sheened, mirrored glass. Yet the person reflected in them was not Gaunt, nor was the moment this one. Instead she beheld a scene from an hour ago.

A man leapt to and fro upon buildings of bone. There was a strange style to his movements. Though he chose his destinations in a boyish rush, his rooftop dance obeyed a strict economy, as though an old man carefully doled out a youth's energy. When he paused, Gaunt could see the two scars of his lean, ferretlike face, one made by steel, one by fire. He gazed out from Master Salt's eyes as if searching for her. Then he leapt to a new height.

"The thief Imago Bone, your lover and sometimes your mentor, prancing about on bone rooftops. Sup-

47

pose he couldn't resist." Salt blinked his eyes back to their former, glowing state. "But you knew he might be gone for hours. Impatient, you continued alone."

Gaunt's breathing quickened. She found she could not evade Master Salt, nor lie. "Yes. For all Bone's skill…"

"…he is a boy," Master Salt said. "Yes, I see. I can taste sorrows, poet. Imago Bone's life is an accident, is it not? Bizarre magics stretched his adolescence nearly a century. Only now is he aging normally. He is a great thief; but he is a child in many ways. You fear for him. You are as often his guardian as his student. An unlikely pair, following foolish quests."

"They are not foolish." Gaunt shivered, staring into the shimmering blue eyes. "Not all…."

"Quests are excuses, poet. You must live as you wish. As I have done. You do not need bards, or Imago Bone, or King Rainjoy to justify your wanderlust."

Gaunt imagined she felt the tug of the trade winds. Or perhaps it was the clatter of a horse beneath her, the taste of bow-spray from a river canoe, the scent of a thousand fragile mountain wildflowers.

"A true wanderer," Salt said, "needs no nation, no captain, no hope of gold to answer the siren lure."

And Gaunt wondered, why had she tried to refashion Bone and herself as heroes, when they could simply travel, drink in the world?

But no, this quest was *not* foolish. She must resist Salt's words. "There—will be war," she stammered, "unless Rainjoy can learn compassion.…And he never can, without you."

"I see also," Salt said unmoved, "why you help him." Gaunt lowered her eyes.

"Abandon that guilt, poet. Abandon all that imprisons you! Leave this quest; join Bone as a thief if it suits you, or shirk him as well—either way, seize your freedom, and do not abuse mine." Salt lifted his hand to Gaunt's mouth. "I did not ask to become a *someone*, any more than humans do. Yet here I am, and I will set my own course. I will hear the sea, and trap its cries."

Now Master Salt scraped a thumbnail against the tip of an index finger, and a blue droplet fell against Gaunt's lips. As the salty tang kissed her, she imagined the rocking of a deck underfoot, heard the songs of seamen raising sail, smelled the stinging brine upon the lines. Her heart skipped once and her eyelids drooped, as she slipped toward a dream of adventure in distant waters, not merely losing her existence, but casting it aside like soiled clothes.

But then from somewhere came Imago Bone's easy voice. "You should listen to him, Gaunt," Bone said. "He makes perfect sense."

With a start, Gaunt opened her eyes. Bone crawled through the passage leading to the dragon-skull's nostrils, face blue from the cliffside winds and sweaty from carrying his many pouches of esoteric tools: ironsilk lines, quicksap adhesive, a spectrum of camouflaging dyes.

As Master Salt turned, Bone sprang to the bottle sheltering the miniature *Darkfast Dreamweaver*. The thief shattered it against the table's edge.

Salt cried out.

So did the broken bottle.

The miniature ocean within the glass spilled onto the dirt floor, foaming and dwindling like a tendril of surf dying upon shore. A chorus of drowning sailors arose, dimly, like an old memory. Then water and voices were gone.

"Curse you," spat Master Salt, and the spittle boiled upon the table, and gave a sound like maddened seagulls as it vanished. He seized the thief, pressing pale blue thumbs against Bone's throat, thumbs that grew foam-white even as Bone went purple.

"Allow..." the thief gurgled, "allow me to introduce...."

"No," said Master Salt.

"Rude...." Bone's voice trailed off, and he flailed uselessly in Salt's grip.

Bone had saved her. Bone was friend, lover, companion on the road. Nevertheless Gaunt hesitated one moment as he suffocated; so much poetry did the shelves of bottles hold, they might have cradled densely inked scrolls from ancient libraries.

But she knew what she must do. She shut her eyes and yanked.

The shelves toppled, shattering glass, breaking small ships, spilling the trapped substance of Master Salt. The room filled with the despairing cries of lost sailors.

Master Salt shrieked and released Bone, who crumpled, hacking saltwater. Salt knelt as well, trying to clutch the tiny oceans as they misted into nothingness. His knees crunched glass and crushed ships.

Gaunt trembled with the destruction she'd caused. But soon the sailors' voices faded to dim wailing, and she regained her voice.

"Dead sailors move you?" she asked. "Expect more. War is brewing. To prevent it, King Rainjoy will need the compassion he lost. The compassion you bear."

"You speak of compassion? You, who can do this?"

"These voices are of men already lost. But if war comes, they will seem just a drop in a surgeon's pail."

Salt lowered his head.

"I will go," he said at last. "If only to prevent your crushing more dreams."

Imago Bone rose with a look of gratitude, put his hand upon Gaunt's shoulder.

"I regret I did not arrive sooner," he whispered, then smiled ruefully. "The skeletal rooftops, they beckoned...."

"We'll talk of it later," Gaunt said. "No one can help being who they are." She leaned against him, but could not bear to look at him, nor at Master Salt, who gathered broken ships, tenderly, bone by scattered bone.

"The first is found," sighed the man upon the ivory chair.

An older man, shuffling through the chamber of mists, stopped and coughed. "Majesty?"

"Persimmon Gaunt. And her companion thief." The voice was dim, and flat. "They have found the first. Soon, all will be well."

"The reports I bring, ah, belie such optimism." The older man scuttled closer. His robes fluttered with no regard to the drafts. "The nobles, hm, demand war with the Eldshore, if you cannot secure an alliance by marriage. I suggest you build ships, raise troops." He raised a wrinkled hand before the king's nose, then snatched at something only he could see.

He inverted the hand, revealing an *enfleshment* from the king's memory, the tiny image of a red-haired woman, proud and bejeweled. She spat in the king's direction. Her voice rose dimly: *You are cold, with no soul within you. You shall never have me.* Turning on her heel, she stalked off the palm and into nonexistence.

"Eldshore's princess *will* marry me;" said the king, "once I am a better man. Once *they* make me a better man."

"Strange, mm?—that you can sense their doings while I cannot."

Mirthlessly, the king smiled. "You may have made them, sorcerer, but they belong to me."

"Do not hope for too much, my king. War is in the air."

"When you are here, Spawnsworth, the air smells of worse. Leave your reports and go."

When the older man had retreated up a staircase, the king said in a toneless voice without conviction, "I *will* feel again."

From the staircase descended the sounds of tortured things.

The journey to Lornbridge took two weeks, but they felt like two years to the thief Imago Bone.

Master Salt spoke only in grunts. Surely thousands of subjects were capable of grunting for their king; why should Rainjoy need this entity in particular?

Gaunt walked as though shouldering a treasure chest of guilt (Bone often pictured metaphorical treasure chests, feeling deprived of real ones) and there was a distance in her eyes even as she lay nights upon his shoulder.

So it was a relief, finally, to risk his neck reaching a well-guarded noblewoman noted for feathering suitors with arrows.

Seen through tall grass, the battlement looked sickly

and moist in the moonlight. (Bone's cloak, after a treatment of saps and powders, matched it.) He slithered beside it, scrambled halfway up, paused for heavy bootfalls to pass, then scurried atop. Time for one gulp of manure-scented air, then he was over the other side, hurling a ball of sticky grain as he dove.

He thudded onto a haycart exactly as the pigpen filled with squealing. By the time the guards investigated, the animals would have devoured the evidence. He slipped into courtyard shadows.

This was more like it: sparks of danger against the steel of brilliant planning. A shame he wasn't stealing anything.

My beloved's doing, Bone thought as he climbed atop a stable. When they met he was a legend, perhaps the greatest second-story man of the Spiral Sea. (The higher stories went of course without question.) Though she could pay little, he'd accepted enormous risk recovering a manuscript of hers from a pair of sorcerous bibliophiles, a task that had required another book, a tome of the coldest kind of magic. That matter concluded, he'd undertaken an absurdly noble quest, the accursed tome's destruction.

Absurd nobility impressed Persimmon Gaunt.

Bone smirked, reversed his cloak to the side stained with berry juice, then leapt from the stable roof onto Duskvale Keep itself, clinging to irregularities in the russet stone. His slow corkscrew toward the highest window allowed him time to review six months of inquiries along the Spiral Sea, a process garnering nothing but scars, empty pockets, and a list of enemies who wouldn't at all mind the damnable book for themselves.

Half jesting, half desperate, Bone had proposed consulting the court wizard of Swanisle.

He'd expected scowls. Swanisle was notorious for persecuting the bards of its county Gaunt (a society of women compared to witches, and similarly treated) formerly by burning, today by exile. He'd assumed Persimmon left with her teachers, would seethe at the thought of returning. But she had assented with a strange look.

Bone should have worried more at that look.

Distracted by such thoughts, Bone froze upon hearing a bright *swish*. Presently, from afar, came a dim *thunk*.

Lady Duskvale was firing off correspondence.

There was not one keep at Lornbridge but two, separated by the narrow, abysmal Groangorge. Westward stood Duskvale Keep and eastward rose the sandstone tower of Mountdawn. For generations, Gaunt had explained to Bone, the youth of Duskvale and Mountdawn had swooned for each other, sighing and pining across the impassable deep.

Then, four years ago, the keeps' masters paupered themselves constructing a bridge. The fortresses became one small town. Not merely did a stone span connect the castle; dozens of hundred-foot ropes, cables, and pulleys twisted overhead with messages, squirrels, nobles' drying underwear.

Yet today the bridge was guarded, the ropes cut, the youth forbidden to mix.

Swish.

Thunk.

Bone smirked and climbed beside the topmost window.

"Oh, why does he not write me?" he heard a voice exclaim.

Bone craned his head. "Perhaps because—"

"Ay!"

An arrow shot past, a roll of paper wound upon the shaft.

This time there followed no *thunk* but a dim clatter upon the stone bridge.

"Perhaps," Bone said, heart pounding, "because he is not as good a shot as yourself. Though I am pleased even you must aim."

"Who are you?" the voice demanded.

Bone crouched upon the sill, and bowed. "Bone: acquirer of oddities."

Lady Duskvale regarded him with hawk-dark eyes framed by stern cheekbones and black rivulets of hair. "Do you plan mischief? I warn you, I will tolerate mischief with but one man, and he I fire arrows at. For you I have a knife for stabbing, and lungs for screaming."

"I have no wish for mischief, stabs, or screams."

"Are you...are you a messenger from Lord Mountdawn?"

"Better than that, my lady. I am Bone. I and the poet Gaunt have come to comfort Lornbridge. May I enter?"

"I would be more comforted with you outside."

"Even a footpad's foot may fall asleep."

"One moment." She nocked an arrow, drew, and aimed. Then she backed into the room. "All right."

Bone leapt inside. "I admire your caution—and more, the strength of your arm—but it is not thieves at your window you must fear. It is the embodiment of sorrow."

She raised her eyebrows, and Bone helped himself to a chair beside a small table serviceable as a shield. He drummed his fingers upon it. "Consider, my lady. In your father's day, these keeps were famous for romance. Men and women pined hopelessly from across the gulf. But that has changed."

"You mock me, thief?" Duskvale's fingers quivered upon the bowstring, as did Bone's upon the table. "Of course it has changed."

"Explain."

"Very well, though my arm grows weaker. Four years ago my father and old Lord Mountdawn, rest their souls, heard identical whispers in their sleep, imploring them to build the bridge. For a time all was glorious. Yet if there are whispers now, they implore weeping. Bravos duel for damsels, spurned paramours hurl themselves into the gorge. Only I and my love, young Lord Mountdawn, are spared these frenzies, for we are calculating and circumspect."

A carrier pigeon fluttered through the window, alighting upon a perch near Duskvale. She regarded it and Bone, then sighed and set down her bow. (Bone released a long breath.) Removing a note from the pigeon's foot, Duskvale read, "'*Soon I must fight my way across the bridge to your side. Each arrow is a caress, but I would kiss the callouses of the hand that fired it. Dear one! Alive or dead, my bloody hide arrives in the morning!*'" She looked up in vexation. "You are interrupting a private conversation, you know. Explain your purpose."

"Are you aware," Bone asked, "that your monarch was once called the Weeping King?"

"Rainjoy?" she mused. "I heard Father say as much. A sensitive boy crushed by the crown's weight,

weeping at the consequences of all commands." She
crushed Mountdawn's note. "Men *can* be overwrought
at times. But the king has changed. Now they call him
Rainjoy the Stonefaced. What does it matter?"

"Did your father speak of the Pale Council?"

"Everyone knows of them," Duskvale said impa-
tiently. "Rainjoy's wise advisors. They came from far
away and never went among the people. But the
people loved them, for they counseled compassion,
and kept the king's cruel wizard at bay. But they departed four years ago and this is of no consequence
and my beloved is about to die for me."

"Hear this: the Council did not come from a far
land, nor did they return there. One member dwells
nearby."

"What?"

"They are creatures of magic, my dear, born of a
bargain between Rainjoy and his wizard."

"What bargain?"

"That Rainjoy, so wracked by conscience he could
not function as king, should weep but three more
tears in his life. Yet those tears would be given human
form, so when Rainjoy wished he could safely seek
the insights of sorrow."

Duskvale fingered her bow. "Impossible."

"No, merely quite ill-advised. I've met one such
tear. Another dwells here. We will need your help,
and your paramour's, to snare it. Tell me, do you retain builders' plans for the bridge?"

In the end it was the sincerity in Bone's eyes, or
(more likely) the desperation in Duskvale's heart, that
bade her send a pointed message to Mountdawn and
then summon servants to make certain preparations.
Bone was relieved not to relate stealing her father's

ship-in-a-bottle and rifling his memoirs. For it was Lord Duskvale who had owned the faux *Darkfast Dreamweaver*, its surging in harmony with the whispers of Lornbridge.

Soon the moonlight found the thief whistling, strolling across that great stone arch. At midpoint he squeezed a tiny sack of quicksap, which he smeared full across his gloves, then applied to his shoes.

He descended the bridge's side, enjoying the brisk mountain air, the churning murmur of the river far below, the tickle of vertigo. Presently there came a swish from the west and a thunk to the east.

At this signal Bone crawled underneath the span, hairs pointing toward watery, rocky doom. Where the plans indicated it would be, he discovered a square opening. He crawled inside.

Blue light surrounded him. "Who?" called a bleak voice, like a hollow wind through a shattered house.

The chamber was like a monk's cell, a cold stone sitting room with a few books (with such titles as *Ballad of the Poisoned Paramour* and *The Tragickal History of Violet Swoon*), some decoration (withered roses), odd mementos (lockets with strands of hair inside), and a lamp (bearing not oil but a pale blue liquid glimmering like glacial moonlight).

"I had gambled," Bone said, shedding his gloves, "you would not wish to miss the romantic play of light upon the river. I am Imago Bone," he added, changing his shoes, "and I bring greetings from the king."

The quicksap discarded, Bone gazed upon Rainjoy's tear. She resembled a spindly, large-eyed maiden in a white shift. She shimmered gently in the blue light, reflecting and echoing it. Her long white hair fluttered and frayed, blending into the chamber's dim mists.

She regarded Bone with incomprehension. "Rainjoy abandoned us."

"He would enjoy your counsel again."

"I cannot give it. I am not his anymore, a slave, nameless...now I am Mistress Mist. This is my home. There must be love in the world, you see. Lonely were these keeps, but I whispered of this bridge, and they are lonely no longer. Still do I whisper of love."

"You whisper of more than that. Men and women have perished."

"*I* do not slay them," Mist answered sadly. "In my presence they sense what purest love could be, and how far short they fall." She frowned at Bone. "But you—why are *you* here? When your true love is elsewhere, waiting and worrying. Why while your precious moments with me? Do you abandon her for me? Do you betray?"

A chill enveloped him; he could not evade those eyes.

He thought of Persimmon Gaunt. Of course he would not betray her for this apparition. And yet—was he not flippant, unheedful of her? His dallying upon the rooftops of Serpenttooth nearly caused her death. Did he not repay devotion with childish disregard? Was he not cruel?

He did not deserve her, he realized, nor life. Better to end his existence now, than risk wounding her further. Bone yearned for the abyss at his back.

But even as the impulse for annihilation took over, his old lust for living cried out. He could not prevent his leap, but he modified the angle and, falling, grasped the ironsilk strand fired by Lady Duskvale.

The thread bent, rose, bent, held. It sliced his palm, and he trembled with the urge to release it, dash himself to bits far below. Fortunately the impulse weakened away from Mist.

He saw Gaunt leaning over the bridge's side. "I am sorry...."

"What?" she shouted.

He shook his head, cried instead: "Pigeon!"

Gaunt raised her arm. From the Mountdawn side of the chasm a pigeon fluttered to alight upon Bone's shoulder, a poem of Gaunt's affixed to its leg. Bone shrugged the bird upward and it fluttered into the hidden chamber. Presently Bone heard a sad voice, reading.

> *"Love floating skyward is earthly no longer*
> *Braced with selfishness, ardor is stronger*
> *On solid ground let rest love's wonder—*
> *And so your bridge we break asunder."*

"Picks!" Bone shouted, and at once there sang a chorus of metal biting stone.

"No!"

A large silvery blob, like a pool of mercury ignorant of gravity, flowed from beneath the bridge and oozed upward to the span. Blue light rose from that spot, and although Bone could not see her, he heard Mist shout, "I concede! The bridge will be mute without me. Please do not break it. Keep it, and find love if you can. I will go."

A voice like lonely seabirds answered, "They snared me likewise, sister. For we cannot destroy as they do."

"Yes, brother. They ruin themselves, and each other. We only awaken their sorrow."

"But the last tear will defeat them, sister. The last is the strongest of all."

"The second is found," said the king in the room of mists.

Framing the ivory throne, twin pillars of rainwater poured from funnels and spilled into a pool with a swan's outline, wingtips catching the water, nose aimed at the throne's foot, a drain where the heart should be. Just as they believed distress strengthened the spirit, the royal house of Swanisle believed chill weather quickened the flame within a man.

The king rose, undressed, and waded in, his pensive expression unchanged.

From beside the throne his companion said carefully, "This poet is, ah, resourceful."

"Of course. She is a bard of Gaunt."

"Mm. Never forget, majesty, her ilk caused you great pain."

The king shivered in his pool. It gave him a look that resembled passion. "Great pain. And great wonder. I remember how every spider in its shimmering, dew-splattered web was an architect of genius to be cherished, not squashed. I remember a defiant spark in the eyes, a stony strength in the limbs of every maiden men declared ugly. I remember the disbelieving child in the faces of condemned men, a child whose mind might yet encompass creation, were that infinite head still upon that foreshortened neck. I remember knowing these things, Spawnsworth, but I can no longer *feel* them. But *they* will help. Soon."

"Soon," the wizard murmured, scratching his chin.

His robe quivered, jerked, as though pained by needlepricks.

Nightswan Abbey formed the outline of a soaring bird, and although its crumbling bulk no longer suggested flight of any kind, the music pouring from its high windows did much to compensate.

A crowd of the young and elderly gathered beneath the sanctuary windows every evening to hear the sweet polyphony, as the purple sunset kissed the first of the night's stars. The sisterhood could sing only within these walls; all else would be vanity. Even so, during the last four years their music had rekindled some of Nightswan's fame, long dimmed in this age of grim, conquering kings.

It was as if those hundred mortal throats conjured the spirit of the Swan Goddess of the Night and the Stars, she who plunged into the sun, seawater glistening upon her wings, to cool its fire and make the Earth temperate and fit for life, she whose charred body fell back into the sea, to become Swanisle.

The music ceased and the listeners drifted away, murmuring to one another—all save four, who slipped among the bushes. Soon, two reemerged, one casting a line to a window, the second glancing backward. "They will not flee," Gaunt whispered. "They are contemptuous, certain their sister will humble us. I am uneasy."

Bone shrugged. "We will handle her. We've seen worse, we two."

Gaunt did not reply.

They ascended to the vast sanctuary, slipping behind the winged marble altar of the Swan. In the pews a lone nun prayed. Her white cap, cut in the outline of a swan, enhanced the rich darkness of a robe embroidered with tiny stars. The intruders made hand signals: they would pause until she departed.

Then the nun looked up, her face still shadowed by her hood, and sang in a voice sweet as any of the abbey's chorus, yet with an unexpected pain, as though a delicate aperitif were served too hot. The first stanza was muted, but her voice rose with the second:

King Stormproud fell to war's caress,
Left Swanisle to his boy,
Who had not learned to love distress:
Soft-hearted was Rainjoy.

Gaunt gave Bone a sharp look, listening.

His shivering toes just touched the floor
When he claimed his father's chair.
When the sad queen's heart would beat no more
He tore his silky hair.

The nun rose. The intruders hid themselves behind the onyx, speckled pulpit as she approached the altar, still singing.

Yet when a wizard of county Gaunt
(Spawnsworth was his name)
Tried his wicked strength to flaunt
The boy king's heart took flame.
For all Gaunt's fear, and all its horror
Marched as Rainjoy's foe.
Enfleshment was the wizard's lore—
To fashion warriors from woe.

The sister knelt where the wine was kept, the wine that symbolized the goddess's blood, shed to make all life possible. She cast a surreptitious glance over her shoulder. Her face was a pale, dimly glowing blue, growing brighter as she sang.

Rainjoy led his armies north,
Felled the work of Spawnsworth's hands,
Yet surely more would soon ride forth
Till they conquered all his lands.
Now the bards of Gaunt were rightly known
To clasp old secrets to the breast.
So the army overturned every stone
Till the king beheld the best.

The nun passed her hand over the wine vessel, and shining droplets fell into the dark liquid. They quickly dimmed, and the wine appeared as before.

"Gaunt's ancient thanes," King Rainjoy spoke,
"The very land would quick obey.
"To free it from the wizard's yoke
"I must know Gaunt as did they."
The woman said, "What you seek takes years,
"A lifetime spent in Gaunt,
"A knowledge born of woe and tears,
"Not a young man's morning jaunt."
"My father died on Eldshore's strand.
"My mother died of loss.
"A wizard makes to seize my land—
"This die I'll gladly toss."

At last Gaunt could stand waiting no more, and stepped forward. The run ceased singing, caught her breath.

Gaunt curtsied. Meanwhile Bone leapt forward, tumbled, rolled, and stood where he blocked the nun's best retreat. He bowed low, eyes upon her.

In a hot, dusky voice more evocative of tavern than tabernacle, the nun said, "You are agents of the king, I take it?" She raised her head, showing a weary blue face and sapphire smile like a dagger-cut. "I've sensed my siblings being gathered."

"You are correct. I am Persimmon...of Gaunt. A poet. This is my companion, Bone. We bear Rainjoy's plea for your help. He must marry Eldshore's princess to stop a war, but she refuses. She senses Rainjoy feels no sorrow, knows no compassion."

"A wise woman." The tear laughed, one sharp, jarring note. "I am Sister Scald. You are a poet of Gaunt? Did Gaunt's bards train you, before Rainjoy exiled them?"

"They did," Gaunt said, "before exiling *me*."

Glimmering eyes widened. "Did you learn 'Rainjoy's Curse?'"

"Yes," Gaunt said. And she did not sing, but continued Scald's song in speech.

She led him then, where doomed ships had lunged
At cliffs where white foam churned;
To chasms where young suitors plunged;
To pyres where bards had burned.
She wooed him with rhymes of sailors drowned,
And songs of lovers dead,
And poems of bards long in the ground,
Until she wooed him to her bed.
Into a fevered dream he fell
Of the web that snares all lives—
One soul's joy breeds another's hell.
One suffers, and one thrives.
He woke to slaps: For bedding her so,
She offered jibe and taunt.

He trembled chill as she did go;
For now he knew the soul of Gaunt.
And when the nightmare horde returned,
Raised from Gaunt's old pain,
He told it, "Sleep, for I have learned:
"Let the land swallow you again."
The warriors melted into earth
And the wizard quick was seized.
Spawnsworth said, "O king of worth,
"How might you be appeased?"
Rainjoy trembled. "I feel each death.
"All paths shine slick with blood.
"I cannot bear to end your breath."
The mage swore fealty where he stood.
A king of Swanisle delights in rue
And his name's a smirking groan.
But in Rainjoy endless tears did brew
And he longed for eyes of stone.

Scald's voice bit the silence. "He has those eyes now. The bards gave him knowledge of all life's woe, but Spawnsworth tricked him out of his tears. For a time he still consulted us, but who willingly seeks out sorrow? At last he consulted us no more. He became the sort of king Spawnsworth could control."

"He senses what he's lost. Serve him again."

"I serve others now."

Bone broke in. "Indeed? Your brother served others with bottled grief, your sister with a bridge of doomed desire. We threatened these contrivances; the tears surrendered. I say good riddance."

"You mock *their* work, thief?" Scald seized Bone's chin, locked eyes with his. "I see into your soul, decrepit boy. You've begun aging at last, yet you fritter away your moments impressing this foolish girl. And *you*—" She released Bone, snatched Gaunt's ear—"you forsook the glory of voice and memory for clumsy meanderings of ink. Now you neglect even that dubious craft following this great mistake of a man." Scald stepped back, dismissing poet and thief with a wave. "What a pair you are, what a waste of wind your love! Who are *you*, to lecture me?"

Shivering, Gaunt looked away, toward the tall windows and bright stars. But she replied. "I will tell you, tear of Rainjoy. I was a girl who saw the boy king rescue county Gaunt from the creatures who tore her family to bits. I was a bard's apprentice who loved him from afar. And when my teacher *boasted* of how she granted his request by breaking his spirit, I knew I'd follow her no more."

She looked at Bone, who regarded her wonderingly. "I'd not guard secret lore in my skull, but offer my words in ink, telling of grief such that anyone could understand. I would tarry in graveyards and let tombs inspire my verse. For if the bards hoarded living song, I would peddle the dead, written word." Gaunt returned her gaze to Scald. "When Spawnsworth made an end to Rainjoy's weeping, the king's first act was to exile the bards. And how I laughed that day. Come, tear. You cannot shame me. I will repay my teachers' debt."

"You surprise me," Scald said, "but I think you will not take me. I have no bottles, no bridge to harm. My substance passes into the sacramental wine, inspiring the sisters' music. Would you destroy all grapes in the world?"

"I do not need to." Gaunt gestured toward the door.

Scald turned, saw a cluster of black, star-speckled habits underneath white swan hats.

A nun with a silver swan necklace stepped forward, old hands trembling. "We have listened, Sister Scald. Gaunt and Bone sent warning by carrier pigeon that they would seek a king's tear this night, unaware we'd knowingly given you sanctuary. I have been torn, until this moment. I might defy even Rainjoy to honor our pledge, Scald....But you have meddled with our sacraments. You must go."

"*Oathbreaker*," Scald snarled. She looked right and left. "All of you—all humans are traitors, to yourselves, to others. Listen then, and understand."

And Scald sang.

This song was wordless. It was as though the earlier music was simply the white breakers of this, the churning ocean, or the moonlit fog-wisps crossing the lip of this, the crevasse. Now the cold depths were revealed. They roared the truth of human treachery, of weakness, of pain.

Before that song the humans crumpled.

"No...." Gaunt whimpered, covering her face.

"Nothing...." whispered Bone. "I am nothing...not man, not boy. A waste...."

Somehow, Bone's anguish bestirred Gaunt to defy her own. "You are something." She wrenched each word from her throat like splinters torn from her own flesh. "You are not a waste."

The sisters knelt, some mouthing broken regretful words, some clawing for something sharp, something hard, to make an end. But Gaunt raised her head to the singer. "Scald...." It should have been a defiant cry, but it emerged like a child's plea. "Look what you do, to those who sheltered you...."

Scald's eyes were hard, lifted ceilingward in a kind of bitter ecstasy. Yet she looked, and for a time watched the nuns cringing upon the stone floor.

She went silent.

She walked to one of the high windows. "I am no better than you," she murmured. "I sense my siblings, like me born of regret. It seems we cannot escape it." Scald removed her swan cap and lowered her head. "We will go."

Gaunt helped Bone to his feet. He clutched her shoulders as though grasping some idea rare and strange. "Why did you not tell me," he said, "of your family?"

She lowered her gaze. "When you suggested Spawnsworth might deal with that accursed tome we've locked away, Bone, I believed his skills were not appropriate and his character untrustworthy. But I realized we two might somehow repay the debt I felt to Rainjoy. It was a deception, Bone, one that deepened with time. I feared you would be angry."

He nodded. "Perhaps later. Now I am merely glad there is still a Gaunt to perhaps be angry with. It is done. For better or worse, we've recovered Rainjoy's tears."

She met his look. "Are they, Bone? Are they Rainjoy's? Or are they more like grown children? I think whatever their faults, they have seized control of their existence. I think they are people." She scowled in frustration. "I fear Scald is right; I am never consistent."

"You cannot deliver them up, now, can you?"

She shook her head. "Forgive me, Bone. We've gained nothing."

"I disagree." He leaned forward, kissed her.

Startled, she kissed him back, then pulled away.

"You are changing the subject! You can never focus on one thing; you are forever a boy."

"Fair enough, but I say you are the subject, and you are what I've gained. I know you better, now. And I would rather know you better, Persimmon Gaunt, than plunder all the treasure-vaults of Brightcairn. Though I'd cheerfully do both."

She gaped at him. "Then...you have your wish. Whatever Scald may think of us." She gazed at the bent figure beside the window. "To risk losing you three times this journey—it makes me care nothing for how odd is our love, our life. It is ours, and precious."

"Then my dear," Bone said, "let's discuss how we'll evade the king's assassins, when we break our pledge."

"How precious...." Gaunt murmured, still watching Scald, and her eyebrows rose. "No, we will not break it, Bone! We will fulfill it too well."

A storm frothed against King Rainjoy's palace, and the hall of mists felt like a ship deck at foggy dawn. Salt, Mist, and Scald stepped toward the ivory throne, knelt beside the swan pool. Behind the Pale Council stood Persimmon Gaunt and Imago Bone.

Upon the throne, the king studied his prodigal tears.

"So," he said.

The tears blinked back.

"Gaunt and Bone," said the wizard Spawnsworth from beside the throne, his cloak twisting as though with suppressed annoyance. "I, ah, congratulate you. You have accomplished a great deed."

"Not so difficult," Bone said easily. "Send us to fetch the morning star's shyer cousin, or the last honest man's business partner, and we might have surrendered. These three were not so well hidden." He smiled. "Anyone might have found them."

"Whatever," Spawnsworth said with a dismissive wave. "Your, um, modesty covers mighty deeds. Now, Majesty, I would examine these three in private. They have dwelled apart too long, and I fear they might be, ah, unbalanced. It might be years before I dare release them."

The tears said nothing, watching only Rainjoy.

"Yes," Rainjoy murmured, staring back, agreeing to something Spawnsworth had not said. "Yes, I would...speak with them."

Before the sorcerer could object, Gaunt said, "Alas, my king, Spawnsworth's fears are quite justified. I regret where duty leads."

With that, she drew a dagger and stabbed Sister Scald where her heart ought to have been.

By then Bone had sliced the glistening throats of Master Salt and Mistress Mist.

The king's tears lost their forms, spilling at once from their robes, flowing like pale blue quicksilver into the swan pool, where they spiraled down into the drain and were lost to sight.

"What?" King Rainjoy whispered, shaking, rising to his feet. "What?"

"It was necessary, Majesty," Gaunt said. "They had become mad. They meant you harm."

"We suspected," Bone said, "that only in your presence could they die."

"Die," echoed Rainjoy. He sank back onto the throne.

Spawnsworth had gone pale, his cloak twitching in agitated spasms. But his voice was calm as he said, "I will wish to investigate the matter, of course...but, it seems you have done the kingdom a great, ah, service. It is not too late, I would say, to consider a reward. You sought my advice?"

Rainjoy cradled his head in his hands.

"Alas," said Gaunt, her eyes on the king, "our time with the tears has been instructive regarding your art. It is powerful, to be sure, but not suited to our problem. No offense is meant."

Spawnsworth frowned. "Then gold, perhaps? Jewels?"

Bone swallowed, but said nothing.

"My king," said the sorcerer, "what do you...." Then he bit his lip.

Rainjoy wept.

"My king," repeated Spawnsworth, looking more nonplused than when Salt, Mist, and Scald vanished down the drains.

It was little more than a sparkling wetness along the left eye, a sheen that had barely begun to streak. Rainjoy wiped it with a silken sleeve. "It is nothing," Rainjoy said, voice cold.

Gaunt strode around the pool and up to the throne, ignoring Spawnsworth's warning look. She touched Rainjoy's shoulder.

"It is something," she said.

He stared at her wide-eyed, like a boy. "It is simply....I let them go for so long. I never imagined I would lose them forever. They did not obey."

"Oh my king," Gaunt said, "my dear king. Tears cannot obey. If they could, they would be saltwater only."

He held up the sleeve, dotted with a tiny wet stain. "I have tears again....I do not deserve them."

"Yet here they are. Listen to them, King Rainjoy,

even though these tears are mute. And never be parted from them."

The king watched as Gaunt returned to Bone's side. The poet gave the thief one nod, and Imago Bone offered the king an unexpectedly formal bow, before the two clasped hands and walked slowly toward the door. Rainjoy thought perhaps he heard the thief saying, *Your penance, Gaunt, will consist of a six-city larcenous spree which I shall now outline*, and the poet's answering laugh. Perhaps she cast a final look back, but the mists embraced her, and he would never be sure. He regretted it, that he'd never be sure.

"I am sad, Spawnsworth," he said, wondering. "I do not sense life's infinite sorrow. But I am sad."

But Spawnsworth did not answer, and the light in his eyes was not nascent tears but a murderous glint. He stalked up the stairs.

In his tower there twitched a menagerie of personifications: howling griefs, snarling passions, a stormy nature blustering in a crystal dome, a dark night of the soul shrouding the glass of a mirror. In places there lurked experiments that twitched and mewled. Here a flower of innocence sprouted from the forehead of a gargoyle of cynicism. There a phoenix of renewal locked eyes forever with a basilisk of stasis.

Spawnsworth arrived in this sanctum, teeth grinding, and began assembling the vials of love's betrayal and friendship's gloom, the vials he would form into an instrument of revenge upon Gaunt and Bone.

There came a cough behind him.

He whirled and beheld three shining intruders.

"We are not easily slain, as you should know," Master Salt said. He opened a cage.

"We, clearly, are more easily forgotten," said Mistress Mist. She unstoppered a flask.

"But we will see you never forget us," said Sister Scald, pushing a glass sphere to shatter against the floor. "We believe you could use our counsel. Ah, I see there are many here who agree."

As his creations swarmed toward him, it occurred to Spawnsworth that the many grates in the floor, used to drain away blood and more exotic fluids, fed the same sewers as those in the hall of mists. "You cannot do this," he hissed. "You are Rainjoy's, and he would never harm me."

"We are Rainjoy's no longer," the tears said.

He turned to flee, and felt his own cloak tremble with excitement and spill upward over his face.

Of the many voices heard from the sorcerer's tower that hour, the one most human, the palace servants agreed, was the one most frightening. When they found Spawnsworth's body in the room of empty cages, all remarked how the face was contorted with sorrow, yet the eyes were dry.

"Social Dreaming of the Frin"

Ursula K. Le Guin

On the Frinthian Plane dreams are not private property. There is no such thing as a dream of one's own. A troubled Frin has no need to lie on a couch recounting dreams to a psychoanalist, for the doctor already knows what the patient dreamed last night, because the doctor dreamed it too; and the patient also dreamed what the doctor dreamed; and so did everyone else in the neighborhood.

To escape from the dreams of others or to have a secret dream, the Frin must go out alone into the wilderness. And even in the wilderness, their sleep may be invaded by the strange dream-visions of lions, antelope, bears, or mice.

While awake, and during much of their sleep, the Frin are as dream-deaf as we are. Only sleepers who are in or approaching REM sleep can participate in the dreams of others also in REM sleep.

REM is an acronym for "rapid eye movement," a visible accompaniment of this stage of sleep; its signal in the brain is a characteristic type of electro-encephalic wave. Most of our rememberable dreams occur during REM sleep.

Frinthian REM sleep and that of people on our

75

plane yield very similar EEG traces, though there are some significant differences, in which may lie the key to their ability to share dreams.

To share, the dreamers must be fairly close to one another. The carrying power of the average Frinthian dream is about that of the average human voice. A dream can be received easily within a hundred-meter radius, and bits and fragments of it may carry a good deal farther. A strong dream in a solitary place may well carry for two kilometers or even farther.

In a lonely farmhouse a Frin's dreams mingle only with those of the rest of the family, along with echoes, whiffs, and glimpses of what the cattle in the barn and the dog dozing on the doorstep hear, smell, and see in their sleep.

In a village or town, with people asleep in all the houses round, the Frin spend at least part of every night in a shifting phantasmagoria of their own and other people's dreams which I find it hard to imagine.

I asked an acquaintance in a small town to tell me any dreams she could recall from the past night. At first she demurred, saying that they'd all been nonsense, and only "strong" dreams ought to be thought about and talked over. She was evidently reluctant to tell me, an outsider, things that had been going on in her neighbors' heads. I managed at last to convince her that my interest was genuine and not voyeuristic. She thought a while and said, "Well, there was a woman—it was me in the dream, or sort of me, but I think it was the mayor's wife's dream, actually, they live at the corner—this woman, anyhow, and she was trying to find a baby that she'd had last year. She had put the baby into a dresser drawer and forgotten all about it, and now I was, she was, feeling worried about it—Had it had anything to eat? Since last year?

O my word, how stupid we are in dreams! And then, oh, yes, then there was an awful argument between a naked man and a dwarf, they were in an empty cistern. That may have been my own dream, at least to start with. Because I know that cistern. It was on my grandfather's farm where I used to stay when I was a child. But they both turned into lizards, I think. And then—oh yes!"—she laughed—"I was being squashed by a pair of giant breasts, huge ones, with pointy nipples. I think that was the teenage boy next door, because I was terrified but kind of ecstatic, too. And what else was there? Oh, a mouse, it looked so delicious, and it didn't know I was there, and I was just about to pounce, but then there was a horrible thing, a nightmare—a face without any eyes—and huge, hairy hands groping at me—and then I heard the three-year-old next door screaming, because I woke up too. That poor child has so many nightmares, she drives us all crazy. Oh, I don't really like thinking about that one. I'm glad you forget most dreams. Wouldn't it be awful if you had to remember them all!"

Dreaming is a cyclical, not a continuous activity, and so in small communities there are hours when one's sleep-theater, if one may call it so, is dark. REM sleep among settled, local groups of Frin tends to synchronize. As the cycles peak, about five times a night, several or many dreams may be going on simultaneously in everybody's head, intermingling and influencing one another with their mad, inarguable logic, so that (as my friend in the village described it) the baby turns up in the cistern and the mouse hides between the breasts, while the eyeless monster disappears in the dust kicked up by a pig trotting past through a new dream, perhaps a dog's, since the pig is rather dimly seen, but is smelt with enormous particularity. But after such episodes comes a period when everyone can sleep in peace, without anything exciting happening at all.

In Frinthian cities, where one may be within dream-range of hundreds of people every night, the layering and overlap of insubstantial imagery is, I'm told, so continual and so confusing that the dreams cancel out, like brushfuls of colors slapped one over the other without design; even one's own dream blurs at once into the meaningless commotion, as if projected on a screen where a hundred films were already being shown, their soundtracks all running together. Only occasionally does a gesture, a voice, ring clear for a moment, or a particularly vivid wet dream or ghastly nightmare cause all the sleepers in a neighborhood to sigh, ejaculate, shudder, or wake up with a gasp.

Frin whose dreams are mostly troubling or disagreeable say they like living in the city for the very reason that their dreams are all but lost in the "stew," as they call it. But others are upset by the constant oneiric noise and dislike spending even a few nights in a metropolis. "I hate to dream strangers' dreams!" my village informant told me. "Ugh! When I come back from staying in the city, I wish I could wash out the inside of my head!"

Even on Our Plane, young children often have trouble understanding that the experiences they had just before they woke up aren't "real." It must be far more bewildering for Frinthian children, into whose innocent sleep enter the sensations and preoccupations of adults—accidents relived, griefs renewed, rapes reenacted, wrathful conversations with people fifty years in the grave. But adult Frin are ready to answer children's questions about the shared dreams and to discuss them, defining them always as dream, though not as unreal. There is no word corresponding to "unreal" in Frinthian; the nearest is "bodiless." So the children learn to live with adults' incomprehensible memories, unmentionable acts, and inexplicable emotions, much as do children who grow up on our plane amid the terrible incoherence of civil war or in times of plague and famine; or, indeed, children anywhere, at any time. Children learn what is real and what isn't, what to notice and what to ignore, as a survival tactic, a means of staying alive. It is hard for an outsider to judge, but my impression of Frinthian children is that they mature early, psychologically; and by the age of seven or eight they are treated by adults as equals.

As for the animals, no one knows what they make of the human dreams they evidently participate in. The domestic beasts of the Frin seemed to me to be remarkably pleasant, trustful, and intelligent. They are generally well looked after. The fact that they share their dreams with their animals might explain why the Frin use animals to haul and plow and for milk and wool, but not as meat.

The Frin say that animals are more sensitive dream-receivers than human beings, and can receive dreams even from people from other planes. Frinthian farmers have assured me that their cattle and swine are deeply disturbed by visits from people from carnivorous planes. When I stayed at a farm in Enya Valley the chicken-house was in an uproar half the night. I thought it was a fox, but my hosts said it was me.

People who have mingled their dreams all their lives say they are often uncertain where a dream began, whether it was originally theirs or somebody else's; but within a family or village the author of a particularly erotic or ridiculous dream may be all too easily identified. People who know one another well can recognize the source-dreamer from the tone or events of the dream, its style. But after all, it has become their own as they dream it. Each dream may be shaped differently in each mind. And, as with us, the personality of the dreamer, the oneiric I, is often tenuous, strangely disguised, or unpredictably different from the daylight person. Very puzzling dreams or those with powerful emotional affect may be discussed on and off all day by the community, without the origin of the dream ever being mentioned.

But most dreams, as with us, are forgotten at waking. Dreams elude their dreamers, on every plane.

It might seem to us that the Frin have very little psychic privacy; but they are protected by this common amnesia, as well as by doubt as to any particular dream's origin, and by the obscurity of dream itself. And their dreams are truly common property. The sight of a red and black bird pecking at the ear of a bearded human head lying on a plate on a marble table and the rush of almost gleeful horror that accompanied it—did that come from Aunt Unia's sleep, or Uncle Tu's, or Grandfather's, or the cook's, or the girl next door's? A child might ask, "Auntie, did you dream that head?" The stock answer is, "We all did." Which is, of course, the truth.

Frinthian families and small communities are close-knit and generally harmonious, though quarrels and feuds occur. The research group from Mills College that traveled to the Frinthian plane to record and study oneiric brainwave synchrony agreed that (like the synchronization of menstrual and other cycles within groups on our plane) communal dreaming may serve to strengthen the social bond. They did not speculate as to its psychological or moral effects.

From time to time a Frin is born with unusual powers of projecting and receiving dreams—never one without the other. The Frin call such a dreamer whose "signal" is unusually clear and powerful a strong mind. That strong-minded dreamers can receive dreams from non-Frinthian humans is a proven fact. Some of them apparently can share dreams with fish, with insects, even with trees. A legendary strong mind named Du Ir claimed that he "dreamed with the mountains and the rivers," but his boast is generally regarded as poetry.

Strong minds are recognized even before birth, when the mother begins to dream that she lives in a warm, amber-colored palace without directions or gravity, full of shadows and complex rhythms and musical vibrations, and shaken often by slow peaceful earthquakes—a dream the whole community enjoys, though late in the pregnancy it may be accompanied by a sense of pressure, of urgency, that rouses claustrophobia in some.

As the strong-minded child grows, its dreams reach two or three times farther than those of ordinary people, and tend to override or co-opt local dreams going on at the same time. The nightmares and inchoate, passionate deliria of a strong-minded child who is sick, abused, or unhappy can disturb everyone in the neighborhood, even in the next village. Such children, therefore, are treated with care; every effort is made to make their life one of good cheer and disciplined serenity. If the family is incompetent or uncaring, the village or town may intervene, the whole community earnestly seeking to ensure the child peaceful days and nights of pleasant dreams.

"World-strong minds" are legendary figures, whose dreams supposedly came to everyone in the world, and who therefore also dreamed the dreams of everyone in the world. Such men and women are revered as holy people, ideals and models for the strong dreamers of today. The moral pressure on strong-minded people is in fact intense, and so must be the psychic pressure. None of them lives in a city: they would go mad, dreaming a whole city's dreams. Mostly they gather in small communities where they live very quietly, widely dispersed from one another at night, practicing the art of "dreaming well," which mostly means dreaming harmlessly. But some of them become guides, philosophers, visionary leaders.

There are still many tribal societies on the Frinthian plane, and the Mills researchers visited several. They reported that among these peoples, strong minds are regarded as seers or shamans, with the usual perquisites and penalties of such eminence. If during a famine the tribe's strong mind dreams of traveling clear down the river and feasting by the sea, the whole tribe may share the vision of the journey and the feast so vividly, with such conviction, that they decide to pack up and start downriver. If they find food along the way, or shellfish and edible seaweeds on the beach, their strong mind gets rewarded with the choice bits; but if they find nothing or run into trouble with other tribes, the seer, now called "twisted mind," may be beaten or driven out.

The elders told the researchers that tribal councils usually follow the guidance of dream only if other indications favor it. The strong minds themselves urge caution. A seer among the Eastern zhud-Byu told the researchers, "This is what I say to my people: Some dreams tell us what we wish to believe. Some dreams tell us what we fear. Some dreams are of what we know though we may not know we knew it. The rarest dream is the dream that tells us what we did not know."

Frinthia has been open to other planes for over a century, but the rural scenery and quiet lifestyle have brought no great influx of visitors. Many tourists avoid the plane under the impression that the Frin are a race of "mindsuckers" and "psychovoyeurs."

Most Frin are still farmers, villagers, or town-dwellers, but the cities and their material technologies are growing fast. Though technologies and techniques can be imported only with the permission of the All-Frin government, requests for such permission by Frinthian companies and individuals have become increasingly frequent. Many Frin welcome this growth of urbanism and materialism, justifying it as the result of the interpretation of dreams received by their strong minds from visitors from other planes. "People came here with strange dreams," says the historian Tubar of Kaps, himself a strong mind. "Our strongest minds joined in them, and joined us with them. So we all began to see things we had never dreamed of. Vast gatherings of people, cybernets, ice cream, much commerce, many pleasant belongings and useful arti-facts. 'Shall these remain only dreams?' we said. 'Shall we not bring these things into wakeful being?' So we have done that."

Other thinkers take a more dubious attitude toward alien hypnogogia. What troubles them most is that the dreaming is not reciprocal. For though a strong mind can share the dreams of an alien visitor and "broadcast" them to other Frin, nobody from another plane has been capable of sharing the dreams of the Frin. We cannot enter their nightly festival of fantasies. We are not on their wavelength.

The investigators from Mills hoped to be able to reveal the mechanism by which communal dreaming is effected, but they failed, as Frinthian scientists have also failed, so far. "Telepathy," much hyped in the literature of the interplanary travel agents, is a label, not an explanation. Researchers have established that the genetic programming of all Frinthian mammals includes the capacity for dream-sharing, but its operation, though clearly linked to the brainwave synchrony of sleepers, remains obscure. Visiting foreigners do not synchronize; they do not participate in that nightly ghost-chorus of electric impulses dancing to the same beat. But unwittingly, unwillingly—like a deaf child shouting—they send out their own dreams to the strong minds asleep nearby. And to many of the Frin, this seems not so much a sharing as a pollution or infection.

"The purpose of our dreams," says the philosopher Sorrdja of Farfrit, a strong dreamer of the ancient Deyu Retreat, "is to enlarge our souls by letting us imagine all that can be imagined: to release us from the tyranny and bigotry of the individual self by letting us feel the fears, desires, and delights of every mind in every living body near us." The duty of the strong-minded person, she holds, is to strengthen dreams, to focus them—not with a view to practical results or new inventions, but as a means of understanding the world through a myriad of experiences and sentiences (not only human). The dreams of the greatest dreamers may offer to those who share them a glimpse of an order underlying all the chaotic stimuli, responses, acts, words, intentions, imaginings of daily and nightly existence.

"In the day we are apart," she says. "In the night we are together. We should follow our own dreams, not those of strangers who cannot join us in the dark. With such people we can talk; we can learn from them and teach them. We should do so, for that is the way of the daylight. But the way of the night is different. We go together then, apart from them. The dream we dream is our road through the night. They know our day, but not our night, nor the ways we go there. Only we can find our own way, showing one another, following the lantern of the strong mind, following our dreams in darkness."

The resemblance of Sorrdja's phrase "road through the night" to Freud's "royal road to the unconscious" is interesting but, I believe, superficial. Visitors from my plane have discussed psychological theory with the Frin, but neither Freud's nor Jung's views of dream are of much interest to them. The Frinthian "royal road" is trodden not by one secret soul but a multitude. Repressed feelings, however distorted, disguised, and symbolic, are the common property of everybody in one's household and neighborhood. The Frinthian unconscious, collective or individual, is not a dark wellspring buried deep under years of evasions and denials, but a kind of great moonlit lake to whose shores everybody comes to swim together naked every night.

And so the interpretation of dreams is not, among the Frin, a means of self-revelation, of private psychic inquiry and readjustment. It is not even species-specific, since animals share the dreams, though only the Frin can talk about them.

For them, dream is a communion of all the sentient

creatures in the world. It puts the notion of self deeply into question. I can imagine only that for them to fall asleep is to abandon the self utterly, to enter or reenter into the limitless community of being, almost as death is for us.

"Agamemnon's Run"
Robert Sheckley

Agamemnon was desperate. Aegisthus and his men had trapped him in Clytemnestra's bedroom. He could hear them stamping through the hallways. He had climbed out a window and made his way down the wall clinging by his fingernails to the tiny chiseled marks the stonecutters had left in the stone. Once in the street, he thought he'd be all right, steal a horse, get the hell out of Mycenae. It was late afternoon when he made his descent from the bedroom window. The sun was low in the west, and the narrow streets were half in shadow.

He thought he had got away free and clear. But no: Aegisthus had posted a man in the street, and he called out as soon as Agamemnon was on the pavement.

"He's here! Agamemnon's here! Bring help!"

The man was a beefy Spartan, clad in armor and helmet, with a sword and shield. Agamemnon had no armor, nothing but his sword and knife. But he was ready to tackle the man anyhow, because his rage was up, and although Homer hadn't mentioned it, Agamemnon was a fighter to beware of when his rage was up.

The soldier must have thought so. He retreated, darting into a doorway, still crying the alarm. Agamemnon decided to get out of there.

A little disoriented, he looked up and down the street. Mycenae was his own city, but he'd been away in Troy for ten years. If he turned to his left, would the street take him to the Lion Gate? And would Aegisthus have guards there?

Just that morning he had ridden into the city in triumph. It was hateful, how quickly things could fall apart.

He had entered Mycenae with Cassandra beside him in the chariot. Her hands were bound for form's sake, since she was technically a captive. But they had been bedmates for some weeks, ever since he had bought her from Ajax after they sacked Troy. Agamemnon thought she liked him, even though Greek soldiers had killed her parents and family. But that had been while their blood rage was still high; their rage at so many of their companions killed, and for the ten long wasted years camped outside Troy's walls, until Odysseus and his big wooden horse had done the trick. Then they'd opened the city gates from the inside and given the place over to rage, rape, and ruin.

None of them were very proud of what they'd done. But Agamemnon thought Cassandra understood it hadn't been personal. It wasn't that he was expecting forgiveness from her. But he thought she understood that the important ones—Agamemnon himself, Achilles, Hector, Odysseus—were not bound by the rules of common men.

They were special people, and it was easy to forget that he was not the original Agamemnon, not the first. The lottery had put them into this position, the damnable lottery which the aliens had set over them, with its crazed purpose of replaying events of the ancient world, only this time with the possibility of changing the outcomes.

He was Chris Johnson, but he had been Agamemnon for so long that he had nearly forgotten his life before the lottery chose him for this role.

And then there had been all the trouble of getting to Troy, the unfortunate matter of Iphigenia, the ten years waiting in front of the city, the quarrel with Achilles, and finally, Odysseus' wooden horse and the capture and destruction of Troy and nearly all its inhabitants, and then the long journey home over the wine-dark sea; his return to Mycenae, and now this.

And before that? He remembered a dusty, small town not far from the Mexican border. Amos' water tower had been the tallest building on the prairie for 200 miles in any direction. Ma's Pancake House had been the only restaurant. When he made his lucky draw in the lottery, he remembered thinking it would be worth life itself just to get out of here, just to live a little.

It had never been easy to get out of Mycenae. The city's heart was a maze of narrow streets and alleys. The district he was in, close to the palace, had an Oriental look—tiny shops on twisting streets. Many of the shopkeepers wore turbans. Agamemnon had never researched the life of the ancient Greeks, but he supposed this was accurate. The creators of the lottery did what they did for a reason.

The street Agamemnon was on came out on a broad boulevard lined with marble statues. Among them, Agamemnon recognized Perseus and Achilles, Athena and Artemis. The statues had been painted in bright colors. He was surprised to see a statue to himself. It didn't look much like him, but it had his name on it. In English letters, not Greek. It was a concession the lottery had made to modern times: everyone in this Greece spoke English. He wondered if the statue represented the first Agamemnon. He knew that the lottery was always repeating the classical roles. Had there ever been a first Agamemnon? With myths and legends, you could never be quite sure.

He saw that a procession was coming down the boulevard. There were musicians playing clarinet and trumpet. Timpani players. Even a piano, on a little cart, drawn by a donkey.

That was obviously not legitimate. But he reminded himself that the lottery was staging this, and they could make it any way they wanted it. He didn't even know where their Greece was. Behind the musicians there were dancing girls, in scanty tunics, with wreaths around their heads and flowers in their hair. They looked drunk. He realized that these must be maenads, the crazed followers of Dionysus, and behind them came Dionysus himself. As he came closer, Agamemnon recognized him. It was Ed Carter from Centerville, Illinois. They had met in one of the lottery staging rooms, where they had gone for their first assignments.

"Dionysus!" Agamemnon called out.

"Hello, Agamemnon, long time no see. You're looking good." Dionysus was obviously drunk. There were wine stains on his mouth and his tunic. He didn't seem able to pause in his dancing march, so Agamemnon walked along beside him.

"Going to join me?" Dionysus asked. "We're having

a feast later, and then we're going to tear apart King Pentheus."

"Is that strictly necessary?"

Dionysus nodded. "I was given specific orders. Pentheus gets it. Unless he can figure something out. But I doubt this one's up to it."

Agamemnon asked, a bit formally, "How is it going with you, Dionysus?"

Dionysus said, "Pretty well, Agamemnon. I'm getting into this. Though it was no fun being killed last week. A real bummer."

"I didn't hear about that."

"I didn't anticipate it myself," Dionysus said. "But they jump you around in time, you know, to make sure you cover all the salient points of your character's life. No sooner had I been married to Ariadne—did you ever meet her? Lovely girl. Abandoned by Theseus on the isle of Naxos, you know—and then I came along and married her. A bit sudden on both our parts, but what a time we had! Naxos is a lovely place—I recommend it for a holiday—anyhow, immediately after that, I found myself newborn in the Dictean cave. I think it was the Dictean. And these guys, these Titans with white faces were coming at me, obviously intending murder. I put up a hell of a struggle. I changed into a bird, a fish, a tree. I could have pulled it off, but the contest was rigged against me. I had to die in order to be reborn. They seized me at last and tore me apart, as my maenads will do for Pentheus. But Apollo gathered my bits, and Zeus took me into himself, and in due course I was reborn. And here I am, leading my procession of crazy ladies down the main street of Mycenae. Not bad for a kid from Centerville, Illinois, huh? And what about you, Agamemnon?"

"I've got some trouble," Agamemnon said. "Remember my wife, Clytemnestra? Well, she's sore as hell at me because she thinks I sacrificed our daughter Iphigenia."

"Why did you do that?"

"To call up a wind so the fleet could get to Troy. But I didn't really do it! I made it look like a sacrifice, but then I arranged for Artemis to carry Iphigenia away to Aulis, where she has a nice job as high priestess."

"Everyone thinks you had your daughter killed," Dionysus said.

"They're wrong! There's that version of the story that says I didn't. That's the one I'm going with. But that bitch Clytemnestra and her sleazy boyfriend Aegisthus won't buy it. They've got guards out all over the city with orders to kill me on sight."

"So what are you going to do?"

"I need a way out of this! Can you help me? Isn't there some way I can get out of this whole mess?"

"Maybe there is," Dionysus said. "But you'd have to ask Tiresias for specifics."

"Tiresias? He's dead, isn't he?"

"What does that matter? He was the supreme magician of the ancient world. He'd be glad to talk to you. He likes talking to live ones."

"But how do I get to the underworld?"

"You must kill someone, then intercept the Charon-function when it comes to carry off the shade, and accompany them across the Styx."

"I don't want to kill anyone. I've had enough of that."

"Then find someone on the point of death and it'll still work."

"But who?"

"What about Cassandra?"

"No, not Cassandra."

"She's doomed anyway."

"We think we've figured an out for her. Anyhow, I won't kill her."

"Suit yourself. Actually, anybody will do."

"I'm not going to just grab some person off the street and kill him!"

"Agamemnon, it's really not a time to be finicky....What about a plague victim? One not quite dead, but on the way?"

"Where would I find a plague victim?"

"Follow a plague doctor."

"How will I know Charon when he comes? His appearance is always invisible to any but the dead."

Dionysus frowned for a moment, then his brow cleared. He reached inside his tunic and took out a purple stone on a chain.

"They gave me this in Egypt. It's an Egyptian psychopomp stone. Some kind of amethyst, I believe. Take it. There's a doctor over there! Good luck, Agamemnon! I really must go now."

And with a wave of his hand, Dionysus danced off after his maenads.

Agamemnon saw the person Dionysus had been referring to: a tall, middle-aged man in a long black cloak, carrying an ivory cane, and wearing a conical felt cap on which was the symbol of Asclepius.

Agamemnon hurried over to him. "Are you a doctor?"

"I am. Strepsiades of Cos. But I can't stop and chat with you. I am on my way to a call."

"To a plague victim?"

"Yes, as it happens. A terminal case, I fear. The

family waited too long to send for me. Still, I'll do what I can."

"I want to go with you!"

"Are you a doctor? Or a relative?"

"Neither. I am—a reporter!" Agamemnon said in a burst of inspiration.

"How can that be? You have no newspapers here in Mycenae. I've heard that Argive Press managed to run for a while, but the price of copper went through the ceiling, and Egypt stopped exporting papyrus..."

"It's a new venture!"

The doctor made no comment when Agamemnon fell into step beside him. Agammemnon could tell the man wasn't pleased. But there was nothing he could do about it. He might even have been furious; but Agamemnon wore a sword, and the doctor appeared to be unarmed.

After several blocks, Agamemnon saw they were going into one of the slum areas of the city. *Great*, he thought. *What am I getting myself into?*

They went down a narrow alley, to a small hut at the end of it. Strepsiades pushed open the door and they entered. Within, visible by the gray light from a narrow overhead window and a single flickering oil lamp on the floor, a man lay on a tattered blanket on the ground. He appeared to be very old, and very wasted. Strepsiades knelt to examine him, then shook his head and stood up again.

"How long does he have?" Agamemnon asked.

"Not long, poor fellow. He's approaching the final crisis. You can tell by the skin color. Sometimes these cases linger on for a few hours more, half a day, even a day. But no longer."

"Let me look at him," Agamemnon said and knelt

down beside the sick man. The man's skin was bluish gray. His lips were parched and cracked. Thin lines of blood oozed from his nostrils and the corners of his eyes. The turgid blood was the only sign of life in the man.

Agamemnon was acutely aware that he had little time in which to make his escape from Mycenae. But the man was still alive. How long did he have to wait until he died? A minute? An hour? How long before Aegisthus' soldiers found him? He had to get it over with. He tried to make up his mind whether to smother or strangle the man.

He started to reach toward the man's throat. The man opened his eyes. With the man suddenly staring at him with bloodshot blue eyes, Agamemnon hesitated—

"King Agamemnon!" the sick man whispered. "Can it be you? I am Pyliades. I was a hoplite in the first rank of the Argolis Phalanx. I served under you in the Trojan War. What are you doing here, sir?"

Agamemnon heard himself say, "I heard of your plight, Pyliades, and came to wish you well."

"Very good of you, sire. But then, you always were a good man and a benevolent commander. I'm surprised you remember me. I was only a common soldier. My parents had to sell the farm in order to purchase my panoply, so I could march with the others and avenge Greece for the unfair abduction of our Helen."

"I remembered you, Pyliades, and came to say farewell. Our war is won. The might of Greece has prevailed. Of course, we had Achilles. But what good would Achilles have been if it weren't for men in the ranks like you?"

"I remember Prince Achilles well, and the burial

fires we lit for him when he was killed. I hope to see him again, in Hades. They say—"

The sick man's meandering discourse was broken as the door to his room was suddenly slammed open. Two armed soldiers pushed their way in. They hesitated, seeing the doctor in his long robe. Then they spotted Agamemnon.

The leading soldier, a burly red-bearded man, said, "Kill them all. Aegisthus wants no witnesses. I'll take care of Agamemnon myself."

The second soldier was the one who had spotted Agamemnon coming out of the palace window, and had run from him. He advanced now on the doctor, who raised his ivory cane to protect himself, saying, "There's no need for this. I am a neutral, a physician from Cos, here only to treat the sick and injured. Let me go, I'll never say a word about what's going on here."

The soldier glanced at the red-bearded man, evidently his officer, who muttered, "No witnesses!" Then he turned back to Agamemnon.

Agamemnon saw the doctor suddenly lift his staff and bring it down on the soldier's head. The rod broke. Growling, sword poised, the soldier advanced on the doctor.

Agamemnon could see no more, because the red-bearded man was coming at him. Agamemnon had his sword out, but without armor, he knew he stood little chance against an experienced hoplite. He circled around the sick man on his blanket, and the red-bearded soldier pursued, cautiously but relentlessly.

Agamemnon heard a scream. The doctor had been wounded, but was still fighting, trying to stab his assailant with the stub of his ivory cane. Agamemnon continued circling, winding his cloak around his left arm, but he knew it was hopeless, utterly hopeless....

And then, in an instant, everything changed.

Pyliades, with the last vestige of his strength, reached out and clutched the red-bearded soldier around the legs. The soldier staggered and cut viciously at the sick man. That moment offered Agamemnon's only chance, and he took it. With a hoarse cry he threw himself against the soldier, overbalancing him. The weight of the man's armor did the rest. He fell heavily over Pyliades' body, his sword caught in the sick man's chest, trapped between two ribs.

Agamemnon was on top of him. Releasing his own sword, Agamemnon pulled the knife from his belt and tried to stab the man in the face. The knife bounced off the metal nose guard, breaking at the tip. Agamemnon took better aim and pushed the knife through an opening in the helmet, past a missing cheek guard, into the man's cheek, up into his eye socket, and then, with a twist, into his brain.

Pyliades was croaking, "Good for you, Commander. We'll show these Trojan swine a thing or two..."

Agamemnon was already rolling to his feet, just in time to see the other soldier thrust his sword deep into the doctor's belly. The soldier's helmet had come off in the fight. Agamemnon seized him from behind, bent back his head, and cut his throat. There was silence in the house of the sick man.

There were four corpses on the floor. The doctor had just passed away. Pyliades was dead, but with a grin on his face. Agamemnon hoped it was a grin of triumph rather than the sardonic grin of the plague victim.

The soldier whose throat he'd cut lay in a pool of his own blood. Steam was rising from it. The red-bearded soldier, with the knife in his brain, wasn't bleeding much. But he was as dead as the others. Agamemnon himself was uninjured. He could scarcely believe it. He shook himself to make sure.

He was fine. Now, to find Charon.

He reached inside his tunic, pulled out the amethyst that Dionysus had given him. He looked around the room through it.

The room was a dark violet. The proportions weren't as he remembered them. The amethyst seemed to have distorting properties. Agamemnon experienced a wave of dizziness. He sat down on the floor. Taking a deep breath, he calmed himself with an effort of will and looked around the room again.

He saw what looked like a wisp of smoke taking shape. Was it from the oil lamp? No, that had been broken during the fight—a wonder it hadn't set the place on fire.

At the same time he felt the walls of the hovel changing, expanding, dissolving.

Agamemnon blinked. The room was transforming fast. He was disoriented. He could no longer see the walls. He was outside. He lowered the amethyst to reorient himself.

He was indeed outside. Not even in Mycenae. He was sitting on a boulder on a low, marshy shore. There was a river in front of him. Its waters were black, sleek, oily. It appeared to be twilight or early evening. The sun was nowhere in sight, although it had been afternoon when all this began. There were no stars in the darkness, no light anywhere. Yet he could see. Some distance ahead of him, on a low ridge of rock poking out of the mud, there were four figures. Agamemnon thought he knew who they were. In the gloom he could also make out a sort of dock on the shore beyond the four figures. A long, low boat was tied to one of its pillars, and a man was standing in it.

The man was gesturing, and his voice came through clearly. "Come on, you guys! You know the drill. Come to the boat. The boat's not going to come to you."

The four rose and began walking to the dock. Their steps were the slow, unhurried footsteps of the dead. Agamemnon got up and hurried to join them.

He reached the dock at the same time they did. He recognized the doctor, Pyliades, and the two soldiers.

The man in the boat was urging them to move along, get aboard, get on with it.

"Come on," he said, "I have no time to waste. Do you think you're the only dead awaiting transportation? Move along now, get aboard...You there," he said to Agamemnon, "you've got no business here. You're still living."

Agamemnon held up the amethyst. "I need to come aboard. You're Charon, aren't you?"

"His son," the man said. "One of his sons. We're all called Charon. Too much work for the old man alone. Too much for us now, too! But we do what we can. You've got the psychopomp stone, so I guess you can come aboard." He turned to the others. Did you bring any money for the passage?"

They shook their heads. "It was all too sudden," the doctor said.

"I will stand surety for them," Agamemnon said. "And for myself as well. I'll deposit the money wherever you want upon my return. You have the word of Agamemnon, king of kings."

"Make sure you don't forget, or when your time comes, your shade will be left here on the shore."

"How much do you want?" Agamemnon asked.

"The fee is one obol per dead man, but five obols for you because you're alive and weigh more. Go to any Thomas Cook, have them convert your currency into the obol, and deposit it in the Infernal Account."

"Thomas Cook has an infernal account."

"Didn't know that, did you?"

Agamemnon and the others got on Charon's boat. It was narrow, with two rows of built-in benches facing each other. Agamemnon and Pyliades sat on one side, the two soldiers on the other, and the doctor, after a moment's hesitation, sat on a little bench in front of a shelter cabin, at right angles to the benches. Charon untied the mooring line and pushed the boat away from the dock. Once free, he set a steering oar in place, and stood on the decked stern and began to gently scull the boat.

They sat in silence for a while as the boat glided over the dark waters.

At last Agamemnon said, "Is this going to take long?"

"It'll take as long as it takes," Charon said. "Why? You in a rush?"

"Not exactly," Agamemnon said. "Just curious. And interested in getting to the bottom of these mysteries."

"Give your curiosity a rest," Charon said. "Here in the land of the dead, just as in the land of the living, no sooner do you understand one mystery than another comes up to replace it. There's no satisfying curiosity. I remember when Heracles came through here. He was in a tearing hurry, couldn't wait to wrestle with Cerberus and bring him up to the world of the living."

"They say he succeeded," Agamemnon said.

"Sure. But what good did it do him? When he got back, King Eurystheus just had another job for him. There's no end of things to do when you're alive."

The red-bearded soldier abruptly said, "I just want you to know, Agamemnon, that I bear you no ill will for having killed me."

"That's good of you," Agamemnon said. "After you tried so hard to kill me."

"There was nothing personal about it," the red-beard said. "I am Sallices, commander of Aegithus' bodyguard in Mycenae. I was ordered to kill you. I follow orders."

"And look where they have brought you!" Agamemnon said.

"Where else would I be going but here? If not this year, then the next, or the one after that."

"I didn't expect to be killed," the other soldier said. "I am Creonides. My time in Aegisthus' service was over at the end of the week. I was going back to my little farm outside Argos. Returning to my wife and baby daughter."

"I can't believe this self-pitying nonsense," the doctor said. "My name is Strepsiades. I am a respected doctor of Cos, an island famous for its healers. I came to Mycenae for purely humanitarian reasons, to give what help I could to victims of the plague that you fellows carried back from Asia. And how am I rewarded? A villainous soldier kills me so there should be no witnesses to the illegal and immoral execution of his lord."

"But I was just following orders," Creonides said. "My immediate commander, Sallices here, ordered me to do it."

"And I," Sallices said, "was following the orders of my commander, the noble Aegisthus."

"But those were immoral orders!" Pyliades said, sitting up and speaking now for the first time in a firm deep voice, with no signs of plague on him. "Any man can see that!"

"Do you really think so?" Sallices asked. "And what if the orders were immoral? What is a soldier supposed to do, question and decide on each order given to him by his superiors? I've heard that you fellows did a few things you weren't so proud of during the Trojan War. Killing the whole population of Troy, and burning the city."

"We were avenging ourselve for the theft of Helen!" Plyiades declared hotly.

"And what was Helen to you?" Sallices asked. "Your wife or daughter? Not a bit of it! The wife of a king not even of your own country, since you are Argives, not Spartans. And anyhow, according to all accounts, the lady left Menelaus and went away with Paris willingly. So what were you avenging?"

"Our slain companions," Pyliades said. "Achilles, our beloved leader."

"Now that is really a laugh," Sallices said. "Your companions were there for the booty, and Achilles was there for the glory. Furthermore, he made his choice. It was prophesied he'd die gloriously at Troy, or lead a long inglorious life if he stayed home. No one had to die for poor Achilles! He made his choice to die for himself."

There was silence for a while. Then Doctor Strepsiades said, "It must all have seemed different at the time. Men's choices are not presented to them in a reflective space. They come in the clamor and fury of the moment, when a choice must be made at once, for better or worse."

"Is it the same with you, Doctor?" Agamemnon asked. "Or are you alone blameless among us?"

Dr. Strepsiades was silent for a long while. At last he said, "My motives were not entirely humanitarian. I might as well confess this to you, since I will have to tell it to the Judges of the Dead. Queen Clytemnestra sent a herald to our school of physicians on Cos, imploring us for help with the plague, and offering a recompense. I was able to buy a nice little house in the city for my wife and children before I embarked."

"Clytemnestra!" Agamemnon said. "That murderous bitch!"

"She was trying to look out for her people," Strepsiades said. "And besides, she had her reasons. We have it on good authority that you sacrificed your daughter Iphigenia to call up a breeze to carry you and your men to Troy."

"Now wait a minute," Agamemnon said. "There's another version of the story in which the goddess Artemis took Iphigenia to Aulis, to be high priestess to the Taurians."

"I don't care about your face-saving version," Strepsiades said. "It was probably inspired by political reasons. In your heart you know you sacrificed your daughter."

Agamemnon sighed and did not answer.

"And not only did you do that, but you also involved your son, Orestes, in matricide, from which came his agony and his madness."

"None of that could be predicted at the time," Agamemnon said. "Charon, what do you think?"

Charon said, "We have been doing this ferrying for a long time, my father, my brothers, and I, and we share all the information we pick up. We have some questions, too, first and foremost about ourselves."

Charon took a drink of wine from a leather flask lying in the bottom of the boat, and continued.

"What are we here for? Why is there a Charon, or a Charon-function? Are we anything apart from our function? Just as you might ask, Agamemnon, whether you are anything apart from the morally ambiguous story of your life? A story which, for all intents and purposes, has no end and no beginning, and which in one guise or another is always contemporaneous, always happening. Do you ever get any time off from being the Agamemnon-function, do you ever have a chance for some good meaningless fun? Or do you always have to operate your character? Can you do anything without your act proposing a moral question, a dilemma for the ages, ethically unanswerable by its very nature?"

"What about the rest of us?" Strepsiades asked. "Are our lives negligible just because they don't pose a great moral question like Agamemnon's?"

"You and Agamemnon alike are equally negligible," Charon said. "You are merely the actors of old stories, which have more or less significance as the fashions of the times dictate. You are human beings, and you cannot be said to be with or without significance. But one like you, Agamemnon, is a symbol and a question mark to the human race, just as the human race is to all intelligent life in the Kosmos."

A chilling thought crossed Agamemnon's mind.

"And you, Charon? What are you? Are you human? Are you one of those who brought us the lottery?"

"We are living beings of some sort," Charon said. "There are more questions than answers in this matter of living. And now, gentlemen, I hope this conversation has diverted you, because we are at our destination."

Looking over the side of the boat, Agamemnon could see a dark shoreline coming up. It was low, like the one they had left, but this one had a bright fringe of sandy beach.

The boat made a soft grating sound as Charon ran it onto the sand.

"You are here," Charon said, and then to Agamemnon: "Don't forget you owe me payment."

"Farewell, Commander," said Pyliades. "I hope for a favorable judgment, and to see you again in the palace of Achilles, where they say he lives with Helen, the most beautiful woman who ever was or ever will be. They say the two of them feast the heroes of the Trojan War, and declaim the verses of Homer in pure Greek. I was not a hero, nor do I even speak Greek; but Achilles and Helen may welcome people like me—I have a cheery face now that death has removed the plague from me—and can be counted upon to applaud the great heroes of our Trojan enterprise."

"I hope it turns out so," Agamemnon said. It may be a while before I come there myself, since I am still alive."

The others said their farewells to Agamemnon, and assured him they bore him no ill will for their deaths. Then the four walked in the direction of the Judges' seats, which were visible on a rise of land. But Agamemnon followed a sign that read, "This way to the Orchards of Elysium and the Islands of the Blest."

For these were the regions where he expected to find Tiresias.

He walked through pleasant meadowlands, with cattle grazing in the distance. These, he had been told, were part of Helios' herd, which were always straying into this part of Hades, where the grass was greener.

After a while he came to a valley. In the middle of the valley was a small lake. A man stood in the middle of the lake with water up to his mouth. There were trees growing along the lakeshore, fruit trees, and their branches hung over the man in the water, and ripe fruit drooped low over his head. But when he reached up to pick a banana or an apple—both grew on the same tree—the fruit shrank back out of his reach.

Agamemnon thought he knew who this was, so he walked to the shore of the lake and called out, "Hello, Tantalus!" The man in the water said, "Why, if it isn't Agamemnon, ruler of men! Have you come to rule here in hell, Agamemnon?"

"Certainly not," Agamemnon said. "I'm just here for a visit. I've come to talk with Tiresias. Would you happen to know where I might find him?"

"Tirisias keeps a suite in Hades' palace. It's just to your left, over that rise. You can't miss it."

"Thanks very much, Tantalus. Is it very onerous, this punishment the gods have decreed for you? Is there anything I can do?"

"Good of you to ask," Tantalus said. "But there's nothing you could do for me. Besides, this punishment is not as terrible as it might seem. The gods are relentless in decreeing punishment, but they don't much care who actually does it. So a couple of us swap punishments, and thus get some relief from the same thing over and over."

"Who do you trade with, if you don't mind my asking?"

"By no means. A bit of conversation is a welcome diversion. Sisyphus, Prometheus, and I from time to time take over one another's punishments. The exercise of pushing Sisyphus' boulder does me good—otherwise I might get fat—I tend to gorge when I get the chance."

"But to have your liver torn out by a vulture when you take over for Prometheus—that can't be much fun."

"You'd be surprised. The vulture often misses the liver, chews at a kidney instead, much less hurtful. Especially when you consider that here in hell, sensation is difficult to come by. Even King Achilles and Queen Helen, each blessed with the unsurpassed beauty of the other, have a bit of trouble feeling desire without bodies. Pain is a welcome change to feeling nothing."

Agamemnon set out again in the direction Tantalus had indicated. He went across a high upland path, and saw below a pleasant grove of pine trees. There were a dozen or so men and women in white robes, strolling around and engaging in animated conversation.

Agamemnon walked over to them and announced who he was. A woman said, "We know who you are. We were expecting you, since your trip here was mentioned in several of the books that were lost when the great library at Alexandria burned. In honor of your arrival, several of us have written philosophical speeches entitled 'Agamemnon's Lament.' These speeches are about the sort of things we thought we would hear from you."

"Since you knew I was coming, why didn't you wait and hear what I actually did say?"

"Because, Agamemnon, what we did is the philosophical way, and the way of action. We wrote your speech ourselves, instead of passively waiting for you to write it, if you ever would. And, since you are not a philosopher yourself, we thought you were unlikely to cast your thoughts into a presentation sufficiently rigorous for an intelligent and disinterested observer. Nor were you a dramatist, so your thoughts were unlikely to have either the rigor or beauty of a philosophical dramatist such as Aeschylus or Sophocles. Since words once said cannot be unsaid, as conversation permits no time for reflection and revision, we took the liberty of putting what we thought you would be likely to say into proper grammatical form, carefully revised, and with a plethora of footnotes to make the meaning of your life and opinions clear to even the meanest understanding."

"Very good of you, I'm sure," said Agamemnon, who, although deficient in philosophy, had a small but useful talent for irony.

"We don't expect our work will represent you, Agamemnon, the man," another philosopher said. "But we hope we've done justly by you, Agamemnon, the position."

"This is all very interesting," Agamemnon said. "But could you tell me now how I might find Tiresias?"

The philosophers conferred briefly. Then one of them said, "We do not recognize Tiresias as a philosopher. He is a mere shaman."

"Is that bad?" Agamemnon asked.

"Shamans may know some true things, but they are not to be relied upon because they do not know why or how they know. Lacking this—"

"Hey," Agamemnon said, "The critique of shamanism is unnecessary. I just want to talk to the guy."

"He's usually in the little grove behind Achilles' palace. Come back if you want a copy of our book of your opinions."

"I'll do that," Agamemnon said, and walked away in the direction indicated.

Agamemnon passed through a little wood. He noticed it was brighter here than in the other parts of Hades he had visited. Although no sun was visible, there was a brightness and sparkle to the air. He figured he was in one of the better parts of the underworld. He was not entirely surprised when he saw, ahead of him, a table loaded with food and drink, and a masked man in a long cloak sitting at it, with an empty chair beside him.

The man waved. "Agamemnon? I heard you were looking for me, so I've made it easy by setting myself in your path. Come have a chair, and let me give you some refreshment."

Agamemnon walked over and sat down. "You are Tiresias?"

"I am. Would you like some wine?"

"A glass of wine would be nice." He waited while Tiresias poured, then said, "May I ask why you are masked?"

"A whim," Tiresias said. "And something more. I am a magician, or shaman, to use a term popular in your time. Upon occasion I go traveling, not just here in ancient Greece, but elsewhere in space and time."

"And you don't want to be recognized?"

"It can be convenient, to be not too well known. But that's not the real reason. You see, Agamemnon, knowing someone's face can give you a measure of power over him. So Merlin discovered when he consorted with the witch Nimue, and she was able to enchant him. I do not give anyone power over me if I can help it."

"I can't imagine anyone having power over you."

"I could have said the same for Merlin, and one or two others. Caution is never out of place. Now tell me why you seek me out. I know, of course. But I want to hear it from your own lips."

"It's no secret," Agamemnon said. "My wife, Clytemnestra, and her lover, Aegisthus, have sworn to kill me. I come to you to ask if there is some way out of this Greek trap I am in."

"You are supposed to be slain for having sacrificed your daughter Iphigenia, so your fleet could sail to Troy."

"Now wait a minute!" Agamemnon said. "There's another version in which I did not kill Iphigenia. She's alive now in Aulis!"

"Don't try to deceive me with tricky words," Tiresias said. "Both versions of your story are true. You both killed and did not kill your daughter. But you are guilty in either version, or both. Have you ever heard of Schrödinger's cat? It was a scientific fable popular in your day and age."

"I've heard of it," Agamemnon said. "I can't pretend I ever really understood it."

"The man who concocted the fable is condemned, though no cat was ever slain. And this is true in the two worlds."

Agamemnon was silent for a while. He had been

watching Tiresias' mask, which at times seemed made of beaten gold, at other times of golden cloth that billowed when he spoke.

After a while, Agamemnon asked, "What two worlds are you speaking of?"

"The world of Earth with its various time lines, and the world of the lottery."

"So there's no escape?"

"My dear fellow, I never said that. I only wanted to point out that you're in a far more complicated and devious game than you had imagined."

"Why have the people of the lottery done this to us?"

"For the simplest and most obvious of reasons. Because it seemed a good idea to them at the time. Here was Earth, a perfect test case for those who could manipulate the time lines. Here were the stories of the Greeks, which the human world is not finished with yet. It seemed to the makers of the lottery that here was a perfect test case. They decided to live it through again, and again, to see if the moral equations would come out the same."

"And have they?"

The tall figure of Tiresias shrugged, and Agamemnon had the momentary impression that it was not a man's form beneath the cloak.

"As I said, it seemed a good idea at the time. But that was then, and yesterday's good idea doesn't look so good today."

"Can you tell me how to get out of here?"

Tiresias nodded. "You'll have to travel on the River of Time."

"I never heard of it."

"It's a metaphor. But the underworld is a place where metaphors become realities."

"Metaphor or not, I don't see any river around here," Agamemnon said.

"I'll show you how to get to it. There's a direct connection, a tunnel from here to Scylla and Charybdis, both of which border the ocean. You'll go through the tunnel which will lead you there."

"Isn't there some other way to get there?"

Tiresias continued, "This is the only way. Once past Scylla and Charybdis, you'll see a line of white breakers. Cross them. You will be crossing the river in the ocean that goes into the past. You don't want that one. You'll see another line of breakers. Cross these and you will be in the river that will carry you from the past into the future."

"The past...but where in the future?"

"To a place you will know, Agamemnon. Wait no longer. Do this now."

Agamemnon got up and walked in the direction Tiresias had indicated. When he looked back, the magician was gone. Had he been there in the first place? Agamemnon wasn't sure. The indirections of the lottery were bad enough. But when you added magic...

He saw something light-colored, almost hidden beneath shrubbery. It was the entrance to a tube burrowing down into the earth. Wide enough so he could get into it. A tube of some light-colored metal, aluminum, perhaps, and probably built by the lottery people, since aluminum hadn't been used in the ancient world.

Was he really supposed to climb through it? He hesitated, and then saw that there was a woman standing close to the tube. From the look of her, he knew it could only be one woman.

"Helen!"

"Hello, Agamemnon. I don't believe we ever got to meet properly before. I have come to thank you for sending me home to Menelaus. And to offer you my hospitality here in the Elysian Fields."

"You are too kind, Queen Helen. But I must go home now."

"Must you?"

Agamemnon hesitated. Never had he been so sorely tempted. The woman was the epitome of all his dreams. There could be nothing as wonderful as to be loved by Helen.

"But your new husband, Achilles—"

"Achilles has a great reputation, but he is dead, Agamemnon, just as I am. A dead hero does not even compare to a live dog. You are alive. Alive and in hell! Such a wonderful circumstance is rare. When Heracles and Theseus were here, they were only passing through. Besides, I was not here then. Things might have been different if I had been!"

"I am alive, yes," Agamemnon said. "But I will not be allowed to stay here."

"I'll talk Hades into it. He likes me—especially with his wife Persephone gone for half a year at a time."

Agamemnon could glimpse the future. It thrilled him and frightened him. But he knew what he wanted. To stay here with Helen—as much of Helen as he could get....

She held out her hand. He reached toward her—

And heard voices in the distance.

And then he saw shapes in the sky. One was a tall, handsome, thickset middle-aged woman, with long loose dark hair. The other was young, tall, slim, with fair hair piled up on her head and bound with silver ornaments.

The women seemed to be walking down the sky toward him, and they were in vehement discussion.

"You must tell him to his face what he did!" the older woman was saying.

"Mummy, there's no reason to make a scene."

"But he had you killed, can't you understand that? Your throat cut on the altar! You must tell him so to his face."

"Mummy, I don't want to accuse Daddy of so gross a crime. Anyhow, there's another version that says that Artemis rescued me and carried me to the Taurians, where I served as high priestess."

"Agamemnon killed you! If not literally, then figuratively, no matter which version of the story you're following. He's guilty in either version."

"Mummy, calm down, I don't want to accuse him."

"You little idiot, you'll do as I tell you. Look, we're here. There he is, the great killer. Ho, Agamemnon!"

Agamemnon could listen no longer. Letting go of Helen's hand, aware that he was forsaking the good things of death for the pain and uncertainty of life, he plunged into the underbrush and hurled himself into the white metal tube.

Agamemnon had been prepared for a precipitous passage downward, but not for the circling movement he underwent as the tube spiraled in its descent. It was dark, and he could see no light from either end. He was moving rapidly, and there seemed nothing he could do to hasten or slow his progress. He was carried along by gravity, and his fear was that his wife and daughter would enter the tube in pursuit of him. He thought that would be more than he could bear.

He continued to fall through the darkness, scraping against the sides of the tube. The ride came to an abrupt end when he suddenly fell through the end of it. He had a heart-stopping moment in the air, then he was in the water.

The shock of that cold water was so great that he found himself paralyzed, unable to make a move.

And he came out on a corner of a small south Texas town. There was José, standing beside the pickup parked in front of the general store. José gasped when he saw Chris. For a moment he was frozen. Then he hurried over to him. "Senor Chrees! Is it you?" There were hugs, embraces. When he'd left for the lottery and distant places, he'd left them to run the ranch. Make what they could out of it. But it was still his ranch, and he was home. Maria said, "I make your favorite, turkey mole tonight!" And then she talked about their cousins in Mexico, some of whom he'd known as a boy.

There was more shopping, and then they were driving down the familiar dirt road with its cardboard stretches, to the ranch. José drove them to the ranch in his old pickup. The ranch looked a little rundown, but very good. Chris lounged around in the kitchen. Chris dozed on the big old sofa, and dreamed of Greece and Troy. And then dinner was served.

After dinner, Chris went into the front room and lay down on the old horsehair sofa. It was deliciously comfortable, and the smells were familiar and soothing. He drifted into sleep, and knew that he was sleeping. He also knew when the dream began: it was when he saw the tall, robed figure of Tiresias.

Tiresias nodded to him and sat down on the end of the couch. It crossed Chris' mind that he might be in danger from a dream-figure, but there was nothing he could do about it.

"I came here to make sure you got home all right. When you enter the River of Time, you can never be too sure."

"Yes, I am back where I ought to be. Tell me, Tiresias, is there a danger of Clytemnestra finding me here?"

"She will not find you here. But punishment will. It is inescapable."

"What am I to be punished for? I didn't do anything!"

"When you were Agamemnon, you killed your daughter. For that deed, you owe Necessity a death."

"But the version I'm going by—"

"Forget such puerile nonsense. A young woman has been killed. In Homer, whose rules we're going by, there is no guilt. But there is punishment. Punishment is symbolic of the need for guilt, which still hadn't been invented in Homer's time. We learn through guilt. Thus we return to innocence."

"I thought, if I came home, I'd be free of all that. And anyhow, Artemis—"

"Forget such specious nonsense. It shows why Plato hated sophists. No one learns anything by making the worse case the better. The Agamemnon situation is a curse, and it goes on and on, gathering energy through expiation and repetition. The Greeks had a predilection for creating these situations—Oedipus, Tantalus, Sisyphus, Prometheus, the list is endless. One character after another falls into a situation that must be solved unfairly. The case is never clear, but punishment always follows."

"Does it end here?"

"The expiation for mythic conditions never ends. Opening into the unknowable is the essence of humanity."

Then Chris dreamed that he sat up on his couch, opened his shirt, and said, "Very well, then—strike!"

"A truly Agamemnon-like gesture, Chris. But I am not going to kill you."

"You're not? Why are you here then?"

"At these times, a magician is always present to draw the moral."

"Which is?"

"It is an exciting thing to be a human being."

"You're here to tell me that? So Clytemnestra gets her revenge!"

"And is killed in turn by Orestes. Nobody wins in these dreams, Chris."

"So that's what you came here to tell me."

"That, and to take care of some loose ends. Goodbye, Chris. See you in hell."

And with that, Tiresias was gone.

Chris woke up with a start. The dream of Tiresias had been very real. But it was over now, and he was back at his Texas ranch. He sat up. It was evening. It had turned cold after the sun went down. He got up. Hearing his footsteps, Maria came running in from the kitchen. She was carrying his old suede jacket.

"You put this on, Mr. Chris," she said, and threw the jacket around his shoulders.

The jacket was curiously constricting. Chris couldn't

move his arms. And then José was there, and somehow they were bending his head back.

"What are you doing?" Chris asked, but he really didn't have to be told when he caught the flash of steel in José's hand.

"How could you?" he asked.

"Hey, Mr. Chris, we join the lottery, me and Maria!" José said. "I'm going to be the new Agamemnon, she's Clytemnestra, but we take care of the trouble before it begins. We kill the old Agamemnon, so it doesn't have to happen again!"

Chris thought it was just like José to get things mixed up, to try to solve a myth before it began. He wondered if Cassandra had hinted at this outcome, and if he had ignored her, since that was her curse. He sank to the floor. The pain was sharp and brief, and he had the feeling that there was something he had left undone, though he couldn't remember what it was....

He couldn't know it, not at that time, that a man in a yellow buffalo-hide coat had gone to the local branch of Thomas Cook and put in a payment. He had it directed to the Infernal Account. The clerk had never heard of that account, but when he checked with the manager, there it was.

The payment ensured that Chris wouldn't be left for eternity on the wrong shore of Styx, and that the other four were paid for, too.

It was a little nicety on the part of Tiresias. He hadn't had to do it, but he did it anyhow. Those old magicians had class. And anyhow, that's what a good magician does—he ties up loose ends.

"Creation"
Jeffrey Ford

I learned about Creation from Mrs. Grimm, in the basement of her house around the corner from ours. The room was dimly lit by a stained-glass lamp positioned above the pool table. There was also a bar in the corner, behind which hung an electric sign that read *Rheingold* and held a can that endlessly poured golden beer into a pilsner glass that never seemed to overflow. That brew was liquid light, bright bubbles never ceasing to rise.

"Who made you?" she would ask, consulting that little book with the pastel-colored depictions of agony in hell and the angel-strewn clouds of heaven. She had the nose of a witch, one continuous eyebrow, and tea-cup-shiny skin—even the wrinkles seemed capable of cracking. Her smile was merely the absence of a frown, but she made candy apples for us at Halloween and marshmallow bricks in the shapes of wise men at Christmas. I often wondered how she had come to know so much about God and pictured saints with halos and cassocks playing pool and drinking beer in her basement at night.

We kids would page through our own copies of the catechism book to find the appropriate response, but before anyone else could answer, Amy Lash would already be saying, "God made me."

Then Richard Antonelli would get up and jump

around, making fart noises through his mouth, and Mrs. Grimm would shake her head and tell him God was watching. I never jumped around, never spoke out of turn, for two reasons, neither of which had to do with God. One was what my father called his size ten, referring to his shoe, and the other was that I was too busy watching that sign over the bar, waiting to see the beer finally spill.

The only time I was ever distracted from my vigilance was when she told us about the creation of Adam and Eve. After God had made the world, he made them too, because he had so much love and not enough places to put it. He made Adam out of clay and blew life into him, and once he came to life, God made him sleep and then stole a rib and made the woman. After the illustration of a naked couple consumed in flame, being bitten by black snakes and poked by the fork of a pink demon with horns and bat wings, the picture for the story of the creation of Adam was my favorite. A bearded God in flowing robes leaned over a clay man, breathing blue-gray life into him.

That breath of life was like a great autumn wind blowing through my imagination, carrying with it all sorts of questions like pastel leaves that momentarily obscured my view of the beautiful flow of beer: Was dirt the first thing Adam tasted? Was God's beard brushing against his chin the first thing he felt? When he slept, did he dream of God stealing his rib and did it crack when it came away from him? What did he make of Eve and the fact that she was the only woman for him to marry? Was he thankful it wasn't Amy Lash?

Later on, I asked my father what he thought about the creation of Adam, and he gave me his usual response to any questions concerning religion. "Look," he said, "it's a nice story, but when you die you're food for the worms." One time my mother made him take me to church when she was sick, and he sat in the front row, directly in front of the priest. While everyone else was genuflecting and standing and singing, he just sat there staring, his arms folded and one leg crossed over the other. When they rang the little bell and everyone beat their chest, he laughed out loud.

No matter what I had learned in catechism about God and hell and the ten commandments, my father was hard to ignore. He worked two jobs, his muscles were huge, and once, when the neighbors' Doberman, big as a pony, went crazy and attacked a girl walking her poodle down our street, I saw him run outside with a baseball bat, grab the girl in one arm and then beat the dog to death as it tried to go for his throat. Throughout all of this he never lost the cigarette in the corner of his mouth and only put it out in order to hug the girl and quiet her crying.

"Food for the worms," I thought and took that thought along with a brown paper bag of equipment through the hole in the chain link fence into the woods that lay behind the school yard. Those woods were deep, and you could travel through them for miles and miles, never coming out from under the trees or seeing a backyard. Richard Antonelli hunted squirrels with a BB gun in them, and Bobby Lenon and his gang went there at night, lit a little fire and drank beer. Once, while exploring, I discovered a rain-sogged *Playboy*; once, a dead fox. Kids said there was gold in the creek that wound among the trees and that there was a far-flung acre that sank down into a deep valley where the deer went to die. For many years it was rumored that a monkey, escaped from a traveling carnival over in Brightwaters, lived in the treetops.

It was mid-summer and the dragonflies buzzed, the squirrels leaped from branch to branch, frightened sparrows darted away. The sun beamed in through gaps in the green above, leaving, here and there, shifting puddles of light on the pine-needle floor. Within one of those patches of light, I practiced creation. There was no clay, so I used an old log for the body. The arms were long, five-fingered branches that I positioned jutting out from the torso. The legs were two large birch saplings with plenty of spring for running and jumping. These I laid angled to the base of the log.

A large hunk of bark that had peeled off an oak was the head. On this I laid red mushroom eyes, curved barnacles of fungus for ears, a dried seed pod for a nose. The mouth was merely a hole I punched through the bark with my pen knife. Before affixing the fern hair to the top of the head, I slid beneath the curve of the sheet of bark those things I thought might help to confer life—a dandelion gone to ghostly seed, a cardinal's wing feather, a see-through quartz pebble, a twenty-five-cent compass. The ferns made a striking hairdo, the weeds, with their burr-like ends, formed a venerable beard. I gave him a weapon to hunt with: a long pointed stick that was my exact height.

When I was finished putting my man together, I stood and looked down upon him. He looked good. He looked ready to come to life. I went to the brown paper bag and took out my catechism book. Then kneeling near his right ear, I whispered to him all of the questions Mrs. Grimm would ever ask. When I got to the one, "What is Hell?" his left eye rolled off his face, and I had to put it back. I followed up the last answer with a quick promise never to steal a rib.

Putting the book back into the bag, I then retrieved a capped, cleaned-out baby-food jar. It had once held vanilla pudding, my little sister's favorite, but now it was filled with breath. I had asked my father to blow into it. Without asking any questions, he never looked away from the racing form, but took a drag from his cigarette and blew a long, blue-gray stream of air into it. I capped it quickly and thanked him. "Don't say I never gave you anything," he mumbled as I ran to my room to look at it beneath a bare light bulb. The spirit swirled within and then slowly became invisible.

I held the jar down to the mouth of my man, and when I couldn't get it any closer, I unscrewed the lid and carefully poured out every atom of breath. There was nothing to see, so I held it there a long time and let him drink it in. As I pulled the jar away, I heard a breeze blowing through the leaves; felt it on the back of my neck. I stood up quickly and turned around with a keen sense that someone was watching me. I got scared. When the breeze came again, it chilled me, for wrapped in it was the quietest whisper ever. I dropped the jar and ran all the way home.

That night as I lay in bed, the lights out, my mother sitting next to me, stroking my crewcut and softly singing, "Until the Real Thing Comes Along," I remembered that I had left my catechism book in the brown bag next to the body of the man. I immediately made believe I was asleep so that my mother would leave. Had she stayed, she would have eventually felt my guilt through the top of my head. When the door was closed over, I began to toss and turn, thinking of my man lying out there in the dark woods by himself. I promised God that I would go out there in the morning, get my book, and take my creation apart. With the first bird song in the dark of the new day, I fell asleep and dreamed I was in Mrs. Grimm's basement with the saints. A beautiful woman saint with a big rose bush thorn sticking right in the middle of her forehead told me, "Your man's name is Cavanaugh."

"Hey, that's the name of the guy who owns the deli in town," I told her.

"Great head cheese at that place," said a saint with a baby lamb under his arm.

Another big bearded saint used the end of a pool cue to cock back his halo. He leaned over me and asked, "Why did God make you?"

I reached for my book but realized I had left it in the woods.

"Come on," he said, "that's one of the easiest ones."

I looked away at the bar, stalling for time while I tried to remember the answer, and just then the glass on the sign overflowed and spilled onto the floor.

The next day, my man, Cavanaugh, was gone. Not a scrap of him left behind. No sign of the red feather or the clear pebble. This wasn't a case of someone having come along and maliciously scattered him. I searched the entire area. It was a certainty that he had risen up, taken his spear and the brown paper bag containing my religious instruction book, and walked off into the heart of the woods.

Standing in the spot where I had given him life, my mind spiraled with visions of him loping along on his birch legs, branch fingers pushing aside sticker bushes and low hanging leaves, his fern hair slicked back by the wind. Through those red mushroom eyes, he was seeing his first day. I wondered if he was as frightened to be alive as I was to have made him, or had the breath of my father imbued him with a grim food-for-the-worms courage? Either way, there was no dismantling him now—Thou shalt not kill. I felt a grave responsibility and went in search of him.

I followed the creek, thinking he would do the same, and traveled deeper and deeper into the woods. What was I going to say to him, I wondered, when I finally found him and his simple hole of a mouth formed a question? It wasn't clear to me why I had made him, but it had something to do with my father's idea of death—a slow rotting underground; a cold dreamless sleep longer than the universe. I passed the place where I had discovered the dead fox and there picked up Cavanaugh's trail—holes poked in the damp ground by the stride of his birch legs. Stopping, I looked all around through the jumbled stickers and bushes, past the trees, and detected no movement but for a single leaf silently falling.

I journeyed beyond the Antonelli brothers' lean-to temple where they hung their squirrel skins to dry and brewed sassafras tea. I even circled the pond, passed the tree whose bark had been stripped in a spiral by lightning, and entered territory I had never seen before. Cavanaugh seemed to stay always just ahead of me, out of sight. His snake-hole footprints, bent and broken branches, and that barely audible and constant whisper on the breeze that trailed in his wake drew me on into the late afternoon until the woods began to slowly fill with night. Then I had a thought of home: my mother cooking dinner and my sister playing on a blanket on the kitchen floor; the Victrola turning out The Ink Spots. I ran back along my path, and somewhere in my flight I heard a loud cry, not bird nor animal nor human, but like a thick limb splintering free from an ancient oak.

I ignored the woods as best I could for the rest of the summer. There was basketball, and games of guns with all of the children in the neighborhood ranging across everyone's backyard, trips to the candy store for comic books, late night horror movies on Chiller Theatre. I caught a demon jab of hell for having lost my religious instruction book, and all of my allowance for four weeks went toward another. Mrs. Grimm told me God knew I had lost it and that it would be a few weeks before she could get me a replacement. I imagined her addressing an envelope to heaven. In the meantime, I had to look on with Amy Lash. She'd lean close to me, pointing out every word that was read aloud, and when Mrs. Grimm asked me a question, catching me concentrating on the infinite beer, Amy would whisper the answers without moving her lips and save me. Still, no matter what happened, I could not completely forget about Cavanaugh. I thought my feeling of responsibility would wither as the days swept by; instead it grew like a weed.

On a hot afternoon at the end of July, I was sitting in my secret hideout, a bower formed by forsythia bushes in the corner of my backyard, reading the latest installment of *Nick Fury*. I only closed my eyes to rest them for a moment, but there was Cavanaugh's rough-barked face. Now that he was alive, leaves had sprouted all over his trunk and limbs. He wore a strand of wild blueberries around where his neck should have been, and his hair ferns had grown and deepened their shade of green. It wasn't just a day-dream, I tell you. I knew that I was seeing him, what he was doing, where he was, at that very minute. He held his spear as a walking stick, and it came to me then that he was, of course, a vegetarian. His long thin legs bowed slightly, his log of a body shifted, as he cocked back his curled, wooden parchment of a head and stared with mushroom eyes into a beam of sunlight slipping through the branches above. Motes of pollen swirled in the light, chipmunks, squirrels, deer silently gathered, sparrows landed for a brief moment to nibble at his hair and then were gone. All around him, the woods looked on in awe as one of its own reckoned the beauty of the sun. What lungs, what vocal chords, gave birth to it, I'm not sure, but he groaned; a sound I had witnessed one other time while watching my father asleep, wrapped in a nightmare.

I visited that spot within the yellow blossomed forsythias once a day to check up on my man's progress. All that was necessary was that I sit quietly for a time until in a state of near-nap and then close my eyes and fly my brain around the corner, past the school, over the treetops, then down into the cool green shadow of the woods. Many times I saw him just standing, as if stunned by life, and many times traipsing through some unknown quadrant of his Eden. With each viewing came a confused emotion of wonder and dread, like on the beautiful windy day at the beginning of August when I saw him sitting beside the pond, holding the catechism book upside down, a twig finger of one hand pointing to each word on the page, while the other hand covered all but one red eye of his face.

I was there when he came across the blackened patch of earth and scattered beers from one of the Lenon gang's nights in the woods. He lifted a partially crushed can with backwash still sloshing in the bottom and drank it down. The bark around his usually indistinct hole of a mouth magically widened into a smile. It was when he uncovered a half a pack of Camels and a book of matches that I realized he must have been spying on the revels of Lenon, Cho-cho, Mike Stone, and Jake Harwood from the safety of the night trees. He lit up and the smoke swirled out the back of his head. In a voice like the creaking of a rotted branch, he pronounced, "Fuck."

And most remarkable of all was the time he came to the edge of the woods, to the hole in the chain link fence. There, in the playground across the field, he saw Amy Lash, gliding up and back on the swing, her red gingham dress billowing, her bright hair full of motion. He trembled as if planted in earthquake earth, and squeaked the way the sparrows did. For a long time, he crouched in that portal to the outside world and watched. Then, gathering his courage, he stepped onto the field. The instant he was out of the woods, Amy must have felt his presence, and she looked up and saw him approaching. She screamed, jumped off the swing, and ran out of the playground. Cavanaugh, frightened by her scream, retreated to the woods, and did not stop running until he reached the tree struck by lightning.

My religious instruction book finally arrived from above, summer ended and school began, but still I went every day to my hideout and watched him for a little while as he fished gold coins from the creek or tracked, from the ground, something moving through the treetops. I know it was close to Halloween, because I sat in my hideout loosening my teeth on one of Mrs. Grimm's candy apples when I realized that my secret seeing place was no longer a secret. The forsythias had long since dropped their flowers. As I sat there in the skeletal blind, I could feel the cold creeping into me. "Winter is coming," I said in a puff of steam and had one fleeting vision of Cavanaugh, his leaves gone flame red, his fern hair drooping brown, discovering the temple of dead squirrels. I saw him gently touch the fur of a stretched-out corpse hung on the wall. His birch legs bent to nearly breaking as he fell to his knees and let out a wail that drilled into me and lived there.

It was late night, a few weeks later, but that cry still echoed through me and I could not sleep. I heard, above the sound of the dreaming house, my father come in from his second job. I don't know what made me think I could tell him, but I had to tell someone. If I kept to myself what I had done any longer, I thought I would have to run away. Crawling out of bed, I crept down the darkened hallway past my sister's room and heard her breathing. I found my father sitting in the dining room, eating a cold dinner and reading the paper by only the light coming through from the kitchen. All he had to do was look up at me and I started crying. Next thing I knew, he had his arm around me and I was enveloped in the familiar aroma of machine oil. I thought he might laugh, I thought he might yell, but I told him everything all at once. What he did was pull out the chair next to his. I sat down, drying my eyes.

"What can we do?" he asked.

"I just need to tell him something," I said.

"Okay," he said. "This Saturday, we'll go to the woods and see if we can find him." Then he had me describe Cavanaugh, and when I was done he said, "Sounds like a sturdy fellow."

We moved into the living room and sat on the couch in the dark. He lit a cigarette and told me about the woods when he was a boy; how vast they were, how he trapped mink, saw eagles, how he and his brother lived for a week by their wits alone out in nature. I eventually dozed off and only half woke when he carried me to my bed.

The week passed and I went to sleep Friday night, hoping he wouldn't forget his promise and go to the track instead. But the next morning, he woke me early from a dream of Amy Lash by tapping my shoulder and saying, "Move your laggardly ass." He made bacon and eggs, the only two things he knew how to make, and let me drink coffee. Then we put on our coats and were off. It was the second week in November and the day was cold and overcast. "Brisk," he said as we rounded the corner toward the school, and that was all he said until we were well in beneath the trees.

I showed him around the woods like a tour guide, pointing out the creek, the spot where I had created my man, the temple of dead squirrels. "Interesting," he said to each of these, and once in a while mentioned the name of some bush or tree. Waves of leaves blew amidst the trunks in the cold wind, and with stronger gusts, showers of them fell around us. He could really walk and we walked for what seemed ten miles, out of the morning and into the afternoon, way past any place I had ever dreamed of going. We discovered a spot where an enormous tree had fallen, exposing the gnarled brainwork of its roots, and another two acres where there were no trees but only smooth sand hills. All the time, I was alert to even the slightest sound, a cracking twig, the caw of a crow, hoping I might hear the whisper.

As it grew later, the sky darkened and what was cold before became colder still.

"Listen," my father said, "I have a feeling like the one when we used to track deer. He's nearby, somewhere. We'll have to outsmart him."

I nodded.

"I'm going to stay here and wait," he said. "You keep going along the path here for a while, but, for Christ's sake, be quiet. Maybe if he sees you, he'll double back to get away, and I'll be here to catch him."

I wasn't sure this plan made sense, but I knew we needed to do something. It was getting late. "Be careful," I said, "he's big and he has a stick."

My father smiled. "Don't worry," he said and lifted his foot to indicate the size ten.

This made me laugh, and I turned and started down the path, taking careful steps. "Go on for about ten minutes or so and see if you see anything," he called to me before I rounded a bend.

Once I was by myself, I wasn't so sure I wanted to find my man. Because of the overcast sky the woods were dark and lonely. As I walked I pictured my father and Cavanaugh wrestling each other and wondered who would win. When I had gone far enough to want to stop and run back, I forced myself around one more turn. Just this little more, I thought. He's probably already fallen apart anyway, dismantled by winter. But then I saw it up ahead, treetops at eye level, and I knew I had found the valley where the deer went to die.

Cautiously, I inched up to the rim, and peered down the steep dirt wall overgrown with roots and stickers, into the trees and the shadowed undergrowth beneath them. The valley was a large hole as if a meteor had struck there long ago. I thought of the treasure trove of antlers and bones that lay hidden in the leaves at its base. Standing there, staring, I felt I almost understood the secret life and age of the woods. I had to show this to my father, but before I could move away, I saw something, heard something moving below. Squinting to see more clearly through the darkness down there, I could just about make out a shadowed figure standing, half hidden by the trunk of a tall pine.

"Cavanaugh?" I called. "Is that you?"

In the silence, I heard acorns dropping.

"Are you there?" I asked.

There was a reply, an eerie sound that was part voice, part wind. It was very quiet but I distinctly heard it ask, "Why?"

"Are you okay?" I asked.

"Why?" came the same question.

I didn't know why, and wished I had read him the book's answers instead of the questions the day of his birth. I stood for a long time and watched as snow began to fall around me.

His question came again, weaker this time, and I was on the verge of tears, ashamed of what I had done. Suddenly, I had a strange memory flash of the endless beer in Mrs. Grimm's basement. At least it was something. I leaned out over the edge and, almost certain I was lying, yelled, "I had too much love."

Then, so I could barely make it out, I heard him whisper, "Thank you."

After that, there came from below the thud of branches hitting together, hitting the ground, and I knew he had come undone. When I squinted again, the figure was gone.

I found my father sitting on a fallen tree trunk back along the trail, smoking a cigarette. "Hey," he said when he saw me coming, "did you find anything?"

"No," I said, "let's go home."

He must have seen something in my eyes, because he asked, "Are you sure?"

"I'm sure," I said.

The snow fell during our journey home and seemed to continue falling all winter long.

Now, twenty-one years married with two crewcut boys of my own, I went back to the old neighborhood last week. The woods and even the school have been obliterated, replaced by new developments with streets named for the things they banished—Crow Lane, Deer Street, Gold Creek Road. My father still lives in the same house by himself. My mother passed away some years back. My baby sister is married with two boys of her own and lives upstate. The old man has something growing on his kidney, and he has lost far too much weight, his once huge arms having shrunk to the width of branches. He sat at the kitchen table, the racing form in front of him. I tried to convince him to quit working, but he shook his head and said, "Boring."

"How long do you think you can keep going to the shop?" I asked him.

"How about until the last second," he said.

"How's the health?" I asked.

"Soon I'll be food for the worms," he said, laughing.

"How do you really feel about that?" I asked.

He shrugged. "All part of the game," he said. "I thought when things got bad enough I would build a coffin and sleep in it. That way, when I die, you can just nail the lid on and bury me in the backyard."

Later, when we were watching the Giants on TV and I had had a few beers, I asked him if he remembered that time in the woods.

He closed his eyes and lit a cigarette as though it

would help his memory. "Oh, yeah, I think I remember that," he said.

I had never asked him before. "Was that you down there in those trees?"

He took a drag and slowly turned his head and stared hard, without a smile, directly into my eyes. "I don't know what the hell you're talking about," he said and exhaled a long, blue-gray stream of life.

"The Face of an Angel"
Brian Stableford

When Mrs. Allison had gone, taking the photo-quality A4 sheet from the printer with her, Hugo Victory took another look at the image on his computer screen, which displayed her face as it would appear when the surgery she had requested had been carried out.

The software Victory used to perform that task had started out as a standard commercial package intended as much for advertisement purposes as to assist him to plan his procedures, but he had modified it considerably in order to take aboard his own innovations and the idiosyncrasies of his technique. Like all great artists, Victory was one of a kind; no other plastic surgeon in the world plied his scalpels with exactly the same style. He had been forced to learn programming in order to reconstruct the software to meet his own standards of perfection, but he had always been prepared to make sacrifices in the cause of his art.

Victory considered the contours of Mrs. Allison's as-yet-imaginary face for six minutes, using his imagination to investigate the possibility that more might be done to refresh her fading charms. He decided in the end that there was not. Given the limitations of his material, the image on the screen was the best attainable result. It only remained to reproduce in practice what the computer defined as attainable. He only had to click the mouse twice to replace the image of the face with an image of the musculature beneath, already marked up with diagrammatic indications of the required incisions, excisions and reconnections. Some were so delicate that he would have to use a robotic arm to carry out the necessary microsurgery, collaborating with the computer in its guidance.

Victory printed out the specifications, and laid the page in the case-file, on top of his copy of the image that Mrs. Allison had taken with her. Then he buzzed Janice and asked her whether his next potential client had arrived.

There was a slight tremor in the secretary's voice when she confirmed that a Mr. Gwynplaine had indeed arrived. Victory frowned when he heard it, because the first duty of an employee in her situation was to remain pleasantly impassive in the face of any deformation—but he forgave her as soon as the client appeared before him. If ever there was a man in need of plastic surgery, Victory thought, it was the man who had replaced Mrs. Allison in the chair on the far side of his desk. And if there was one man in the world who could give him exactly what he needed, Victory also thought, it was Dr. Hugo Victory.

"I'm sorry you had to wait so long for an appointment, Mr. Gwynplaine," Victory said, smoothly. "I'm a very busy man."

"I know," said Gwynplaine, unsmilingly. Victory judged that the damage inflicted on Gwynplaine's face—obviously by fire—had paralysed some muscles while twisting others into permanent contraction, leaving the man incapable of smiling. The injuries were by no means fresh; Gwynplaine might not be quite as old as he looked, but Victory judged that he must be at least fifty, and that the hideous scars must have been in place for at least half his lifetime. If he'd acquired the injuries in the Falklands the army's plastic surgeons would have undone at least some of the damage, and all employers had to carry insurance against injuries inflicted by industrial fires, so the accident must have been a private affair. Victory had never seen anyone hurt in quite that way by a house fire—not, at any rate, anyone who had survived the experience.

"Your problem is very evident," Victory said, rising to his feet and readying himself to take a closer look, "but I wonder why you've left it so long before seeking treatment."

"You mistake the reason for my visit, Doctor," Gwynplaine said, in a voice that was eerily distorted by his inability to make full use of his lips, although long practice had evidently enabled him to find a way of pronouncing every syllable in a comprehensible manner. When Victory glanced down at the note Janice had made, the slightly monstrous voice added: "As your secretary also did. I fear that I allowed her to make the assumption, rather than state my real business, lest she turn me away."

As he spoke, the paragon of ugliness lifted the briefcase that he had brought with him and snapped the catch.

Victory sat down again. He was annoyed, because Janice had strict instructions never to permit salesmen or journalists to fill appointment-slots reserved for potential patients—but the mistake was understandable. Victory had never seen a salesman or journalist so unfashionably dressed, and the ancient briefcase was something a fossilized academic might have carried defiantly through a long career of eccentricity.

The object which Gwynplaine produced from the worn bag was a book, but its pages were not made of paper and its leather binding bore no title. It was not the product of a printing-press—but it was not Medieval either. Victory guessed, on the basis of the condition of the binding, that it might be eighteenth century, or seventeenth, but not earlier.

Gwynplaine laid the book on the desk, and pushed it towards Victory. Victory accepted it, but did not open it immediately.

"You seem to have mistaken the nature of my collection," Victory said, frostily. "Nineteenth-century portraiture is my speciality. Pre-Raphaelite and Symbolist. I don't collect books, except for products of the Kelmscott Press. In any case, I don't pursue my hobbies during working hours."

"This is to do with your work, not your hobby," Gwynplaine told him. "Nor am I trying to make a sale—the book isn't mine to sell, but if it were, I'd deem it priceless."

"What is it?" the doctor asked, curiously. He opened the volume as he spoke, but the first page on which his eyes fell was inscribed in a language he had never seen before.

"It's a record of the secrets of the comprachicos," Gwynplaine told him. "It appears to be complete—which is to say that it includes the last secret of all: the purpose for which the organization was founded, long before it became notorious."

"I have no idea what you're talking about," Victory told his mysterious visitor. "If you're hoping to barter for my services I'm afraid you've come to the wrong plastic surgeon." But he had turned to another page now, and although the script remained utterly inscrutable, this one bore an illustrative diagram.

Victory had seen a great many anatomical texts in his time, but he had never seen an account of the musculature of the human face as finely detailed as the one he was looking at. It was easily the equal of Durer's anatomical studies, although it was more intricate and seemed indicative of an uncanny appreciation of the inner architecture of the human face. It seemed to Victory that the author of the diagram addressed him as one genius of plastic surgery to another, even though the message emanated from an era in which plastic surgery had been unknown. His interest increased by a sudden order of magnitude.

"I hope you will permit me to explain," Gwynplaine said, mildly.

Victory turned to another illustration. This one had been carefully modified in a manner that was impossibly similar to the print he had taken from his computer only a few minutes earlier. A layman might have seen nothing but a confusion of arbitrary lines scrawled on the image of facial musculature, but Hugo Victory saw a set of clear and ingenious instructions for surgical intervention. Victory decided that he wanted this book as desperately as he had ever wanted anything. If Gwynplaine could not sell it, then he wanted a photocopy, and a translation.

If this is genuine, Victory thought, *it will rewrite the history of plastic surgery. If the text lives up to the promise of the illustrations I've so far seen, it might help to rewrite modern textbooks as well. And even if it turns out to be a fake, manufactured as recently as yesterday, the ingenuity of the instructions testifies to the existence of an unknown master of my art.*

"Please go on, Mr. Gwynplaine," the surgeon said, his eyes transfixed by the illustration. "Tell me what you came here to say."

"Comprachicos means *child-buyers*," Gwynplaine

said, his strange voice taking on an oddly musical quality. "Even in their decadence, in the eighteenth century, the comprachicos took pride in being tradesmen, not thieves. They were wanderers by then, often confused with gypsies, but they were a very different breed. Even nineteenth century accounts take care to point out that while true gypsies were pagans, the comprachicos were devout Catholics.

"Those same sources identify the comprachicos' last protector in England as James II, and state that they were never heard of again after fleeing the country when William of Orange took the throne. The retreat into obscurity is understandable. The Pope had ex-communicated the entire organization—one reason why the Protestant William was secretly supported by Rome against his Catholic rival—and such succour as those who fled from England could receive in France was limited and covert. The entire society re-treated to Spain, and even then found it politic to vanish into the Basque country of the southern Pyrenees. They have remained invisible to history ever since—but they had been invisible before, and the wonder may be that they were ever glimpsed at all.

"Almost everything written about the comprachicos was written by their enemies, and was intended to demonize them. They were attacked as mutilators of the children they bought, charged with using their techniques to produce dwarfs and hunchbacks, ac-robats and contortionists, freaks and horrors. It was true that they could and did produce monsters—but even in the Age of Reason and the Age of Enlighten-ment the demand for such products came from the courts of Europe, which still delighted in the antics of clowns and clever fools. The comprachicos sold wares of those kinds to Popes and Kings as well as

Tsars and Sultans. The clowns which caper in our circuses even to this day use make-up to produce simulacra of the faces that the comprachicos once teased out of raw flesh.

"Yes, the comprachicos used their plastic arts—arts which men like you are only beginning to rediscover—for purposes that you or I might consider evil or perverse. But that was not their primary aim. That was not the reason for which the organization was founded, in the days when the Goths still ruled Iberia."

Hugo Victory had never heard of comprachicos, but he had heard that families of beggars in ancient times had sometimes mutilated their children in order to make them more piteous, and he had heard too that the acrobats of Imperial Rome had trained the joints of their children so that they could be dislocated and relocated at will, preparing them for life as extraordinary gymnasts. For this reason, he was not inclined to dismiss Gwynplaine's story entirely—and he was still turning the parchment pages with reverential fingers, still marveling at the anatomical diagrams and the fanciful surgical schemes superimposed upon them. "What *was* the reason for the organization's existence?" he asked.

"To reproduce the face and figure of Adam."

That startled the surgeon into looking up. "What?"

"Adam, you will recall, was supposed to have been made in God's image," Gwynplaine said. "The comprachicos believed that the face Adam wore before the Fall was a replica of the Divine Countenance itself, as were the faces of the angels; when Adam and Eve ate from the tree of the knowledge of good and evil, however, their features and forms became contorted—and when God expelled them from Eden, he made that contortion permanent, so that they and their children would never see his image again in one another's faces and figures.

"The comprachicos believed that if only they could find a means of undoing that contortion, thus unmasking the ultimate beauty of which humans were once capable, they would give their fellows the opportunity to see God. That sight, they believed, would provide a powerful incentive to seek salvation, and would prepare the way for Christ's return and the end of the world. Without such preparation, they feared, men would stray so far from the path of their religion that God would despair of them, and leave them to make their own future and their own fate."

"But there never was an Adam or an Eden," Victory pointed out, still meeting the oddly plaintive eyes of his frightful visitor, although he knew that there was not a man in England who could win a staring-match against such opposition. "We know the history of our species," he added, as he dropped his gaze to the book again. "*Genesis* is a myth."

But this book is not a myth, Victory said to himself, silently. *This is, at the very least, a record of experiments of which the accepted history of medicine has no inkling.*

"The comprachicos had a different opinion as to the history of our species," Gwynplaine told him, flatly. "They knew, of course, that there were other men on Earth besides Adam—how else would Cain have found them in the east of Eden?—but they trusted the word of scripture that Adam alone had been made in God's image, and that Adam's face was the face of all the angels, the ultimate in imaginable beauty. Not that it was just the face that they were anxious to reproduce, of course. They wanted to recover the design of Adam's entire body—but the face was the most important element of that design."

"This is nonsense," Victory said—but he could not muster as much conviction as he would have desired, or thought reasonable. There was something about Gwynplaine's peculiar voice that was corrosive of scepticism.

Gwynplaine leaned forward and placed the palms of his hands flat upon the open pages of the book that he had laid on Victory's desk, preventing the doctor from turning the next page. "All the secrets of the comprachicos are recorded here," he said. "Including the last."

"If they knew how to achieve their object," Victory objected, "why did they not do so? If they did it, why did they not succeed in bringing about their renaissance of faith and the salvation of mankind?"

"According to the book, the operation was a success," Gwynplaine told him, "but the child died while the scars were still fresh. The surgeon who carried out the operation died too, not long afterwards. The project was carried out here in London, not two miles east of Harley Street but the timing was disastrous. The year was 1665. Plague took them both. There was no one else in England with the requisite skill to make a second attempt, so a summons was sent to Spain—but by the time the call was answered, London had been destroyed by the great fire. The record of the operation was thought to have been lost.

"When William came to power and the comprachicos fled to the continent they no longer had the book, and their subsequent experiments failed—but the book had not burned in the fire. It was saved, and secreted by a thief, who did not know its nature because he could not read the language in which it was written. It was only recently rediscovered by someone who understood what it was. You will not find a dozen scholars in Europe who could read it—in a century's time, there might be none at all—but I am one. What I need as well is a man with the skill necessary to carry out those of its instructions that require an expert hand and surgical instruments. I have been told that I might do well to take it to California, but I have also been told that I might not need to do that, if only you will agree to help me. I already have a child." He added the last sentence in a negligent tone, as if that consideration were a mere bagatelle.

"Have you also been advised that you might be insane?" Victory inquired.

"Often. I will admit to being a criminal, given that it is illegal to buy children in England now, or even to import children that have been bought elsewhere—but as to the rest, I admit nothing but curiosity. Perhaps the instructions are false, and the whole tale is but an invention. Perhaps the judgment of success was premature and the child would not have grown up to display the face of Adam at all. But I am curious—and so are you."

"If you wanted me to operate on you," Victory said, "I might take the risk—but I can't operate on a child using a set of instructions written by some seventeenth century barber."

"The child I have acquired is direly in need of your services," Gwynplaine told him. "So far as anyone in England can tell, I am his legal guardian—and no one in the place where I bought him will ever dispute the fact. The manipulations of the body and the training of the facial flesh that require no cutting I can do myself—but I am no surgeon, and even if I could master the pattern of incision and excision I would not dare attempt the grafts and reconnections. Your part is the minor one by comparison with mine, requiring no more than a few hours of your time once you have fully understood the instructions—but it is the heart and soul of the process, and it requires a near-superhuman sureness of touch. You cannot do this as a matter of mere business, of course. I cannot and will not pay you. If you do it, you must do it because you need to know what the result will be. If you say no, you will never see me again—but I do not believe that you will say no. I can read your face, Dr Victory. You wear your thoughts and desires openly."

As he tore his avid gaze away from Gwynplaine's censorious fingers Victory became acutely conscious of his own reflexive frown." Who the hell are you?" he asked, roughly.

"Gwynplaine is as good a name as any," the man with the unreadable face informed him, teasingly.

"I want the book," Victory said, his own perfectly ordinary voice sounding suddenly unnatural by comparison with the other's strangely-contrived locutions. "A copy, at least. And a key to the script."

Gwynplaine could not smile, so there was no surprise in the fact that his face did not change. "You may make a copy of it afterwards, if you take care to do no damage," he agreed. "I will give you the name of a man who can translate the script for you. Have no fear that you might do harm. If you achieve nothing else, you might prevent the child from growing up a scarecrow. I think you understand well enough what costs that involves—though not, of course, as well as I."

Victory felt—knew, in fact—that he was on the threshold of the most momentous decision of his life. He had seen enough of the book to know that he had to see all of it. He was faced with an irresistible temptation.

"I'll need to see the child as soon as possible," Victory said, slightly astonished at his own recklessness, but proud of his readiness to seize the utterly unexpected opportunity. "I'll tell Janice to fix an emergency appointment for tomorrow."

Even at a mere thirteen weeks old, the child—to whom Gwynplaine referred as Dust—was as hideous as his guardian, although his ugliness was very different in kind. The baby had never been burned in a fire; the distortion of his features was partly due to a hereditary dysfunction and partly to the careless use of forceps by the midwife who had delivered him, presumably in some Eastern European hellhole.

Had the child been brought to him in the ordinary course of affairs, Hugo Victory would have been reasonably confident that he could achieve a modest reconstruction of the skull and do some repair work on the mouth and nose, but he would only have been able to reduce the grotesquerie of the face to the margins of tolerability. Normality would have been out of the question, let alone beauty. Nor could Victory see, to begin with, how the procedures outlined in the diagrams illustrating the final chapter of Gwynplaine's book would assist in overcoming the limitations of his own experience and understanding.

"This is an extremely ambitious series of interventions," he told Gwynplaine. "It requires me to sever and relocate the anchorages of a dozen different muscles. There can be no guarantee that the nerves will function at all once the reconnections heal, even assuming that they do heal. On the other hand, these instructions make no provision for repairing the damage done to the boy's skull. I'll have to use my own procedures for that, and I'm not at all sure that they're compatible. At the very least, they'll increase the danger of nervous disconnections that will render the muscles impotent."

"My part of the work will replenish and strengthen his body's ability to heal itself," Gwynplaine assured him. "But the groundwork has to be done with scalpel and suture. If you can follow the instructions, all will be well."

"The instructions aren't completely clear," Victory objected. "I don't doubt your translation, but the original seems to have been written in some haste, by a man who was took a little too much for granted. There's potential for serious mistakes to be made. I'll have to make further modifications to my computer software to take aboard the untried procedures, and it will be extremely difficult to obtain an accurate preview of the results."

"It won't be necessary to preview the results," Gwynplaine assured him. "Nor would it be desirable. You must modify the software that controls the robotic microscalpel, of course, but that's all."

"That won't take as long, admittedly," Victory said. "Amending the imaging software isn't *strictly* necessary....but working without a preview will increase the uncertainty dramatically. The robotic arm ought to make the delicate procedures feasible, but guiding it will stretch my resources as well as the computer's to the full. If a seventeenth-century surgeon really did set out to follow this plan with nothing but his own hand to guide the blades he must have had a uniquely steady hand and the eyes of a hawk."

"You only have to step into the National Gallery to witness the fact that there were men in the past with steadier hands and keener eyes than anyone alive today," Gwynplaine said. "But your technology will compensate for the deterioration of the species, as it does in every other compartment of modern life. As to the lack of specificity in the instructions, I'm prepared to trust your instincts. If you'll only study the procedures with due care, and incorporate them into your computer programmes with due diligence, I'm certain that their logic will eventually become clear to you—and their creativity too. There's as much art in this business as science, as you know full well."

Victory did know that, and always had; it was Gwynplaine's comprehension of the art and science that he doubted. But Gwynplaine would not permit him to photocopy a single page of the book until the work was done. So Victory imported his own diagrams and his own calculations into his modified computer programmes, embodying within them as much arcane knowledge as the specific task required. He wanted far more than that—he wanted the whole register of secrets, the full description of every item of the comprachicos' arts—but he had to be patient.

There was a great deal of preparatory work to be done before Victory could even contemplate taking a scalpel to the infant's face, but the surgeon was as determined to get the job done as Gwynplaine was. He cleared his diary by rescheduling all the operations he had planned, in order to devote himself utterly to the study of the diagrams Gwynplaine allowed him to see and Gwynplaine's translations of the text. He practised unfamiliar elements of procedure on a rat and a pig as well as running dozens of simulations on the computer. But time was short, because the child called Dust was growing older with every day that passed, and the bones of the baby's face were hardening inexorably hour by hour.

Under normal circumstances Victory would have required a team of three to assist with the operation, in addition to an anaesthetist, but as things were he had to be content to work with Gwynplaine alone—and, of course, the computer to guide the robotic arm. It was as well that Gwynplaine proved exceedingly adept in an assistant role.

The first operation took four hours, the second three and the third nearly six....but in the end, Victory's part was complete.

Victory had never been so exhausted in his life, but he did not want to retire to bed. Gwynplaine insisted that he could watch over the boy while the surgeon slept, but if Victory had not been at the very end of his tether he would never have consented to the arrangement. "If there's any change in his condition," Victory said, "wake me immediately. If all's well, there'll be time in the morning take a final series of X-rays and to finalise the post-operative procedures."

But when the doctor woke up again Gwynplaine had vanished, taking the child and the book with him. He had also taken every scrap of paper on which Victory had made notes or drawings of his own—every one, at least, that he could find. Nor had the computer been spared. The instructions for the operation had been deleted and a virus had been set to work that would have trashed the hard disk—thus obliterating all the other notes Victory had covertly copied on to the machine and photographs of several pages from the book that he had taken unobtrusively with a digital camera—had it been allowed to run its course.

Fortunately, it seemed that Gwynplaine did not understand the workings of computers well enough to ensure the completion of this particular task of destruction. Victory was able to purge his machine of the virus before it had done too much damage, saving numerous precious remnants of the imperilled data.

A good deal of work would need to be done to recover and piece together the data he had contrived to steal, let alone to extrapolate that data into further fields of implication, but Victory had never been afraid of hard work. Although the material he had contrived to keep was only a tiny fraction of what he had been promised, he had enough information already to serve as fodder for half a dozen papers. Given time, his genius would allow him to build considerably on that legacy. Even if he could not recover all the secrets of the comprachicos, he felt certain that he could duplicate the majority of their discoveries—including, and especially, the last.

In the years that followed, Hugo Victory's skill and fame increased considerably. He was second to none as a pioneer in the fast-advancing art of plastic surgery, and he forced tabloid headline-writers to unprecedented excesses as they sought to wring yet more puns from his unusually helpful name. He lacked nothing—except, of course, for the one thing he wanted most of all: Gwynplaine's book.

On occasion, Victory paused to wonder how the experiment had turned out, and what the child's face might look like now that he was growing slowly towards the threshold of manhood—but he did not believe in Adam, or angels, or the existence of God. The existence of the book, on the other hand, was beyond doubt. He still wanted it, more than anything his money could buy or his celebrity could command.

He did all the obvious things. He hired private detectives, and he scoured the internet for any information at all connected with the name of Gwynplaine, or the society of comprachicos. He also published a painstakingly-compiled photo fit of Gwynplaine's remarkable face, asking for any information at all from anyone who had seen him.

Despite the accuracy of the image he had published, not one of the reports of sightings that he received produced any further evidence of Gwynplaine's existence. The detectives could not find anything either, even though they checked the records of every single burn victim through all the hospitals of Europe for half a century and more.

In the meantime, his internet searches found far too much. There were more Gwynplaines in the world than Victory had ever imagined possible, and the comprachicos were as well known to every assiduous hunter of great historical conspiracies as the Knights Templar and the Rosicrucians. Somewhere in the millions of words that were written about their exploits there might have been a few grains of truth, but any such kernels were well and truly buried within a vast incoherent chaff of speculations, fictions, and downright lies.

Victory tracked down no less than a dozen copies of books allegedly containing the teratological secrets of the comprachicos, but none of them bore more than the faintest resemblance to the one Gwynplaine had shown him. Some of the diagrams in the older specimens gave some slight evidence that their forgers might have seen the original, but it seemed that none of them had been able to make a meticulous copy of a single image, and that none had had sufficient understanding of anatomy to make a good job of reproducing them from memory.

He had all but given up his quest when it finally bore fruit—but it was not the sort of fruit he had been expecting, and it was not a development that he was prepared to welcome.

When Janice's successor handed him the card bearing the name of Monsignor Torricelli, and told him that the priest in question wanted to talk to him about the fate of a certain mutilated child, Victory felt an inexplicable shudder of alarm, and it was on the tip of his tongue to ask the secretary to send the man away—but his curiosity was as powerful as it had ever been.

"Send him in, Meg," he said, calmly. "And hold my other appointments till I've done with him."

The Monsignor was a small dark man dressed in black-and-purple clerical garb. Meg took his cape and his little rounded hat away with her when she had shown him to his chair.

"You have some information for me, Father?" Victory asked, abruptly.

"None that you'll thank me for, I fear," Monsignor Torricelli countered. He was not a man incapable of smiling, and he demonstrated the fact. "But I hope you might be generous enough to do me a small service in return."

"What service would that be?" Victory enquired,

warily—but the priest wasn't ready to spell that out without preamble.

"We've observed the progress of your search with interest," the little man told him. "Although you've never publicly specified the reason for your determination to find the individual you call Gwynplaine, it wasn't too difficult to deduce. He obviously showed you the book of the secrets of the comprachicos, and you've indicated by the terms of your search that he had a child with him. We assume that he persuaded you, by one means or another, to operate on the child. We also assume that he spoke to you about the face of Adam, and that you did not believe what he said. Am I right so far?"

"I'm not a Catholic," Victory said, without bothering to offer any formal sign of assent, "but I have a vague notion that a Monsignor is a member of the Pope's own staff. Is that true?"

"Not necessarily, nowadays," the priest replied. "But in this particular case, yes. I am attached to the papal household as well as to the Holy Office."

"The Holy Office? You mean the Inquisition?"

"Your reading, though doubtless wide, is a little out of date, Dr Victory. There is no Inquisition. There has been no Inquisition for two hundred years, just as there has been no society of comprachicos for two hundred years."

"Do you know where Gwynplaine is?" Victory asked, abruptly.

"Yes." The answer seemed perfectly frank.

"Where?"

"Where he has always been—in hell."

Somehow, Victory felt less astonished by that statement than he should have been, although he did not suppose for a moment that Monsignor Torricelli meant to signify merely that Gwynplaine was dead.

"He wasn't in hell nine years ago," Victory said. "He was sitting where you are. And he spent the next ten days with me, in the lab and the theatre."

"From his point of view," Torricelli counted, still smiling, "this was hell, nor was he out of it. I am borrowing from Marlowe, of course, but the description is sound."

"You're telling me that Gwynplaine was—is—the devil."

"Of course. Had you really not understood that, or are you in what fashionable parlance calls *denial*?"

"I don't believe in the devil," Victory said, flatly.

"Of course you do," the Monsignor replied. "You can doubt the existence of God, but you can't doubt the existence of the devil. You're only human, after all. Good may be elusive within your experience, but not temptation. You may doubt that the devil can take human form, even though you and he were in such close and protracted proximity for ten long days, but you cannot possibly doubt the temptation to sin. You know pride, covetousness, envy—you, of all people, must have a very keen appreciation of the force of envy—and all the rest. Or is it only their deadliness that you doubt?"

"What other information do you have for me, Monsignor?" Victory tried to sound weary, but he couldn't entirely remove the edge of unease from his voice. He wondered whether there was a level somewhere beneath his conscious mind in which he did indeed retain a certain childlike faith in the devil, and an equally childlike certainty that he had once met him in human guise—but the thought was difficult to bear. If the devil existed, then God presumably existed too, and that possibility was too horrible to contemplate.

"The child died," Torricelli said, bluntly.

Strangely enough, that seemed more surprising than the allegation that Gwynplaine was the devil. Victory sat a little straighter in his chair, and stared harder at the man whose smile, even now, had not quite disappeared. "How do you know?" he asked.

"You hired a dozen private detectives to search for you, who hadn't the slightest idea what they were up against. We have a worldwide organization at our disposal, who knew exactly what to look for as soon as your postings had alerted us. The child died before he was a year old. Don't be alarmed, Dr Victory—you weren't responsible. So far as we could judge, the operations you performed were probably successful. It was the adversary's part that went awry. It's all happened before, of course, a dozen times over. If it's any comfort to you, this was the first time since 1665 that the cutter's part was properly done. If he'd only been prepared to honour his bargain and let you help with the part that remained to be done...but that's not his way. You may think yourself a proud and covetous man, but you're only the faintest echo of your model."

"If you weren't a priest," Victory observed, "I'd suspect you of being insane. Given that you are a priest, I suppose delusions of that kind are merely part and parcel of the faith."

"Perhaps," the little man conceded, refreshing his cherubic smile. "I wonder if, perchance, you suspected Mr. Gwynplaine of being insane, when he too was only suffering the delusions of his faith."

Victory didn't smile in return. "I don't see how I

can help you," he said. "If the resources of your worldwide organization have enabled you to discover that the child's dead and that Gwynplaine's safe in hell, what can you possibly want from me?"

"We've been monitoring your publications and your operations for the last few years, Dr Victory," Torricelli said, letting his smile die in a peculiarly graceful manner. "We know how hard you've worked to make full use of the scraps of information that you plundered from the devil's book, while labouring under the delusion that he didn't mean to let you keep them. We know how ingeniously you've sought to use the separate elements of the operation you carried out on his behalf. I'm sure he's been watching you just as intently. We suspect that your busy hands have done almost all of the work that he found for them and that he's ready to pay you another visit, to offer you a new bargain. We don't suppose that it will do any good to warn you, although we'd be delighted to be surprised…but we do hope that you might be prepared to give the incomplete programme to us instead of completing it for him."

Until the priest used the word "programme" Victory had been perfectly prepared to believe that the whole conversation was so much hot air, generated by the fact that the lunatic fringe of the Holy Office was every bit as interested in crazy conspiracy theories as all the other obsessive internet users who were fascinated by the imaginary histories of the Templars, the Rosicrucians, the Illuminati and the comprachicos. Even then, he struggled against the suspicion that he had been rumbled.

"What programme?" He said.

"The most recently updated version of the software you use to show your clients what they'll look like when you've completed the courses of surgery you've outlined for them. The one whose code has finally been modified to take in all but one of the novel procedures to which the adversary introduced you. The one which would reproduce the face of Adam, if you could only insert that last missing element into the code—the tantalising element that the devil has carefully reserved to his own custody."

Victory tried hard to control his own expression, lest it give too much away. He had known, of course, that he had come close to a final resolution of the comprachicos' last secret, but he had not been able to determine that he was only one step short. But on what authority, he wondered, had the Monsignor decided that he was almost home? Did the Vatican have plastic surgeons and computer hackers at its disposal? If it did, would they be set to work on tasks of this bizarre sort? If so, had the men in question genius enough not only to steal his work but to read it more accurately than he had read it himself?

It was too absurd.

"Why would I give my work to anyone while it's incomplete?" Victory asked. "And why shouldn't I show it to everyone, when I've perfected it? Surely that's what you ought to want—if what Gwynplaine told me is true, it ought to put humankind back on the path to salvation."

"He's not called the father of lies without reason," the priest observed. "He was an angel himself, before his own fall. He doesn't remember what he and Adam looked like, but he knows full well that the comprachicos weren't searching for a way to set mankind on the path to salvation. Quite the reverse, in fact. Why do you think they were condemned as heretics and annihilated?"

"I understand the politics of persecution well enough to know that so-called heretics didn't need to be guilty of anything to be hounded to extinction by the Church," Victory retorted.

"I doubt that you do," Torricelli said, with a slight regretful sigh. "But that's by the by. We'll pay you for the programme as it presently exists, if you wish—provided that we can obtain all rights in the intellectual property, and that you agree to desist from all further work on the project."

Victory was slightly curious to know what price the Vatican might be willing to pay, but he didn't want to waste time. "I already have more money than I can spend," he said, proudly. "The only thing I want that I don't have is the book I saw nine years ago—and I'm not entirely sure that I need it any longer. I don't have any particular interest in the faces of angels but I'm extremely curious to know what the results of the operation I performed might have been, if the boy had lived."

"You're making a mistake, Dr Victory," said Monsignor Torricelli.

"You needn't worry about me selling out to the opposition," Victory said. "I've dealt with Gwynplaine before. This time, I'll need copies made in advance—and then we'll be even. Afterwards, I *might* let him look at what the programme produces—but I'm certainly not going to let him walk off with it while I have the strength to stop him."

"I wish you'd reconsider," the priest persisted. "No harm will be done if you stop now, even though you're so close. The Adversary might be able to complete the programme himself if he steals the present version, but he wants more than a computer-generated image. He'd still need an artist in flesh, and that he isn't. He isn't even as clever with computers as he'd like to be."

"I find *that* difficult to believe," Victory observed, sarcastically.

"The reason he makes so much work for other idle hands," Monsignor Torricelli said sadly, "is that his own are afflicted with too many obsolete habits. It was his part of the scheme that went wrong, remember, not yours. It's as dangerous to overestimate him as it is to underestimate him. Don't do his work for him, Dr Victory. Don't give him what he wants. You know he doesn't play fair. You know who and what he is, if you'll only admit it to yourself. You still have a choice in this matter. Use it wisely, I beg of you."

"That's what I'm trying to do," Victory assured him. "It's just that my wisdom and your faith don't see eye to eye."

"We're prepared to give you more than money," Torricelli said, with the air of one who obliged to play his last card, even though the game had been lost for some considerable time. "You're an art collector, I believe."

"I'm not prepared to be bribed, even with works of art," Victory said. "I'm an artist myself, and my own creativity comes first."

"Human creativity is always secondary to God's," Monsignor Torricelli riposted. "I hope you'll remember that, when the time comes."

In the wake of Torricelli's visit Victory returned to his computer model with renewed zest. There was so much obvious nonsense in what the priest had told him that there was no real reason to believe the assurance that he was only one step short of being able to reproduce—at least on paper—the face of Adam, but Victory had no need of faith to season his curiosity. He felt that he was, indeed, close to that particular goal, and the feeling was enough to lend urgency to his endeavours.

Part of his problem lay in the fact that the transformative software had to begin with the image of a child only a few weeks old. When Victory used computer imaging to inform a forty-year-old woman what she would look like when he had worked his magic, the new image was constructed on the same finished bone-structure, modifying muscles that were already in their final form, removing superfluous fat and re-modelling skin whose flexibility was limited. A baby's face, by contrast, was as yet unmade. The bones were still soft, the muscles were vulnerable to all manner of influence by use and habit, the minutely-layered fat still had vital metabolic functions to perform, and the overlying skin had a great deal of growing and stretching yet to do.

Even the best conventional software could only offer the vaguest impression of the adult face that would eventually emerge from infantile innocence, because that emergence was no mere matter of predestined revelation. Integrating the effects of early surgery into conventional software usually made the results even more uncertain—and no matter how ingeniously Victory had laboured to overcome these difficulties, he had not been able to set them entirely aside. He had to suppose that if and when he could produce a perfect duplicate of the comprachicos' instructions the surgical modifications specified therein would somehow obliterate the potential variability that infant faces usually had, but every hypothetical alteration he made by way of experiment had the opposite effect, increasing the margin of causation left to chance and circumstance.

Whatever the missing piece of the puzzle was, if there was indeed only one, it was obviously a piece of magical—perhaps miraculous—subtlety and power.

There were, in the meantime, other aspects of the comprachicos' field of expertise that continued to reveal interesting results and applications, but Victory had lost his ability to content himself with petty triumphs. No matter how much nonsense Torricelli had spouted, he had been right to call the project "tantalising".

The five weeks that elapsed between Torricelli's attempt to bribe him and Gwynplaine's reappearance were the most tortuous of Victory's life, and the fact that the torture in question was entirely self-inflicted did not make it any easier to bear.

This time, Gwynplaine did not bother to telephone for an appointment. He simply turned up one evening, long after Meg had gone home, when Victory was still working at his computer. He was not carrying his briefcase.

"You're a very difficult man to find, Mr. Gwynplaine," Victory observed, as his visitor settled himself into the chair on the far side of his desk.

"Not according to my detractors," Gwynplaine observed, as unsmilingly as ever. "According to them, I'm impossible to avoid—urgently present in every malicious impulse and every self-indulgent whim."

"Are you telling me that you really are the devil?"

"Don't be ridiculous, Dr Victory. There is no devil. He's an invention of the Church—an instrument of moral terrorism. Priests have always embraced the defeatist belief that the only way to persuade people to be good is to threaten them with eternal torment. You and I know better than that. We understand that the only worthwhile way to persuade people to be good is to show them the rewards that will flow from virtuous endeavour. There has to be more to hope for than vague promises of bliss beyond death. If anyone's living proof of that, it's you."

"So who are you, really?" Victory tried, as he said it, to meet Gwynplaine's disconcerting stare with the kind of detachment that befitted a man who could repair every horror and enhance every beauty, but it wasn't easy.

"I was sold as a child," Gwynplaine said, his eerie voice becoming peculiarly musical again. "Adam's is not the only face the comprachicos tried to reproduce. The society is not yet extinct, no matter what the Pope may think—but its members are mere butchers nowadays, while men like you follow other paths."

"That was done to you deliberately?"

"It wasn't quite the effect they intended to produce."

"And before? Were you...like the boy you brought me nine years ago?"

"No. I was healthy, and fair of face. Angelic, even. I might have become....well, that's water under the bridge. Even you could not help me now, Dr Victory. I hope to see the face of Adam before I die, but not in a mirror."

In spite of his impatience, Victory could not help asking one more question. "Was Torricelli lying?" he asked. "Or did he really believe what he told me?"

"He believed it," Gwynplaine told him, his gaze never wavering within his frightful mask. "He still believes it—but he won't interfere again, because he also believes that the devil operates on Earth with the permission of God."

Victory decided that it was time to get down to business. "Where's the book?" he demanded.

"Safe in the custody of its rightful owners," Gwynplaine told him. "You don't need it. Nine years of nurturing the seeds I lent you has prepared you for what needs to be done. All you need now is the master key—and a child."

Victory shook his head. "No," he said. "That's not the way it's going to be done. Not this time. This time, I get all the information first. This time, I get to see the face on my computer before I make a single cut. No arguments—it's my way, or not at all. You cheated me once; I won't trust you again."

"If I broke my promise," Gwynplaine said, "it was for your own good. If I'd succeeded in my part of the project...but that's more water under the bridge. You're not the only one who's being doing things the hard way these last nine years. We're almost there—but I'd be doing you a grave disservice if I didn't warn you that you're in danger. If you'll condescend to take my advice you'll leave the programme incomplete until you have to use it to guide the robot arm. Don't attempt to preview the result. No harm can come to you if you work in the flesh of a child and allow me to take him away when you've finished—but I can't protect you if you refuse to take my advice."

"And what, exactly, will become of me if I look at the face of Adam on my computer before I attempt to reproduce it in the flesh?"

"I don't know. Nobody knows—certainly not Monsignor Torricelli. In contrast to the fanciful claims of legend, the Church has never had the slightest contact with the world of the angels."

"So your warning is just so much bluster?" Victory said.

"No. I'm trying to protect my own interests. I don't want anything unfortunate to happen to you before you repeat the experiment—or afterwards, for that matter."

"But you said before that the face of Adam would bring about a religious renaissance—that it would inspire everyone who saw it to forsake sin and seek salvation."

"I said nothing of the kind," Gwynplaine said, equably. "I only said that the comprachicos believed that. You already know that the Church believes otherwise. So do I. I may be privy to the comprachicos' secrets, but I'm not one of them. I'm their victim and their emissary, but I'm also my own person. For myself, I haven't the slightest interest in the salvation or damnation of humankind."

"So what *do* you want out of this?"

"That's my business. The question is, doctor—what do *you* want out of it, and what are you prepared to risk in order to get it? I've given you the warning that I was duty bound to offer. If you're prepared to take the risk, having had fair warning, so am I. I can't give you the book, but I can give you the last piece that's missing from your painstaking reconstruction of its final secret. If you insist on seeing an image before you attempt to produce the real thing I won't try again to prevent it. If, after seeing the image, you're unable to conduct the operation, I'll simply take the results of all your hard work to California. My advice to you is that you should find a suitable child, and conduct the operation as before, without a preview of the likely result. Take it or leave it—in either case, I intend to proceed."

"I'll leave the advice," Victory said. "But I'll take the missing piece of the puzzle."

Gwynplaine reached into the inside pocket of his ridiculously unfashionable jacket and produced a folded piece of paper. If he really had been in hell the inferno was obviously equipped with photocopiers. Victory unfolded the piece of paper and looked at the diagram thus revealed.

He stared at it for a minute and a half, and then he let out his breath.

"Of course," he said. "So simple, so neat—and yet I'd never have found it without the cue. Diabolically ingenious."

Gwynplaine did not take the trouble to contradict him.

Gwynplaine sat languidly in the chair, a perfect exhibition of patience, while Victory's busy fingers flew over the keyboard and clicked the mouse again and again, weaving the final ingredient into the model that would reproduce the face of Adam when the programme was run.

It was not a simple matter of addition, because the code had to be modified in a dozen different places to accommodate the formulas describing the final incision-and-connection.

Victory had half-expected the code itself to be mysteriously beautified, but it remained mere code, symbolising a string of ones and zeroes as impenetrable to the naked eye and innocent mind as any other. Until the machine converted it into pictures it was inherently lifeless and vague—but when the job was done....

In the end, Victory looked up. He didn't bother to look at his wristwatch, but it was pitch dark outside and Harley Street was in the grip of the kind of silence that only fell for a brief interval in the small hours. "It's ready," he said. "You'd better join me if you want to watch."

"If you don't mind," Gwynplaine said, "I'll stay on this side of the desk and watch you. I have patience enough to wait for the real thing."

"If Torricelli were here," Victory said, "he'd probably remind me of the second commandment." He was looking at the screen as he said it, where he had set up the face of a three-week-old child. He had chosen the child at random; any one, he supposed, would do as well as another.

"If Torricelli were here," Gwynplaine said, "neither of us would give a fig for anything he said."

Victory drew the mouse across the pad, and launched the programme.

He had watched its predecessors run a thousand times before, without seeing anything unusual in the adult face that formed in consequence. He had run them so many times, in fact, that he had ceased to believe that there was any conceivable human face that could have any unusual effect on his inquiring eye and mind. When he tried to imagine what the face of Adam might look like, all he could summon to mind was the image painted by Michelangelo on the ceiling of the Sistine Chapel.

But Adam did not look like that at all.

Adam's face was unimaginable by any ordinary mortal—even an artist of genius.

While learning the basics of medicine forty-two

years before, Hugo Victory had been informed that each of his eyes had a blind spot where the neurones of the optic nerve spread out to connect to the rods and cones in the retina. Because he had always been slightly myopic, his blind spots had been slightly larger than those of people with perfect vision, but they still did not show up in the image of the world formulated by his brain. Even if he placed a hand over one eye, to eliminate the exchange of visual information between the hemispheres of his cerebral cortex, he still saw the world entire and unblemished, free of any void. That, he had been told, was an illusion. It was not that the brain "filled in" the missing data to complete the image, but rather that the brain ignored the part of the image that was not there, so efficiently that its absence was imperceptible. And yet, the blindspot *was* there. Anything eclipsed by it was not merely invisible, but left no clue as to its absence.

It was a blind spot of sorts—albeit a trivial one—that had prevented Victory from being able to see or deduce the missing element in his model of the comprachicos' final secret. It was likewise a blind spot of sorts—but by no means a trivial one—that had prevented him and every other man in the world from extrapolating the face of Adam and the angels from his knowledge of the vast spectrum of ordinary human faces.

Now, the blind spot was removed. His mind was no longer able to ignore that which had previously been hidden even from the power of imagination. Hugo Victory saw an image of the proto-human face that had been made in God's image.

Quietly, he began to weep—but his tears dried up much sooner than he could have wished.

His right hand—acting, apparently, without the benefit of any conscious command—moved the mouse, very carefully, across its mat, and clicked it again in order to exit from the programme.

He watched without the slightest reservation or complaint as Gwynplaine, who had waited until then to move around the desk, carefully burned the programme on to a CD that he had appropriated from the storage cabinet.

"I told you so," the man with the hideous face murmured, not unkindly, as he carefully set the computer to reformat the hard disk. "I played as fair as I dared to be. That wasn't the real thing, of course. It was just a photograph, lacking even the resolution it might have had. You should have done as I asked and worked directly on a child, Dr Victory. It might require a dozen more attempts, or a hundred, but in time, one of them will survive to adulthood. *That* will be the real thing. At least, I hope so. The comprachicos might not have got it absolutely right, of course. Even now, I still have to bear that possibility in mind. But I remain hopeful—and now I have something that's worth taking to California, I'm one step nearer to my goal."

"It's strange," Victory said, wondering why he had utterly ceased to care. "When you first came into my office, nine years ago, I thought you were the most awfully disfigured man I'd ever seen. I couldn't imagine why the doctors who'd treated you after your accident hadn't done more to ameliorate the effect of the burns. But now I've grown used to you, you seem perfectly ordinary. Hideous, but perfectly ordinary. I thought nine years ago—and still thought, ninety minutes ago—that I could do something for you, if you'd only permit me to try, but now I see that I couldn't....that there's simply nothing to be done."

"It's not strange to me," Gwynplaine assured him. "I've lived among the comprachicos. I understand these things better than any man alive...with one possible exception, now. I hope you can find it in your heart to forgive me for that enlightenment."

"I don't feel capable of forgiveness any more," Victory said. "Or hatred either. Or...."

"Much as I'd like to hear the rest of the list," Gwynplaine said, apologetically, "I really must be going. If you see Monsignor Torricelli again, please give him my fondest regards. Unlike him, you see, I really have learned to love my enemies."

It was not until Meg arrived at half past eight that Victory had the opportunity to assess the full extent of the change that had come over him, but once the evidence was before him he understood its consequences easily enough.

Meg, like Janice before her, was an unusually beautiful young woman. A plastic surgeon had to surround himself with beautiful people, in order to advertise and emphasize his powers as a healer. But Meg now seemed, to Victory's unprejudiced and fully awakened sight, not one iota more or less beautiful than Gwynplaine. She looked, in fact, absolutely ordinary: aesthetically indistinguishable from every other member of the human race. Nor could Victory imagine any practicable transformation that would bring about the slightest improvement.

It was, he realised, going to be rather difficult to function efficiently as a plastic surgeon from now on. So extreme was the devastation of his aesthetic capacity, in fact, that Victory could not think of any field of human endeavour in which he might be able to function creatively or productively—but the inability did not cause him any distress.

Even the idea that he was now in a kind of hell, beyond any possibility of escape or redemption, could not trouble him in the least.

Nor could the faintly absurd suspicion that he might have provided the means for the devil to free himself, at long last, from the voracious burden of his envy of humankind.

"Dating Secrets
of the Dead"
David Prill

Hey, *Jerry, there's THAT new girl.*

Oh, yes. Her name's Caroline May Ames. She's a swell kid.

Why? Do you know her?

Not very well, Bud. I wish I did.

I don't know what it is, but there's something about her you like.

Well, she always looks nice for one thing.

They all look nice, at first....

Jerry hadn't had a date in an eternity. He didn't know why. They had dressed him so stylishly. His black dress shoes had such a sheen to them. His wispy brown hair was trimmed and combed. His cheeks had a ruddy, outdoorsy hue. His fingernails had once been nicely manicured—now they had grown long. Too long. Maybe that was it. Maybe his uncut fingernails were turning off the girls.

No, it had to be more than that.

All in all, I look pretty sharp, he thought.

Then maybe it's my personality or personal habits.

I'm soft-spoken—my breath would hardly fog a mirror.

Polite. To a fault.

171

Interesting experiences to share. Absolutely. My life review was a gripping melodrama.

Jerry didn't want to face rejection again, but he did like that new girl, Caroline May Ames. They had exchanged small talk once before, the day she arrived. They were in the same row, after all. She was so pretty. Her white dress had ivory beads and lace. Her blonde hair cascaded comfortably over her shoulders. She had such a peaceful look on her face.

He called for her.

Hi, Caroline. This is Jerry.

Oh hi, Jerry.

I was wondering, Caroline, if you want to go out with me tonight?

Tonight? I'm sorry, I can't, Jerry. I already have a date for tonight. Why don't you call some other time?

Oh, okay. Thanks anyway, Caroline. Bye.

Goodbye, Jerry.

Strike out, Jerry thought, feeling dejected. Didn't she like him? She acted like she did. Then why didn't she want to go out with him?

He decided to ask Bud about it. Bud had been around longer than Jerry, and always seemed to have good advice to share.

...so I don't know what happened. I asked Caroline for a date, and she turned me down flat.

How long did the conversation last?

Not long. A minute or so.

That's good. Your call shouldn't go on for hours. That's a pretty sensible attitude. When did you ask her to go out with you?

Tonight.

There's your problem. Be sure not to wait until the last minute to ask a girl for a date. It's no compliment

172

to any girl to call her so late that she thinks she's the last resort.

I never thought of that. Thanks a lot, Bud.

Glad to help, fella.

Jerry tried again the next day.

Hi, Caroline, this is Jerry.

Hi, Jerry.

Caroline, uh, I don't suppose you'd want to go out with me sometime.

Oh, I suppose we could. Call me sometime.

That was better. A real step in the right direction. He told Bud about his success.

That's great, Jerry. When are you two going out, then?

Uh, we didn't exactly set a day.

How did you ask her?

Jerry told him.

Don't ask a girl out in a backhanded way that makes her feel uncomfortable. It's a mark of your insecurity, too. And one other tip: Don't ask a girl if she is busy on a certain night. That puts her on the spot.

Boy, this is more complicated than I thought, Jerry mused. *So how should I ask her then?*

Think of something to do that she might like. Don't leave it entirely up to her. Suggest two or three activities, and see how she responds. Perhaps go out with a group of friends.

There's a skating party on Friday. Maybe Caroline would want to do that.

Now you've got the hang of it.

He called for Caroline again.

Hi, Jerry.

Hi, Caroline. Say, the gang is going to a skating party on Friday. I was wondering if you'd want to go with me. We'd have to leave early, but we'd get back by eleven. Or else we could spend the evening watching the flesh rot off our bones. We'd get back later if we did that.

Gee, Jerry, the skating party sounds like loads of fun. I'd love to go.

Great. I'll come for you around six.

Jerry was smart. He kept a date calendar, and checked it before asking Caroline to the party. Not a bad idea.

Good boy! Bud congratulated Jerry when told of his success with Caroline. *I wish I could go to the skating party but I told my folks I'd spend the evening with them. They don't get out much anymore.*

I really appreciate your help, said Jerry. *I just wish I could take you with me!*

Jerry was joshing Bud, but it was true. His friend knew the proper habit patterns, and what it took to be popular.

The days leading up to his date with Caroline seemed to crawl and creep. Throughout the week Jerry quizzed Bud on how he should behave on his date, what to say, what a girl expects. Finally, the weekend rolled in, and Jerry grew stiff with anticipation.

Wardrobe. Jerry decided to wear what he had on. His dark suit. It made him look more mature. A few holes, hardly noticeable, some mild staining in the crotch area, but Caroline would understand. She was that kind of girl.

A few minutes before six Jerry showed up where Caroline lived. He didn't need Bud to tell him the importance of promptness. He wanted to make a good impression on her folks, too.

Her parents were side by side when he arrived.

Good evening, Mr. and Mrs. Ames. I'm Jerry Weathers, Caroline's friend.

Even though they were Midwestern stoic, Jerry felt at ease with her mom and dad. There wasn't enough left of them to make trouble.

Jerry, how nice to see you.

Caroline.

She looked wonderful. White dress. Beads. Blonde hair. Shoulders. A portrayal of peace on her face.

Hi, Caroline. You look so natural.

Thanks. How nice of you to notice. She addressed her parents. *We should be back from the skating party by eleven.*

There is no magic formula about when to come home from a date. The hour Jerry and Caroline would return was decided by where they were going on their date, whether tomorrow was a school day, how many dates she had had recently, and so forth.

I'll take good care of her, Mr. and Mrs. Ames, said Jerry. *Good night.*

'Night, Mom and Dad. Don't wait up for us.

As they met up with the gang for the skating party, Jerry felt relaxed and sociable. It had helped knowing Caroline, even just a little, before they went on their first date. Jerry had been on blind dates before. Most of them were dumb and deaf, too, and then there was that headless girl. A midwayride mishap, he had overheard during her interment. She was fun, but not really Jerry's type.

The skating party. It seemed unreal, that's how entranced he was with Caroline.

He felt light on his feet, Dead Astaire, his skate blades cutting into the dark sheet on the pond. They skated in a long loop, hand in hand. Caroline's hand was colder than Hell. He tried warming it up with his own, but it didn't seem to help much.

As they skated beneath the festering full moon, they seemed to get into a rhythm with each other, carried away with the dance. Jerry would release Caroline, just the tips of their fingers touching, then he would draw her back in, and they would spin around, laughing inside, and skate on down the ice. Caroline seemed to be enjoying herself a lot. She was a good kid.

Jerry had been concentrating on Caroline so much that he was surprised when he looked away and saw that the whole gang was watching them waltz across the pond.

We're a big hit, he said, nodding to the onlookers.

When Caroline realized they had an audience, she self-consciously tried to stop, her blade catching a ridge on the ice. She lost her balance, and they fell in time, too.

The gang rushed over.

Are you guys all right?

I think so, said Jerry. *Caroline, are you hurt?*

I'm fine. Just a little bump.

We should probably sit and watch the others skate for a while.

No, don't stop, the gang said. *You two were skating so beautifully.*

Yes, how long have you been skating together?

Well, actually this is our first date, Jerry explained.

You're kidding! Wow. Talk about a perfect match.

Caroline got a blushing expression on her face, although no blood filled her cheeks. It was pretty cold out there on the pond.

I think we'll catch our breaths, Jerry said, helping Caroline back up onto her feet.

They skated carefully over to the edge of the pond, stepping through the snowbank to a concrete bench. A weather-worn angel watched over them, a dollop of snow on her nose.

Jerry tried to call up the advice Bud had passed on to him. What did he say to talk about? A popular movie, friends they have in common, anything that is of mutual interest.

Movies were out. He hadn't seen one in ages. Friends? She was new in his neighborhood. Anything they were both interested in. That was the solution, but what did they share other than their place of residence? He didn't know.

Say something....

Uh, Caroline....

Yes, Jerry?

That's a lovely dress you're wearing.

Why, thank you. You look very nice, too.

Do I really? I mean, it's my only suit....

It looks fine.

And my skin. The flaking...the bugs....

She took both of his hands in hers. *Jerry, I like you. For yourself. I don't care about the bugs. Forget about the bugs. You'd have to be looking for them to see them. You have a good heart. I'm glad you asked me out. I'm having a fun time. I really am.*

Gosh, Caroline, you're really a neat person.

Silence, and then Jerry began to feel awkward. Think of something.

Then it struck him. How could I have missed it? The perfect topic for first date small talk. He knew Bud would be proud.

I like the smell of...dirt. Do you?

I didn't at first. But I think I'm getting used to it.

Me, too. I mean, I didn't like it at first either. But after a while, it kind of, you know, gets under your skin.

Yes, I suppose it does.

In the springtime, they bring flowers.

I love flowers.

Sometimes, you can smell the rain.

I always liked rain. Rain makes the whole world fresh and new.

Sometimes, there are leaks.

I suppose so.

They chatted for a while longer, swapping death stories—she and her folks expiring in a car wreck on an ice-coated highway, he succumbing to an inoperable brain tumor—then returned to the pond. The skating party broke up as the moon went down. Things were going so well with Caroline that he didn't want to break the spell.

Caroline's mom and dad were inert when they got back. It was only a quarter to eleven.

I had a swell time tonight, said Caroline.

I'm glad you enjoyed the skating, Jerry said. *I'm glad you weren't hurt when you fell on the ice.*

I was more surprised than anything. All those people staring at us: It was like a dream.

They were having a good time together. But all good things, like life itself, must eventually come to an end.

Thank you for our date, Jerry said. *I had fun, too. I hope we can see each other again.*

So do I, Caroline said. *Please call for me anytime.*

In many communities, a good night kiss is expected

as the customary way of ending a date. It can mean any number of things. A token of friendship, a simple way of saying thank you for the evening, a sign of affection. What it means depends on the two people and their definition of their relationship and themselves.

Jerry took the safe route. When Caroline rose, he squeezed her hand and searched for a smile.

The look on her face said she had a smile inside her.

And the date was over.

The next day, he told Bud about his evening with Caroline. Not in too much detail, because he didn't want to be one of those boys who doesn't respect a girl's privacy and reputation, and most importantly her personal feelings.

Your advice really helped me a lot, he told Bud.

Glad to be of service, guy.

I'm not sure what to do next. Should I wait a few days before calling her again? I don't feel like waiting. But I don't want her to think I'm too pushy either.

There's no perfect answer to your question. It depends on the two people and their definition of their relationship and themselves.

Gosh, I don't know, Bud. It all sounds pretty complicated.

It's the easiest thing in the world. You could call her today just to thank her for going with you to the skating party. That's a common courtesy. A girl would appreciate the gesture. Remember, though, to have a sensible attitude. Your call shouldn't go on for hours.

Should I ask her out again when I call?

After your courtesy call, I would wait a couple of days. By then it will be mid-week, and it will still give her several days notice. Remember, though, not to call her so late that she thinks she's the last resort.

So Jerry did call Caroline later that day, and handled it just the way Bud suggested. Although he yearned to talk to Caroline for hours, he kept it short. She seemed to genuinely appreciate his thoughtfulness.

Her receptive attitude toward him made his next call easy.

Hi Caroline, it's Jerry.

Hi, Jerry. How are you?

I'm doing very well, thank you. And yourself?

Just fine, thanks.

I was wondering, Caroline, if you would like to go on a hay ride this Saturday? The whole gang is going.

Oh, I'd love to, Jerry.

Great. I'll come for you around six, if that's okay.

That would be perfect. I'll see you then, Jerry.

Thank you, Caroline. Good-bye.

Jerry passed the week in a daze. A wonderful new world was opening up for him. He thought about Caroline constantly, and eagerly anticipated their next engagement. A hay ride would be the ideal second date. You don't ask just anyone to go on a hayride. Skating is something you do separately, but a hayride is something you do...together. There could be several opportunities for floating his arm around her shoulder. Sweet. Bud strongly approved, too. Everything was going to be a shining golden sky.

And then disaster turned his social life on its ear.

Actually, more toward the front of his head.

One moment his left eyeball was tucked snugly into its socket where it belonged; the next moment it had migrated down his cheek, like a mouse peeking out of its hole.

The rotting must have progressed further than he realized. Jerry knew it was inevitable, although he hadn't cared to dwell on it, but why did it have to happen now? This week? So close to the hayride?

He tried to look on the bright side. The eye was still attached. That was worth something. Jerry tried to recall anatomy. Was it the optic nerve that secured the eyeball to the socket? And when that disintegrated...

What a fix.

Jerry immediately sought out Bud. He had to help. He just had to. Both of his eyes had long since vacated the premises. He must know what to do.

After hearing his dilemma, Bud said, *Well heck, I'd lend you mine, if I still had any.*

Can't we just pop it back in?

Afraid not. The normal rotting of tissue, plus the bugs, plus....

Okay, okay. So what am I going to do? I have a date with Caroline on Saturday. We're going on a hayride. I can't let her see me like this.

Don't call attention to it and she'll hardly notice.

How could she not notice? My eye is hanging halfway down my face for gosh sake.

Try to keep her on the side of your good eye.

I don't think that's going to solve much.

Listen, Jerry. This is just in the nature of things. You can't stop it. I can't stop it. We just do the best we can with what we have left of ourselves. Death goes on.

But Caroline...

You think she really likes you?

Yes. I do.

Then it won't matter. Consider this: if one of her eyes fell out of her head, would you stop seeing her?

Well, no…

There, you see? She probably feels exactly the same way.

But she's so pretty.

They're always pretty, in the beginning.

But what should I say to her?

Be straightforward. Girls appreciate that. There's no need to get graphic, of course. Avoid the temptation to seek sympathy. Have a positive, accepting attitude. You still have one good eye, don't you?

Well, yes….

If you let her know you're disturbed by it, then you'll just end up making her feel uncomfortable. She'll be glad to follow your lead. Once you explain the situation, don't bring it up again. Soon, you won't even remember that your eye is out of its socket, dangling there.

I don't know, Bud….

It will work, Jerry. Trust me. I haven't steered you wrong so far, have I?

Bud was right. His advice had been invaluable. He had common sense in bushels.

Jerry didn't want to spring any surprises on Caroline, so on Saturday morning he called for her.

Hi, Caroline. This is Jerry.

Well hi, Jerry. How are you?

I'm fine, Caroline. And yourself?

Fine, thank you. We're still on for tonight, aren't we?

Yes, of course. But, uh, there's a little problem.

A problem?

I'm just having some trouble with my eye.

Nothing too serious, I hope.

Oh, no, no....It's just, well, not exactly in the socket anymore. It's sort of...hanging down.

My goodness.

I mean, it's still attached. No doubt about that.

Yes, of course.

Silence.

I'm sorry, Jerry said.

It's okay. I understand, I really do.

You do?

I sure do. You still have one good eye, don't you?

Yes.

Well, there you go.

You mean you don't mind, Caroline? You'll still go on the hayride with me?

Yes, I'll still go on the hayride with you, silly. You're still the same person I went skating with, aren't you?

Gosh, Caroline, you're really a swell girl.

So I'll see you this evening and I don't want to hear another word about it.

So long, Caroline. And thank you.

Jerry put the eye out of his mind.

A few minutes before six he came to Caroline. It's wise to leave a little early for a date. That way, there's no need to rush when you arrive at your date's residence. Makes for a more relaxed and enjoyable experience for everyone.

Hi, Jerry.

Hi, Caroline. Good evening, Mr. and Mrs. Ames.

He felt a warm greeting. Apparently he met with their approval.

Caroline looked beautiful. White dress, beads, peace, etc.

You look just like yourself, said Jerry.

Thank you, Jerry. That's sweet of you to say.

183

Are you all ready then? Jerry asked.

All set. 'Night mom and dad. We'll be back by ten-thirty.

Good night, Mr. and Mrs. Ames. Don't worry, I'll take good care of Caroline.

When they arrived at the hayride, the gang was already piling into the rotting hay wagon. Jerry had a few kernels of uneasiness as they approached the wagon. Someone was hooking a chestnut mare into its bridle. Large chunks of flesh were missing from the horse's flanks. Much of its head was eaten away, a part of the jawbone showing. Nobody was making a fuss about it. Jerry felt his self-confidence soar.

When they reached the business end of the wagon, Jerry stepped up first, and offered Caroline a hand. She took it and he pulled her up.

Hi, gang! Jerry said.

Hi, Jerry! the gang replied. *Nice to see you, Caroline!*

Hi, everybody! Caroline said.

Jerry found a spot for them in the hay. He positioned himself so that Caroline had to sit on the side of his good eye. No sense drawing attention to the flaw if it could be easily avoided.

In a short time the driver hopped up on the front of the wagon, and gently shook the frayed reins. The skeletal horse broke into a trot, its sleigh bells sounding like a death rattle, the wagon rocking forward with the motion.

The driver guided the horse along the narrow trail that wound around the frozen pond and through the snowy field. Pine trees, statuary, and ornate white buildings passed by.

What a wonderful idea this was, Caroline said. *This is really fun. I'm glad you came along.*

Caroline patted Jerry on the forearm, then her fingers began to slide down toward his wrist, a clear sign that she was interested in holding hands.

Fortunately, Jerry first glanced down at her hand, then saw his own....

Immediately, he brought his arm across his chest and thrust his hand into the hay. Then, he reached across with his left hand and took hers.

I think I got a sliver, he explained.

Oh, let me see. I can take it out.

Well it's in pretty deep. I'll remove it later. It doesn't hurt much at all, really.

This seemed to satisfy her.

Her fingers were cold, and his were gone.

Not all of them, perhaps two, possibly three. All he saw were black, rotted stumps. The digits must have fallen off after he hoisted her up onto the wagon. He hadn't even felt their departure. Were they in the wagon? He scanned the bed in the vicinity of where he had been standing, but he couldn't spot them amid the hay and snow. They must have fallen into the snow back on the trail. He'd never find them. And even if he did, what good would they do him now?

The rest of the hayride Jerry spent in nervous preoccupation with his missing appendages. The eye was bad enough. He didn't want Caroline to think he was coming apart on her.

Why now? Why all of a sudden? It was almost like the more he tried to have a social life, the more his body rebelled.

When the hay wagon returned to their point of departure, the horse collapsing into dust, Jerry helped

Caroline down to the ground with his left hand, keeping his right tucked into the pocket of his best suit. He didn't dare search the vicinity for his fingers now.

The gang hung out afterward, gossiping and cracking wise like dead teenagers do. Jerry struggled to keep in good spirits. When they got back to her place, it was later than he expected.

Say, look at the time, said Jerry. *I told your folks I'd get you home by ten-thirty and here it is, almost eleven.*

I'm sure they'd understand. We aren't very late at all. There was nothing we could do about it, really.

I don't want your parents to think I'm taking advantage of you.

They won't think that. You can stay for a while. I mean it.

Thank you for the offer, Caroline. I would just feel better if I took a rain check. You understand, don't you?

Oh, of course. You're such a gentleman, Jerry. Next time, I won't let you off the hook so easily.

Good night, Caroline.

Good night, Jerry. She leaned over and kissed him on the cheek, deftly avoiding his droopy eye. Her lips were still chilly from the hayride.

Jerry told Bud the rotten news when he returned to his plot.

Fingers falling off, eh? Join the club.

But what can I do about it? I can't keep company with Caroline like this. She was okay with my eye, but I can't expect her to pretend forever. How are we supposed to hold hands?

Do it spiritually. Girls like a boy who has a kind heart. It makes them feel special.

I want to feel Caroline, touch her.

Use your other hand.

I did, but how long will that last? I'm surprised it's still attached.

There's no turning back, Jerry. There's an old saying around here: If you don't rest in peace, you'll come apart in pieces.

Look, my prospects aren't too good anyway. I appreciate your willingness to help me, Bud. I'll think of something. Maybe if we can keep going on group dates I can hide it from her.

And then what?

I don't know. I don't know. I'll come up with something.

Jerry knew he had to apologize to Caroline, after his behavior on the hayride.

The next day he called for her, trying to inject sunshine into his voice. He remembered sunshine, wistfully.

Hi, Caroline, this is Jerry.

Hello, Jerry. How are you?

Very well, thanks.

That's good. I had a really fun time on the hayride, Jerry. Thank you for taking me.

I enjoyed it, too. That's why I was calling, Caroline. I wanted to apologize for my behavior at your place. I shouldn't have run off like that. You said it was okay if I hung around, and I should have trusted you.

Oh, gosh Jerry, there's no need to apologize. I understand. You were just trying to be sweet.

You're not mad at me then?

Of course not.

Wow, that's great to hear, Caroline. I wasn't sure. I mean, I didn't know. My eye....

You're fine, Jerry.

How about if I make it up to you anyway? The gang is going sledding this afternoon. Do you want to go?

Well, to be honest, Jerry, I was hoping we could do something by ourselves once.

Oh no....

Uh, what did you have in mind?

Why don't we just go for a walk? What do you say?

Jerry knew what he had to say.

Sure, Caroline, that sounds swell. What time do you want me to come over?

How about three?

Three it is.

Terrific. I'll see you then.

Good-bye, Caroline.

Jerry spent the rest of the day wringing his hand.

He couldn't keep his problem in his pocket all afternoon. He had to be honest with Caroline. If only they had given me gloves, he thought with high melancholy.

Three o' clock came like it couldn't wait to see him humiliated.

Jerry hated the fact that he felt trepidation about seeing Caroline. He wanted to feel excitement, anticipation, affection. Not this squeamish, nervous feeling.

On the way over to Caroline's, Jerry felt an odd sensation and it had nothing to do with his interior life. Something in the region of his feet. Suddenly he had trouble walking. And he didn't have to look to know that his toes had been eaten away by time or worms or some burrowing creature.

Jerry didn't get upset, just philosophical. He had hit some kind of plateau, gone from a being with one foot in this world and the other foot in the next, to a decaying corpse with both feet on the verge of rotting off his legs.

When his deterioration had been easy to hide, it had been possible to keep up appearances, pass as something he was not.

But now, with a dangling eye, stumps instead of fingers, a lot of extra space down at the end of his polished black shoes, there was only one path to take.

Jerry presented himself to Caroline as he was, a young man on the downside of his death.

He hobbled the rest of the way to her place.

She was waiting for him, smelling the plastic flowers. An ice-crusted bouquet of pale purples, reds and yellows.

Hi, Caroline.

Oh hi, Jerry. I didn't hear you coming. She looked at him with concern. *Are you okay? You're walking so strangely.*

This was it.

Well, Caroline, you see, my feet are rotting away. And my hand. He displayed it for her. And tried to force a smile on his natural and peaceful face. *I'm a real mess, aren't I?*

Maybe we should just stay here today. We could talk or something.

I want to walk, said Jerry. *Please walk with me, Caroline.*

Sure, Jerry. I'll walk with you.

They slowly strolled among the monuments and trees, stark oaks coated with ice, evergreens hanging heavy with snow. The moon was circled by a pale orange halo.

Why is it happening now, so fast? Caroline gently asked him. *Just the other day you were fine.*

Bud says it's because I won't rest in peace.

Have I met Bud?

I'm not sure. Bud Pollard. 1959–1976. Loving son devoted student friend of the community.

Oh, yes, I remember seeing him.

He's a good guy. He's always given me helpful advice.

I'm so sorry, Jerry. What are you going to do?

They had reached a bench sheltered by a hedge planted in an arc. With every step it seemed harder for Jerry to walk properly. His gait was a rolling, teetering travesty.

Let's sit down, Jerry said, and she helped him do that.

She was seated on his left, so he was able to hold her hand properly.

Caroline put her head on his shoulder. The decay hadn't hit there yet. *We need to have a talk*, Jerry said.

Okay.

They looked at each other, his dangling eye trying to get into the act, too.

You know, Caroline, you're the first girl I've kept company with since I came here. And even if I would have known that dating you would make me decompose to beat the band, I wouldn't have changed a thing, that's how much I've treasured our time together.

I feel the same way. Listen, Jerry, pretty soon what's happening to you will overtake me, too. My eyeballs will go pop, toes and fingers fall off, bits and pieces eaten away. And the bugs....

We have this time together. We have the present, before all that happens.

Yes, isn't it wonderful?

Yes, but I'm withering away so quickly, said Jerry. *I don't know how long I've got before I won't be able to go for walks, or ice skating, or anything.*

Your suit still looks sharp.

I don't want to rush us, Caroline, but those are the facts. If we let the days go by thinking things will always be the way they are now, one day we'll wake up and I'll just be a pile of sludge you used to call a friend.

Oh, Jerry, please, don't talk like that.

We have to face it, Caroline. We can't deny this. He reached out for her with his rotting stump. She drew her hand away.

He gazed grimly at her. *This is our future, Caroline. In a few days you're going to be afraid to even look at me.*

A few remnant tears squeezed themselves from her barren ducts. *I won't be afraid, Jerry. I promise.*

Jerry hesitated for a moment. *What I'm saying, Caroline, is that if you want us to have any sort of...physical relationship, we can't wait.*

Caroline's peaceful, natural face was clouded with sadness.

I'm sorry it has to be like this, said Jerry. *I know this isn't considered good dating etiquette. It's not proper to pressure a girl into intimate relations. If there was another way....*

No, you're right, she said. *We have to face this. I don't want death to be denial, too.*

They sat in quiet spaces for a time, holding hands. A nuthatch lit on an evergreen branch, then flew off when it realized it wasn't alone. Its weight disturbed the branch, sending a dusting of snow down upon the heads of the dead.

So, Caroline, Jerry said shyly, *do you want to go back to my place?*

I'd love to.

Jerry's place was in bad need of a dusting.

It's not much, he said, *but it's home.*

I like it. It's cozy.

Are you comfortable? he asked her.

I'm just fine. It's nice to be so close to you.

Don't worry about hurting me.

I won't. Can we do something about that eye? It's sort of in the way.

Oh, sure. Hang on...got it. Is that better?

Much better. Now I can touch your face all over.

He began to touch her, too.

You don't think I'm easy, Jerry, do you?

No, of course not.

Have there been other girls...like me?

No, only the living.

That makes me feel good.

As they began to probe and pet, and then proceed to the most private of realms, Jerry felt parts of himself break away, disintegrate. His fine suit slowly collapsed in upon itself, soaking up what remained of his bodily fluids.

Jerry suddenly felt disgusted, even horrified, and he didn't know why.

I have very strong feelings for you, Caroline whispered to him.

I feel the same about you.

What's wrong with me? he wondered. This should be the crowning moment of my death. Why do I feel so terrible, so guilt-wracked, so...wrong?

Caroline sensed it, too. *What's going on? Are you okay?*

I'm okay, he said. *I'm okay.*

But he wasn't. This felt so illicit, so...immoral.

At the very moment they consummated their deaths, as his body rotted away to utter uselessness, a shock of awareness hit him, as he understood what had disturbed him, why everything had felt so wrong.

And why now everything was feeling so right.

The final dating secret.

Jerry realized, as both of Caroline's eyes popped out upon her climax, and their precious ooze commingled, that if a living person has intimate relations with a dead body, it's called necrophilia.

If two dead bodies have intimate relations, it must be love.

"Luck"
James Patrick Kelly

Thumb sat on a rock, soothing his sore feet in the river, in no hurry to get home. The stories the shell people had told filled him with foreboding. Meanwhile, he was certain that the spirits had taken Onion's soul down into the belly of the earth while he'd been gone. The sun was still two hands from the edge of the sky. There was plenty of time before dark. Before he reached the summer camp of the people. Before they would tell him his lover was dead. While he tried not to think of her, a dream found him.

In his dream, a great herd of mammoths tracked down from the stony northern hills through the pine forest all the way to the river. There were five and five and five and *five* mammoths...and then more, more than Thumb could have ever counted, even if he used the fingers and toes of all of the people. They were huge, almost too big to fit in the eye of his mind. They trampled trees like tall grass, dropped turds the size of boulders.

Old Owl told a story about the spirit who became a mammoth. He called the beast a *furry mountain of meat*. Owl had been the last to see a mammoth, years ago when he was just a boy. The rest of the people knew mammoths only from the drawings in the long cave.

An animal the size of a mountain–how could that be?

When Thumb's herd of mammoths reached the river, they dipped their trunks into the water. In a dream moment, they drank the river dry. Turtles scrambled into the reeds for shelter. Fish flopped in the mud and died.

After her last baby had been born dead, Onion flopped on her mat like a fish.

Ruc-ruc-ruc-ruc-ruc!

The dream turned to smoke at the sound. Thumb leapt up and almost fell into the river. His feet had gone numb in the cold water and he couldn't feel the ground beneath them. He pulled on his boots, snatched his spear, fit it to his throwing stick.

Ruc-ruc-ruc!

The rumbling came from upriver, around the bend. Thumb had never heard anything like it. An earth sound, like the crack of a falling tree or a boulder crashing off a cliff, except it was wet and hot and alive. A sound that only an animal could make.

He crept deeper into the thicket before he started upriver. Hunting courage pounded in his chest. He strained ear and eye and nose after the quarry. He was ready to jump over the sky. It was hard to make himself go quietly but he parted branches and slid through the leaves.

Man. Come out, man.

The whisper rasped inside his head. He felt it on the tip of his nose, on the hair of his scalp, at the root of his cock and on the bottoms of his tingling feet. It had to be the whisper of a spirit. This was his luck then, whether good or bad. He had no choice. He must obey. Thumb rose up and pushed through the undergrowth toward the water. He knew that he might be about to have his soul stripped from his body. The thought did not much bother him. If Onion were really dead, he would be with her in the belly of the earth.

I am, man.

Thumb was not surprised to see a mammoth standing on the opposite bank. It must have sent the dream and whispered to him in a spirit voice. The surprise was what he felt as he gazed into its round, black eyes. This was no monster that could break trees and drain rivers. It wasn't much taller than he was. Yes, the trunk snaked like a nightmare and the tusks were long and curved and dangerous, but as Thumb took its measure, his confidence surged. The people had no weapon that could wound a mountain or strike at a spirit. But this was an animal that men might dare to hunt and bring down. Thumb let a laugh bubble out of his chest.

"I am Thumb," he shouted across the river at it, "keeper of the caves!" Then he danced, five hops on the spongy bank. He finished by striking the butt of his spear against an alder.

The mammoth raised its trunk and trumpeted in reply. The piercing cry sent a shiver through Thumb. But he was not cowed. He had heard the death scream of a bison and a cave bear's roar.

"This is the valley of the people." He struck the alder again.

At that moment, something at the far edge of his vision jumped. A blur that might have been a deer, or a man in deerskin, plunged into the woods. Was it the spirit? Then why had it run away from him? The mammoth didn't seem to care. It turned away from Thumb, curled its trunk around a willow branch, stripped it from the tree and stuffed it into its mouth. Thumb studied the mammoth as it ate, knowing that he would have to report everything he saw to Owl, the storyteller, and Blue, who spoke for the people. Besides, someday he might paint it on the wall of the cleft, if such was his luck.

It had to be the hairiest animal he had ever seen. The coarse fur was the color of bloodstone. It had thinned along the slope of the backbone but was matted and thick at the flanks. When the mammoth brushed against a low hanging branch, a swarm of flies buzzed out of its mangy coat. Thumb decided that it must be a full-grown animal because of the size of its tusks. The tip of the left one was broken off. The top of its skull was a round bump, like half of an onion.

Suddenly Thumb went very still. He knew why the mammoth had appeared to him, of all people. It was a sign. A turn of luck.

"Is that it, great one?" he said. "Is that why you called me?"

The mammoth dipped its trunk into the river, sucked up water and then squirted it into its mouth. Thumb could see the tongue, gray in the middle, pink on the sides. Then he turned and ran hard for home. For the first time since the thin moon rose, he thought he might see his lover again.

The people made their main summer camp near the top of a low cliff overlooking the river. A rock outcrop sheltered the ledge where they chipped their knives and cooked their meals and laid their mats. When rain came, they ducked into a long lean-to covered with bison hides. The main hearth was at the center of the ledge. In the summer camp, the smoke of their fires could become sky and not sting the eyes and settle in the chest as it did in the winter lodge.

Five and five and five and three of the people gathered close around the hearth that night. Ash and Quick and Spear and Robin and Moon and Bone were away, trading chert with the horse people and waiting with them for the arrival of the reindeer herd. It was the Moon of the Falling Leaves. Thumb's breath made clouds in the cool air.

"Are you warm yet?" he said.

"My heart is," said Onion. He had his arm around her waist and they snuggled beneath a bearskin blanket. She was thin as grass. He could feel her ribs beneath his moist hands. Even when she was pregnant, she was never as big as the other women. Now her breasts were like those of a girl. Thumb had not known Onion when she was young. She had come to them from the horse people five and three summers ago, a round and beautiful woman. Since then she had given birth to three babies, all dead, and had gotten thinner and thinner. Thumb kissed her pale face. The last had almost killed her. But she was still beautiful. He could wait until she was stronger before they would lie together as lovers. That would be soon, he hoped. Her breath tickled his neck.

Bead finished whispering to Owl. The storyteller got up painfully, carrying his years like a skin filled with stones. He hobbled around to the back of the hearth and turned so that the flames were between him and the people. Firelight caught in the creases on his face. Just before he spoke, he straightened and squared his shoulders. Then his voice boomed as it had for all the summers Thumb could remember.

"This is a story of Thumb," he said, "who is the son of my sister and who walks both in the light of the sun and the darkness of the two caves. He gave his story to me so that I could give it to you. It has become a story of the people. I will tell it to you now, even though it doesn't have an ending."

The people yipped and grunted with unease. A story without an ending was bad luck.

Actually, Thumb had told his story mostly to Bead, Owl's lover, and Blue, who spoke for the people. Owl had listened for a while but then had dozed off, as he often did late in the day.

"We know," said Owl, "that Thumb loves Onion and Onion loves Thumb. They have slept nose to nose, belly to belly for five and three winters. She eats the meat he brings her. He eats the roots she digs for him."

"When you find time to hunt," whispered Onion.

"When you dig something besides stones." Thumb gave her a gentle nudge.

"Thumb needed to make paint for the new cave, which some call the cleft. For the red, he had to collect blood stones from the shell people's land. But after bearing a baby that never breathed, his lover became sick with a fever. He had a hard choice. No one ever wants such a choice. Thumb loves Onion, but because he loves the people too, he left her and went to the shell people's land."

Quail gave a low whistle of approval. Thumb was pleased when everyone joined in. Even Owl. Even Onion. Thumb's cheeks were warm.

"While Thumb was gone, a stranger came to us. He brought food gifts of two eels and a badger skin filled with apples, so we welcomed him. He told us his name was Singer. He was an old man, with white and gray and not much brown in his beard. He wore a headdress of the feather people and the deerskins of our people. But he didn't say where he came from and we didn't ask. Although we are a curious people, we are also polite."

Owl paused and waited for the laugh.

"When Singer saw Onion bundled by the fire, he told us that she was going to die. We all thought that he was right. Singer said that he could use his luck to turn hers, but that we must let him do whatever he wanted with her. We talked about what he said. It seemed strange that a man could turn his own luck or anyone else's. But none of us could help Onion. Finally we let Blue speak for us. He told Singer to use his luck.

"Singer crushed herbs from his pouch in a wooden bowl, mixed them with water and gave them to Onion to drink. She went limp but her eyes stayed open. It was as if her soul had left her body. Then he picked her up in his arms and carried her to the river. He laid her on the bank and took off her deerskin shirt and pants. With his two hands he scooped mud onto her naked body, covering her until all we could see was her mouth and her nose. There were some of us who thought this was bad luck." Owl struck his chest with his fist. "Or at least crazy luck. But we said nothing. When Singer finished with the mud, he began to sing."

Owl paused, gathered himself. His voice quavered under and around and sometimes on the notes.

"'Spirits, look at this woman!
I have buried her for you.
She has learned what it is like
in the belly of the earth.
Now you won't have to teach her.

Leave her in the world awhile.

Let her wake with her people.'"

Onion had gone stiff as a tree stump beside him. "Are you all right?" said Thumb. She nodded and squeezed his hand. With a feeling of dread, Thumb understood that even though she seemed better, his lover was still tangled in the stranger's luck.

The effort of singing Onion back to life, even though it was just part of the story, left Owl exhausted. He sat down abruptly and fell silent. Bead dipped a dried gourd into a water skin and scrabbled across the ledge to him. As he drank, she whispered to him. The old man's eyes were as distant as the ice mountains. The people sat in polite silence for several moments, waiting for him to begin again. Bead's talk grew more heated; Thumb could make out words. *Lose...Foolish...Let me!* Finally Owl grunted and pushed her away.

"A fly is buzzing in my ear," he said. "It asks if a woman can tell a man's story." A few people laughed. Bead's smile was tight. She scooted backward but did not rejoin those around the fire. Instead she crouched a few paces away from Owl and waited.

"Then Singer finished his luck song." The storyteller spoke from where he sat, which made everyone nervous. But it was better that he tell the story sitting down rather than stop. It was very bad luck to stop in the middle of a story, especially a story that had no end. "He took off his own clothes, picked Onion up and waded into the water. When the river had rinsed her of the mud, he climbed out of the river and dressed her. Then he kissed her as if she were his lover. She was asleep now, with her eyes closed. A deep sleep, yes, but not the almost-death that had squeezed her before. We could see her breathing. She didn't wake up until the next day. By then, Singer had left us." Owl lowered his voice so that everyone had to lean forward to hear him. "Nobody saw him go. Did he melt like snow? Blow away like smoke?"

He paused, even though he knew no one would answer.

"He was gone." Owl stared into the fire. "All he left was his luck."

The people waited again.

"And this story," he muttered finally, as if speaking to himself.

Silence.

"Is that all?" said little Flamesgirl, who had just lost her baby teeth and still didn't have her name. She had been squirming on her mother's lap during Owl's story. "What about Thumb? What about the big beastie?"

Flame pinched the girl's cheek hard. Everyone knew that she talked more than her mother ought to allow.

"The mammoth, old man," Bead called to Owl, loud enough for everyone to hear. "I think you haven't told about the mammoth."

Owl grunted. "Old man." He struggled to his feet. "She calls me old man." He shook his head in disbelief. "But when I was young, just five and four summers old, I saw a mammoth. Maybe the last one. I will never forget it. Such a fearsome creature...a nose like a great snake and tusks that curved to the clouds. It was covered with shaggy brown fur. When it roared, birds fell out of the sky. It was so huge that the earth shook when it walked...and its foot, one foot could crush three men...because it was bigger than the trees, I saw it...a furry mountain of meat...What?"

As Owl was speaking, Blue rose and approached him. "I would like to finish this story, Owl." Blue touched his arm; he looked very embarrassed. Thumb was embarrassed too. "Will you let me?"

Owl puffed himself up. "Are you the storyteller now?"

"Thumb saw a mammoth today," said Blue gently. "Remember?"

Owl snorted and then glanced over at Bead. Her head was down, as if she were counting her toes. Owl's jaw muscles worked but he made no sound. Blue waited. Then Owl said, "Tell them whatever you want." He turned away, brushed past Bead and stalked into the darkness. Thumb could hear him climb the path to the top of the cliff. A few heartbeats later, Bead went after him.

"He has seen many summers," said Blue, "They have filled him up, I think. Still, it is luck to have him with us."

Then Blue reported to the people what had happened between Thumb and the mammoth. His words didn't sing like Owl's did and his voice never touched the moon, but the story was finished. Afterward there was not much discussion of what had happened that day. A sadness had fallen on the people like a cold rain. The mothers huddled briefly, no doubt talking about whether it was time to change storytellers. Most of the people lay down on their sleeping mats, glad to let the day pass into story.

Onion curled next to Thumb under their bearskin. They were so excited to see each other that they couldn't get to sleep. They talked in lovers' whispers, so as not to disturb the others.

"Owl was right to tie the luck of the mammoth to the stranger's luck," said Thumb, "even if he did forget what he was trying to say. I feel like I'm still bound to it." He sifted her hair through his hands. "And you to this Singer?"

"Maybe. I don't know." She shifted around to face him. "I'm sorry, but I don't remember much about him. They told me what he did but I heard the story as if it had happened to someone else. All I know is that I am better now. And that you're here with me."

"What do you remember?"

"I remember my baby was dead. It was a boy," she said.

"I know. I was with you." Thumb rested his hand on her hip. "But then I had to leave."

"After that all I remember are faces and lots of talk that I couldn't quite understand. And just a bit of a dream." Onion stroked his cheek, as if to assure herself that he was still there. "I was in a cave. I had no lamp and it was dark but I could see a tiny light, far off, like a star and the light called my name. I think it might have been Singer. I tried to crawl toward the light but my arms and legs wouldn't move. Then I heard a wind sound, but it wasn't wind. It was the cave, breathing." She shivered. "That's all."

"It was the long cave," said Thumb, although he didn't believe this, "and it was me, looking for you."

Someone was playing a bone flute. Probably Oak, who usually had trouble sleeping. The notes were soft and drowsy and a little downcast. It was a song of leaves dropping from trees and birds flying south, a song of the end of summer.

The next morning, Blue asked Thumb and Oak to

walk with him to the river for a hunting council. Although Oak was Thumb's half-brother, they had never been close. Oak was younger than Thumb. Their mother had died giving birth to him and their luck had been tangled ever since. But with Quick and the others tracking the reindeer herd, Oak was the best hunter in camp.

He was a simple man, better with his hands than his head. He could throw a spear farther than any of the people, but he could scarcely tell a story straight through. He had no lover and so was always restless. The mothers said that he would leave the valley some day.

The three men carried water skins down the path to the river. Since Blue had called the council, Oak and Thumb waited for him to begin it. At the river, instead of filling his skin, he hung it on a branch. The others did the same and then the three sat facing each other.

"So, do we hunt it?" said Blue.

Oak snorted in disgust. "The question answers itself."

"We could," said Thumb, "if it's just an animal."

"What else would it be?"

"A spirit."

Blue frowned. "You think it is?"

"My thoughts are thick as mud," said Thumb. "I heard a voice in my head. But as soon as I saw the beast, I knew that we could kill it." He shrugged. "You can't kill a spirit."

Oak touched Thumb's knee. "How many men would it take, brother?"

"Five and five, at least. It was feeding, so I'm not sure how fast it charges. More would be better. It'll be dangerous."

"So we had better wait for Quick to come back," said Blue.

Oak made a sour face. "And let it wander off? Blue, this is a mammoth. Think of what people will say of the ones who bring it down. You want to give those stories to the shell people? The horse people?"

Blue shook his head. "Men may die unless we hunt at full strength."

"You could die on the way back to camp if you trip over a stone. I'm not afraid."

"I'm not afraid, either. I'm just not stupid."

Thumb's attention drifted. Their argument was like the chitter of magpies. There was something that he needed to understand about the mammoth. Something that he couldn't talk or think his way to, something that hid underneath words. He began to clear the ground in front of him, pulling grass, sweeping away rotted leaves.

"We've got Horn and Quail and Bright and Rabbit," said Oak. "And you two, if you both agree,"

"Bright is still a boy."

"He has his name."

"He was born the summer before Onion came to us!"

Thumb fluffed the exposed dirt and then began to work with his drawing thumb. The lines were swift and sure. Round head, sloping back, trunk, long tusks.

"What is it?" Oak's voice came from a great distance.

Thumb opened himself and a dream found him.

"Quiet!" said Blue. Thumb could barely hear him over the blood pounding in his ears.

In his dream, the mammoth was already dead. It was lying on its side in a clearing. Flies buzzed the wounds on its neck. Two spears stuck out of its broad chest. The blood was dry.

Thumb was alone with the mammoth. There were no other hunters, no one to thank the mammoth for giving its life to the people and to speed its soul. He knelt beside the mammoth and put his hand on its flank. "I thank you, great one, for the sacrifice you have made. Your death is as precious to us as your life was to you. We needed you and so we killed you. We will use your flesh and bones to make our lives better. Someday when the spirits come to take us from our bodies, we will see you again in the belly of the earth." Then he got up, his nose full of the stink of the mammoth. It was already beginning to rot.

He walked around it once, then walked around it in the opposite direction. In his dream, Thumb was uneasy. It was bad luck to waste any kill, and this was a *mammoth*. Where was everyone?

An elm tree stirred at the edge of the clearing. In a dream moment, its roots gathered into two legs and its branches became the arms of a man. Leaves grew into long gray hair and a beard. The tree man was wearing a deerskin shirt and leggings. He did not speak but held out open hands to show he meant no harm. Thumb thought this might be the stranger who had saved Onion.

Man, I am. It was the voice Thumb had heard by the river.

Singer approached the mammoth. He touched one of the dark eyes and the lid closed. He whispered to the mammoth and its trunk twitched. When he shouted, the sound staggered Thumb and he fell backward.

The mammoth shivered, rolled over, and got to its

knees. Thumb let out a strangled cry of joy and surprise and fear. No animal had ever come back from the dead. The mammoth stood and shook the spears out of its side. Thumb's eyes burned.

Singer loomed over Thumb and started kicking at the ground. He bent to uproot grass, clear leaves. The mammoth trumpeted and lumbered into the forest as Singer squatted. He began to draw in the dirt.

The lines were swift and sure. Round head, sloping back, trunk, long tusks.

"Thumb, are you all right?" Oak was trying to sit him up.

"You shouldn't touch him," said Blue, but he didn't interfere.

Thumb's ears still rang with Singer's shout. He tried to focus on Blue and Oak. They shimmered like they were under water.

"He's crying," said Oak. "Brother, what's wrong?"

Thumb wiped at the wetness under his eye and touched the fingertip to his tongue. In the taste of his tears he saw mammoths flickering on the walls of the long cave. The vision shook him. It was dream knowledge, but the dream was over. The spirits must be very close. They had come to push him to his luck.

Thumb struggled up and pulled his water skin from the tree. "No more talking." He dipped the skin into the current and let it fill. "I'm going to the long cave." He slung it over his shoulder and started toward the camp at a trot. "I'll know what we should do when I get back."

Owl liked to call the cleft *the new cave*, but then he liked to stretch words. Actually it was a place where two huge rocks had fallen against one another, and it was mostly open to the sky. All the paintings and marks on the walls of the cleft had been made either by Thumb, or his teacher, Looker, or Looker's teacher Thorn. They had painted reindeer and red deer and ibex and horses and bison and the secret names of spirits.

But no mammoths. The mammoths were in the long cave.

The long cave was a mystery. Nobody knew who had put their dreams on its walls. Nobody knew how big it was. Owl told a story about the time old Thorn had found a tunnel that led from the long cave to the belly of the earth. The keeper had blocked it with stones to keep the dead from coming back to life. The women told stories about souls without bodies, who wandered the earth, forever alone, but none of the people had ever seen one. Thumb had looked many times for Thorn's tunnel. He had never found it. But even though he knew the long cave better than any of the people, there were still parts of it that he had yet to see. He had never quite gotten the courage to lower himself into the well in the Lodge of Mother Mammoth. And he was too wide in the shoulders to wriggle through the narrows past the abandoned bear nests.

"I don't care," said Onion. "I'm coming with you."

Two mothers who were chipping new stone scrapers covered smiles with their hands.

Thumb wrapped a lump of boar fat in a maple leaf and bound it with braided grass. "But I don't want you to." He put it with his lamp.

Onion didn't bother to answer. She was already

packing food for the trip, a handful of hazel nuts, a parsnip, salsify root, and a dried fish.

"You're not strong enough." Thumb didn't like to quarrel in front of other people.

Onion liked nothing better, especially since his shyness gave her an advantage. "I'm strong enough to sit and tend fire." She stooped to tie the sinew laces of her boots. "And that's all I'll do if I stay here."

Thumb made his best argument. "It's too far." The long cave was a good day's hike from the river. Its mouth was set into the stony ridge that divided the river valley from the lands of the horse people. "Besides, I might be gone all night. Maybe longer." Thumb continued to wrap leaves around pale chunks of fat for the lamp. "I don't know where the dreams will take me."

When he glanced up, Onion was standing with her hips cocked to support the bulging skin she had slung over her shoulder. She smiled at him and he shrugged. He knew that smile. The argument was over.

It was not yet midday when they started out. They talked at first. He told her about his trip to the country of the shell people. They were telling stories about a new people who had come down from the ice mountains. The shell people had not yet seen these strangers themselves, but had heard about them from their distant neighbors, the sky people. The newcomers were said to have four arms. Dogs followed them and obeyed their orders.

"Then we'll call them the dog people," said Onion.

"That wouldn't be very polite." Dogs were scavengers, like crows and rats. The only thing they were good for was eating, and they were often too stringy for that.

"Then call them the ice people." Onion laughed.

"Maybe they melt in the summer and their dogs drink them."

Thumb was pleased to see Onion keep good pace and good conversation. She was definitely getting better.

Onion told him that the mothers had decided to ask Owl's son Bone to become the storyteller, even though he was still learning stories. He had only begun training with his father four summers ago but he a big voice and an easy laugh. His words didn't always light the stars, but he was still young and he would have Owl to teach him.

As they climbed farther away from the river, they dropped into hunting order. Game was scarce near the summer camp, but here they might surprise a hare or a squirrel or even a deer. Thumb moved ahead, stepping quietly, spear at the ready. Onion trailed behind, picking mushrooms and stopping to roll logs over in search of grubs and salamanders.

That night they lay together as lovers. Afterward Thumb wept for their dead baby boy.

The sun was three hands from the dawn edge of the sky when they reached the cave the next day. Onion gathered tinder and kindling while Thumb pulled dead branches from trees and dragged them into a pile. The people visited the long cave regularly and had built a good hearth just inside the entrance. Thumb watched Onion take the smoldering coal she had brought from the hearthfire and set it on the tinder.

"I thank the first mother for this fire," she said. "She makes the warmth of the world." She blew on the coal until it smoked and the tinder caught fire.

When the pile of firewood reached Thumb's waist, he went out to gather birch bark. He peeled what he could and cut the rest with his chert knife. He was careful not to cut a complete circle of bark, which would girdle a tree and kill it. Thumb folded the bark again and again into a wad and then wedged it into the cleft of a green stick. When he had made three of these birch torches he returned to the cave. He was surprised to find Bead, Owl's lover, sitting at the fire next to Onion. She was rocking back and forth, as if in mourning.

"I tried to talk to Owl last night, but he wouldn't hear me," she told them. She looked as if she had slept on a sharp rock. "This morning I followed him here. He walked into the cave without fire or food, with empty hands. When I called for him to stop, he ran from me. I tried to find him but I have no light. I've been looking…I don't know. Most of the day." Her hands and face were dirty and her doeskin shirt was smeared with chalky mud. "He's gone, I think."

"I'll find him." Thumb gestured at the torches he had made. "And I have a lamp."

"What if he doesn't want to be found?" said Bead. "He is ashamed, Thumb. And afraid." She tugged at her hair hard enough to pull a few gray strands out. "And he is an old fool."

"He wants to die in there?" said Onion.

"I think," she said. "Where no one can see him. Where he can't even see himself."

"The spirits will see him," said Thumb. "They are thick in this cave. It will make bad luck for the people."

"If he thinks his own luck has run," said Onion, "maybe he doesn't care."

They sat for a minute in silence, listening to the fire, watching sparks fly up to become sky. In his mind's eye, Thumb tried to see Owl as someone who would knowingly make bad luck for all of them. He couldn't. It wasn't the kind of story Owl would want people to tell about him.

"He isn't like that," he said. "He's gone to the cave as any of us would. To open himself to a dream. To find his luck, not to be done with it."

"Maybe," said Bead.

Was this why he had been brought to the cave? To save Owl? Thumb stood and touched one of the birch bark torches to the fire. "I'll find him." He tucked the other two torches into his belt. "I'll bring him out." The way the two women were looking up at him almost made him believe what he was saying. "And then we'll tell him his own story, again and again, until he understands why we need him."

Some of the people were afraid of the long cave. Most thought it a cold, forbidding place. Thumb didn't understand this. Yes, it was crushingly dark. But the cave was ever untouched by the outside. It was always the same, always itself. In the heat of the summer, it was cool and free of bugs. When wind screamed off the ice mountains in the winter, it was the warmest place in the world. Time slowed in its never-ending night. Dreams lurked at every turn.

The mouth of the long cave was wide and welcoming. It opened onto a huge, damp room, with a ceiling too high for torchlight to reach. The mud on the floor was as sticky as pinesap. Before long, black silence closed around Thumb and all he could hear was the hiss of the torch and mud squishing beneath his boots.

He walked for some time, picking his way down the path trod by countless feet. On his right he passed the Empty Ways, a deep and complicated branch that, for some reason, had never been decorated. He had once asked Looker why they couldn't paint their dreams in this untouched section. Looker had cuffed him with the back of his hand. "This cave belongs to the dead now," said Looker. "Paint here when you're ready to visit the belly of the earth."

Was Owl hiding in one of the Empty Ways? Thumb called to him but got no reply. Owl had been to the cave many times. He would find his way to the Mother's Lodge. To the place of dreams.

Thumb's first torch began to gutter and he lit the second as he came to the underground river, where the main passage veered sharply to the right. This was not a true river like that of the people, more like a stream, but it filled the cave with its gurgle. The ceiling was low here, and the chalk walls were moist and yielding. After a while, Thumb came to First Mammoth.

First Mammoth had been scratched in the soft surface of the wall with a stick, or maybe even a finger. It was about as long as a marmot. Thumb could have carved it himself in a few minutes, if such had been his luck. First Mammoth had to be very old. Its lines weren't as sharp as most of the other carvings. The moisture in the cave had blurred them over countless summers. A long dead cave bear had once sharpened its claws on top of First Mammoth, and even its marks had begun to fade.

Thumb switched the torch to his left hand and with his thumb traced First Mammoth's lines just above the soft surface of the wall.

"I honor you and the one who carved you," he said. "May I meet both of your souls someday when I leave my body." He tugged the last torch out of his belt and leaned it against the wall. "Keep my torch safe and dry, First Mammoth, so I can use it to find my way back to the sun."

A little further on he entered the Council Room, where the cave branched in two directions. The walls of the Council Room were covered with wonders. To one side was the chiseled profile of Father Mammoth, whose eye saw all that happened in the cave. To the other were three wooly rhinoceros, one so fat that its belly scraped the ground. Next to them was the Council of Mammoths.

A line of five mammoths marched left. Five more marched right, as if to cut them off. The two leaders faced each other, eye to eye, their trunks touching. They had been drawn by rubbing soot stone right onto the rock, the surface of which was smooth but not flat. Whoever had created these mammoths had used dips and bulges in the rock to make them leap from the wall into the mind's eye. As Thumb passed his torch from one line to the other, the play of light made the mammoths stir.

The first time he'd seen the Council of the Mammoths, Thumb thought that the two herds were about to fight. Then Looker had explained. Each of the herds walked its own land. Where the leaders met was the boundary. The mammoths touched trunks as brothers might touch fists or sisters hug. This was a dream of friendship, not of rancor, and it was meant to speak to the people who kept the cave. The spirits commanded them, said Looker, to live at peace with their neighbors. It was their luck to take lovers from the shell people and send their children to live with the horse people and to welcome all strangers.

Man, whispered a voice in Thumb's head.

Thumb whirled, but he saw no one. "Who are

you?" He felt as if he were standing on the sky and gazing up at the ground. "Tell me!" The walls swallowed his anger. This was the place of true dreams and he was its keeper. "This is the cave of the people! You don't belong here!"

Man, I am.

Thumb staggered across the Council Room and fell to his knees before Father Mammoth. "Father, I've come looking for Owl, the storyteller. Now something in your cave calls me. I don't understand what is happening. Show me what I must do." And then he opened himself.

No dream found him.

Thumb didn't know what to do. Shocked, he knelt there waiting. Waiting. This had never happened before. Father Mammoth stared down at him but sent no dream. The spirits had forsaken him.

The torch began to gutter.

Man. Come to me.

Thumb fumbled for his lamp. Still on his knees, he flattened a wad of boar fat into the bowl, pinched some moss for a wick and pressed it into the fat. He lit the lamp from the failing torch.

Man.

"What?" he muttered as he stood. His knees creaked. How long had he been kneeling on the cold stone? He left the torch behind and started down the passage toward the Lodge of the Mother Mammoth. The world shrank as he left the Council Room. The torch had cast a strong light, but the lamp burned with a single flame. When he held it at eye level, the floor of the cave disappeared. Thumb groped forward, his free hand brushing the wall. He saw more with his feet than with his eyes. Soon he came to one of the narrows. He stooped, and then crawled on hands and knees. He picked his way slowly, holding the lamp level so as not to spill melting fat or snuff the flame.

The ceiling in the Mother's Lodge was low enough that he could reach up and press his palm flat against it. It was decorated with mammoths and bison and ibex and horses and rhinoceros, outlined in black soot stone. Some stood on top of one another. Upside down jostled right side up. Here was a many to make a man's head swim. Thumb could as soon count the leaves on a tree or the hairs of Onion's head. Ordinarily the spirits of the cave were most present in this great gathering of animals. When Thumb guided people to this room, dreams spun from the ceiling like snow from the winter sky. But now he gazed up in vain. He felt as if his soul had turned to stone.

"Why am I here?" He began by searching the edges of the room, carrying the lamp low so he could see the floor. Nothing. "Talk to me!" Then he struck out for the opposite wall, crisscrossing back and forth. On his fourth traverse, his foot nudged the body.

Thumb rolled Owl over and felt his throat for the beat of blood. He was alive. Thumb squatted, thinking of how to get the old man out of the cave. If he slung Owl over his back and tried to carry him, he'd probably douse the lamp. Besides, how would they wriggle through the narrows? He decided that if he couldn't wake Owl up, he would have to leave the cave, build a litter and bring Bead back to help.

"Owl." Thumb chucked the old man's chin. "Can you hear me?" He leaned close and blew on his eyelids. "Uncle?"

"Hmm."

"It's me, Thumb."

Owl stirred and put his hand to his forehead. Then he opened his eyes. Spears of light, brighter than any fire Thumb had ever seen, shot from Owl's eyes and then winked out. Thumb screamed and sprawled backward, spilling hot fat on himself and snuffing the lamp's puny flame.

Darkness closed around him. He felt it press against his skin, stop his nose, slither down his throat. He tried to scream again but the darkness was smothering him. Terrified, he scuttled across the floor until his back was against a wall. He heard a wind sound, but it wasn't the wind. It was the cave, breathing. Then the room erupted with light. The thing that was Owl but wasn't stood before him. He held his hand above his head. It was on fire and his fingers were bright, flickering flames. Thumb looked up and saw something he had never seen before. All the animals of the Mother's Lodge stared down at him. All, all at once. The wonder of it was almost enough to make him forget what was happening. Owl seemed impressed too. For a moment, he paid no attention to Thumb. Instead he strode around the room, taking in the drawings as if they were old friends. Finally he approached Thumb, who tried to press himself into the rock.

Man, this is not a dream.

Thumb couldn't speak. He could barely nod.

The story of Thumb.

The light from Owl's fist was painful. It stabbed through Thumb's head into mind's eye.

He is great, father to many peoples. He lives many summers.

218

Thumb had no children. All Onion's babies died. Owl's skin began to shift like smoke. Thumb could see his bones glowing.

But he kills the last mammoth. This tangles his luck. When he dies, his soul never gets to the belly of the earth.

Fear gave way to rage. "How do you know this? Who are you?"

Owl lowered the shining fist toward Thumb. Thumb couldn't move, couldn't protect himself.

Man, I am.

Thumb had grown roots. His arms were heavy as logs.

But once I was...

All he could do is look up as Owl touched him.

Thumb.

The light filled his head, driving out all thought.

The next thing Thumb knew, he was kneeling in front of Father Mammoth in the Council Room. The spent torch was on the floor beside the lamp, which was lit. Owl curled nearby, snoring noisily.

"It wasn't a dream," Thumb muttered and sat back on his heels. "Then what was it?" He picked up the lamp absently. Had he just talked to his soul, come back from the dead? Did that mean he had had lost his own soul? He shook the thought from his head and wondered what he should do. Probably rouse Owl. Get him out of the cave. "What about it, old man?" Thumb said softly. "Are you going to catch fire again and say crazy things?

Owl snuffled. He slept with his mouth open so that Thumb could count the teeth he had lost. Thumb stretched his foot across the floor of the cave and gave

Owl a nudge. "Owl." He gave Owl a second, firmer nudge. "Wake up." And then he slid back to watch what would happen.

Owl's mouth closed and then opened again "Am not," he said. His voice was thick.

"Owl!"

"What?" When he opened his eyes, it was clear that no spirit lurked behind them. They were the dim, watery eyes of an old man. "Who is that?"

"Thumb."

He thought for a moment and then nodded. "And the woman?"

"Bead is waiting outside."

He grunted as he propped himself up on an elbow. "I think she would follow me to the belly of the earth." He licked his lips. "If only to tell me I was wrong about something."

Thumb laughed politely. "What do you remember?"

"Remember? I came to the cave to find a guiding dream. Instead I got lost. Then I fell asleep."

"But no dream?"

He shook his head. "Not everyone finds dreams as easily as Thumb."

"Where did you fall asleep? Here? In the Lodge of the Mother Mammoth?"

"Thumb, it was dark." Owl sat up. "The mothers want the new storyteller, yes?"

"Yes."

"I thought so." He stretched and then yipped in pain. "I'm getting too old for a bed of stones." He kneaded the muscles of his back.

"I'm taking the lamp," said Thumb. "I left a fresh torch back at First Mammoth. I'll get it and then we should go."

Owl had gotten to his feet by the time Thumb returned. He steadied himself with a hand to the wall of the cave. "Bone," he said. In the torchlight, the old man's face was pale as the moon. "Bone will take my place."

"We expect you to teach him all the stories you know."

"I have tried all these summers." Owl showed Thumb his teeth. "The son won't make anyone forget the father."

The two men stood at the mouth of the cave, blinking in the afternoon sun. Something was wrong. Thumb dropped the spent torch into the hearth. They were hungry and thirsty but there was no fire and the women were gone.

"Where is she? Owl brushed past Thumb into the open air. "*Bead!*"

"Quiet." Thumb clamped his hand over Owl's mouth to keep him from calling out again. "Look at the coals. That fire didn't burn itself out. Somebody put it out. And I left a spear and a throwing stick."

"Why would they leave us?"

"Wait back in the cave. I'll see what I can find."

Thumb drew his knife and ran across the clearing in front of the cave to the cover of the forest. He moved silently through the trees, parallel to the trail but many paces away. After a while he gave the call of a nuthatch, a high two-note whistle repeated three times. The reply came from his left, a three-note whistle repeated twice. He found Onion and Bead waiting in a dry stream bed. They told him quickly what had happened. Part of Thumb was grateful to hear the dreadful story. It meant that he didn't have to think anymore about what had happened in the cave. He ran to fetch Owl. As they hurried back to the summer camp, the two women tried to remember everything they had heard. And when Thumb got home, he heard the story again, this time from Quick himself.

Quick's party had joined the hunters from the horse people and together they had tracked the reindeer herd. As was their custom, they split the herd and had driven part of it into the Killdeer, a steep-walled gorge blocked off with boulders and felled trees at one end. There they had slaughtered the reindeer. There was enough meat to get both peoples through the coming winter. Fresh skins to make clothes and blankets, antlers and bones for tools. It was a good harvest.

But while the hunters were butchering and skinning the reindeer, they were attacked. Bone thought they might have been spirits, but Quick was certain that they were just men. The attackers fought with "feather sticks"—short straight spears with a flint point at one end and feathers at the other. They threw these sticks from a distance and at great speed. They used a throwing stick unlike anything the hunters had seen before. Spears were useless against the attackers. When the hunters tried to charge them, they were turned back by a pack of fierce dogs.

Of the hunting party, Moon was killed and both Quick and Ash were wounded. The horse people had suffered greater losses. Another party of the strangers had sacked their summer camp and carried off some of the women. After they had escaped the Killdeer, Quick and his men had run for home. The attackers might be on their way to the valley of the people next.

As they passed the long cave, Quick had seen the smoke of Onion's fire and had stopped to warn the women.

"I think these must be the people of the ice mountains," said Thumb as he ran his finger down the feather stick that Quick had brought back. "The shell people told me about the dogs." The point was stained with Quick's own blood. He had worked it out of his thigh after the attack.

"You knew about these strangers?" said Blue.

"It was a story told by the sky people to the shell people," said Thumb, "who told it to me. I thought the truth of it might be a little thin."

People stared as if he had betrayed them. Thumb felt the blood rush to his face.

"In the story I heard," he said, "these people had four arms. Did they?"

"No," said Quick.

Bone spat. "Two were more than enough."

"And there was nothing about these." Thumb gave the feather stick back to Quick. "Or about anyone attacking anyone."

Owl held up his hand. "We should send a runner to the shell people to hear their story again," he said, "and to tell ours. Maybe he should visit the sky people too."

Everyone thought this was a good idea. Blue asked young Bright to start the next morning. Quick said that they should think about striking the summer camp early. The winter lodge, a day's walk upriver, was in a natural terrace that the people walled up with stones. It would be easier to defend. This idea caused a stir among the women. Flame held up her hand.

"The mothers have asked me to speak for them,"

she said. "We're still taking in the harvest. The winter camp is a long way from the best gathering places. That's why we make the summer camp here."

There was no answer to this argument and the men all knew it. They also knew what was coming next.

"There's plenty to harvest this summer," said Flame. "We can fill many skins with good things to eat—if we're here at the summer camp. But now Quick tells us that there will be no reindeer. We'll do our best, but unless there's meat, there will come a time this winter when we'll all go hungry."

Quick drew himself up. "The hunters will bring in meat enough for all." Normally, when Quick said something would be done, everyone stopped worrying about it. But dark blood soaked through the deerskin bandage around his thigh and he looked haggard. He had lost the winter's meat supply. A man was dead.

Oak raised his hand. "I am sure that the mothers can make some delicious rat stews and roasted squirrels, but there is bigger game to hunt. While Thumb was in the cave, I looked for his mammoth. It must like our valley, because I found it just last night. It's less than a day's walk away, on the dawn shore by the sandbar."

"But you can't." Thumb's voice was sharp. "I mean, maybe we should wait,"

Everyone was watching him again. Even Onion seemed troubled by his outburst.

"You asked us to wait once already," said Blue carefully. "We did, because you are keeper of the caves. You went to the long cave and now you're back. What happened? Did you have a dream about the mammoth?"

"I...." Thumb didn't know what to say, in part because he wasn't sure what had happened to him. "It wasn't a dream."

Owl raised his hand again. "He saved me, is what happened." The old man probably thought he was helping Thumb. Paying him back. "I was lost and he found me." He reached over to hug Thumb. "And now I know why. Let me tell you a story of long ago, before we were a people. A story about how my great-grandfather hunted mammoths."

The strength of the people would be tested. Blue had sent a party of scouts to watch for the strangers at the far edges of the valley. That meant that the women would have to help with the hunt. Thumb had doubts about Owl's scheme, especially since Quick could take no part in it. The day after the council, a fever took him. He sprawled on his mat at the camp, senseless, sometimes thrashing in pain. His lover Cloud packed mustard leaves on his wound but it continued to ooze. Oak would take charge of the hunt.

In Owl's story, the old ones had hunted mammoths at night. The beasts were scared of fire, Owl claimed, and could easily be driven with torches. The surest kill would have been to chase the mammoth off a cliff. But the mammoth was finding good forage along the banks of the river. Oak saw the risk in trying to drive it all the way into the hills. Owl's story had the answer. They would dig a pit, force the mammoth into it and slaughter it while it struggled to get out.

Thumb had his own plan. He would stay as far away from the mammoth as he could. Let this story be about Oak, or one of the other men. If he didn't kill it, none of what had happened in the cave would matter.

Oak was calling for a fan of hunters to get the mammoth moving. Two lines of women were to move toward each other, closing its path off with their torches. They would force it into the pit, where the main party of hunters would be waiting to finish it. Thumb asked to be one of the hunters who walked the flanks to protect the women. Everyone thought that this was because he was worried about Onion.

Although she would not let anyone see it, he knew that she was distraught. The horse people were her first people. She had a mother, a sister and cousins who she had kept up with, even after she had come to the valley. The two peoples traded and hunted together and they told each other's stories. Now her birth family might be hurt or dead or taken. There were dark circles under Onion's eyes and she rarely spoke unless spoken to.

It took three days to dig the pit. Owl said it must be covered with brush, or the prey would see its danger. Meanwhile a pair of hunters tracked the mammoth. When it strayed too far from the killing ground, they would show themselves and turn it back. By the night of the third day the trap was set. The people left camp just before dusk.

Thumb had strapped his two best spears and his throwing stick to his back. He offered to help Onion carry her three birch bark torches but she refused. Her eyes were wide and the line of her mouth was straight. She and the other women were jittery walking through the forest in the dark. Thumb didn't blame them. Everyone knew that luck turned at night, often for the bad. When the fat moon rose, everyone felt a little safer.

"Stop!"

Some of the women jumped. Even Thumb gave a yip of surprise. Oak came out of the darkness looking as if he had rolled around in the coals of a dead fire. His face was black and his deerskins filthy.

"This is where Thumb's group builds their fire. A small fire, yes?"

"We know this," said Thumb. "You've told us enough times."

"Then form your line running in that direction." Oak pointed. "Five and five paces apart. Don't light the torches until you get the call. Robin's group, come with me."

Thumb thought Oak must be unsure of himself. That was why he was treating everyone as if they were children.

The women built the fire, thanking the first mother for the light of the world. Then Thumb helped them take their places. He put Onion farthest from the pit and waited with her.

"Are you afraid?" she said.

He was taken aback. Fear was not something men talked about, certainly not just before a hunt. "A little," he said. "Yes."

"Why have you closed yourself off from me?" She took his hand.

"Me? You're the silent one. Are you worried about your family?"

"You are my family, Thumb, and I *am* worried. Something happened in the cave. Something you haven't told me."

He felt his throat tighten. "I've tried not to think about it."

She waited for him to continue.

"It wasn't a dream. It wasn't." He sighed. "It was like we are speaking now, except I was talking to a spirit. A crazy spirit."

"Can spirits be crazy?'

"People can be crazy, so why can't spirits? I don't know. That's why I'm scared, Onion. Because I don't know what to think."

"So what did it say?"

He laughed. "That I am great."

"That wasn't crazy."

He leaned over to kiss her in the darkness. "That I will be father to many peoples," he said softly.

She shrank away from him momentarily, as if he had said something wrong. Then she closed her eyes and kissed him back.

They heard the call of a nuthatch, a high two-note whistle repeated three times. Thumb replied, a three-note whistle repeated twice.

"I'll come back," he said. He lit a torch from the fire and dashed down the line of women, lighting theirs. As he peered into the night, he could just make out the shimmer of the second line. Now Thumb could hear the chants of the fan of hunters driving the mammoth toward them. He threw his torch into the fire and fitted a spear into his throwing stick.

"*We are the people*," the hunters cried, "*We need you, great one.*"

"Let's go," Thumb called, loud enough for everyone to hear, "Walk slowly toward the other lights."

The mammoth trumpeted. It was caught between the lines and headed toward the pit.

"It's working," Thumb called. "The mammoth will pass, then the hunters will be right behind. Close in after them."

"We are the people."

Thumb saw a mammoth-sized shadow lope close by. It was breathing in great, ragged *chuffs*. He could almost taste its fear.

"We need you, great one," called the hunters. Smaller shadows rippled through the trees.

"Follow them," he called. "Not too close."

The two lines of lights came together and Thumb saw Robin wave. Ahead of them the mammoth shrieked and the main group of hunters roared in triumph. Thumb flew down the line to find Onion.

"Are you all right?" he said.

Her eyes shone in the torchlight. "We did it." She was excited.

Man.

The mammoth trumpeted again and Thumb heard a different note in the voices of the hunters. Later, he would learn that the pit wasn't wide enough. That the mammoth had skirted it without falling in. But that moment, all Thumb knew was that something was wrong.

A man screamed in agony. The shouts filled with fear. The luck of the people had turned.

"It's coming back," said Thumb. Hunting courage hammered through his body. "It can't get past Oak and the others but it can break through the chase group." He felt as if his legs were growing longer.

"But our torches," said Onion. "It's afraid of fire."

Man.

"Not if it's wounded." The muscles in his arms bunched and swelled. "It's probably crazy with fear." His hair rose straight from his head.

"Robin!" he called. "It's coming."

Robin pumped his spear to show he was ready.

"Thumb, what are you going to do?

You are.

"I can't die, Onion," said Thumb. "The spirit told me." He gulped air as if he were drowning. "Not until I'm old."

Then he saw it bearing down on him. On Onion. He realized that Owl had been right after all. It *was* a furry mountain, a mountain that galloped.

"Thumb!" cried Onion.

But she was behind him now. He took three effortless steps toward the mammoth. It was as if he were going down to the river for water. He couldn't die tonight. His old life was behind him too, what he had been before he had met himself in the long cave. The new Thumb had great things to do. *The last.* Oh, the stories they would tell about him! *But his soul would never.* The mammoth loomed. *Never.* He planted himself, drew back his throwing stick and screamed at it.

"*I am!*"

This is the story of Thumb the Great. He killed a mammoth with a single thrust of his spear. He gave his people the bow and arrow and taught them the ways of war. When the battle madness took him, there was no one so fierce. He led the people of the valley against the dog people and drove them back to the ice mountains. He lived a long life, fathered many children and mourned two lovers. The spirits treated him as if he were one of their own. One night they came and took him from the people. We believe he still watches over us.

He was a man filled with luck.

"The Majesty of Angels"
Robert Reed

The dead are dressed to travel. Their clothes come in every fashion, but always comfortable and practical and familiar. None of them are carrying luggage, because what are possessions? Temporary, and imperfect. Everything worthwhile has come here. These people are here, and nothing else matters.

So many, I declare.

Too many! we blurt in astonishment.

The overseer explains what has happened. An ancient soul wearing a big woman's body, she relates the horrific and tragic with effortless, even graceful dignity. Dignity is vital to our work. She tells us what she knows and nothing else, and it is only our training and our dignified nature that keep us from screaming in anguish, demanding to know how such awful things can happen.

How many teams will be helping us today?

I have to ask it.

The overseer admits that every available team has been assembled, plus the full corps of reserves, and every trainee, and the trainees' teachers, and even the most venerable members of the old administrative echelons.

And they won't be enough, I'm thinking. Not nearly enough.

But with a steadying voice, she reminds us of who

we are. Do your walk-throughs, she urges. Go on, now. Go!

Walk-throughs are essential.

We show ourselves to the newly dead. That's how it begins. Let them see a face. Let them feel close to you. Give them an opportunity to find qualities familiar and reassuring in that very careful picture you present to them.

Our team is a dozen, including our overseer: Two male bodies, and the rest female. Humans accept these proportions best. They also prefer uniforms, and on this wicked day, we wear dark blue-gray suits with false pockets and narrow gold trim and neat little buttons of brass. To every eye, we look important. Ennobled. Creatures of thorough and perfect competence. I normally cherish this ritual. This walk-through business. My body is tall and young and decidedly female. The crowd parts for me and the dead men can't help but stare. I have long legs and a long, sturdy gait. Countless penises stiffen in my presence. It makes the men grateful, discovering that in death they have held on to this most treasured magic.

A thousand languages carry up toward the illusion of a ceiling.

"She looks like a stewardess," the multitude declares.

One man forgets to step out of my way. He stares at me, particularly at the pin riding above my left breast. He expects to see a crucifix or an Islamic crescent, but the pin is neither. Wearing a puzzled expression, he stands in my way, and I gracefully dance around him, and after I have passed by, he blurts, "Did you see her jewelry?"

"The sideways eight?" says a young woman. "So what's that about?"

"It's mathematical," he explains. "To me, it means infinity."

"Huh," says the woman. "I guess that makes sense, doesn't it?"

Something about the man catches my interest. I'm past him, but I'm lingering, too. His name is Tom. He lived in Oregon. He has two ex-wives and no children, and since he was ten years old, he hasn't believed either in God or Heaven.

"Isn't this just wonderful?" asks the young woman.

Her name is Julianna and she was raised Catholic.

"Things looked so awful," she says with a beaming smile. "And suddenly, this...!"

Tom nods, asking, "So how'd you die?"

Surprised by his question, Julianna blinks and stares.

With a crooked grin, Tom explains himself. "I was riding my bike. It was...I don't know...sometime last week. I tried to beat the light, and a city bus plowed into me." He laughs amiably, faintly embarrassed by his incompetence. "Right now, just being able to stand and hold my guts inside me...well, that's a major accomplishment!" His laughter thins. Squinting, he adds, "The last thing I remember, I was being wheeled back to surgery. Internal bleeding, I guess...I couldn't breathe...and I remember the orderly pushing me down this long, long hallway...."

Julianna touches him. Her hand is warm and a little sticky.

"You really don't know," she says. "Do you?"

"Know what?"

"Something went wrong in the sky," she tells him. "A few days ago, without warning...it just sort of happened...."

"In the sky?"

233

"Something exploded," she admits.

"What something? A star?"

"No, it wasn't that," says Julianna. "On the news, they said it might be a quasar. A little one that happened to be close to the Earth—"

"A quasar?"

People grow quiet, eavesdropping on their conversation.

"A black hole started eating gas clouds and stars," Julianna explains, "and there was this terrific light—"

"I know what a quasar is," Tom says. "It's bright, sure, but it's also very, very distant. Billions of light-years removed from us, and perfectly safe, and I don't see how one of them can just appear one day, without warning."

Julianna shrugs. "Maybe our quasar didn't know your rules."

With his own kind of dignity, Tom absorbs the horrific news. Sad brown eyes look at the surrounding faces. Perhaps he notices that most of the faces are young. Children outnumber the elderly by a long measure. Finally with a soft, hurting voice, he asks, "What about the world? And the people?"

"Dead," says Julianna. "All dead."

More than six billion souls were killed in a heartbeat.

"You were sick," she promises. "Nobody told you what was happening, I bet. I bet not." And again, she touches him.

An enormous machine assembles itself around the multitudes. Our passengers find themselves standing inside what resembles the cabin of an airliner or a modern train; yet this machine feels infinitely superior to anything human-built. The ceiling is low but not smothering and feels soft to the touch like treasured old leather. The floor is a carpet of ankle-deep green grass. Ambient sounds hint at power below and great encompassing strength. This interior is a single round room. An enormous room. Padded seats are laid out in neat concentric rings. Normally there is a healthy distance between seats, save in cases where a family or a group of dear friends died in the same accident or a shared plague. But emergency standards rule today. The seats are packed close, as if everyone is someone's brother or sister. Even a graceful creature has to move with constant care, her long legs dancing from place to place to place.

A routine voyage carries several hundred thousand compliant and thankful souls. But this soul-carriage, built according to our meticulous worst-case scenarios, makes the routine appear simple and small.

Every passenger has a seat waiting. Their name and portrait show in the padded headrest, and everyone begins close to their destination. But even normal days bring problems. Children always run off. Adults want to hunt the loved ones who died before them. My first duty is to help everyone settle, and it is a daunting task. Besides the crush of bodies and the armies of kinetic children, I have to cope with our desperate lack of time.

"If you cannot find your seat," I call out, "take another. Take the first empty seat you come across. Please. You must be sitting and restrained before we can begin our voyage. Please. And make the children sit too. Your child, and everyone else's. We're bound for the same place. A shared destination. We must cooperate to make it an easy voyage."

I have a bright, strong voice. A voice worth hearing.

But I need to be in many places at once, and my skills reach only so far.

Six billion people drop into some seat, adults taking responsibility for the young ones. Those left standing beg for help, and I do my absolute best, smiling as I do with every little part of my job.

People call me "the angel" fondly, with easy trust.

Finally, once everyone is sitting somewhere, I stand in front of my passengers. "Yes," I admit, "you have died. You are dead."

Tom sits in my audience. And Julianna has taken the seat beside him.

"Yet you obviously aren't dead," I tell them. "There is a network, a set of embedded and eternal machines that stretch throughout your galaxy. These machines do nothing but rescue sentient souls as they die, then transport them to a place where they will be safe and happy for all time."

In a stew of language, voices blurt out, "Heaven!"

"Call it what you will," I warn, using the same tongues. "Maybe you're right, yes. Your gods could have built the soul-snaring machines and the wormholes that we are going to use. Since I don't know who actually built them, every answer is valid to me."

That attitude rarely makes people sit easier. Yet it has the delicious advantage of being my honest opinion.

"I'm here to serve you," I promise, showing them my warmest smile. "To make your journey easier, I will do everything I can for you."

Always, a few men giggle in a vulgar way.

Not Tom. He sits quietly, dark eyes never blinking while thick hands wrestle nervously in his lap. He is a brown man with receding black hair worn as a ponytail. I touch his armrest and a glassy round screen appears in the air in front of him. "You may watch any movie or television program, read any book, listen to a favorite song, or if you wish, choose any moment in your own life and watch it replayed as your own eyes saw it, in full. The controls on your armrest will explain themselves—"

A hand jumps up.

"Yes, Quincy," I say. "Do you have a question?"

The man is small and pudgy, wearing shorts and a tan safari hat, and he is thrilled that I know his name. "Do we eat?" Quincy asks. "Because I'm feeling awfully hungry."

"Any meal you can think of, we can make." I promise everyone, "I'll take your orders later. Though I should add, nobody needs to eat or drink anymore."

Another hand lifts.

"Yes, Jean."

She's a young mother with two tiny children. Custom and common sense have set her between her babies. Quite reasonably, she asks, "Will this be a long trip?"

"It will be, yes. I'm sorry, Jean. We have a tremendous distance ahead of us."

Tom makes a low sound.

I look at him. I smile, always. "Do you have a question, Tom?"

He lies, telling me, "I don't. No."

I won't press him. We have run out of time. Lifting my gaze, I stare at the grateful multitudes. "The infinity button on your armrest will summon me or one of my colleagues. Once we're underway, don't hesitate to press the button." Then before anyone can throw out another good question, I close my eyes, vanishing from their gaze.

Again I hear the word, "Angel."

Julianna says it with an easy reverence.

Tom says nothing. Nothing. He never saw the sky catch fire. He never heard the black warnings, the torrent of hard radiations and fantastic heat chasing after the light. As he was dying in the hospital, his family and friends, doctors and nurses, conspired to keep this one worry from him. Alone among my passengers, Tom was unaware. Innocent.

He's likely grieving for his dead world, a reasonable anger festering inside him.

"Our angel's beautiful," says Julianna. "Don't you think, Tom?"

He shrugs and says, "Very," while his hands continue to wrestle in his lap. He glances across the aisle. One of Jean's babies looks up at him, smiling gamely. Leaning low, Tom whispers to the wide-eyed three-year-old, saying, "Hey there, kid. Hey. So what about this whole crock of shit bothers you the most?"

The early vibrations are honest and important. Space and time are being manipulated by means both decisive and violent. Dimensions without human names are being traversed. For safety's sake, everyone must remain in his seat. No exceptions. Tiny variations of mass disrupt the intricate calculations, and our ship is cumbersome enough, thank you.

My team and overseer sit together.

As is customary, we discuss what has happened and what we can anticipate, the overseer nourishing a mood of cautious optimism.

You don't remember, she says to me. You haven't worked with humans long enough. But there was a period when we wondered if this was inevitable. Bringing all of them, I mean. Because they had some brutal weapons, and with a few buttons pushed, they would have killed most of their world.

I show her that I'm listening, thinking hard about what she's telling me. Then, letting my worry show, I ask, How do I respond to certain questions?

She knows which questions. Showing a narrow smile, she asks, Do you think they're likely to ask them?

No, I admit.

Haven't we taken the sensible steps?

Always, I say.

But make yourselves ready, she advises all of us. Examine your manifest. Don't let anyone catch you unprepared.

Easily said. But nobody mentions that each of us, standing alone on the grassy floor, is responsible for thousands upon thousands of souls.

We are successfully underway. People are encouraged to stand if they wish, and if they don't move too far, they may wander. A constant trembling passes through the floor, and from overhead a whispering roar comes, reminding them of a distant and irresistible wind. These are artificial sensations. They bring the sense of motion, of distance won. Sentience doesn't mean sophistication; humans would find the perfect stillness of interstellar travel unnerving, which is why we supply them with every comforting illusion.

Being sophisticated doesn't give me the right to think small thoughts about those who are otherwise.

That's what I remind myself as a thousand fingers call to me.

Wherever I am, I watch Tom. I listen to his voice and the voices swirling around him. In life, the man

239

was a reader. He enjoyed a broad if rather haphazard love for science and mathematical puzzles. "Tell me what happened," he says to the English-speaking strangers. "What did you see? Read? Hear? And what do you absolutely know as fact?"

His neighbors have few facts to offer. But that doesn't stop some of them from declaring, "It was God's judgment, plain and simple."

Tom never listens to the plain and simple.

Others repeat the magical word, "Quasar," and shrug their shoulders. "That's what everyone says it was."

Tom explains his doubts. In clear, crisp terms, he teaches dozens of people about the universe and its brutal, amoral past. "Quasars are far away because they live in the deepest past," he explains. Then with grim urgency, he adds, "The part of the sky you're talking about doesn't have a big black hole. It's too close to us. We'd see its gravity at work. And even if something like that was hiding near us, there isn't nearly enough gas and dust to fuel the monster."

Once, then again, I happen by. I show Tom my best smile, and with a warm but firm voice, I suggest that he move back near his seat again. "I'll show you the way," I remark. "Or if you'd rather, I can just put you there."

Tom is a bright, determined skeptic, but he's also a male. His eyes betray interest.

Lust is a vapor that I can inhale, and then enlarge by assorted means, flinging luscious, intoxicating molecules back at the man, feeding his lust until his penis quivers and his breathing comes up short.

After a third visit, the male animal is a little bit in love with me.

On my fourth visit, he stops interrogating the passengers, watching as I deliver a dish of kale and potatoes to a fellow passenger.

The passenger asks, "Do you know how old I am, dear?"

"One hundred and three," I reply, "and your name is Bernice. But your good friends call you Bernie."

With giddy amazement, the old woman says, "Do you know? I outlived three husbands and as many children. But that's fine, because now I'm traveling to Heaven to see them again. Isn't that right, dear?"

I nod. And smile. "Your husbands are there. And your children. And everyone else who made this journey before you." I lift my gaze, smiling only at Tom, forcing him to stare back at me. "How can anything that perfect be anything but beautiful?"

The male animal licks his lips.

Again I urge Tom to return to his empty seat. But he gathers himself, then tells me, "No," with a cool determination. "No, I want to talk to you. Just to you."

I pretend to misunderstand his intentions.

"Me? Really?" I bubble, letting my nipples engorge.

But the man puts on a cold, uncompromising face and declares "Alone."

He asks, "Is it possible?"

Then with his shoulders squared, he says, "Because if you won't do this, Miss Angel...if you don't pay attention to me, I'm screaming with whatever I've got for lungs...!"

I can see the man that he seems to be. In an instant, I examine the enormity of Tom's brief life—everything that he has said and done, and everything done and said to him. Obvious strategies present themselves to me, begging to be used. Yet I hesitate. I know better.

This man was assaulted by a bus, his belly ripped open, candy-colored guts spilling across the hot black asphalt. For that horrible instant, Tom was conscious. Despite misery and spreading shock, he managed to look at his mangled insides...and what he thought at that particular instant, I do not know. I cannot know. Every soul's thoughts are always its own; no eye can peer into a mind's foggy depths. Which is why the soul is precious. Is worth this kind of sacrifice and expense. What we cannot know perfectly must be preserved, at all costs. That's what this soul-carriage means.

This is what I'll tell him, in some fashion or another.

But he speaks first. "How does this all work?" Tom asks. "You and your angel friends carry the dead off to this heaven place? Is that it?"

We're standing in the chamber where I sat with my colleagues. By all appearances, we are alone.

"Is this your job?" he presses.

"This is my life," I purr. "My purpose. My calling."

Something in those words amuses him. He stares at my face, occasionally glancing at my nipples. Then with a little snort, he asks, "Are there other alien species? And when they die, do you whisk them off to wherever?"

"There are others, but I don't whisk them anywhere," I explain. "My calling is here, with your noble species."

"You help us travel to the afterlife?"

"Yes."

"And you've always done this?"

"Not always," I confess. "Not for very long, considering."

He doesn't ask the obvious questions. How long?

Where did you work before? And why did you change posts? Instead Tom points out, "You won't be making the human run anymore. Will you?"

I say, "No, I won't," with obvious, honest sadness.

Tom nods. Considers.

Then I take hold of our conversation, telling him, "Yes, this is a tragedy. A tragedy. But aren't you just a little pleased to find yourself alive and bound for places that you can't even imagine?"

Dark eyes narrow. Then he calmly and firmly says, "Dolphins."

"What about them?"

"Are their souls saved, too?"

"Of course. Yes."

"And they're riding toward their afterlife...what...? Inside a starship that masquerades as a saltwater lagoon...?"

His guess is rather near the truth.

"There are many species of cetaceans," I explain. "Some are sentient. But others, sadly, have nothing for a soul-saver to latch onto."

I expect Tom to ask about other species. Elephants, dogs, and the like. But he returns to me, remarking, "You're going to have to be reassigned."

"I'll take the calling that suits me," I declare.

He doesn't seem to hear me. His mouth opens, teeth a little crooked and yellowed. Their imperfections make his face seem more handsome. Because it helps my strategy, I fall in love with him. Or is it my strategy that's to blame? Love needs to feel genuine to be love; isn't that what every overseer and every poet claims?

"What killed my world?" he mutters.

I pretend not to understand the question. "Pardon—" I begin.

"It wasn't a quasar," he maintains with aloud, knowing voice. "Or an exploding star. Or anything else normal."

I say nothing.

He stares at my chest. At the infinity pin riding on my breast. A slow tongue wets his lips, and with his next breath, Tom asks, "Are you a robot?"

"No," I blurt.

"A projection? A fantasy? What?"

This is a perfect moment. With my warm, slightly dampened hand, I touch his chin and then the soft back of his ear, teasing him for a little moment before saying, "I could be any of those things. How would I know? But what I believe I am is an immortal soul, and a good soul…at least good enough to be entrusted with your little species…."

Tom shivers, nods.

I take back my hand.

He wants the hand, and everything else. But he denies himself, almost sobbing when he explains, "I had this professor in college. A brilliant man. He spent an entire class talking about black holes and white holes and wormholes, and how it might be possible to leap through space and time…and all the reasons why you don't want to do it, because of the places where everything could go to shit…."

I could undress myself, and then undress him. I could win this man with a few simple acts of geometry.

Yet I do nothing but listen.

"What happened in the sky…it sounds like a wormhole turning unstable…."

We are alone here. My team and the overseer are busy with the multitudes.

"If it was a wormhole," he tells me, "then that ex-

244

plains why an empty piece of the sky can explode, without warning."

I could lie. And maybe he would believe me.

Or I could take emergency measures, easing Tom into a quarantine region of the ship. He would enjoy himself. He hasn't seen his professor in twenty years; perhaps he would leap at the chance.

But for good reasons, I do something else.

I grasp his hand and lift it easily, straightening his first two fingers, making their brown tips fondle the warm brass of the infinity pin. Beneath the pin, he feels the firm breast. Beneath the breast, a heart drums along. And with a pleading and soft and absolutely honest voice, I beg, "Please, tell nobody. Nobody."

He tries to lift his hand, but I won't let him.

"There was a malfunction," I confess. "A mistake and a tragedy, and everything's in a shambles. We were caught by surprise. The radiation could have destroyed us before we launched. We haven't nearly enough staff and it's going to be a terribly long, long journey, and please, don't tell anybody what you know." My heart beats; my lungs rise and fall. "Unless you really want to make a mess of things," I concede. "But I don't think...I can't believe, Tom...that there's even a little bit of that kind of man lurking inside you...."

I watch him, but not as closely now.

In part, I believe we have a pact. An understanding. If I cannot trust this person, then I haven't the skill necessary to do my job, and that is a revelation I'd rather not endure.

Yet more is at work here than trust. I haven't the time or resources to hover beside a lone soul, deciphering his every whisper. The multitudes are begging for delicious meals, and they ask the same few questions, hungry for my smile and my musical reassurances. Many men and the occasional woman hope to see what is beneath my skirt. There is nothing dishonorable in that. A moment's flirt buys a wealth of good tidings and durable hopes. An arm brushing against an arm is the easiest trick. The human face is fluid and rich, capable of its own language, and I've always been adept at making the most from a single expression, from a lifted eyebrow and the flash of my perfect white teeth.

By all appearances, I am relentlessly cheerful and seamlessly kind—an expert in every facet of my endless work. But the real soul always hides behind an impenetrable shroud. Who we are is our only genuine secret, and my secret self grows weary and bored, and in odd ways, terrified.

The children scare me. There are too many babies, too many toddlers. Countless souls whose sentience is minimal by any measure. Older children can be bribed with movies and bright games and the vague promise of greater pleasures to come. But the littlest ones are sociopaths demanding nothing but the undiluted attention of everyone else. They scream and whine and cry, and they build fierce little rages that refuse to die. Out of habit, mothers press them to their breasts, and for a little while, they nurse with the same habitual dedication. But diapers remain unsoiled, thankfully; messy old metabolisms were left on the dead world. And after the first long while, the eating habit always falters. Always fails. The adults quit asking for feasts and snacks, and their babies grow tired of drinking without the pleasures of the toilet. The cycle breaks, at least temporarily, and now an equally treasured habit takes hold.

Sleep comes to everyone, or nearly so.

I move among my slumbering souls. Seats have plunged backward, forming beds. The ambient light falls away into a delicious gloom, save for those little pools of colored light where someone fights the urge. Tom is one of the fighters. With bleary, blood-dashed eyes, he sits upright, chin to palm, watching moments culled from his own life. Drifting beside him, my smile goes unnoticed. "She's beautiful," I mention in a whisper.

Tom acts startled. He blinks and takes a quick deep breath—another unnecessary and treasured habit. To prevent misunderstandings, he explains, "She was my mother. She died a few days after this."

"I know that," I promise.

A dark brown woman looks at her son, singing and smiling. She has a beautiful voice perfectly suited for the hymn. God and Christ are her passions. That's plain to see. When she finishes the verse, she stops singing and straightens her hospital gown, and she gasps with a drowning vigor, then kisses her ten-year-old between his blinking and embarrassed eyes.

"Where is she?" he asks.

"Waiting for you," I reply instantly.

But that won't satisfy Tom. He shakes his leaden head, glancing at the girl beside him. At the sleeping Julianna. "What's this place?" he whispers. "This afterlife place...what really happens there...?"

"Imagine," I begin. Then I hold my tongue against the damp roof of my mouth, waiting for his eyes to come around, meeting my fond gaze. Then I say, "Imagine," again. Firmly, as if uttering a command. "Your home will remind you very much of the Earth, and you can build any life for yourself there. Any life you can imagine. Your neighbors will be human souls and alien souls. With a word or a thought, you can learn anything you wish about the universe. Those enduring questions that your college professors could not answer...refused to answer...? They will be transparently obvious, if you wish. With more astonishing questions looming behind them, revealing themselves to you for the first time."

An intelligent soul can't help but be seduced by such a promise. Yet Tom buries his curiosity beside his eagerness. Looking only at me, he says, "This place. Whatever you call it. Have you ever actually lived there yourself?"

"No, I haven't."

Then in the next moment, I confess, "I never joined with the Afterlife. Honestly. Honestly, no."

Again, this man continues to surprise me. He nods as if he fully anticipated my answer, as if he already knew all about me. Then he gives his tired eyes a brutal massage, fingers digging at the sockets as he says to me, or maybe to himself, "I don't know what I'm scared of. But I am. Absolutely, rip-shitting scared."

But I am not scared any longer.

Everyone grows bored of sleep, and they wake by the millions. And again I am swimming in my work, answering summonses and the same few precious questions and delivering treats as well as ease-of-mind. I coax children toward their abandoned seats. I explain to harried parents that no, I cannot slip sedatives into milk or cake. Nothing metabolic is happening inside our ship. Hearts and heads are illusions, seamlessly convincing but perfectly unreal. Stripped of meat and blood, souls are invulnerable to every chemical assault. But the same souls can always be distracted, which is why I keep generating great heaps of fancy colored blocks and soft dolls with soft voices, plus intricate, wondrous puzzles that change their nature, always building some new conundrum as the old conundrum collapses under hard scrutiny.

Adults settle into a mood of sturdy contemplation. Of review and reappraisal. Every soul passes through this normally comforting stage. Tom simply arrived early. People are sitting forward in their seats, watching little snatches of their thoroughly recorded lives. Most seek out special days that they've always treasured, and then later, they hunt out moments filled with regrets, weighing what they see now against the emotionally charged events that they've never been able to forget.

For me, this is always the best part of the journey. Not just the easiest, but the most fulfilling. How can it be anything but beautiful, watching the multitude gradually and inexorably come to terms with its enormous past?

I mention this to my overseer.

She doesn't seem to hear my thoughts.

I am confident, I confess to her. Aren't things going exceptionally well?

She looks at me, and hesitates. Then in an almost glancing fashion, she mentions, Two of your contemplative souls are fighting now. Brawling.

The man with the floppy hat, Quincy, is trading blows with a teenage boy named Gene. They can't hurt each other, but their little mayhem is unseemly. Alarming. And absolutely foolish.

I place myself next to them, and I glare.

They barely notice me. Quincy says, "You son-of-a-bitch liar," and takes a careless swing at the boy's angry face. Gene steps back, avoiding the blow. Then he moves forward, delivering matching blows to the wide soft belly. And Quincy doubles up and crumbles for no better reason than he expects pain. The idea of misery pulls him down to the floor, and curled up like an embryo, he moans. Then with a plaintive and exhausted voice, he says, "You're still." He says, "A son-of-a-bitch liar."

Gene tries to kick the man, but a second foot clips his foot, deflecting it.

I'm standing nearby, watching. What I want is to show everyone else my disapproval. My scalding rage. This is not seemly behavior and I intend to make that point incandescently clear. And then I'll punish both souls, making them look pathetic in front of the others and hopefully putting an end to this particular nonsense.

I am not the agent who stops the fight.

Tom is.

And Tom is the one who barks, "Leave him alone," while stepping between the two combatants. "Back away, and walk away. Okay, son?"

"Liar," Quincy mutters from the safety of the floor.

The boy fumes and spits, then finally looks in my direction. Dark eyes widen until his young face is mostly eyes, and a scared and furious voice says, "Bitch. You. You did it to our world, didn't you?"

For too long, I say nothing.

"Enough," is what Tom tells him.

Then I manage to ask, "What do you mean? What are you talking about?"

"I heard. I know." The young man's anger is seamless and irresistible. "Your damned machines are what killed us all! Isn't that right, bitch?"

What I need to say is perfectly obvious.

"You are mistaken," I tell him.

Then to everyone in earshot, I say, "Someone must have lied to you. Or you heard things wrong."

"See?" Quincy moans. "Told you!"

Then I give Tom a good hard stare. Waiting for him to look at me. Waiting for some trace of shame. But the man simply stands motionless, hands at his sides, wearing a sturdy expression that implies concentration, and concern, as his eyes rise, looking into my gaze, those staring eyes telling me:

No, I did not. I did not. I did not.

My team and overseer are waiting for me.

Who did you bring with you? the overseer asks.

Everyone, I say.

But she sees that for herself. I'm holding tight to several hundred souls—everyone who might have seen the fight or heard the ugly rumor—and Tom is at the front of the heap, saying to the old woman's face, "Like I told your girl here. It wasn't me."

Is the damage contained? the overseer asks me.

I believe. so, yes. I heard nothing else from anywhere else, and nobody except Quincy and Gene spoke about our complicity.

Complicity? the overseer responds.

Yes, I say. What else is it?

She looks at Tom. "What did you tell the others?"

"Nothing," he promises.

The overseer searches the seating charts, and then summons Julianna. With a warning sneer, she asks the girl, "What did Tom tell you?"

"About what?" Julianna asks. She acts nervous, but no more than anyone who is in the presence of someone important. "He told me about the bus hitting him. About a thousand times, he told me that story." Then she glances at Tom, adding, "You're dead. Okay? So get over it!"

"What were those two men fighting about?" the overseer asks.

Julianna shrugs and says, "Who knows?"

"You don't know?"

"Something about how the Earth died." Again, she shrugs. Then she grudgingly admits, "Yeah, I heard talk. Whispers, mostly. They were saying—"

"Who was speaking—?"

"People. Three, four seats over. This kid was standing there—"

"This child?" The overseer shows her Gene. "Is this the one?"

Julianna says, "No," without a shred of doubt. "It was a younger kid. He was talking about how the Earth died. He heard it from some angel—"

"Do you see that boy here? Anywhere?"

Julianna looks at the souls that I brought with me. She is thorough and slow, shaking her head when she finishes, telling us, "He was moving through, I think. On foot. He said he wanted to see as many people as possible before we got where we were going—"

Search for this boy! the overseer cries out.

It takes an instant, and too long. A teammate retrieves the boy and places him in front of us. He is a Sikh, perhaps thirteen years old. He is handsome and bright-eyed and a little fearless. When asked, he is nothing but forthright about what he knows. "The explosion came when a shipment of souls were taken away. Their wormhole turned unstable—"

"Who told you this?" the overseer demands to know.

The boy looks at my team, lifts his arm in my direction, and then points at the man-angel beside me.

My colleague collapses, and sobs, saying, "I did not. I told you—"

"That my calculations were wrong." The boy smiles with genuine pride, then tells the overseer, "I like math and relativity. Neat things like that. I watched the fire in the sky, and did calculations, and I told this angel that it made sense, if our ship employs some kind of superluminal transportation system—"

The boy has walked a very long distance. In the general confusion, he went unnoticed. Each of us is to blame and we know it, and by every means available we look back along his likely course, listening to everything that's being said. Particularly to the whispers.

"And they were wrong," he confesses. "My math was. I wasn't taking into account the effects of—"

A million whispers wash over me.

"They murdered our world," the multitudes are telling each other.

"The angels slaughtered us all…!"

I feel horrible. Wicked, and weak. Useless. And doomed.

Then Tom steps forward, looking only at me. "It wouldn't kill you to apologize to me," he says. "But before you get around to that, maybe you experts should figure out what you're going to do next. Now that this tiger's crawled out of her bag."

Again, I stand before my souls.

My shoulders slump, and I consciously keep my

face from showing anything that might be confused for a smile. I am apologetic. Contrite. Hands opened, palms upturned, I bow before thousands of glowering faces, and with a hurting voice admit, "It's all true. This rumor that you're hearing…that we tried to keep from you…it is true, and it is awful, and perhaps it would help if you took out your anger on me…."

I tell them, "Attack me. Brutalize me. Do whatever you wish to me and to my body, please."

Of course, no one moves. Or remembers to breathe. With others watching, even the most vicious soul is incapable of acting on his worst impulses.

I kneel. Dip my sorry head. Wait.

Then I raise my head, looking through genuine tears. "I don't know who built the wormholes," I admit, "or if they were the same entities who built this place where you are being taken now. I don't even know what you are feeling now. Souls are sanctuaries. Citadels with windows but no gates. Each of you feels hatred and rage and a choking sense of betrayal that I can only imagine, and all I can do is remind you, each of you…remind you that for ten million years, creatures such as I have been saving your ancestors whenever they perished…whisking them to immortality…and without our hard labor, your souls and their souls would have been thrown away by this enormous and very extraordinarily cruel universe…."

Faces stare. Even the children sense the importance of my words, if not what the words mean.

"As promised," I continue, "you may live as you wish in this safe place. In this heaven. Which means that if you desire it, you may rebuild the Earth that you've left. Every brick in its place. Every mote of dust and blue river and the towering mountains and the scuttling beetles. Every little feature can be made real again, and you will return to your old lives. Which, I might add, is not that unusual for a species in your particular circumstance."

That brings a roaring silence.

"Build a new Earth," I tell them. "But this time, the sky doesn't explode. You will grow up and grow old and die, each in your own time. And that's when each of you discovers that you're already living in your afterlife."

The silence quiets. Grows reflective.

"Which reminds me," I mention, casually but not. And again, I show my smile. "It has been suggested...suggested by better minds than mine...that every living world and every conscious mind always exists in someone's heaven...and Death simply moves each of us along an endless chain of Heavens....

"Now isn't it pretty to think so...?"

"How's the general mood?" Tom asks.

I am back in the chamber again. It is just the two of us, again.

"Better?" he asks.

"Better," I admit. Then I give him a look, and too late by long ways, I tell him, "I'm sorry for suspecting you—"

"No need for apologies," he remarks, laughing mildly.

Then before I speak again, he mentions, "It seems you can use some help. You're so thin, and there's so many people out there...I'm just thinking that maybe it would be best to pull a few passengers out of their seats and train them fast and give them little duties they can't screw up too badly—"

"Are you interested in that work?" I ask.

The man doesn't answer me. Not immediately or directly, he won't. But his dark eyes grow distant now, and with a distracted voice, he explains, "I was in the hospital, dying. And thinking about everything. My life. Its purpose, and its worth, and all the usual bullshit. Then they were wheeling me down the hall-way…and I was sure that I was dying…and what I kept thinking, over and over, was that the orderly pushing the gurney had the best job in the universe. You know? Bearing the dead along like that. It just seemed so natural. So lovely. I just felt envious, all of a sudden. And that was my last thought. My only thought, really. I just wished that in my life I could have done something simple and noble like that guy got to do every damned day.…"

I stare at him. And I wait.

"You never actually entered that afterlife place," he says to me. "Did you?"

"Never."

"Is that typical of your profession?"

"It is," I confess. "You don't happen upon many souls who wish to leave, once they're actually there."

He nods. Sucks on his teeth. And finally, looking into my eyes, he says, "Well," with a deft finality. He says, "I never believed in that place anyway." And he smiles, touching me, squeezing my elbow with one damp hand while the other hand fingers that symbol of boundless forever.

"Ailoura"

Paul Di Filippo

The small aircraft swiftly bisected the cloudless chartreuse sky. Invisible encrypted transmissions raced ahead of it. Clearance returned immediately from the distant, turreted manse—Stoessl House—looming in the otherwise empty riven landscape like some precipice-perching raptor. The ever-unsleeping family marchwarden obligingly shut down the manse's defenses, allowing an approach and landing. Within minutes, Geisen Stoessl had docked his small deltoid zipflyte on one of the tenth-floor platforms of Stoessl House, cantilevered over the flood-sculpted, candy-colored arroyos of the Subliminal Desert.

Geisen unseamed the canopy and leaped easily out onto the broad sintered terrace, unpeopled at this tragic, necessary, hopeful moment. Still clad in his dusty expeditionary clothes, goggles slung around his neck, Geisen resembled a living marble version of some young roughneck godling. Slim, wiry, and alert, with his laughter-creased, soil-powdered face now set in solemn lines absurdly counterpointed by a mask of clean skin around his recently shielded green eyes, Geisen paused a moment to brush from his protective suit the heaviest evidence of his recent wildcat digging in the Lustrous Wastes. Satisfied that he had made some small improvement in his appearance upon this weighty occasion, he advanced toward the portal leading inside. But before he could actuate the door, it opened from within.

Framed in the door stood a lanky, robe-draped bestient: Vicuna, his mother's most valued servant. Set squarely in Vicuna's wedge-shaped hirsute face, the haughty maid's broad velveteen nose wrinkled imperiously in disgust at Geisen's appearance, but the moreauvian refrained from voicing her disapproval of that matter in favor of other upbraidings.

"You arrive barely in time, Gep Stoessl. Your father approaches the limits of artificial maintenance, and is due to be reborn any minute. Your mother and brothers already anxiously occupy the Natal Chambers."

Following the inhumanly articulated servant into Stoessl House, Geisen answered, "I'm aware of all that, Vicuna. But traveling halfway around Chalk can't be accomplished in an instant."

"It was your choice to absent yourself during this crucial time."

"Why crucial? This will be Vomacht's third reincarnation. Presumably this one will go as smoothly as the first two."

"So one would hope."

Geisen tried to puzzle out the subtext of Vicuna's ambiguous comment, but could emerge with no clue regarding the current state of the generally complicated affairs within Stoessl House. He had obviously been away too long—too busy enjoying his own lonely but satisfying prospecting trips on behalf of the family enterprise—to be able to grasp the daily political machinations of his relatives.

Vicuna conducted Geisen to the nearest squeezer, and they promptly dropped down fifteen stories, far below the bedrock in which Stoessl House was rooted.

On this secure level, the monitoring marchwarden hunkered down in its cozy low-Kelvin isolation, meaningful matrices of B-E condensates. Here also were the family's Natal Chambers. At these doors blazoned with sacred icons Vicuna left Geisen with a humid snort signifying that her distasteful attendance on the latecomer was complete.

Taking a fortifying breath, Geisen entered the rooms.

Roseate illumination symbolic of new creation softened all within: the complicated apparatus of rebirth as well as the sharp features of his mother, Woda, and the doughy countenances of his two brothers, Gitten and Grafton. Nearly invisible in the background, various bestient bodyguards hulked, inconspicuous yet vigilant.

Woda spoke first. "Well, how very generous of the prodigal to honor us with his unfortunately mandated presence."

Gitten snickered, and Grafton chimed in, pompously ironical. "Exquisitely gracious behavior, and so very typical of our little sibling, I'm sure."

Tethered to various life-support devices, Vomacht Stoessl—unconscious, naked and recumbent on a padded pallet alongside his mindless new body—said nothing. Both he and his clone had their heads wrapped in organic warty sheets of modified Stroonian brain parasite, an organism long ago co-opted for mankind's ambitious and ceaselessly searching program of life extension. Linked via a thick living interparasitical tendril to its younger doppelganger, the withered form of the current Vomacht, having reached the limits of rejuvenation, contrasted strongly with the virginal, soulless vessel.

During Vomacht Stoessl's first lifetime, from 239

to 357 PS, he had sired no children. His second span of existence (357 to 495 PS) saw the birth of Gitten and Grafton, separated by some sixty years and both sired on Woda. Toward the end of his third, current lifetime (495 to 675 PS), a mere thirty years ago, he had fathered Geisen upon a mystery woman whom Geisen had never known. Vanished and unwedded, his mother—or some other oversolicitous guardian—had denied Geisen her name or image. Still, Vomacht had generously attended to all the legalities granting Geisen full parity with his half brothers. Needless to say, little cordiality existed between the older members of the family and the young interloper.

Geisen made the proper obeisances at several altars before responding to the taunts of his stepmother and stepbrothers. "I did not dictate the terms governing Gep Stoessl's latest reincarnation. They came directly from him. If any of you objected, you should have made your grievances known to him face-to-face. I myself am honored that he chose me to initiate the transference of his mind and soul. I regret only that I was not able to attend him during his final moments of awareness in this old body."

Gitten, the middle brother, tittered, and said, "The hand that cradles the rocks will now rock the cradle."

Geisen looked down at his dirty hands, hopelessly ingrained with the soils and stone dusts of Chalk. He resisted an impulse to hide them in his pockets. "There is nothing shameful about my fondness for fieldwork. Lolling about in luxury does not suit me. And I did not hear any of you complaining when the Eventyr Lode that I discovered came on-line and began to swell the family coffers."

Woda intervened with her traditional maternal acerbity. "Enough bickering. Let us acknowledge that no possible arrangement of this day's events would have pleased everyone. The quicker we perform this vital ritual, the quicker we can all return to our duties and pleasures, and the sooner Vomacht's firm hand will regrasp the controls of our business. Geisen, I believe you know what to do."

"I studied the proper *Books of Phowa* en route."

Grafton said, "Always the grind. Whenever do you enjoy yourself, little brother?"

Geisen advanced confidently to the mechanisms that reared at the head of the pallets. "In the proper time and place, Grafton. But I realize that to you, such words imply every minute of your life." The young man turned his attention to the controls before him, forestalling further tart banter.

The tethered and trained Stroonian life-forms had been previously starved to near hibernation in preparation for their sacred duty. A clear cylinder of pink nutrient fluid laced with instructive protein sequences hung from an ornate tripod. The fluid would flow through twin IV lines, once the parasites were hooked up, enlivening their quiescent metabolisms and directing their proper functioning.

Murmuring the requisite holy phrases, Geisen plugged an IV line into each enshrouding creature. He tapped the proper dosage rate into the separate flow-pumps. Then, solemnly capturing the eyes of the onlookers, he activated the pumps.

Almost immediately the parasites began to flex and labor, humping and contorting as they drove an infinity of fractally minuscule auto-anesthetizing tendrils into both full and vacant brains in preparation for the transfer of the vital engrams that comprised a human soul.

But within minutes, it was plain to the observers that something was very wrong. The original Vomacht Stoessl began to writhe in evident pain, ripping away from his life supports.

The all-observant marchwarden triggered alarms. Human and bestient technicians burst into the room. Grafton and Gitten and Woda rushed to the pumps to stop the process. But they were too late. In an instant, both membrane-wrapped skulls collapsed to degenerate chunky slush that plopped to the floor from beneath the suddenly destructive cauls.

The room fell silent. Grafton tilted one of the pumps at an angle so that all the witnesses could see the glowing red numerals.

"He quadrupled the proper volume of nutrient, driving the Stroonians hyperactive. This is murder!"

"Secure him from any escape!" Woda commanded.

Instantly Geisen's arms were pinioned by two burly bestient guards. He opened his mouth to protest, but the sight of his headless father choked off all words.

Gep Vomacht Stoessl's large private study was decorated with ancient relics of his birthworld, Lucerno: the empty, age-brittle coral armature of a deceased personal exoskeleton; a row of printed books bound in sloth-hide; a corroded aurochs-flaying knife large as a canoe paddle. In the wake of their owner's death, the talismans seemed drained of mana.

Geisen sighed, and slumped down hopelessly in the comfortable chair positioned on the far side of the antique desk that had originated on the Crafters' planet, Hulbrouck V. On the far side of the nacreous expanse sat his complacently smirking half brother, Grafton. Just days ago, Geisen knew, his father had hauled himself out of his sickbed for one last appearance at this favorite desk, where he had dictated the terms of his third recincarnation to the recording marchwarden. Geisen had played the affecting scene several times en route from the Lustrous Wastes, noting how, despite his enervated condition, his father spoke with his wonted authority, specifically requesting that Geisen administer the paternal rebirthing procedure.

And now that unique individual—distant and enigmatic as he had been to Geisen throughout the latter's relatively short life—the man who had founded Stoessl House and its fortunes, the man to whom they all owed their luxurious independent lifestyles, was irretrievably gone from this plane of existence.

The human soul could exist only in organic substrates. Intelligent as they might be, condensate-dwelling entities such as the marchwarden exhibited a lesser existential complexity. Impossible to make any kind of static "backup" copy of the human essence, even in the proverbial bottled brain, since Stroonian transcription was fatal to the original. No, if destructive failure occurred during a rebirth, that individual was no more forever.

Grafton interpreted Geisen's sigh as indicative of a need to unburden himself of some secret. "Speak freely, little brother. Ease your soul of guilt. We are completely alone. Not even the marchwarden is listening."

Geisen sat up alertly. "How have you accomplished such a thing? The marchwarden is deemed to be incorruptible, and its duties include constant surveillance of the interior of our home."

Somewhat flustered, Grafton tried to dissemble. "Oh, no, you're quite mistaken. It was always possible to disable the marchwarden selectively. A standard menu option—"

Geisen leaped to his feet, causing Grafton to rear back. "I see it all now! This whole murder, and my seeming complicity, was planned from the start! My father's last testament—faked! The flow codes to the pumps—overriden! My role—stooge and dupe!"

Recovering himself, Grafton managed with soothing motions and noises to induce a fuming Geisen to be seated again. The older man came around to perch on a corner of the desk. He leaned over closer to Geisen and, in a smooth voice, made his own shockingly unrepentant confession.

"Very astute. Too bad for you that you did not see the trap early enough to avoid it. Yes, Vomacht's permanent death and your hand in it were all neatly arranged—by mother, Gitten, and myself. It had to be. You see, Vomacht had become irrationally surly and obnoxious toward us, his true and loving first family. He threatened to remove all our stipends and entitlements and authority, once he occupied his strong new body. But those demented codicils were edited from the version of his speech that you saw, as was his insane proclamation naming you sole factotum of the family business. All of Stoessl Strangelet Mining and its affiliates was to be made your fiefdom. Imagine! A young desert rat at the helm of our venerable corporation!"

Geisen strove to digest all this sudden information. Practical considerations warred with his emotions. Finally he could only ask, "What of Vomacht's desire for me to initiate his soul-transfer?"

"Ah, that was authentic. And it served as the perfect bait to draw you back, as well as the peg on which we could hang a murder plot and charge."

Geisen drew himself up proudly. "You realize that these accusations of deliberate homicide against me will not stand up a minute in court. With what you've told me, I'll certainly be able to dig up plenty of evidence to the contrary."

Smiling like a carrion lizard from the Cerise Ergstrand, Grafton countered, "Oh, will you, now? From your jail cell, without any outside help? Accused murderers cannot profit from the results of their actions. You will have no access to family funds other than your small personal accounts while incarcerated, nor any real partisans, due to your stubbornly asocial existence of many years. The might of the family, including testimony from the grieving widow, will be ranked against you. How do you rate your chances for exculpation under those circumstances?"

Reduced to grim silence, Geisen bunched his muscles prior to launching himself in a futile attack on his brother. But Grafton held up warning hand first.

"There is an agreeable alternative. We really do not care to bring this matter to court. There is, after all, still a chance of one percent or less that you might win the case. And legal matters are so tedious and time-consuming, interfering with more pleasurable pursuits. In fact, notice of Gep Stoessl's death has not yet been released to either the news media or to Chalk's authorities. And if we secure your cooperation, the aftermath of this tragic 'accident' will take a very different form than criminal charges. Upon getting your binding assent to a certain trivial document, you will be free to pursue your own life unencumbered by any obligations to Stoessl House or its residents."

Grafton handed his brother hard copy of several

pages. Geisen perused it swiftly and intently, then looked up at Grafton with high astonishment.

"This document strips me of all my share of the family fortunes, and binds me from any future role in the estate. Basically, I am utterly disenfranchised and disinherited, cast out penniless."

"A fair enough summation. Oh, we might give you a small grubstake when you leave. Say—your zipflyte, a few hundred esscues, and a bestient servant or two. Just enough to pursue the kind of itinerant lifestyle you so evidently prefer."

Geisen pondered but a moment. "All attempts to brand me a patricide will be dropped?"

Grafton shrugged. "What would be the point of whipping a helpless, poverty-stricken nonentity?"

Geisen stood up. "Reactivate the marchwarden. I am ready to comply with your terms."

Gep Bloedwyn Vermeule, of Vermeule House, today wore her long blonde braids arranged in a complicated nest, piled high atop her charming young head and sown with delicate fairylights that blinked in time with various of her body rhythms. Entering the formal reception hall of Stoessl House, she marched confidently down the tiles between ranks of silent bestient guards, the long train dependent from her formfitting scarlet sandworm-fabric gown held an inch above the floor by tiny enwoven agravitic units. She came to a stop some meters away from the man who awaited her with a nervously expectant smile on his rugged face.

Geisen's voice quaked at first, despite his best resolve. "Bloedwyn, my sweetling, you look more alluring than an oasis to a parched man."

The pinlights in the girl's hair raced in chaotic patterns for a moment, then settled down to a stable configurations that somehow radiated a frostiness belied by her neutral facial expression. Her voice, chorded suggestively low and husky by fashionable implants, quavered not at all.

"Gep Stoessl, I hardly know how to approach you. So much has changed since we last trysted."

Throwing decorum to the wind, Geisen closed the gap between them and swept his betrothed up in his arms. The sensation Geisen enjoyed was rather like that derived from hugging a wooden effigy. Nonetheless, he persisted in his attempts to restore their old relations.

"Only superficial matters have changed, my dear! True, as you have no doubt heard by now, I am no longer a scion of Stoessl House. But my heart, mind, and soul remain devoted to you! Can I not assume the same constancy applies to your inner being?"

Bloedwyn slipped out of Geisen's embrace. "How could you assume anything, since I myself do not know how I feel? All these developments have been so sudden and mysterious! Your father's cruelly permanent death, your own capricious and senseless abandonment of your share of his estate—How can I make sense of any of it? What of all our wonderful dreams?"

Geisen gripped Bloedwyn's supple hide-mailed upper arms with perhaps too much fervor, judging from her wince. He released her, then spoke. "All our bright plans for the future will come to pass! Just give me some time to regain my footing in the world. One day I will be at liberty to explain everything to you. But, until then, I ask your trust and faith. Surely you nust share my confidence in my character, in my undiminished capabilities?"

Bloedwyn averted her tranquil blue-eyed gaze from Geisen's imploring green eyes, and he slumped in despair, knowing himself lost. She stepped back a few paces and, with voice steeled, made a formal declaration she had evidently rehearsed prior to this moment.

"The Vermeule marchwarden has already communicated the abrogation of our pending matrimonial agreement to your house's governor. I think such an impartial yet decisive move is all for the best, Geisen. We are both young, with many lives before us. It would be senseless to found such a potentially interminable relationship on such shaky footing. Let us both go ahead—separately—into the days to come, with our extinct love a fond memory."

Again, as at the moment of his father's death, Geisen found himself rendered speechless at a crucial juncture, unable to plead his case any further. He watched in stunned disbelief as Bloedwyn turned gracefully around and walked out of his life, her fluttering scaly train still visible for some seconds after the rest of her had vanished.

The cluttered, steamy, noisy kitchens of Stoessl House exhibited an orderly chaos proportionate to the magnitude of the preparations underway. The planned rebirth dinner for the paterfamilias had been hastily converted to a memorial banquet, once the proper, little-used protocols had been found in a metaphorically dusty lobe of the marchwarden's memory. Now scores of miscegenational bestients under the supervision of the lone human chef, Stine Pursiful, scraped, sliced, chopped, diced, cored, deveined, scrubbed, layered, basted, glazed, microwaved, and pressure-treated various foodstuffs, assembling the imported luxury ingredients into the elaborate fare that would furnish out the solemn buffet for family and friends and business connections of the deceased.

Geisen entered the aromatic atmosphere of the kitchens with a scowl on his face and a bitterness in his throat and heart. Pursiful spotted the young man and, with a fair share of courtesy and deference, considering the circumstances, stepped forward to inquire of his needs. But Geisen rudely brushed the slim punctilious chef aside, and stalked toward the shelves that held various MREs. With blunt motions, he began to shovel the nutri-packets into a dusty shoulder bag that had plainly seen many an expedition into Chalk's treasure-filled deserts.

A small timid bestient belonging to one of the muskrathyrax clades hopped over to the shelves where Geisen fiercely rummaged. Nearsighted, the be-aproned moreauvian strained on tiptoe to identify something on a higher shelf.

With one heavy foot, Geisen kicked the servant out of his way, sending the creature squeaking and sliding across the slops-strewn floor. But before the man could return to his rough provisioning, he was stopped by a voice familiar as his skin.

"I raised you to show more respect to all the Implicate's creatures than you just exhibited, Gep Stoessl. Or if I did not, then I deserve immediately to visit the Unborn's Lowest Abattoir for my criminal negligence."

Geisen turned, the bile in his craw and soul melting to a habitual affection tinged with many memories of juvenile guilt.

Brindled arms folded across her queerly configured chest, Ailoura the bestient stood a head shorter than

Geisen, compact and well-muscled. Her heritage mingled from a thousand feline and quasi-feline strains from a dozen planets, she resembled no single cat species morphed to human status, but rather all cats everywhere, blended and thus ennobled. Rounded ears perched high atop her densely pelted skull. Vertical slitted eyes and her patch of wet leathery nose contrasted with a more-human-seeming mouth and chin. Now anger and disappointment molded her face into a mask almost frightening, her fierce expression magnified by a glint of sharp tooth peeking from beneath a curled lip.

Geisen noted instantly, with a small shock, the newest touches of gray in Ailoura's tortoiseshell fur. These tokens of aging softened his heart even further. He made the second-most-serious conciliatory bow from the Dakini Rituals toward his old nurse. Straightening, Geisen watched with relief as the anger flowed out of her face and stance, to be replaced by concern and solicitude.

"Now," Ailoura demanded, in the same tone with which she had often demanded that little Geisen brush his teeth or do his schoolwork, "what is all this nonsense I hear about your voluntary disinheritance and departure?"

Geisen motioned Ailoura into a secluded corner of the kitchens and revealed everything to her. His account prompted low growls from the bestient that escaped despite her angrily compressed lips. Geisen finished resignedly by saying, "And so, helpless to contest this injustice, I leave now to seek my fortune elsewhere, perhaps even on another world."

Ailoura pondered a moment. "You say that your brother offered you a servant from our house?"

"Yes. But I don't intend to take him up on that

promise. Having another mouth to feed would just hinder me."

Placing one mitteny yet deft hand on his chest, Ailoura said, "Take me, Gep Stoessl."

Geisen experienced a moment of confusion. "But Ailoura—your job of raising me is long past. I am very grateful for the loving care you gave unstintingly to a motherless lad, the guidance and direction you imparted, the indulgent playtimes we enjoyed. Your teachings left me with a wise set of principles, an admirable will and optimism, and a firm moral center—despite the evidence of my thoughtless transgression a moment ago. But your guardian duties lie in the past. And besides, why would you want to leave the comforts and security of Stoessl House?"

"Look at me closely, Gep Stoessl. I wear now the tabard of the scullery crew. My luck in finding you here is due only to this very demotion. And from here the slide to utter inutility is swift and short—despite my remaining vigor and craft. Will you leave me here to face my sorry fate? Or will you allow me to cast my fate with that of the boy I raised from kittenhood?"

Geisen thought a moment. "Some companionship would indeed be welcome. And I don't suppose I could find a more intimate ally."

Ailoura grinned. "Or a slyer one."

"Very well. You may accompany me. But on one condition."

"Yes, Gep Stoessl?"

"Cease calling me 'Gep.' Such formalities were once unknown between us."

Ailoura smiled. "Agreed, little Gei-gei."

The man winced. "No need to regress quite that far. Now, let us return to raiding my family's larder."

"Be sure to take some of that fine fish, if you please, Geisen."

No one knew the origin of the tame strangelets that seeded Chalk's strata. But everyone knew of the immense wealth these cloistered anomalies conferred.

Normal matter was composed of quarks in only two flavors: up and down. But strange-flavor quarks also existed, and the exotic substances formed by these strange quarks in combination with the more domestic flavors were, unconfined, as deadly as the more familiar antimatter. Bringing normal matter into contact with a naked strangelet resulted in the conversion of the feedstock into energy. Owning a strangelet was akin to owning a pet black hole, and just as useful for various purposes, such as powering star cruisers.

Humanity could create strangelets, but only at immense cost per unit. And naked strangelets had to be confined in electromagnetic or gravitic bottles during active use. They could also be quarantined for semipermanent storage in stasis fields. Such was the case with the buried strangelets of Chalk.

Small spherical mirrored nodules—"marbles," in the jargon of Chalk's prospectors—could be found in various recent sedimentary layers of the planet's crust, distributed according to no rational plan. Discovery of the marbles had inaugurated the reign of the various Houses on Chalk.

An early scientific expedition from Preceptimax University to the Shulamith Wadi stumbled upon the strangelets initially. Preceptor Fairservis, the curious discoverer of the first marble, had realized he was dealing with a stasis-bound object and had unluckily managed to open it. The quantum genie inside had promptly eaten the hapless fellow who freed it, along with nine-tenths of the expedition, before beginning a sure but slow descent toward the core of Chalk. Luckily, an emergency response team swiftly dispatched by the planetary authorities had managed to activate a new entrapping marble as big as a small city, its lower hemisphere underground, thus trapping the rogue.

After this incident, the formerly disdained deserts of Chalk had experienced a land rush unparalleled in the galaxy. Soon the entire planet was divided into domains—many consisting of noncontiguous properties—each owned by one House or another. Prospecting began in earnest then. But the practice remained more an art than a science, as the marbles remained stealthy to conventional detectors. Intuition, geological knowledge of strata, and sheer luck proved the determining factors in the individual fortunes of the Houses.

How the strangelets—plainly artifactual—came to be buried beneath Chalk's soils and hardpan remained a mystery. No evidence of native intelligent inhabitants existed on the planet prior to the arrival of humanity. Had a cloud of strangelets been swept up out of space as Chalk made her eternal orbits? Perhaps. Or had alien visitors planted the strangelets for unimaginable reasons of their own? An equally plausible theory.

Whatever the obscure history of the strangelets, their current utility was beyond argument.

They made many people rich.

And some people murderous.

In the shadow of the Tasso Escarpments, adjacent to

the Glabrous Drifts, Carrabas House sat desolate and melancholy, tenanted only by glass-tailed lizards and stilt-crabs, its poverty-overtaken heirs dispersed anonymously across the galaxy after a series of unwise investments, followed by the unpredictable yet inevitable exhaustion of their marble-bearing properties—a day against which Vomacht Stoessl had more providently hedged his own family's fortunes.

Geisen's zipflyte crunched to a landing on one of the manse's grit-blown terraces, beside a gaping portico. The craft's doors swung open and pilot and passenger emerged. Ailoura now wore a set of utilitarian roughneck's clothing, tailored for her bestient physique and matching the outfit worn by her former charge, right down to the boots. Strapped to her waist was an antique yet lovingly maintained variable sword, its terminal bead currently dull and inactive.

"No one will trouble us here," Geisen said with confidence. "And we'll have a roof of sorts over our heads while we plot our next steps. As I recall from a visit some years ago, the west wing was the least damaged."

As Geisen began to haul supplies—a heater-cum-stove, sleeping bags and pads, water condensers—from their craft, Ailoura inhaled deeply the dry tangy air, her nose wrinkling expressively, then exhaled with zest. "Ah, freedom after so many years! It tastes brave, young Geisen!" Her claws slipped from their sheaths as she flexed her pads. She unclipped her sword and flicked it on, the seemingly untethered bead floating outward from the pommel a meter or so.

"You finish the monkey work. I'll clear the rats from our quarters," promised Ailoura, then bounded off before Geisen could stop her. Watching her unfettered tail disappear down a hall and around a corner, Geisen smiled, recalling childhood games of strength and skill where she had allowed him what he now realized were easy triumphs.

After no small time, Ailoura returned, licking her greasy lips.

"All ready for our habitation, Geisen-kitten."

"Very good. If the bold warrior will deign to lend a paw…?"

Soon the pair had established housekeeping in a spacious, weatherproof ground floor room (with several handy exits), where a single leering window frame was easily covered by a sheet of translucent plastic. After distributing their goods and sweeping the floor clean of loess drifts, Geisen and Ailoura took a meal as their reward, the first of many such rude campfire repasts to come.

As they relaxed afterward, Geisen making notes with his stylus in a small pocket diary and Ailoura dragging her left paw continually over one ear, a querulous voice sounded from thin air.

"Who disturbs my weary peace?"

Instantly on their feet, standing back to back, the newcomers looked warily about. Ailoura snarled until Geisen hushed her. Seeing no one, Geisen at last inquired, "Who speaks?"

"I am the Carrabas marchwarden."

The man and bestient relaxed a trifle. "Impossible," said Geisen. "How do you derive your energy after all these years of abandonment and desuetude?"

The marchwarden chuckled with a trace of pride. "Long ago, without any human consent or prompting, while Carrabas House still flourished, I sunk a thermal tap downward hundreds of kilometers. The backup energy thus supplied is not much, compared with my

275

old capacities, but has proved enough for sheer survival, albeit with much dormancy."

Ailoura hung her quiet sword back on her belt. "How have you kept sane since then, marchwarden?"

"Who says I have?"

Coming to terms with the semideranged Carrabas marchwarden required delicate negotiations. The protective majordomo simultaneously resented the trespassers—who did not share the honored Carrabas family lineage—yet on some different level welcomed their company and the satisfying chance to perform some of its programmed functions for them. Alternating ogreish threats with embarrassingly humble supplications, the marchwarden needed to hear just the right mix of defiance and thanks from the squatters to fully come over as their ally. Luckily, Ailoura, employing diplomatic wiles honed by decades of bestient subservience, perfectly supplemented Geisen's rather gruff and patronizing attitude. Eventually, the ghost of Carrabas House accepted them.

"I am afraid I can contribute little enough to your comfort, Gep Carrabas." During the negotiations, the marchwarden had somehow self-deludingly concluded that Geisen was indeed part of the lost lineage. "Some water, certainly, from my active conduits. But no other necessities such as heat or food, or any luxuries either. Alas, the days of my glory are long gone!"

"Are you still in touch with your peers?" asked Ailoura.

"Why, yes. The other Houses have not forgotten me. Many are sympathetic, though a few are haughty and indifferent."

Geisen shook his head in bemusement. "First I learn

that the protective omniscience of the marchwardens may be circumvented. Next, that they keep up a private traffic and society. I begin to wonder who is the master and who is the servant in our global system."

"Leave these conundrums to the preceptors, Geisen. This unexpected mode of contact might come in handy for us some day."

The marchwarden's voice sounded enervated. "Will you require any more of me? I have overtaxed my energies, and need to shut down for a time."

"Please restore yourself fully."

Left alone, Geisen and Ailoura simultaneously realized how late the hour was and how tired they were. They bedded down in warm bodyquilts, and Geisen swiftly drifted off to sleep to the old tune of Ailoura's drowsy purring.

In the chilly viridian morning, over fish and kava, cat and man held a war council.

Geisen led with a bold assertion that nonetheless concealed a note of despair and resignation.

"Given your evident hunting prowess, Ailoura, and my knowledge of the land, I estimate that we can take half a dozen sandworms from those unclaimed public territories proved empty of strangelets, during the course of as many months. We'll peddle the skins for enough to get us both off-planet. I understand that lush homesteads are going begging on Nibbriglung. All that the extensive water meadows there require is a thorough desnailing before they're producing golden rice by the bushel—"

Ailoura's green eyes, so like Geisen's own, flashed with cool fire. "Insipidity! Toothlessness!" she hissed.

"Turn farmer? Grub among the waterweeds like some *platypus*? Run away from those who killed your sire and cheated you out of your inheritance? I didn't raise such an unimaginative, unambitious coward, did I?"

Geisen sipped his drink to avoid making a hasty affronted rejoinder, then calmly said, "What do you recommend, then? I gave my legally binding promise not to contest any of the unfair terms laid down by my family, in return for freedom from prosecution. What choices does such a renunciation leave me? Shall you and I go live in the shabby slums that slump at the feet of the Houses? Or turn thief and raider and prey upon lonely mining encampments? Or shall we become freelance prospectors? I'd be good at the latter job, true, but bargaining with the Houses concerning hard-won information about their own properties in humiliating, and promises only slim returns. They hold all the high cards, and the supplicant offers only a mere saving of time."

"You're onto a true scent with this last idea. But not quite the paltry scheme you envision. What I propose is that we swindle those who swindled you. We won't gain back your whole patrimony, but you'll surely acquire greater sustaining riches than you would by flensing worms or flailing rice."

"Speak on."

"The first step involves a theft. But after that, only chicanery. To begin, we'll need a small lot of strangelets, enough to salt a claim everyone thought exhausted."

Geisen considered, buffing his raspy chin with his knuckles. "The morality is dubious. Still—I found a smallish deposit of marbles on Stoessl property during my aborted trip, and never managed to report it. They were in a flood-plain hard by the Nakhoda Range, newly exposed and ripe for the plucking without any large-scale mining activity that would attract satellite surveillance."

"Perfect! We'll use their own goods to con the ratlings! But once we have this grubstake, we'll need a proxy to deal with the Houses. Your own face and reputation must remain concealed until all deals are sealed airtight. Do you have knowledge of any such suitable foil?"

Geisen began to laugh. "Do I? Only the perfect rogue for the job!"

Ailoura came cleanly to her feet, although she could not repress a small grunt at an arthritic twinge provoked by a night on the hard floor. "Let us collect the strangelets first, and then enlist his help. With luck, we'll be sleeping on feathers and dining off golden plates in a few short weeks."

The sad and spectral voice of the abandoned marchwarden sounded. "Good morning, Gep Carrabas. I regret keenly my own serious incapacities as a host. But I have managed to heat up several liters of water for a bath, if such service appeals."

The eccentric caravan of Marco Bozzarias and his mistress Pigafetta had emerged from its minting pools as a top-of-the-line Baba Yaya model of the year 650 PS. Capacious and agile, larded with amenities, the moderately intelligent stilt-walking cabin had been designed to protect its inhabitants from climatic extremes in unswaying comfort while carrying them surefootedly over the roughest terrain. But plainly, for one reason or another (most likely poverty) Bozzarias had neglected the caravan's maintenance over the twenty-five years of its working life.

Raised now for privacy above the sands where Geisen's zipflyte rested, the vehicle-cum-residence canted several degrees, imparting a funhouse quality to its interior. Swellings at its many knee joints indicated a lack of proper nutrients. Additionally, the cabin itself had been patched with so many different materials—plastic, sandworm hide, canvas, chitin—that it more closely resembled a heap of debris than a deliberately designed domicile.

The caravan's owner, contrastingly, boasted an immaculate and stylish appearance. To judge by his handsome, mustachioed looks, the middle-aged Bozzarias was more stage-door idler than cactus hugger, displaying his trim figure proudly beneath crimson ripstop trews and utility vest over bare hirsute chest. Despite this urban promenader's facade, Bozzarias held a respectable record as a freelance prospector, having pinpointed for their owners several strangelet lodes of note, including the fabled Gosnold Pocket. For these services, he had been recompensed by the tightfisted landowners only a nearly invisible percentage of the eventual wealth claimed from the finds. Despite his current friendly grin, it would be impossible for Bozzarias not to harbor decades-worth of spite and jealousy.

Pigafetta, Bozzarias' bestient paramour, was a voluptuous, pink-skinned geisha clad in blue and green silks. Carrying perhaps a tad too much weight—hardly surprising, given her particular gattaca—Pigafetta radiated a slack and greasy carnality utterly at odds with Ailoura's crisp and dry efficiency. When the visitors had entered the cabin, before either of the humans could intervene, Geisen and Bozzarias had been treated to an instant but decisive bloodless cat-fight that had settled the pecking order between the more-auvians.

Now, while Pigafetta sulked winsomely in canted corner amid her cushions, the furry female victor consulted with the two men around a small table across which lay spilled the stolen strangelets, corralled from rolling by a line of empty liquor bottles.

Bozzarias poked at one of the deceptive marbles with seeming disinterest, while his dark eyes glittered with avarice. "Let me recapitulate. We represent to various buyers that these quantum baubles are merely the camel's nose showing beneath the tent of unconsidered wealth. A newly discovered lode on the Carrabas properties, of which you, Gep Carrabas—" Bozzarias leered at Geisen, "—are the rightful heir. We rook the fools for all we can get, then hie ourselves elsewhere, beyond their injured squawks and retributions. Am I correct in all particulars?"

Ailoura spoke first. "Yes, substantially."

"And what would my share of the take be? To depart forever my cherished Chalk would require a huge stake—"

"Don't try to make your life here sound glamorous or even tolerable, Marco," Geisen said. "Everyone knows you're in debt up to your nose, and haven't had a strike in over a year. It's about time for you to change venues anyway. The days of the freelancer on Chalk are nearly over."

Bozzarias sighed dramatically, picking up a reflective marble and admiring himself in it. "I suppose you speak the truth—as it is commonly perceived. But a man of my talents can carve himself a niche anywhere.

And Pigafetta *had* been begging me of late to launch her on a virtual career—"

"In other words," Ailoura interrupted, "you intend to pimp her as a porn star. Well, you'll need to relocate to a mediapoietic world then for sure. May we assume you'll become part of our scheme?"

Bozzarias set the marble down and said, "My pay?"

"Two strangelets from this very stock."

With the speed of a glass-tailed lizard Bozzarias scooped up and pocketed two spheres before the generous offer could be rescinded. "Done! Now, if you two will excuse me, I'll need to rehearse my role before we begin this deception."

Ailoura smiled, a disconcerting sight to those unfamiliar with her tender side. "Not quite so fast, Gep Bozzarias. If you'll just submit a moment—"

Before Bozzarias could protest, Ailoura had sprayed him about the head and shoulders with the contents of a pressurized can conjured from her pack.

"What! Pixie dust! This is a gross insult!"

Geisen adjusted the controls of his pocket diary. On the small screen appeared a jumbled, jittering image of the caravan's interior. As the self-assembling pixie dust cohesed around Bozzarias' eyes and ears, the image stabilized to reflect the prospector's visual point of view. Echoes of their speech emerged from the diary's speaker.

"As you well know," Ailoura advised, "the pixie dust is ineradicable and self-repairing. Only the ciphers we hold can deactivate it. Until then, all you see and hear will be shared with us. We intend to monitor you around the clock. And the diary's input is being shared with the Carrabas marchwarden, who has been told to watch for any traitorous actions on your part.

That entity, by the way, is a little deranged, and might leap to conclusions about any actions that even verge on treachery. Oh, you'll also find that your left ear hosts a channel for our remote, ah, verbal advice. It would behoove you to follow our directions, since the dust is quite capable of liquefying your eyeballs upon command."

Seemingly inclined to protest further, Bozzarias suddenly thought better of dissenting. With a dispirited wave and nod, he signaled his acquiescence to their plans, becoming quietly businesslike.

"And to what Houses shall I offer this putative wealth?"

Geisen smiled. "To every House at first—except Stoessl."

"I see. Quite clever."

After Bozzarias had caused his caravan to kneel to the earth, he bade his new partners a desultory goodbye. But at the last minute, as Ailoura was stepping into the zipflyte, Bozzarias snagged Geisen by the sleeve and whispered in his ear.

"I'd trade that rude servant in for a mindless pleasure model, my friend, were I you. She's much too tricky for comfort."

"But, Marco—that's exactly why I cherish her."

Three weeks after first employing the wily Bozzarias in their scam, Geisen and Ailoura sat in their primitive quarters at Carrabas House, huddled nervously around Geisen's diary, awaiting transmission of the meeting they had long anticipated. The diary's screen revealed the familiar landscape around Stoessl House as seen from the windows of the speeding zipflyte carrying their agent to his appointment with Woda, Gitten, and Grafton.

During the past weeks, Ailoura's plot had matured, succeeding beyond their highest expectations.

Representing himself as the agent for a mysteriously returned heir of the long-abandoned Carrabas estate—a fellow who preferred anonymity for the moment—Bozzarias had visited all the biggest and most influential Houses—excluding the Stoessls—with his sample strangelets. A major new find had been described, with its coordinates freely given and inspections invited. The visiting teams of geologists reported what appeared to be a rich new lode, deceived by Geisen's expert saltings. And no single House dared attempt a midnight raid on the unprotected new strike, given the vigilance of all the others.

The cooperative and willing playacting of the Carrabas marchwarden had been essential. First, once its existence was revealed, the discarded entity's very survival became a seven-day wonder, compelling a willing suspension of disbelief in all the lies that followed. Confirming the mystery man as a true Carrabas, the marchwarden also added its jiggered testimony to verify the discovery.

Bozzarias had informed the greedily gaping families that the returned Carrabas scion had no desire to play an active role in mining and selling his strangelets. The whole estate—with many more potential strangelet nodes—would be sold to the highest bidder.

Offers began to pour in, steadily escalating. These included feverish bids from the Stoessls, which were rejected without comment. Finally, after such high-handed treatment, the offended clan demanded to know why they were being excluded from the auction.

Bozzarias responded that he would convey that information only in a private meeting.

To this climactic interrogation the wily rogue now flew.

Geisen turned away from the monotonous video on his diary and asked Ailoura a question he had long contemplated but always forborne from voicing.

"Ailoura, what can you tell me of my mother?"

The cat-woman assumed a reflective expression that cloaked more emotions than it revealed. Her whiskers twitched. "Why do you ask such an irrelevant question at this crucial juncture, Gei-gei?"

"I don't know. I've often pondered the matter. Maybe I'm fearful that if our plan explodes in our faces, this might be my final opportunity to learn anything."

Ailoura paused a long while before answering. "I was intimately familiar with the one who bore you. I think her intentions were honorable. I know she loved you dearly. She always wanted to make herself known to you, but circumstances beyond her control did not permit such an honest relationship."

Geisen contemplated this information. Something told him he would get no more from the close-mouthed bestient.

To disrupt the solemn mood, Ailoura reached over to ruffle Geisen's hair. "Enough of the useless past. Didn't anyone ever tell you that curiosity killed the cat? Now, pay attention! Our Judas goat has landed—"

Ursine yet doughy, unctuous yet fleering, Grafton clapped Bozzarias' shoulder heartily and ushered the foppish man to a seat in Vomacht's study. Behind the dead padrone's desk sat his widow, Woda, all motile maquillage and mimicked mourning. Her teeth sported a fashionable gilt. Gitten lounged on the arm of a sofa, plainly bored and resentful, toying with a handheld hologame like some sullen adolescent.

After offering drinks—Bozzarias requested and received the finest vintage of sparkling wine available on Chalk—Grafton drove straight to the heart of the matter.

"Gep Bozzarias, I demand to know why Stoessl House has been denied a chance to bid on the Carrabas estate."

Bozzarias drained his glass and dabbed at his lips with his jabot before replying. "The reason is simple, Gep Stoessl, yet of such delicacy that you would not have cared to have me state it before your peers. Thus this private encounter."

"Go on."

"My employer, Timor Carrabas, you must learn, is a man of punctilio and politesse. Having abandoned Chalk many generations ago, Carrabas House still honors and maintains the old ways prevalent during that golden age. They have not fallen into the lax and immoral fashions of the present, and absolutely contemn such behavior."

Grafton stiffened. "To what do you refer? Stoessl House is guilty of no such infringements on custom."

"That is not how my employer perceives affairs. After all, what is the very first thing he hears upon returning to his ancestral homeworld? Disturbing rumors of patricide, fraternal infighting, and excommunication, all of which emanate from Stoessl House and Stoessl House alone. Leery of stepping beneath the shadow of such a cloud, he could not ethically undertake any dealings with your clan."

Fuming, Grafton started to rebut these charges, but Woda intervened. "Gep Bozzarias, all mandated investigations into the death of my beloved Vomacht resulted in one uncontested conclusion: pump failure produced a kind of alien hyperglycemia that drove the Stroonians insane. No human culpability or intent to harm was ever established."

Bozzarias held his glass up for a refill and obtained one. "Why, then, were all the bestient witnesses to the incident terminally disposed of? What motivated the abdication of your youngest scion? Giger, I believe he was named?"

Trying to be helpful, Gitten jumped into the conversation. "Oh, we use up bestients at a frightful rate! If they're not dying from floggings, they're collapsing from overuse in the mines and brothels. Such a flawed product line, these moreauvians. Why, if they were robots, they'd never pass consumer-lab testing. As for Geisen—that's the boy's name—well, he simply got fed up with our civilized lifestyle. He always did prefer the barbaric outback existence. No doubt he's enjoying himself right now, wallowing in some muddy oasis with a sandworm concubine."

Grafton cut off his brother's tittering with a savage glance. "Gep Bozzarias, I'm certain that if your employer were to meet us, he'd find we are worthy of making an offer on his properties. In fact, he could avoid all the fuss and bother of a full-fledged auction, since I'm prepared right now to trump the highest bid he's yet received. Will you convey to him my invitation to enjoy the hospitality of Stoessl House?"

Bozzarias closed his eyes ruminatively, as if harkening to some inner voice of conscience, then answered, "Yes, I can do that much. And with some small encouragement, I would exert all my powers of persuasiveness—"

Woda spoke. "Why, where did this small but heavy bag of Tancredi moonstones come from? It certainly doesn't belong to us. Gep Bozzarias—would you do me the immense favor of tracking down the rightful owner of these misplaced gems?"

Bozzarias stood and bowed, then accepted the bribe. "My pleasure, madame. I can practically guarantee that Stoessl House will soon receive its just reward."

"Sandworm concubine!" Geisen appeared ready to hurl his eavesdropping device to the hard floor, but restrained himself. "How I'd like to smash their lying mouths in!"

Ailoura grinned. "You must show more restraint than that, Geisen, especially when you come face-to-face with the scoundrels. Take consolation from the fact that mere physical retribution would hurt them far less than the loss of money and face we will inflict."

"Still, there's a certain satisfaction in feeling the impact of fist on flesh."

"My kind calls it 'the joy when teeth meet bone,' so I fully comprehend. Just not this time. Understood?"

Geisen impulsively hugged the old cat. "Still teaching me, Ailoura?"

"Until I die, I suppose."

"You are appallingly obese, Geisen. Your form recalls nothing of the slim blade who cut such wide swaths among the girls of the various Houses before his engagement."

"And your polecat coloration, fair Ailoura, along with those tinted lenses and tooth caps, speak not of a bold mouser, but of a scavenger through garbage tips."

Regarding each other with satisfaction, Ailoura and Geisen thus approved of their disguises.

With the aid of Bozzarias, who had purchased for them various sophisticated, semiliving prosthetics, dyes, and off-world clothing, the man and his servant—Timor Carrabas and Hepzibah—resembled no one ever seen before on Chalk. His pasty face rouged, Geisen wobbled as he waddled, breathing stertorously, while the limping Ailoura diffused a moderately repulsive scent calculated to keep the curious at a certain remove.

The Carrabas marchwarden now spoke, a touch of excitement in its artificial voice. "I have just notified my Stoessl House counterpart that you are departing within the hour. You will be expected in time for essences and banquet, with a half hour allotted to freshen up and settle into your guest rooms."

"Very good. Rehearse the rest of the plan for me."

"Once the funds are transferred from Stoessl House to me, I will in turn upload them to the Bourse on Feuilles Mortes under the name of Geisen Stoessl, where they will be immune from attachment. I will then retreat to my soulcanister, readying it for removal by your agent, Bozzarias, who will bring it to the space field—specifically the terminal hosting Gravkosmos Interstellar. Beyond that point, I cannot be of service until I am haptically enabled once more."

"You have the scheme perfectly. Now we thank you,

and leave with the promise that we shall talk again in the near future, in a more pleasant place."

"Good-bye, Gep Carrabas, and good luck."

Within a short time the hired zipflyte arrived. (It would hardly do for the eminent Timor Carrabas to appear in Geisen's battered craft, which had, in point of fact, already been sold to raise additional funds to aid their subterfuge.) After clambering clumsily on board, the schemers settled themselves in the spacious rear seat while the chauffeur—a neat-plumaged and discreet raptor-derived bestient—lifted off and flew at a swift clip toward Stoessl House.

Ailoura's comment about Geisen's attractiveness to his female peers had set an unhealed sore spot within him aching. "Do you imagine, Hepzibah, that other local luminaries might attend this evening's dinner party? I had in mind a certain Gep Bloedwyn Vermeule."

"I suspect she will. The Stoessls and the Vermeules have bonds and alliances dating back centuries."

Geisen mused dreamily. "I wonder if she will be as beautiful and sensitive and angelic as I have heard tell she is."

Ailoura began to hack from deep in her throat. Recovering, she apologized, "Excuse me, Gep Carrabas. Something unpleasant in my throat. No doubt a simple hairball."

Geisen did not look amused. "You cannot deny reports of the lady's beauty, Hepzibah."

"Beauty is as beauty does, master."

The largest ballroom in Stoessl House had been extravagantly bedecked for the arrival of Timor Carrabas. Living luminescent lianas in dozens of neon tones festooned the heavy-beamed rafters. Decorator dust migrated invisibly about the chamber, cohering at random into wallscreens showing various entertaining videos from the mediapoietic worlds. Responsive carpets the texture of moss crept warily along the tessellated floor, consuming any spilled food and drink wasted from the large collation spread out across a servitor-staffed table long as a playing field. (House chef Stine Pursiful oversaw all with a meticulous eye, his upraised ladle serving as baton of command. After some argument among the family members and chef, a buffet had been chosen over a sit-down meal, as being more informal, relaxed, and conducive to easy dealings.) The floor space was thronged with over a hundred gaily caparisoned representatives of the Houses most closely allied to the Stoessls, some dancing in stately pavanes to the music from the throats of the octet of avian bestients perched on their multibranched stand. But despite the many diversions of music, food, drink, and chatter, all eyes had strayed ineluctably to the form of the mysterious Timor Carrabas when he entered, and from time to time thereafter.

Beneath his prosthetics, Geisen now sweated copiously, both from nervousness and the heat. Luckily, his disguising adjuncts quite capably metabolized this betraying moisture before it ever reached his clothing.

The initial meeting with his brothers and stepmother had gone well. Hands were shaken all around without anyone suspecting that the flabby hand of Timor Carrabas concealed a slimmer one that ached to deliver vengeful blows.

Geisen could see immediately that since Vomacht's death, Grafton had easily assumed the role of head of household, with Woda patently the power behind the throne and Gitten content to act the wastrel princeling.

"So, Gep Carrabas," Grafton oleaginously purred, "now you finally perceive with your own eyes that we Stoessls are no monsters. It's never wise to give gossip any credence."

Gitten said, "But gossip is the only kind of talk that makes life worth liv—oof!"

Woda took a second step forward, relieving the painful pressure she had inflicted on her younger son's foot. "Excuse my clumsiness, Gep Carrabas, in my eagerness to enhance my proximity to a living reminder of the fine old ways of Chalk. I'm sure you can teach us much about how our forefathers lived. Despite personal longevity, we have lost the institutional rigor your clan has reputedly preserved."

In his device-modulated, rather fulsome voice, Geisen answered, "I am always happy to share my treasures with others, be they spiritual or material."

Grafton brightened. "This expansiveness bodes well for our later negotiations, Gep Carrabas. I must say that your attitude is not exactly as your servant Bozzarias conveyed."

Geisen made a dismissive wave. "Simply a local hireling who was not truly privy to my thoughts. But he has the virtue of following my bidding without the need to know any of my ulterior motivations." Geisen felt relieved to have planted that line to protect Bozzarias in the nasty wake of the successful conclusion of their thimblerigging. "Here is my real counselor. Hepzibah, step forward."

Ailoura moved within the circle of speakers, her unnaturally flared and pungent striped musteline tail waving perilously close to the humans. "At your service, Gep."

The Stoessls involuntarily cringed away from the unpleasant odor wafting from Ailoura, then restrained their impolite reaction.

"Ah, quite an, ah, impressive moreauvian. Positively, um, redolent of the ribosartor's art. Perhaps your, erm, adviser would care to dine with others of her kind."

"Hepzibah, you are dismissed until I need you."

"As you wish."

Soon Geisen was swept up in a round of introductions to people he had known all his life. Eventually he reached the food, and fell to eating rather too greedily. After weeks spent subsisting on MREs alone, he could hardly restrain himself. And his glutton's disguise allowed all excess. Let the other guests gape at his immoderate behavior. They were constrained by their own greed for his putative fortune from saying a word.

After satisfying his hunger, Geisen finally looked up from his empty plate.

There stood Bloedwyn Vermeule.

Geisen's ex-fiancée had never shone more alluringly. Threaded with invisible flexing pseudo-myofibrils, her long unfettered hair waved in continual delicate movement, as if she were a mermaid underwater. She wore a gown tonight loomed from golden spider silk. Her lips were verdigris, matched by her nails and eye shadow.

Geisen hastily dabbed at his own lips with his napkin, and was mortified to see the clean cloth come away with enough stains to represent a child's immoderate battle with an entire chocolate cake.

"Oh, Gep Carrabas, I hope I am not interrupting your gustatory pleasures."

"Nuh—no, young lady, not at all. I am fully sated. And you are?"

"Gep Bloedwyn Vermeule. You may call me by my first name, if you grant me the same privilege."

"But naturally."

"May I offer an alternative pleasure, Timor, in the form of a dance? Assuming your satiation does not extend to *all* recreations."

"Certainly. If you'll make allowances in advance for my clumsiness."

Bloedwyn allowed the tip of her tongue delicately to traverse her patinaed lips. "As the Dompatta says, 'An earnest rider compensates for a balky steed.'"

This bit of familiar gospel had never sounded so lascivious. Geisen was shocked at this unexpected temptress behavior from his ex-fiancée. But before he could react with real or mock indignation, Bloedwyn had whirled him out onto the floor.

They essayed several complicated dances before Geisen, pleading fatigue, could convince his partner to call a halt to the activity.

"Let us recover ourselves in solitude on the terrace," Bloedwyn said, and conducted Geisen by the arm through a pressure curtain and onto an unlit open-air patio. Alone in the shadows, they took up positions braced against a balustrade. The view of the moon-drenched arroyos below occupied them in silence for a time. Then Bloedwyn spoke huskily.

"You exude a foreign, experienced sensuality, Timor, to which I find myself vulnerable. Perhaps you would indulge my weakness with an assignation tonight, in a private chamber of Stoessl House known to me? After any important business dealings are successfully concluded, of course."

Geisen seethed inwardly, but managed to control his voice. "I am flattered that you find a seasoned fellow of my girth so attractive, Bloedwyn. But I do not wish to cause any intermural incidents. Surely you are affianced to someone, a young lad both bold and wiry, jealous and strong."

"Pah! I do not care for young men, they are all chowderheads! Pawing, puling, insensitive, shallow, and vain, to a man! I was betrothed to one such, but luckily he revealed his true colors and I was able to cast him aside like the churl he proved to be."

Now Geisen felt only miserable self-pity. He could summon no words, and Bloedwyn took his silence for assent. She planted a kiss on his cheek, then whispered directly into his ear. "Here's a map to the boudoir where I'll be waiting. Simply take the east squeezer down three levels, then follow the hot dust." She pressed a slip of paper into his hand, supplementing her message with extra pressure in his palm, then sashayed away like a tainted sylph.

Geisen spent half an hour with his mind roiling before he regained the confidence to return to the party.

Before too long, Grafton corralled him.

"Are you enjoying yourself, Timor? The food agrees? The essences elevate? The ladies are pliant? Haw! But perhaps we should turn our minds to business now, before we both grow too muzzy-headed. After conducting our dull commerce, we can cut loose."

"I am ready. Let me summon my aide."

"That skun—That is, if you absolutely insist. But surely our marchwarden can offer any support services you need. Notarization, citation of past deeds, and so forth."

"No. I rely on Hepzibah implicitly."

Grafton partially suppressed a frown. "Very well, then."

Once Ailoura arrived from the servants' table, the trio headed toward Vomacht's old study. Geisen had to remind himself not to turn down any "unknown" corridor before Grafton himself did.

Seated in the very room where he had been fleeced of his patrimony and threatened with false charges of murder, Geisen listened with half an ear while Grafton outlined the terms of the prospective sale: all the Carrabas properties and whatever wealth of strangelets they contained, in exchange for a sum greater than the Gross Plantetary Product of many smaller worlds.

Ailoura attended more carefully to the contract, even pointing out to Geisen a buried clause that would have made payment contingent on the first month's production from the new fields. After some arguing, the conspirators succeeded in having the objectionable codicil removed. The transfer of funds would be complete and instantaneous.

When Grafton had finally finished explaining the conditions, Geisen roused himself. He found it easy to sound bored with the whole deal, since his elaborate scam, at its moment of triumph, afforded him surprisingly little vengeful pleasure.

"All the details seem perfectly managed, Gep Stoessl, with that one small change of ours included. I have but one question. How do I know that the black sheep of your House, Geisen, will not contest our agreement? He seems a contrary sort, from what I've heard, and I would hate to be involved in judicial proceedings, should he get a whim in his head."

Grafton settled back in his chair with a broad smile.

"Fear not, Timor! That wild hair will get up no one's arse! Geisen has been effectively rendered powerless. As was only proper and correct, I assure you, for he was not a true Stoessl at all."

Geisen's heart skipped a cycle. "Oh? How so?"

"The lad was a chimera! A product of the ribosartors! Old Vomacht was unsatisfied with the vagaries of honest mating that had produced Gitten and myself from the noble stock of our mother. Traditional methods of reproduction had not delivered him a suitable toady. So he resolved to craft a better heir. He used most of his own germ plasm as foundation, but supplemented his nucleotides with dozens of other snippets. Why, that hybrid boy even carried bestient genes. Rat and weasel, I'm willing to bet! Haw! No, Geisen had no place in our family."

"And his mother?"

"Once the egg was crafted and fertilized, Vomacht implanted it in a host bitch. One of our own bestients. I misapprehend her name now, after all these years. Amorica, Orella, something of that nature. I never really paid attention to her fate after she delivered her human whelp. I have more important properties to look after. No doubt she ended up on the offal heap, like all the rest of her kind."

A red curtain drifting across Geisen's vision failed to occlude the shape of the massive aurochs-flaying blade hanging on the wall. One swift leap and it would be in his hands. Then Grafton would know sweet murderous pain, and Geisen's bitter heart would applaud—

Standing beside Geisen, Ailoura let slip the quietest cough.

Geisen looked into her face.

A lone tear crept from the corner of one feline eye.

Geisen gathered himself and stood up, unspeaking.

Grafton grew a trifle alarmed. "Is there anything the matter, Gep Carrabas?"

"No, Gep Stoessl, not at all. Merely that old hurts pain me, and I would fain relieve them. Let us close our deal. I am content."

The star liner carrying Geisen, Ailoura, and the stasis-bound Carrabas marchwarden to a new life sped through the interstices of the cosmos, powered perhaps by a strangelet mined from Stoessl lands. In one of the lounges, the man and his cat nursed drinks and snacks, admiring the exotic variety of their fellow passengers and reveling in their hard-won liberty and security.

"Where from here—son?" asked Ailoura with a hint of unwonted shyness.

Geisen smiled. "Why, wherever we wish, Mother dear."

"Rowr! A world with plenty of fish, then, for me!"

"Mr. Gaunt"
John Langan

I

It was not until five weeks after his father's funeral that Henry Farange was able to remove the white plastic milk crate containing the old man's final effects from the garage. His reticence was a surprise: his father had been sick—dying, really—for the better part of two years and Henry had known it, had known of the enlarged heart, the failing kidneys, the brain jolted by mini-strokes. He had known it was, in the nursing home doctor's favorite cliché, only a matter of time, and if there were moments Henry could not believe the old man had held on for as long or as well as he had, that didn't mean he expected his father to walk out of the institution to which his steadily declining health had consigned him. For all that, the inevitable phone call, the one telling him that his father had suffered what appeared to be a heart attack, caught him off guard, and when his father's nurse had approached him at the gravesite, her short arms cradling the milk crate into which the few items the old man had taken with him to the nursing home had been deposited, Henry's chest had tightened, his eyes filled with burning tears. Upon his return home from the post-funeral brunch, he had removed the crate from his back seat and carried it into the garage,

299

where he set it atop his workbench, telling himself he couldn't face what it contained today, but would see to it tomorrow.

Tomorrow, though, turned into the day after tomorrow, which became the day after that, and then the following day, and so on, until a two-week period passed during which Henry didn't think of the white plastic milk crate at all, and was only reminded of it when a broken cabinet hinge necessitated his sliding up the garage door. The sight of the milk crate was a reproach, and in a sudden burst of repentance he rushed up to it, hauled it off the workbench, and ran into the house with it as if it were a pot of boiling water and he without gloves. He half-dropped it onto the kitchen table and stood over it, panting. Now that he let his gaze wander over the crate's contents, he could see that it was not as full as he had feared. A dozen hardcover books: his father's favorite Henry James novels, which, he had claimed, were all that he wanted to read in his remaining time. Henry lifted them from the crate one by one, glancing at their titles. *The Ambassadors. The Wings of the Dove. The Golden Bowl. The Turn of the Screw. What Maisie Knew.* He recognized that last one: the old man had tried twice to convince him to read it, sending him a copy when he was at college, and again a couple of years ago, a month or two before the old man entered the nursing home. It was his father's favorite book of his favorite writer, and, although he was no English scholar, Henry had done his best, both times, to read it. But he rapidly became lost in the labyrinth of the book's prose, in sentences that wound on for what felt like days, so that by the time you arrived at the end, you had forgotten the beginning and had to start over again. He hadn't finished *What Maisie Knew*, had given up the attempt after Chapter One the first time, Chapter Three the second, and had had to admit his failures to his father. He had blamed his failures on other obligations, on school and work, promising he would give the book another try when he was less busy. He might make good his promise yet: there might be a third attempt, possibly even success, but when he was done, his father would not be waiting to discuss it with him. Henry removed the rest of the books from the crate rapidly.

Here was a framed photo of Henry receiving his MBA, a smaller black and white picture of a man and woman he recognized as his grandparents tucked into its lower right corner. Here was a gray cardboard shoebox filled with assorted snapshots that appeared to stretch back over his father's lifetime, as well as four old letters folded in their original envelopes. Here was a postcard showing the view up the High Street to Edinburgh Castle. Here was the undersized saltire, the blue and white flag of Scotland, he had bought for his father when he had stopped off for a weekend in Edinburgh on his way home from Frankfurt, just last summer. Here was a cassette tape wrapped in a piece of ruled notebook paper bound to it by a thick rubber band, his name written on the paper in his father's rolling hand.

His heart leapt, and Henry slid the rubber band from around the paper with fingers suddenly dumb. There was more writing on the other side of the paper, a brief note. He read, "Dear Son, I'm making this tape *just in case*. Listen to *it as soon as possible*. It's all true. Love, Dad." That was all. He turned the tape over: it was plain and black, no label on either side.

Leaving the note on the table, he carried the tape into the living room, to the stereo. He slid the tape into the deck, pushed PLAY, adjusted the volume, and stood back, arms crossed.

For a moment, there was only the hum of blank tape, then a loud snap and clatter and the sound of his father's voice, low, resonant, and slightly graveled, the way it sounded when he was tired. His father said, "I think I have this thing working. Yes, that's it." He cleared his throat. "Hello, Henry, it's your father. If you're listening to this, then I'm gone. I realize this may seem strange, but there are facts of which you need to be aware, and I'm concerned I don't have much time to tell you them. I've tried to write it all down for you, but my hand's shaking so badly I can't make any progress. To tell the truth, I don't know if the matter's sufficiently clear in my head for me to write it. So, I've borrowed this machine from the night-duty nurse. I suppose I should have told you all this—oh, years ago, but I didn't, because—well, let's get to what I have to say first. I can fill in my motivations along the way. I hope you have the time to listen to this all at once, because I don't think it'll make much sense in bits and pieces. I'm not sure it makes much sense all together.

"The other night, I saw your uncle on television: not David, your mother's brother, but George, my brother. I'm sure you won't remember him: the last and only time you saw him, you were four. I saw him, and I saw his butler. You know how little I sleep these days, no matter, it seems, how tired I am. Much of the time between sunset and sunrise I pass read-ing—re-reading James, and watching more television than I should. Last night, unable to concentrate on

"MR. GAUNT"

What Maisie Knew any longer, I found myself watching a documentary about Edinburgh on public television. If I watch PBS, I can convince myself I'm being mildly virtuous, and I was eager to see one of my favorite cities, if only on the screen. It's the city my parents came from; I know you know that. Sadly, the documentary was a failure, so spectacularly insipid that it almost succeeded in delivering me to sleep a good three hours ahead of schedule. Then I saw George walk across the screen. The shot was of Prince's Street during the Edinburgh festival. The street was crowded, but I recognized my brother. He was slightly stooped, his hair and beard bone-white, though his step was still lively. He was followed by his butler, who stood as tall and unbending as ever. Just as he was about to walk off the screen, George stopped, turned his head to the camera, and winked, slowly and deliberately.

"From the edge of sleep, I was wide awake, filled with such fear my shaking hands fumbled the remote control onto the floor. I couldn't muster the courage to retrieve it, and it lay there until the morning nurse picked it up. I didn't sleep: I couldn't. Your uncle kept walking across that screen, his butler close behind. Though I hadn't heard the news of his death, I had assumed he must be gone by now. More than assumed: I had hoped it. I should have guessed, however, that George would not have slipped so gently into that good night; indeed, although he's just this side of ninety, I now suspect he'll be around for quite some time to come.

"Seeing him—does it sound too mad to say that I half-think he saw me? More than half-think: I know he saw me. Seeing my not-dead older brother walk

303

across the screen, to say nothing of his butler, I became obsessed with the thought of you. Your uncle may try to contact you, especially once I'm gone, which I have the most unreasonable premonition may be sooner rather than later. Before he does, you must know about him. You must know who, and what, he is. You must know his history, and you must know about his butler, about that...monster. For reasons you'll understand later, I can't simply tell you what I have to tell you, or perhaps I should say I can't tell you what I have to tell you simply. If I were to come right out with it in two sentences, you wouldn't believe me; you'd think I had suffered one TIA too many. I can't warn you to stay away from your uncle and leave it at that: I know you, and I know the effect such prohibitions have on you; I've no desire to arouse your famous curiosity. So I'm going to ask you to bear with me, to let me tell you about my brother in what I think is the manner best suited to it. Indulge me, Henry, indulge your old father."

Henry paused the tape. He walked out of the living room back into the kitchen, where he rummaged the refrigerator for a beer while his father's words echoed in his ears. The old man knew him, all right: his "famous" curiosity was aroused, enough that he would sit down and listen to the rest of the tape now, in one sitting. His dinner date was not for another hour and a half, and, even if he were a few minutes late, that wouldn't be a problem. He smiled, thinking that despite his father's protestations of fear, once the old man warmed up to talking, you could hear the James scholar taking over, his words, his phrasing, his sentences, bearing subtle witness to a lifetime spent with the writer he had called "the Master." Henry pried the cap off the beer, checked to be sure the answering machine was on, switched the phone's ringer off, and returned to the living room, where he released the PAUSE button and settled himself on the couch.

His father's voice returned.

II

Once upon a time, there was a boy who lived with his father and his father's butler in a very large house. As the boy's father was frequently away, and often for long periods of time, he was left alone in the large house with the butler, whose name was Mr. Gaunt. While he was away, the boy's father allowed him to roam through every room in the house except one. He could run through the kitchen; he could bounce on his father's bed; he could leap from the tall chairs in the living room. But he must never, ever, under any circumstances, go into his father's study. His father was most insistent on this point. If the boy entered the study...hisfather refused to say what would happen, but the tone of his voice and the look on his face hinted that it would be something terrible.

That was how the story used to begin, as if it were a fairy tale that someone else had written and I just happened to remember. I suppose it sounds generic enough: the traditional, almost incantatory, beginning; the nondescript boy, father, butler, and house. Do you remember the first time I told it to you? I don't imagine so: you were five, although you were precocious, which was what necessitated the tale in the first place. You were staying with me for the summer—your mother and her second husband were in Greece—in the house in Highland. That house! All those rooms, the high ceilings, the porch with its view of the Hudson: how I wish you didn't have to sell it to afford the cost of putting me in this place. I had hoped you might choose to live there. Ah well, as you yourself said, what use is a house of that size to you, with no wife or family? Another regret....

But I was talking about the story, and the first time you heard it. Like some second-rate Bluebeard, I had permitted you free access to every room in the house save one: my study, which contained not the head of my previous wife (if only! Sorry, I know she's your mother), but extensive notes, four years' worth of notes toward the book I was about to write on Henry James's portrayal of family relations. Yes, yes, I should have known that declaring it forbidden would only pique your interest; it's one of those mistakes you not only can't believe you made, but that seems so fundamentally obvious you doubt whether in fact it occurred. The room was kept locked when I wasn't working in it, and I believed it secure. All this time later, I have yet to discover how you broke into it. I can see you sitting in the middle of the hardwood floor, four years' work scattered and shredded around you, a look of the most intense concentration upon your face as you dragged a pen across my first edition of *The Wings of the Dove*. I'm not sure how, but I remained calm, if not quite cheerful, as I escorted you from my study up the stairs to your bedroom. I sat you on the bed and told you I had a story for you. You were very excited: you loved it when I told you stories. Was it another one about Hercules? No, it wasn't; it was another kind of story. It was the story of a little boy just about your age, a little boy who had opened a door he was not supposed to.

Then and there, my brain racing, I told you the

story of Mr. Gaunt and his terrible secret, speaking
slowly, deliberately, so that I would have time to
shape the next event. Does it surprise you to hear that
the story has no written antecedent? It became such
a part of our lives after that. It frightened you out of
my study for the rest of that summer; you avoided
that entire side of the house. Then the next summer,
when your friend Brad came to stay for the weekend
and the three of us stayed up late while I told you
stories, you actually requested it. "Tell about Mr.
Gaunt," you said. I can't tell you how shocked I was.
I was shocked that you remembered: children forget
much, and it's difficult to predict what will lodge in
their minds; plus you had been with your mother and
husband number two without interruption for almost
nine months. I was shocked, too, that you would
want to hear a narrative expressly crafted to frighten
you. It frightened poor Brad; we had to leave the light
on for him, which you treated with a bit more con-
tempt than really was fair.

After that: how many times did I tell you that story?
Several that same summer, and several every summer
for the next six or seven years. Even when you were
a teenager, and grew your hair long and refused to
remove that denim jacket that you wore down to an
indistinct shade of pale, even then you requested the
story, albeit with less frequency. It's never gone that
far from us, has it? At dinner, the visit before last, we
talked about it. Strange that in all this time you never
asked me how I came by it, in what volume I first
read it. Perhaps you're used to my having an esoteric
source for everything and assume this to be the case
here. Or perhaps you don't want to know: you find
it adds to the story not to know its origin. Or perhaps
you're just not interested: literary scholarship never

has been your strong point. That's not a reproach: investment banking has been very good for and to you, and you know how proud I am of you.

There is more to the story, though: there is more to every story. You can always work your way down, peel back the layers till you discover, as it were, the skull beneath the skin. Whatever you thought about the story's roots, whatever you would answer if I were to ask you where you thought I had plucked it from, I'm sure you never guessed that it grew out of an event that occurred in our family. That *donnée*, as James would've called it, involved George, George and his butler and Peter, George's son and your cousin. Yes, you haven't heard of Peter before: I haven't ever mentioned his name to you. He's been dead a long time now.

You met George when you were four, at the house in Highland. I had just moved into it from the apartment in Huguenot I occupied after your mother and I separated. George was in Manhattan for a couple of days, doing research at one of the museums, and took the train up to spend the afternoon with us. He was short, stocky verging on portly, and he kept his beard trimmed in a Vandyke, which combined with his deep-set eyes and sharp nose leant him rather a Satanic appearance: the effect, I'm sure, intended. He wore a vest and a pocket watch with which you were fascinated, not having seen a pocket watch before. Throughout the afternoon and into the evening, you kept asking George what time it was. He responded to each question by slowly withdrawing the watch from his pocket by its chain, popping open its cover, carefully scrutinizing its face, and announcing, "Why, Hank," (he insisted on calling you Hank; he appeared to find it most amusing), "it's three o'clock." He was patient with you; I will grant him that.

After I put you to bed, he and I sat on the back porch looking at the Hudson, drinking Scotch, and talking, the end result of which was that he made a confession—confession! it was more of a boast!—and I demanded he leave the house, leave it then and there and never return, never speak to me or communicate in any way with me again. He didn't believe I was serious, but he went. I've no idea how or if he made his train. I haven't heard from him since, all these years, nor have I have heard of him, until last night.

But this is all out of order. You don't know anything about your uncle. I've been careful not to mention his name lest I arouse that curiosity of yours. Indeed, maybe I shouldn't be doing so now. That's assuming, of course, that you'll take any of the story I'm going to relate seriously, that you won't think I've confused my Henry James with M.R. James, or, worse, think it a sign of mental or emotional decay, the first hint of senility or depression. The more I insist on the truth of what I tell, the more shrill and empty my voice will sound; I know the scenario well. I risk, then, a story that might be taken as little more than a prolonged symptom of mental impairment or illness; though really, how interesting is that? In any event, it's not as if I have to worry about you putting me in a home. Yes, I know you had no choice. Let's start with the background, the condensed information the author delivers, after an interesting opening, in one or two well-written chapters.

George was ten years older than I, the child of what in those days was considered our parents' middle age, as I was the child of their old age. This is to say that Mother was thirty-five when George was born, and forty-five when I was. Father was close to fifty at my birth, about the same age I was when you were born. Funny—as a boy and a young man, I used to swear that, if I were to have children, I would not wait until I was old enough to be their grandfather, and despite those vows that was exactly what I did. Do you suppose that's why you haven't married yet? We like to think we're masters of our own fates, but the fact is, our parents' examples exert far more influence on us than we realize or are prepared to realize. I like to think I was a much more youthful father to you than my father was to me, but in all fairness, fifty was a different age for me than it was for him. For me, fifty was the age of my maturity, a time of ripeness, a balance point between youth and old age; for Father, fifty was a room with an unsettlingly clear view of the grave. He died when I was fifteen, you know, while here I am, thanks to a daily assortment of colored pills, closer to eighty than anyone in my family before me, with the exception, of course, of my brother.

I have few childhood memories of George: an unusually intelligent student, he left the house and the country for Oxford at the age of fifteen. Particularly gifted in foreign languages, he achieved minor fame for his translation and commentary on *Les mystères du ver*, a fifteenth-century French translation of a much older Latin work. England suited him well; he returned to see us in Poughkeepsie infrequently. He did, however, visit our parents' brothers and sisters, our uncles and aunts, in and around Edinburgh on holidays, which appeared to mollify Father and Mother. (Their trips back to Scotland were fewer than George's trips back to them.) My brother also voyaged to the Continent: France, first, which irritated Father (he was possessed by an almost pathological hatred of all things French, whose cause I never could discover, since our name is French; you can be sure, he would not have read my book on Flaubert); then Italy, which worried Mother (she was afraid the Catholics would have him); then beyond, on to those countries that for the greater part of my life were known as Yugoslavia: Croatia, Bosnia-Herzegovina, Serbia, and past them to the nations bordering the Black Sea. He made this trip and others like it, to Finland, to Turkey, to Persia as it was then called, often enough. I have no idea how he afforded any of it. Our parents sent him little enough money, and his scholarship was no source of wealth. I have no idea, either, of the purpose of these trips; when I asked him, George answered, "Research," and said no more. He wrote once a month, never more and occasionally less, short letters in which a single nugget of information was buried beneath layers of formality and pleasantry; not like those letters I wrote to you while you were at Harvard. It was in such a letter that he told us he was engaged to be married.

Aside from the fact that it lasted barely two years, the most remarkable thing about your uncle's marriage was your cousin, Peter, who was born seven months after it. Mother's face wore a suspicious frown for several days after the news of his birth reached us (I think it came by telegram; your grandparents were very late installing a phone); Father was too excited by the birth of his first grandson to care. I didn't feel much except a kind of disinterested curiosity. I was an uncle, but I was thirteen, so the role didn't have the significance for me it might have had I been only a few years older. The chances of my seeing my nephew any time in the near future were sufficiently slim to justify my reserve; as it happened, however, my brother and his wife, whose name was Clarissa, visited us the following summer with Peter. Clarissa was quite wealthy; she was also, I believe, quite a bit older than George, though by how much I couldn't say. Even now, after a lifetime's practice, I'm not much good at deciphering people's ages, which causes me no end of trouble, I can assure you. Their visit went smoothly enough, though your grandparents showed, I noticed, the razor edge of uneasiness with their new daughter-in-law's crisp accent and equally crisp manners. Your grandmother used her wedding china every night, while your grandfather, whose speech usually was peppered with Scots words and expressions, spoke what my mother used to call "the King's English." Their working class origins, I suspect, rising up to haunt them.

Peter was fat and blond, a pleasant child who appeared to enjoy his place on your grandmother's hip, which from the moment he arrived was where he spent most of his days. Any reservations Mother might have had concerning the circumstances of his birth were wiped away at the sight of him. When he returned from work, Father had a privileged place for his grandson on his knee: holding each of the baby's hands in his hands, Father sat Peter upright on his knee, then jiggled his leg up and down, bouncing Peter as if he were riding a horse, all the while singing a string of nonsense syllables: "a leedle lidel leedle lidel leedle lidel lum." It was something Father did with any baby who entered the house; he must have done it with me, and with George. I tried it with you, but you were less than amused by it. After what appeared to be some initial doubt at his grandfather's behavior, when he rode up and down with an almost tragic expression on his face, Peter quickly came to enjoy and even anticipate it, and when he saw his grandfather walk in the door, the baby's face would break into an enormous grin, and he waved his arms furiously. Clarissa was good with her son, handling him with more confidence than you might expect from a new mother; George largely ignored Peter, passing him to Clarissa, Mother, Father, or me whenever he could manage it. Much of his days George spent sequestered in his room, working, he said, on a new translation. Of what he did not specify, only that the book was very old, much older than *Les mysteères du ver*. He kept the door to the room locked, which I discovered, of course, trying to open it.

The three of them stayed a month, leaving with promises to write on both sides, and although it was more than a year later, it seemed the next thing anyone heard or knew Clarissa had filed for divorce. Your grandparents were stunned. They refused to tell me the grounds for Clarissa's action, but when I lay awake at night I heard them discussing it downstairs in the living room, their voices faint and indistinguishable except when one or the other of them became agitated and shouted, "It isn't true, for God's sake, it can't be true! We didn't raise him like that!" Clarissa sued for custody of Peter, and somewhat to our parents' surprise, I think, George countersued. It was not only that he did not appear possessed of sufficient funds; he did not appear possessed of sufficient interest. The litigation was interminable and bitter. Your grandfather died before it was through, struck dead in the street as we were walking back from Sunday services by a stroke whose cause, I was and am sure, was his elder son's divorce. George did not return for the funeral; he phoned to say it was absolutely impossible for him to attend—the case and all—he was sure Father would have understood. The divorce and custody battle were not settled for another year after that. When they were, George was triumphant.

I don't know if you remember the opening lines of *What Maisie Knew*. The book begins with a particularly messy divorce and custody fight, in which the father, though "bespattered from head to foot," initially succeeds. The reason, James tells us, is "not so much that the mother's character had been more absolutely damaged as that the brilliancy of a lady's complexion (and this lady's, in court, was immensely remarked) might be more regarded as showing the spots." I can recall reading those lines for the first time: I was a senior in high school, and a jolt of recognition shot up my spine as I recognized George and Clarissa, whose final blows against one another had been struck the previous fall. I think that's when I first had an inclination I might study old James. Unlike James's novel, in which the custody of Maisie is eventually divided between her parents, George won full possession of Peter, which he refused to share in the slightest way with Clarissa. I imagine she must have been devastated. George packed his and Peter's bags and moved north, to Edinburgh, where he purchased a large house on the High Street and engaged the services of a manservant, Mr. Gaunt.

Oh yes, Mr. Gaunt was an actual person. Are you surprised to hear that? I suppose he did seem rather a fantastic creation, didn't he? I can't think of him with anything less than complete revulsion, revulsion and fear, more fear than I wish I felt. I met him when I was in Edinburgh doing research on Stevenson and called on my brother, who had returned from the Shetlands that morning and was preparing to leave for Belgium later that same night. The butler was exactly as I described him to you in the story, only more so.

Mr. Gaunt never said a word. He was very tall, and very thin, and his skin was very white and very tight, as if he were wearing a suit that was too small. He had a long face and long, lank, thin, colorless hair, and a big, thick jaw, and tiny eyes that peered out at you from the deep caverns under his brows. He did not smile, but kept his mouth in a perpetual pucker. He wore a black coat with tails, a gray vest and gray pants, and a white shirt with a gray cravat. He was most quiet, and if you were standing in the kitchen or the living room and did not hear anything behind you, you could expect to turn around and find Mr. Gaunt standing there.

Mr. Gaunt served the meals, though he himself never ate that the boy saw, and escorted visitors to and from the boy's father when the boy's father was home, and, on nights when he was not home, Mr. Gaunt unlocked the door of the forbidden study at precisely nine o'clock and went into it, closing the door behind him. He remained there for an hour. The boy did not know what the butler did in that room, nor was he all that interested in finding out, but he was desperate for a look at his father's study.

Your uncle claimed to have contracted Gaunt's service during one of his many trips, and explained that the reason Gaunt never spoke was a thick accent—I believe George said it was Belgian—that marred his speech and caused him excruciating embarrassment. As Gaunt served us tea and shortbread,

I remember thinking that something about him suggested greed, deep and profound: his hands, whose movements were precise yet eager; his eyes, which remained fixed on the food, and us; his back, which was slightly bent, inclining him toward us but having the opposite effect, making him seem as if he were straining upright, resisting a powerful downward pull. No doubt it was the combination of these things. Whatever the source, I was noticeably glad to see him exit the room; although, after he had left, I had the distinct impression he was listening at the door, hunched down, still greedy.

As you must have guessed, the boy in our fairy tale was Peter, your cousin. He was fourteen when he had his run-in with Mr. Gaunt, older, perhaps, than you had imagined him; the children in fairy tales are always young children, aren't they? I should also say more about the large house in which he lived. It was a seventeenth-century mansion located on the High Street in Edinburgh, across the street and a few doors down from St. Giles's Cathedral. Its inhabitants had included John Jackson, a rather notorious character from the early nineteenth century. There's a mention of him in James's notebooks: he heard Jackson's story while out to dinner in Poughkeepsie, believe it or not, and considered treating it in a story before rejecting it as, "too lurid, too absolutely over the top." The popular legend, of whose origins I'm unsure, is that Jackson, a defrocked Anglican priest, had truck with infernal powers. Robed and hooded men were seen exiting his house who had not been seen entering it. Lights glowed in windows, strange cries and laughter sounded, late at night. A woman who claimed to have worked as Jackson's chambermaid swore there was a door to Hell in a room deep under the basement.

He was suspected in the vanishings of several local children, but nothing was proved against him. He died mysteriously, found, as I recall, at the foot of a flight of stairs, apparently having tumbled down them. His ghost, its neck still broken, was sighted walking in front of the house, looking over at St. Giles and grinning; about what, I've never heard.

Most of this information about the house I had from George during my visit; it was one of the few subjects about which I ever saw him enthused. I don't know how much if any of it your cousin knew; though I suspect his father would have told him all. Despite the picture its history conjures, the house was actually quite pleasant: five stories high including the attic, full of surprisingly large and well-lit rooms, decorated with a taste I wouldn't have believed George possessed. There was indeed a locked study: it comprised the entirety of the attic. I saw the great dark oaken door to it when your uncle took me on a tour of the house: we walked up the flight of stairs to the attic landing and there was the entrance to the study. George did not open it. I asked him if this was where he kept the bodies, and although he cheerfully replied that no, no, that was what the cellar was for, his eyes registered a momentary flash of something that was panic or annoyance. I did not ask him to open the door, in which there was a keyhole of sufficient diameter to afford a good look into the room beyond. Had my visit been longer, had I been his guest overnight, I might have stolen back up to that landing to peak at whatever it was my brother did not wish me to see. Curiosity, it would appear, does not just run in our family: it gallops.

Peter lived in this place, his father's locked secret above him, his only visitors his tutors, his only companion the silent butler. That's a bit much, isn't it? During our final conversation, George told me that Peter had been a friendless boy, but I doubt he knew his son well enough to render such a verdict with either accuracy or authority. Peter didn't know many, if any, other children, but I like to think of your cousin having friends in the various little shops that line the High Street. You know where I'm talking about, the cobbled street that runs in a straight line up to the Castle. You remember those little shops with their flimsy T-shirts, their campy postcards, their overpriced souvenirs. We bought the replica of the Castle that used to sit on the mantelpiece at one of them, along with a rather expensive pin for that girl you were involved with at the time. (What was her name? Jane?) I like to think of Peter, out for a walk, stopping in several shops along the way, chatting with the old men and women behind the counter when business was slow. He was a fine conversationalist for his age, your cousin.

I had met him again, you see, when he was thirteen, the year before the events I'm relating occurred. George was going to be away for the entire summer, so Peter came on his own to stay with your grandmother. I was living in Manhattan—actually, I was living in a cheap apartment across the river in New Jersey and taking the ferry to Manhattan each morning. My days I split teaching and writing my dissertation, which was on the then relatively fresh topic of James's later novels, particularly *The Golden Bowl*, and their modes of narration. Every other week, more often when I could manage it, I took the train up to your grandmother's to spend the day and have dinner with her. This was not as great a kindness as I would like it to seem: my social life was nonexistent, and I was desperately lonely. Thus, I visited Peter several times throughout June, July, and August.

At our first meeting he was unsure what to make of me, spending most of the meal silently staring down at his plate, and asking to be excused as soon as he had finished his dessert. Over subsequent visits, however, our relationship progressed. By our last dinner he was speaking with me freely, shaking my hand vigorously when it was time for me to leave for my bus and telling me that he had greatly enjoyed making my acquaintance. What did he look like? Funny: I don't think I have a picture of him; not from that visit, anyway. He wasn't especially tall; if he was due an adolescent growth-spurt, it had yet to arrive. His hair, while not the same gold color it had been when he was a baby, still was blond, slightly curled, and his eyes were dark brown. His face, well, as is true with all children, his face blended both his parents', although in his case the blend was particularly fine. What I mean is, unlike you, whose eyes and forehead have always been identifiably mine and whose nose and chin have always been identifiably your mother's, Peter's face, depending on the angle and lighting, appeared to be either all his father or all his mother. Even looking at him directly, you could see both faces simultaneously. He spoke with an Edinburgh accent, crisp and clear, and when he was excited or enthusiastic about a subject, his words would stretch out: "That's maaaarvelous." He told your grandmother her accent hadn't slipped in the least, and she smiled for the rest of the day.

He was extremely bright, and extremely interested in ancient Egypt, about which his father had provided him with several surprisingly good books. He could not decide whether to be a philologist, like his father, or an Egyptologist, which sounded more interesting; he inclined to Egyptology, but thought his father would appreciate him following his path. Surprising and heartbreaking—horrifying—as it seems in retrospect, Peter loved and missed his father. He was very proud of George: he knew of and appreciated George's translations, and confided in us his hope that one day he might achieve something comparable. "My father's a genius," I can hear him saying, almost defiantly. We were sitting at your grandmother's dining room table. I can't remember how we had arrived at the subject of George, but he went on, "Aye, a genius. None of his teachers were ever as smart as him. None of them could make head nor tail of *Les mystères duver*, and my father translated the whole thing, on his own. There was this one teacher who thought he was something, and he was pretty smart, but my father was smarter; he showed him."

"Of course he's smart, dear," your grandmother said. "He's a Farange. Just like you and your uncle."

"And your Granny," I said.

"Oh, go on, you," she said.

"He's translated things that no one's even heard of," Peter insisted. "He's translated pre-dynastic Egyptian writing. That's from before the pyramids, even. That's fifty-five centuries ago. Most folk don't even know it exists."

"Has he let you see any of it?" I asked.

"No," Peter said glumly. "He says I'm not ready yet. I have to master Latin and Greek before I can move on to just hieroglyphics."

"I'm sure you will," your grandmother said, and we moved on to some other topic. Later, after Peter was asleep, she said to me, "He's a lovely boy, our Peter, a lovely boy. So polite and well-mannered. But he seems awfully lonely to me. Always with his nose in a book: I don't think his father spends nearly enough time with him."

Peter did not speak of his mother.

He knew ancient Egypt as if he had lived in it: your grandmother and I spent more than one dinner listening to your cousin narrate such events as the building of the Great Pyramid of Giza, the factual accuracy of which I couldn't verify but whose telling kept me enthralled. Peter was a born *raconteur*: as he narrated his history, he would assume the voices of the different figures in it, from Pharaoh to slave. "The Great Pyramid," he would say, addressing the two of us as if we were a crowd at a lecture hall, "was built for the Pharaoh Khufu. The Greeks called him Cheops. He lived during the Fourth Dynasty, which was about four and half thousand years ago. The moment he became Pharaoh, Khufu started planning his pyramid, because, really, it was the most important thing he was ever going to build. The Egyptians were terribly concerned with death, and spent much of their lives preparing for it. He picked a site on the western bank of the Nile. The Egyptians thought the western bank was a special place because the sun set in the west. The west was the place of the dead, if you like, the right place to build your tomb. That's all it was, after all, a pyramid. Not that you'd know that from the name: it's a Greek word, 'pyramid;' it comes from 'wheat cake.' The Greeks thought the pyramids looked like giant pointy wheat cakes. We get a lot of names for Egyptian things from the Greeks: like 'pharaoh,' which they adapted from an Egyptian word that meant 'great house.' And 'sarcophagus,' that comes from the Greek for 'flesh-eating.' Why they called funeral vaults flesh-eaters I'll never know." And so on. He did love a good digression, your cousin: he would have made a fine college professor.

So you see, all this is why I dispute your uncle's claim that he was friendless, solitary: given the right set of circumstances, Peter could be positively garrulous. I have little trouble picturing him keeping the proprietor of a small bookshop, say, entertained with the story of the Pharaoh—I can't remember his name—who angered his people so that after his death his statues and monuments were destroyed and he was not buried in his own tomb; no one knew what had become of his body. No one knew what happened to his son either. I planned to take Peter to the Met, to see their Egyptian collection, but for reasons I can't recall we never went. At our final visit, he suggested we write. Initially, I demurred: I was buried in the last chapter of my dissertation, which I had expected to be forty pages I could write in a month but which rapidly had swelled to eighty-five pages that would consume my every waking moment for the next four months. We could write when I was finished, I explained. Peter pleaded with me, though, and in the end I agreed. We didn't write much, just four letters from him and three replies from me.

I found myself leafing through Peter's letters the winter after his visit, when your uncle telephoned your grandmother to inform her that your cousin was missing: he had run away from home and no one knew where he was. Your grandmother was distraught; I was, too, when she called me with the news of Peter's vanishing. She was upset at George, who apparently had shown only the faintest trace of emotion while delivering to her what she rightly regarded as terrible information. He was sure Peter would turn up, George said, boys will be boys and all that, what can you do? Lack of proper family feeling in anyone bothered your grandmother; it was her pet peeve; and she found it a particularly egregious fault in one of her own, raised to know better. "It's a good thing your father isn't alive to see this," she said to me, and I was unsure whether she referred to Peter's running away or George's understated reaction to it.

At the time, I suspected Peter might be making his way to his mother's, and went so far as to contact Clarissa myself, but if such was her son's plan she knew nothing about it. Through her manners I could hear the distress straining her voice, and another thing, a reserve I initially could not understand. Granted that speaking to your former brother-in-law is bound to be awkward, Clarissa's reticence was still in excess of any such awkwardness. Gradually, as we stumbled our way through a conversation composed of half-starts and long pauses, I understood that she was possessed by a mixture of fear and loathing: fear, because she suspected me of acting in concert with my brother to trick and trap her (though what more she had left to lose at that point I didn't and don't know; her pride, I suppose); loathing, because she thought that I was cut from the same cloth as George. Whatever George had done to prompt her to seek divorce a dozen years before, her memory and repugnance of it remained sufficiently fresh to make talking to me a considerable effort.

Peter didn't appear at his mother's, or any other relative's, nor did he return to his father's house. Against George's wishes, I'm sure, Clarissa involved the police almost immediately. Because of her social standing and the social standing of her family, I'm equally sure, they brought all their resources to bear on Peter's disappearance. The case achieved a notoriety that briefly extended across the Atlantic, scandalizing your grandmother; though I'm not aware that anyone ever connected George to us. Suspecting the worst, the police focused their attentions on George, bringing him in for repeated and intense questioning, investigating his trips abroad, ransacking his house. Strangely, in the midst of all this, Gaunt apparently went unnoticed. After subjecting George to close scrutiny for several weeks—which yielded no clue to where Peter might be or what might have happened to him—the detective in charge of the investigation fell dead of a heart attack while talking to your uncle on the telephone. As the man was no more than thirty, this was a surprise. His replacement was more kindly disposed to George, judging that he had undergone enough and concentrating the police's attentions elsewhere. Your cousin was not found; he was never found. Though your grandmother continued to hold out hope that he was alive until literally the day she died, thinking he might have found his way to Egypt, I didn't share her optimism, and reluctantly concluded that Peter had met his end.

I was correct, though I had no way of knowing how horrible that end had been. What happened to Peter took place while his father was out of the house; in Finland, he said. It was late winter, when Scotland has yet to free itself from its long nights and the sky is dark for much of the day. Peter had been living with his father's locked study for eleven years. So far as I know, he had shown no interest in the room in the past, which strikes me as a bit unusual, although I judge all other children's curiosity against yours, an unfair comparison. Perhaps George had told his own cautionary tale. There was no reason to expect Peter's interest to awaken at that moment, but it did. He became increasingly intrigued by that heavy door and what it concealed. I know this, you see, because it was in the first letter he sent to me, which arrived less than a month after his return home. He decided to confide in me, and I was flattered. Though he didn't write this to me, I believe he must have associated his father's study with those Egyptian tombs he'd been reading about; he must have convinced himself of a parallel between him entering that room and Howard Carter entering Tutankhamun's tomb. His father provided him a generous allowance, so I know he wasn't interested in money, as he himself was quick to reassure me in that same letter. He didn't want me to suspect his motives: he was after knowledge; he wanted to see what was hidden behind the dark door. Exactly how long that desire burned in him I can't say; he admitted that while he'd been wandering the woods behind your grandmother's house, he'd been envisioning himself walking through that room in his father's house, imagining its contents. He didn't specify what he thought those contents might be, and I wonder how accurate his imagination was. Did he picture the squat bookcases overstuffed with books, scrolls, and even stone tablets; the long tables heaped with goblets, boxes, candles, jars; the walls hung with paintings and drawings; the floor chalked with elaborate symbols? (I describe it well, don't I? I've seen it—but that must wait.)

It was with his second letter that Peter first disclosed his plans to satisfy his curiosity; plans I encouraged, if only mildly, when at last I sent him a reply. He would have to be careful, I wrote, if he were caught,

I had no doubt the consequences would be severe. I didn't believe they actually would be, but I enjoyed participating in what I knew was, for your cousin, a great adventure. I suggested that he take things in stages, that he try a brief trip up the attic stairs first and see how that went. What length of time was required for him to amass sufficient daring to venture the narrow flight of stairs to the attic landing I can't say. Perhaps he climbed a few of the warped, creaking stairs one day, before his nerve broke and he bolted down them back to his room; then a few more the next day; another the day after that; and so on, adding a stair or two a day until at last he stood at the landing. Or perhaps he rushed up the staircase all at once, his heart pounding, his stomach weak, taking the stairs two and three at a time, at the great dark door almost before he knew it. Having reached the landing, was he satisfied with his accomplishment? Or were his eyes drawn to the door, to the wide keyhole that offered a view of the room beyond? We hadn't discussed that: did it seem too much, a kind of quantum leap from what he had risked scaling the stairs? Or did it seem the next logical step: in for a penny, in for a pound, as it were? Once he stood outside the door, he couldn't have waited very long to lower his eye to the keyhole. When he did, his mouth dry, his hands shaking slightly, expecting to hear either his father or Mr. Gaunt behind him at every moment, he was disappointed: the windows in the room were heavily curtained, the lights extinguished, leaving it dim to the point of darkness on even the brightest day, the objects inside no more than confused shadows.

Peter boiled down all of this to two lines in his third letter, which I received inside a Christmas card. "I finally went to the door," he wrote, "and even looked in the keyhole! But everything was dark, and I couldn't see at all." Well, I suggested in my response, he would need to spy through the door when the study was occupied. Why not focus on Mr. Gaunt and his nine o'clock visitations? His father's returns home were too infrequent and erratic to be depended upon, and I judged the consequences of discovery by his father to be far in excess of those of discovery by the butler. (If I'd known....) Peter felt none of my unease around Mr. Gaunt, which was understandable, given that the butler had been a fixture in his home and life for more than a decade. In his fourth and final letter, Peter thanked me for my suggestion. He had been pondering a means to pilfer Gaunt's key to the room, only to decide that, for the moment, such an enterprise involved a degree of risk whatever was in the room might not be worth. I had the right idea: best to survey the attic clearly, then plan his next step. He would wait until his father was going to be away for a good couple of weeks, which wouldn't be until February. In the meantime, he was trying to decipher the sounds of Mr. Gaunt's nightly hour in the study: the two heavy clumps, the faint slithering, the staccato clicks like someone walking across the floor wearing tap shoes. I replied that it could be the butler was practicing his dancing, which I thought was much funnier at the time than I realize now it was, but that it seemed more likely what Peter was hearing was some sort of cleaning procedure. He should be careful, I wrote; obviously, the butler knew Peter wasn't supposed to be at the study, and if he caught him there, he might very well become quite upset, as George could hold him responsible for Peter's trespass.

I didn't hear from Peter again. For a time, I assumed this was because his enterprise had been discovered and he punished by his father. Then I thought it must be because he was burdened with too much schoolwork: the tutors his father had brought to the house for him, he had revealed in his second letter, were most demanding. I intended to write to him, to inquire after the status of our plan, but whenever I remembered my intention I was in the middle of something else that absolutely had to be finished and couldn't be interrupted, or so it seemed, and I never managed even to begin a letter. Then George called your grandmother, to tell her Peter was gone.

It was more than a quarter century until I learned Peter's fate. Sitting there on the back porch of the house in Highland, I heard it all from my older brother who, in turn, had had it from Gaunt. Oh yes, from Mr. Gaunt: our story, you see, was never that far from the truth. Indeed, it was closer, much closer, than I wish it were.

George left Scotland for an extended trip to Finland the first week in February. He would be away, he told Peter, for at least two weeks, and possibly a third if the manuscripts he was going to view were as extensive as he hoped. Peter wore an appropriately glum face at his father's departure, which pleased George, who had no idea of his son's secret ambition. For the first week after his father left, Peter maintained his daily routine. When at last the appointed date for his adventure arrived, though, he spent it in a state of almost unbearable anticipation, barely able to maintain conversation with any of his shopkeeper friends, inattentive to his tutors, uninterested in his meals. This last would not have escaped Mr. Gaunt's notice.

After spending the late afternoon and early evening roaming through the first three floors of the house, leafing through the library, practicing his shots at the pool table, spinning the antique globe in the living room, Peter declared he was going to make an early night of it, which also would have caught the butler's attention. From first-hand experience, I can tell you that Peter was something of a night owl, retiring to bed only when your grandmother insisted and called him by his full name, and even then reading under the sheets with a flashlight. Gaunt may have suspected your cousin's intentions; I daresay he must have. This would explain why, an hour and a half after Peter said he was turning in, when his bedroom door softly creaked open and Peter, still fully dressed, crept out and slowly climbed the narrow staircase to the attic landing, he found the door to the study standing wide open. It could also be that the butler had grown careless, but that strikes me as unlikely. Whatever Mr. Gaunt was, he was most attentive.

Your cousin stood there at the top of the stairs, gazing at the room that stretched out like a hall and was lit by globed lights dangling from the slanting ceiling. He saw the overstuffed bookcases. He saw the tables heaped high with assorted objects. He saw the paintings crowding the walls, the chalked symbols swarming over the floor. If there was sufficient time for him to study anything in detail, he may have noticed the small Bosch painting, *The Alchemical Wedding,* hanging across from him. It was—and still is—thought lost. It's the typical Bosch scene, crowded with all manner of people and creatures real and fantastic, most of them merrily dancing around the central figures, a man in red robes and a skeleton holding a rose being married by a figure combining features of a man and an eagle. The nearest table displayed a row of jars, each of them filled with pale, cloudy fluid in which floated a single, pink, misshapen fetus; approaching to examine them, he would have been startled to see the eyes of all the tiny forms open and stare at him. If any object caught his attention, it would have been the great stone sarcophagus leaning against the wall to his left, its carved face not the placid mask familiar to him from photos and drawings, but vivid and angry, its eyes glaring, its nostrils flaring, its mouth open wide and ringed with teeth. That would have chased any fear of discovery from his mind and brought him boldly into the study.

It could be, of course, that Peter's gaze, like the boy in our story's, was immediately captured by what was hanging on the antique coat-stand across from him.

At first, the boy thought it was a coat, for that is, after all, what you expect to find on a coat-stand. He assumed it must be Mr. Gaunt's coat, which the butler must have taken off and hung up when he entered the study. Why the butler should have been wearing a coat as long as this one, and with a hood and gloves attached, inside the house, the boy could not say. The more the boy studied it, however, the more he thought that it was a very strange coat indeed: for one thing, it was not so much that the coat was long as that there appeared to be a pair of pants attached to it, and, for another, its hood and gloves were unlike any he had seen before. Where the coat was black, the hood was a pale color that seemed familiar but that the boy could not immediately place. What was more, the hood seemed to be hairy, at least the back of it did, while the front contained a number of holes whose purpose the boy could not fathom. The gloves were of the same familiar color as the hood.

The boy stood gazing at the strange coat until he heard a noise coming from the other end of the study. He looked toward it, but saw nothing: just a tall skeleton dangling in front of another bookcase. He looked away and the noise repeated, a sound like a baby's rattle, only louder. The boy looked again and again saw nothing, only the bookcase and, in front of it, the skeleton. It took a moment for the boy to recognize that the skeleton was not dangling, but standing. As he watched, its bare, grinning skull turned toward him, and something in the tilt of its head, the crook of its spine, sent the boy's eyes darting back to the odd coat. Now, he saw that it was a coat, and pants, and hands, and a face: Mr. Gaunt's hands and face. Which must mean, he realized, that the skeleton at the other end of the room, which replaced the book it had been holding on top of the bookcase and stepped in his direction, was Mr. Gaunt. The boy stared at the skeleton slowly walking across the room, still far but drawing closer, its blank eyes fixed on him, and, with a scream, ran back down the stairs. Behind him, he heard the rattle of the skeleton's pursuit.

There in his father's study, your cousin Peter saw a human skeleton, Mr. Gaunt's skeleton—or the skeleton that was Gaunt—rush toward him from the other side of the room. The skeleton was tall, slightly stooped, and when it moved, its dull yellow bones clicked against each other like a chorus of baby rattles. Peter screamed, then bolted the room. He leapt down the attic stairs two and three at a time, pausing at the fourth floor landing long enough to throw closed the door to the stairs and grasp at the key that usually rested in its lock but now was gone, taken, he understood, by Mr. Gaunt. Peter ran down the long hallway

to the third floor stairs and half-leapt down them. He
didn't bother with the door at the third floor landing:
he could hear that chorus of rattles clattering down
the stairs, too close already. He raced through the
three rooms that lay between the third floor landing
and the stairway to the second floor, hearing Gaunt
at his back as he hurdled beds, chairs, couches;
ducked drapes; rounded corners. A glance over his
shoulder showed the skeleton running after him like
some great awkward bird, its head bobbing, its knees
raised high. He must have been terrified; there would
have been no way for him not to have been terrified.
Imagine your own response to such a thing. I
wouldn't have been able to run; I would have been
paralyzed, as much by amazement as by fear. As it
was, Gaunt almost had him when Peter tipped over
a globe in his path and the skeleton fell crashing behind him. With a final burst of speed, Peter descended
the last flight of stairs and made the front door, which
he heaved open and dashed through into the street.

Between Peter's house and the house to its left as
you stood looking out the front door was a close, an
alley. Peter rushed to and down it. It could be that
panic drove him, or that he meant to evade Gaunt by
taking a route he thought unknown to the butler. If
the latter was the case, the sound of bones rattling
across the cobblestones, a look back at the naked grin
and the arm grasping at him, would have revealed
his error instantly, with no way for him to double
back safely. I suspect the skeleton did something to
herd Peter to that alley, out of sight of any people
who might be on the street; I mean it worked a spell
of some kind. The alley sloped down, gradually at
first, then steeply, ending at the top of a series of
flights of stone stairs descending the steep hillside to

Market Street below. From Market Street, it's not that far to the train station, which may have been Peter's ultimate destination. His heart pounding, his breath rushing in and out, he sped down the hill, taking the stairs two, three, four at a time, his shoes snapping loudly on the stone, the skeleton close, swiping at him with a claw that tugged the collar of his sweater but failed to hold it.

Halfway down the stairs, not yet to safety but in sight of it, Peter's left foot caught his right foot, tripping and tumbling him down the remaining stairs to the landing below, where he smashed into the bars of an iron guardrail. Suddenly, there was no air in his lungs. As he lay sprawled on his back, trying to breathe, the skeleton was on him, descending like a hawk on a mouse. He cried out, covering his eyes. Seizing him by the sweater front, Gaunt hauled Peter to his feet. For a second that seemed to take years, that fleshless smile was inches from his face, as if it were subjecting him to the most intense scrutiny. He could smell it: an odor of thick dust, with something faintly rancid beneath it, that brought the bile to his throat. He heard a sound like the whisper of sand blowing across a stone floor, and realized it was the skeleton speaking, bringing speech from across what seemed a great distance. It spoke one word, "Yes," drawing it out into a long sigh that did not stop so much as fade away: *Yyyeeeeeessssssss*....Then it jerked its head away, and began pulling him back up the stairs, to the house and, he knew, the study. When, all at once, his lungs inflated and he could breathe again, Peter tried to scream. The skeleton slapped its free hand across his mouth, digging the sharp ends of its fingers and thumb into his cheeks, and Peter desisted. They reached the top of the stairs and made their way up the close. How no one could have noticed them, I can't say, though I suspect the skeleton had done something to insure their invisibility; yes, more magic. At the front door, Peter broke Gaunt's grip and attempted to run, but he had not taken two steps before he was caught by the hair, yanked off his feet, and his head was slammed against the pavement. His vision swimming, the back of his head a knot of agony, Peter was led into the house. His knee cracked on an end-table; his shoulder struck a doorframe. As he was dragged to the study, did he speak to the creature whose claw clenched his arm? A strange question, perhaps, but since first I heard this story myself I have wondered it. Your cousin had a short time left to live, which he may have suspected; even if he did not, he must have known that what awaited him in the study would not be pleasant, to say the least. Did he apologize for his intrusion? Did he try to reason with his captor, promise his secrecy? Or did he threaten it, invoke his father's wrath on his return? Was he quiet, stoic, or stunned? Was his mind buzzing with plans of last minute escape, or had it accepted that such plans were beyond him?

There are moments when the sheer unreality of an event proves overwhelming, when, all at once, the mind can't embrace the situation unfolding around it and refuses to do so, withholding its belief. Do you know what I mean? When your grandfather died, later that same afternoon I can remember feeling that his death was not yet permanent, that there was some means still available by which I could change it, and although I didn't know what that means was, I could feel it trembling on the tip of my brain. When your mother told me that she was leaving me for husband number two, that they already had booked a flight together for the Virgin Islands, even as I thought, Well it's about time: I wondered how long it would take this to arrive, I also was thinking, This is not happening: this is a joke: this is some kind of elaborate prank she's worked up, most likely with someone else, someone at the school, probably one of my colleagues; let's see, who loves practical jokes? While she explained the way my faults as a husband had led her to her decision, I was trying to analyze her sentence structure, word choice, to help me determine who in the department had helped her script her lines. A few years later, when she called to tell me about husband number three, I was much more receptive. All of which is to say that, if it was difficult for me to accommodate events that occur on a daily basis, how much more difficult would it have been for your cousin to accept being dragged to his father's study by a living skeleton?

Once they were in the study, Gaunt wasted no time, making straight for the great stone sarcophagus. Peter screamed with all the force he could muster, calling for help from anyone who could hear him, then wailing in pure animal terror. The skeleton made no effort to silence him. At the sarcophagus with its furious visage, Gaunt brought his stark face down to Peter's a second time, as if for a last look at him. He heard that faint whisper again, what sounded like the driest of chuckles. Then it reached out and slid the massive stone lid open with one spindly arm. The odor of decay, the ripe stench of a dead deer left at the side of the road for too many hot days, filled the room. Gagging, Peter saw that the interior of the sarcophagus was curiously rough, not with the roughness of, say, sandstone, but with a deliberate roughness, as if the stone had been painstakingly carved into row upon row of small sharp points, like teeth. The skeleton flung him into that smell, against those points. Before he could make a final, futile gesture of escape, the lid closed and Peter was in darkness, swathed in the thick smell of rot, his last sight the skeleton's idiot grin. Nor was that the worst. He had been in the stone box only a few seconds, though doubtless it seemed an eternity, when the stone against which he was leaning grew warm. As it warmed, it shifted, the way the hide of an animal awakening from a deep sleep twitches. Peter jerked away from the rough stone, his heart in his throat as movement rippled through the coffin's interior. If he could have been fortunate, his terror would have jolted him into unconsciousness, but I know this was not the case. If he was unlucky, as I know he was, he felt the sides of the sarcophagus abruptly swell toward him, felt the rows of sharp points press against him, lightly at first, then more insistently, then more insistently still, until—

I've mentioned the root of the word "sarcophagus;" it was Peter, ironically enough, who told it to me. It's Greek: it means "flesh eating." Exactly how that word came to be applied to large stone coffins I'm unsure, but in this case it was quite literally true. Peter was enclosed within a kind of mouth, a great stone mouth, and it...consumed him. The process was not quick. By the time George returned to the house almost a week and a half later, however, it was complete. Sometime in the long excruciation before that point, Peter must have realized that his father was implicated in what was happening to him. It was impossible for him not to be. His father had brought Mr. Gaunt into the house, and then left Peter at his mercy. His beloved father had failed, and his failure was Peter's death.

It took George longer than I would have expected, almost two full days, to discover Peter's fate, and to discern the butler's role in it. When he did so, he punished, as he put it, Mr. Gaunt suitably. He did not tell me what such punishment involved, but he did assure me that it was thorough. Peter's running away was, obviously, the ruse invented by George to hide his son's actual fate.

By the time your uncle told me the story I've told you, Clarissa had been dead for several years. I hadn't spoken to her since our phone conversation when Peter first vanished, and, I must confess, she had been absent from my thoughts for quite some time when I stumbled across her obituary on the opposite side of an article a friend in London had clipped and sent me. The obituary stated that she had never recovered from the disappearance of her only son almost two decades prior, and hinted, if I understood its implications, that she had been addicted to antidepressants; although the writer hastened to add that the cause of death had been ruled natural and was under no suspicion from the police.

If George heard the news of his former wife's death, which I assume he must have, he made no mention of it to me, not even during that last conversation, when so much else was said. Although I hadn't planned it, we both became quite intoxicated, making our way through the better part of a bottle of Lagavulin after I had put you to bed. The closer I approach to complete intoxication, the nearer I draw to maudlin sentimentality, and it wasn't long, as I sat beside my older brother looking across the Hudson to Poughkeepsie, the place where we had been born and raised and where our parents were buried, I say it wasn't long before I told George to stay where he was, I had something for him. Swaying like a sailor on a ship in a heavy sea, I made my way into the house and to my study, where I located the shoebox in which I keep those things that have some measure of sentimental value to me, pictures, mostly, but also the letters that your cousin had sent me, tucked in their envelopes. Returning to the porch, I walked over to George and held them out to him, saying, "Here, take them."

He did so, a look that was half-bemusement, half-curiosity on his face. "All right," he said. "What are they?"

"Letters," I declared.

"I can see that, old man," he said. "Letters from whom?"

"From Peter," I said. "From your son. You should have them. I want you to have them."

"Letters from Peter," he said.

"Yes," I said, nodding vigorously.

"I was unaware the two of you had maintained a correspondence."

"It was after the summer he came to stay with Mother. The two of us hit it off, you know, quite well."

"As a matter of fact," George said, "I didn't know." He continued to hold the letters out before him, as if he were weighing them. The look on his face had slid into something else.

Inspired by the Scotch, I found the nerve to ask George what I had wanted to ask him for so long: if he ever had received any word, any kind of hint, as to what had become of Peter? His already flushed face reddened more, as if he were embarrassed, caught off guard, then he laughed and said he knew exactly what had happened to his son. "Exactly," he repeated, letting the letters fall from his hand like so many pieces of paper.

Despite the alcohol in which I was swimming, I was shocked, which I'm sure my face must have shown. All at once, I wanted to tell George not to say anything more, because I had intuited that I was standing at the doorway to a room I did not wish to enter, for, once I stood within it, I would discover my older brother to be someone—something—I would be unable to bear sitting beside. We were not and had never been as close as popular sentiment tells us siblings should be; we were more friendly acquaintances. It was an acquaintance, however, I had increasingly enjoyed as I grew older, and I believe George's feelings may have been similar. But my tongue was thick and sluggish in my mouth, and so, as we sat on the back porch, George related the circumstances of his son's death to me. I listened to him as evening dimmed to night, making no move to switch on the outside lights, holding onto my empty glass as if it were a life-preserver. As his tale progressed, my first thought was that he was indulging in a bizarre joke whose tastelessness was appalling; the more he spoke, however, the more I understood that he believed what he was telling me, and I feared he might be delusional if not outright mad; by the story's conclusion, I was no longer sure he was mad, and worried that I might be. I was unsure when he stopped talking: his words continued to sound in my ears, overlapping each other. A long interval elapsed during which neither of us spoke and the sound of the crickets was thunderous. At last George said, "Well?"

"Gaunt," I said. "Who is he?" It was the first thing to leap to mind.

"Gaunt," he said. "Gaunt was my teacher. I met him when I went to Oxford; the circumstances are not important. He was my master. Once, I should have called him my father." I cannot tell you what the tone of his voice was. "We had a disagreement, which grew into an...altercation, which ended with him inside the stone sarcophagus that had Peter, though not for as long, of course. I released him while there was still enough left to be of service to me. I thought him defeated, no threat to either me or mine, and, I will admit, it amused me to keep him around. I had set what I judged sufficient safeguards against him in place, but he found a way to circumvent them, which I had not thought possible without a tongue. I was in error."

"Why Peter?" I asked.

"To strike at me, obviously. He had been planning something for quite a length of time. I had some idea of the depth of his hate for me, but I had no idea his determination ran to similar depths. His delight at what Peter had suffered was inestimable. He had written a rather extended description of it, which I believe he thought I would find distressing to read. The stone teeth relentlessly pressing every square inch of flesh, until the skin burst and blood poured out; the agony as the teeth continued through into the muscle, organ, and, eventually, bone; the horror at finding oneself still alive, unable to die even after so much pain: he related all of this with great gusto.

"The sarcophagus, in case you're interested, I found in eastern Turkey, not, as you might think, Egypt; though I suspect it has its origins there. I first read about it in *Les mystères du ver*, though the references were highly elliptical, to say the least. It took years, and a small fortune, to locate it. Actually, it's a rather amusing story: it was being employed as a table by a bookseller, if you can believe it, who had received it as payment for a debt owed him by a local banker, who in turn...."

I listened to George's account of the sarcophagus's history, all the while thinking of poor Peter trapped inside it, wrapped in claustrophobic darkness, screaming and pounding on the lid as—what? Although, as I have said, I half-believed the fantastic tale George had told, my belief was only partial. It seemed more likely Peter had suffocated inside the coffin, then Gaunt disposed of the body in such a way that very little, if any, of it remained. When George was done talking, I asked, "What about Peter?"

"What about him?" George answered. "Why, 'What about Peter'? I've already told you, it was too late for me to be able to do anything, even to provide him the kind of half-life Gaunt has, much less successfully restore him. What the sarcophagus takes, it does not surrender."

"He was your son," I said.

"Yes," George said. "And?"

"'And'? My God, man, he was your son, and whatever did happen to him, he's dead and you were responsible for his death, if not directly, then through negligence. Doesn't that mean anything to you?"

"No," George said, his voice growing brittle. "As I have said, Peter's death, while unfortunate, was unintentional."

"But," I went on, less and less able, it seemed, to match thought to word with any proficiency, "but he was your son."

"So?" George said. "Am I supposed to be wracked by guilt, afflicted with remorse?"

"Yes," I said, "yes, you are."

"I'm not, though. When all is said and done, Peter was more trouble than he was worth. A man in my position—and though you might not believe it, my position is considerable—doing my kind of work, can't always be worrying about someone else, especially a child. I should have foreseen that when I divorced Clarissa, and let her have him, but I was too concerned with her absolute defeat to make such a rational decision. Even after I knew the depth of my mistake, I balked at surrendering Peter to her because I knew the satisfaction such an admission on my part would give Clarissa. I simply could not bear that. For a time, I deluded myself that Peter would be my apprentice, despite numerous clear indications that he possessed no aptitude of any kind for my art. He was...temperamentally unsuited. It is a shame: there would have been a certain amount of pleasure in passing on my knowledge to my son, to someone of my own blood. That has always been my problem: too sentimental, too emotional. Nonetheless, while I would not have done anything to him myself, I am forced to admit that Peter's removal from my life has been to the good."

"You can't be serious," I said.

"I am."

"Then you're a monster."

"To you, perhaps," he said.

"You're mad," I said.

"No, I'm not," he said, and from the sharp tone of his voice, I could tell I had touched a nerve, so I repeated myself, adding, "Do you honestly believe you're some kind of great and powerful magician?

Or do you prefer to be called a sorcerer? Perhaps
you're a wizard? A warlock? An alchemist? No, they
worked with chemicals; I don't suppose that would
be you. Do you really expect me to accept that tall
butler as some kind of supernatural creature, an animated skeleton? I won't ask where you obtained his
face and hands: I'm sure Jenner's has a special section
for the black arts." I went on like this for several
minutes, pouring out my scorn on George, feeling the
anger radiating from him. I did not care: I was angry
myself, furious, filled with more rage than ever before
or ever after, for that matter.

When I was through, or when I had paused, anyway, George asked, "Could you fetch me a glass of
water?"

"Excuse me?" I said.

He repeated his request: "Could I have a glass of
water?" explaining, "All this conversation has left my
throat somewhat parched."

Your grandmother's emphasis on good manners,
no matter what the situation, caught me off guard,
and despite myself I heard my voice saying, "Of
course," as I set down my glass, stood, and made my
way across the unlit porch to the back door. "Can I
get you anything else?" I added, trying to sound as
scornful as I felt.

"The water will be fine."

I opened the back door, stepped into the house,
and was someplace else. Instead of the kitchen, I was
standing at one end of a long room lit by globed lights
depending from a slanted ceiling. Short bookcases
filled to bursting with books, scrolls, and an occasional stone tablet jostled with one another for space along
the walls, while tables piled high with goblets,
candles, boxes, rows of jars, models, took up the

floor. I saw paintings crowding the walls, including the Bosch I described to you, and elaborate symbols drawn on the floor. At the other end of the room, a bulky stone sarcophagus with a fierce face reclined against a wall. Behind me, through the open door whose handle I still grasped, I could hear the crickets; in front of me, through the room's curtained windows, I could hear the sound of distant traffic, of brakes squealing and horns blowing. I stood gazing at the room I understood to be my brother's study, and then I felt the hand on my shoulder. Initially, I thought it was George, but when he called, "Is my water coming?" I realized he had not left his seat. Through my shirt, the hand felt wrong: at once too light and too hard, more like wood than flesh. The faintest odor of dust, and beneath it, something foul, filled my nostrils; the sound of a baby's rattle being turned, slowly, filled my ears. I heard another sound, the whisper of sand blowing across a stone floor, and realized it was whatever was behind me—but I knew what it was—speaking, bringing speech from across what seemed a great distance. It spoke one word, "Yes," drawing it out into a long sigh that did not stop so much as fade away: *Yyyeeeeeessssssss....*

"I say," George said, "where's my water?"

Inhaling deeply—the hand tightening on my shoulder as I did—I said, "Tell him—tell it to remove its hand from me."

"Him? It? Whatever are you referring to?"

"Gaunt," I answered. "Tell Gaunt to release my shoulder."

"Gaunt?" George cried, his voice alive with malicious amusement, "Why, Gaunt's on the other side of the ocean."

"This is not entertaining," I said, willing myself to remain where I was.

"You're right," George said. "In fact, it's deeply worrying. Are you certain you're feeling all right? Did you have too much to drink? Or are you, perhaps, not in your right mind? Are you mad, dear brother?"

"Not in the least," I replied. "Nor, it would seem, are you."

"Ahh," George said. "Are you certain?"

"Yes," I said, "I am sure." I might have added, "To my profound regret," but I had no wish to antagonize him any further.

"In that case," George said, and the hand left my shoulder. I heard rattling, as if someone were walking away from me across the porch in tapshoes, followed by silence. "Now that I think on it," George said, "I needn't bother you for that glass of water, after all. Why don't you rejoin me?"

I did as he instructed, closing the door tightly. I walked to George and said, in a voice whose shaking I could not master, "It is time for you to go."

After a pause, George said, "Yes, I suppose it is, isn't it?"

"I will not be asking you back," I said.

"No, I don't suppose you will. I could just appear, you know."

"You will not," I said, vehemently. "You will never come here again. I forbid you."

"You forbid me?"

"Yes, I do."

"I find that most entertaining, as you say. However, I shall respect your wishes, lest it be said I lack fraternal affection. It's a pity: that time you came to visit me after Peter's death, I thought you might be my apprentice, and the notion has never vanished from my mind. It generally surfaces when I'm feeling mawkish. I suppose there's no chance—"

"None," I said, "now or ever." You have Satan's nerve, I thought.

"Yes, of course," George said. "I knew what your reply would be: I merely had to hear you say it. When all is said and done, I don't suppose you have the necessary...temperament either. No matter: there are others, one of them closer than you think."

That was his final remark. George had brought no luggage with him: he stepped off the porch into the night and was gone. I stood staring out into the darkness, listening for I am not sure what, that rattling, perhaps, before rushing to the kitchen door. Gripping the doorknob, I uttered a brief, barely coherent prayer, then opened the door. The kitchen confronted me with its rows of hanging pots and pans, its magnetic knife rack, its sink full of dishes awaiting washing. I raced through it, up the stairs to your room, where I found you asleep, one arm around Mr. James, your bear, the other thrown across your face as if you were seeking to hide your eyes from something. My legs went weak, and I seated myself on your bed, a flood of hot tears rolling down my face. I sat up in your room for the rest of that night, and for a week or so after I slept in it with you. The following morning, I returned to the back porch to retrieve your cousin's letters, which I replaced in the shoebox.

I have not heard from George since, all these years.

When I sat you on your bed after having found you surrounded by the shreds of my work, this was what shaped itself into my cautionary tale. It had been festering in my brain ever since George had told me it. Carrying George's words with me had left me feeling tainted, as if having heard of Peter's end had made me complicit in it in a manner beyond my ability to articulate. In giving that story voice, I sought to exorcise it from me. I recognize the irony of my situation: rather than expunging the story, telling it once led to it being told over and over again, until it had achieved almost the status of ritual. Your subsequent delight in the story did mitigate my guilt somewhat, tempting me to remark that a story's reception may redeem its inception; that, however, would be just a bit too much, too absolutely over the top, as James would put it. I remain incredulous at myself for having told you even the highly edited version you heard. It occurs to me that, if it is a wonder our children survive the mistakes we make with them, it is no less astounding that we are not done in by them ourselves; those of us with any conscience, I should add.

Something else: how much you remember of the literature classes you sat through in college I don't know; I realize you took them to please me. I'm sure, however, that enough of the lectures you actually attended has remained with you for you to be capable of at least a rudimentary analysis of our story. In such an analysis, you would treat the figure of the skeleton as a symbol. I can imagine, for example, a psychoanalytic interpretation such as are so often applied to fairy tales. It would judge our particular story to be a cleverly disguised if overly Oedipal allegory in which the locked room would be equated with the secret of sexuality, jealously guarded by the father against the son, and the butler/skeleton with the father's double, an image of death there to punish the boy for his transgression. If you preferred to steer closer to history, you might postulate the skeleton as a representation of an event: say, Mr. Gaunt and your uncle caught in an embrace, another kind of forbidden knowledge. Neither these nor any other interpretations are correct: the skeleton is not a substitution for something else but in fact real; I must insist, even if in doing so I seem to depart plausibility for fantasy, if not dementia. It could be that I protest too much, that you aren't the rigid realist I'm construing you to be. Perhaps you know how easy it is to find yourself on the other side of the looking glass.

No doubt, you'll wonder why I've waited until now to disclose this information to you, when you've been old enough to have heard it for years. I'd like to attribute my reticence solely to concern for you, to worry that, listening to this outrageous tale, you would lose no time setting out to verify it, which might result in your actually making contact with your uncle, and then God only knows what else. I am anxious for you, but, to be honest, more of my hesitation than I want to admit arises from dread at appearing ridiculous in your eyes, of seeing your face fill with pity at the thought that the old man has plunged over the edge at last. I suppose that's why I'm recording this, when I know it would be easy enough to pick up the phone and give you a call.

I can't believe I could be of any interest to George at this late date (so I tell myself), but I'm less sure about you. Sitting up in my bed last night, not watching the remainder of the documentary, I heard your uncle tell me that there were others to serve as his apprentice, one of them closer than I thought. These words ringing in my ears, I thought of that Ouija board you used to play with in college, the tarot card program you bought for your computer. I understand the Ouija board was because of that girl you were seeing, and I know the computer program is just for fun, but either might be sufficient for

George. Your uncle is old, and if he hasn't yet found
an apprentice—

However belated, this, then, all of this tangled
testament, is my warning to you about your uncle, as
well as a remembrance of a kind of your cousin,
whom you never knew. If you believe me—and you
must, Henry, you must—you'll take heed of my
warning. If you don't believe me, and I suppose that
is a possibility, at least I may have entertained you
one last time. All that remains now is for me to tell
you I love you, son, I love you and please, please,
please be careful, Henry: be careful.

III

With a snap, the stereo reached the end of the tape.
Henry Farange released a breath he hadn't been aware
he was holding and slumped back on the couch. His
beer and the pleasant lassitude it had brought were
long gone; briefly, he contemplated going to the refrigerator for another bottle, and possibly the rest of the
six-pack while he was at it. Heaving himself to his
feet and shaking his head, he murmured, "God."

To say he didn't know what to think was the proverbial understatement. As his father had feared, his
initial impression was that the old man had lost it
there at the end, that he had, in his own words,
suffered one mini-stroke too many. But—what? What
else was there to say? That he had felt some measure
of truth in his father's words? That—mad, yes, as it
sounded—a deeper part of him, a much deeper part,
a half-fossilized fragment buried far beneath his reflexive disbelief, accepted what the old man had been
telling him?

Well, actually, that was it exactly, thank you for

asking. Laughable as it seemed; and he did laugh, a humorless bark; Henry couldn't bring himself to discount completely his father's words. There had been something—no single detail; rather, a quality in the old man's voice—that had affected him, had unearthed that half-ossified part of him, had insinuated itself into his listening until, in the end, he found himself believing there was more to this tape than simple dementia. When Henry had been a child, his father had possessed the unfailing ability to tell when he was lying, or so it seemed; even when there was no obvious evidence of his dishonesty, somehow, the old man had known. Asked the source of this mysterious and frustrating power, his father had shrugged and said, "It's in your voice," as if this were the most obvious of explanations. Now, hearing those words echoing in his mind, Henry thought, It's in his voice.

But—a living skeleton? An uncle who was a black magician? A cousin he'd never heard of devoured by a coffin made of living stone? He shook his head again, sighing: there was some truth here, but it was cloaked in metaphor. It had to be. He walked over to the stereo, popped open the tape deck, slid out the tape, and stood with it in his hand, feeling it still warm. His father's voice….Although the old man had quoted their story's beginning and middle, he had not recited its end. The words rose unbidden to Henry's lips: *"Slowly, the skeleton carried the screaming boy up the stairs to his father's study. It walked through the open doorway, closing the door behind it with a solid click. For a long time, that door stayed closed. When at last it opened again, Mr. Gaunt, looking more pleased with himself than anyone in that house ever had seen him, stepped out and made his way down the stairs, rubbing his hands together briskly. As for the boy who had opened the door he was forbidden to open: he was never seen again. What happened to him, I cannot say, but I can assure you, it was terrible."*

The phone rang, and he jumped, fumbling the tape onto the floor. Hadn't he switched that off? Leaving the cassette where it lay, he ran into the kitchen, catching the phone on the third ring and calling, "Hello."

His Uncle George said, "Hello, Henry."

"Uncle George!" he answered, a smile breaking over his face.

"How is everything?" his uncle asked.

"Fine, fine," he said. "I was just getting ready to call you."

"Uh oh."

"Yeah, it looks like I'm going to be a few minutes late to dinner."

"Can you still make it? Should we wait for another night?"

"No, no," Henry said, "there's no need to reschedule. I was just listening to something, a tape; I got kind of caught up in it, lost track of time."

"Music?"

"No, something my father left me. Actually, I was kind of hoping we could talk about it."

"Of course. What is it?"

"I'd rather wait until we see each other, if that's all right with you. Listen: can you call the restaurant, tell them we're running about fifteen minutes late?"

"Certainly. Will that be enough time for you?"

"I can be very fast when I need to be; you'd be amazed. Do you have their number?"

"I believe so. If not, I can look it up."

"Great, great. Okay. Let me run and get ready, and I'll see you shortly."

"Excellent. I'm looking forward to this, Henry. I haven't seen you in—well, to tell you the truth, I can't remember how long, which means it's been too long."

"Hear hear," he said. "I'm looking forward to it too. There's a lot I want to ask you."

"I'm glad to hear it, son: there's much I have to tell you."

"I'm sure you do. I can't wait to hear it."

"Well, this should be a fine, if melancholic, occasion. A Farange family reunion: there haven't been too many of those, I can assure you. What a pity your poor father can't join us. Oh, and Henry? One more thing?"

"What is it?"

"Would it be too much trouble if my butler joined us for dinner?" As Henry's stomach squeezed, his uncle went on, "I'm embarrassed to ask, but I'm afraid I am getting on in years a bit, and I find I can't do much without his help these days. The joys of aging! He's a very quiet chap, though: won't say two words all evening. I hate to impose when we haven't seen each other…."

His mouth dry, Henry stuttered, "Your butler?"

"Yes," his uncle said. "Butler, manservant: 'personal assistant,' I suppose you would call him. If it's going to be an intrusion—"

Recovering himself, Henry swallowed and said, "Nonsense, it's no trouble at all. I'll be happy to have him there."

"Splendid. To tell the truth, he doesn't get out much anymore: he'll be most pleased."

"I'll see you there."

Henry replaced the phone in its cradle, and hurried

to the shower. As he stood with the hot water streaming down on him, his uncle's voice in one ear, his father's voice in the other, he had a vision, both sudden and intense. He saw a boy, dressed in brown slacks and a brown sweater a half-size too big for him, standing at a landing at the top of a flight of stairs. In front of him was a great oaken door, open the slightest hairsbreadth. The boy stood looking at the door, at the wedge of yellow light spilling out from whatever lay on the other side of it. The light was the color of old bones, and it seemed to form an arrow, pointing the boy forward.

—For Fiona

About the Authors

Ron Wolfe is a feature writer and cartoonist for the *Arkansas Democrat-Gazette* newspaper in Little Rock. He is the co-author (with John Wooley) of the novels *Old Fears* and *Death's Door*. Wolfe is from North Platte, Nebraska, Buffalo Bill Cody's hometown. "My grandmother once saw Buffalo Bill ride a white horse into a saloon," he says. "I wished I could have seen him, too, and through her eyes, I did. I think that's when I realized what storytelling is all about."

Chris Willrich's family's from western Washington State, and the landscape there slips into a lot of his fiction—including the rain. His work has appeared in *Isaac Asimov's Science Fiction Magazine*, *The Mythic Circle*, and *The Magazine of Fantasy & Science Fiction* (where this story and its predecessor, "The Thief With Two Deaths," first appeared). These days he lives with my wife in sunny Silicon Valley, works at a university library, and generally leads a safer life than any of his characters.

Ursula K. Le Guin's intellectually provocative fiction has earned her accolades in general literary circles as well as the fields of fantasy and science fiction. The novels of her Earthsea saga, which includes *A Wizard of Earthsea*, *The Tombs of Atuan*, *The Farthest Shore*, *Tehanu: The Last Book of Earthsea*, and *Tales from Earthsea*, break the boundaries between adult and young adult fiction, and comprise a coming-of-age story featuring Ged, an apprentice magician who grows to maturity and faces many challenges as both man and mage over the course of the saga. Le Guin has been praised for her understanding the importance of rituals and myths that shape individuals and societies, and for the meticulous detail with which she brings her alien cultures to life. She has written other novels including *The Lathe of Heaven*, *The Dispossessed*, *Malafrena*, and *Always Coming Home*. Her short fiction has been collected in *The Wind's Twelve Quarters*, *Orsinian Tales*, *Buffalo Gals Won't You Come Out Tonight*, and *Four Ways to Forgiveness*. Le Guin has also written many celebrated essays on the craft of fantasy and science fiction, some of which have been gathered in *The Language of the Night* and *Dancing at the Edge of the World*.

Robert Sheckley is a writer who is constantly pursuing the unknown in his writing, making his reader rethink the most ordinary situations. He has written almost 20 novels, and has collaborated with such authors as Harry Harrison and the late Roger Zelazny. He was the fiction editor of *Omni* magazine from 1980 to 1982, and has also written many television and radio plays. A winner of the Jupiter award, he lives in Oregon.

Jeffrey Ford is the author of a fantasy trilogy comprised of *The Physiognomy* (winner of the 1998 World Fantasy Award for best novel), *Memoranda*, and *The Beyond* (all from Eos/Harper Collins). His most recent books are *The Portrait of Mrs. Charbuque* (Morrow/Harper Collins, 2002) and the story collection, *The Fantasy Writer's Assistant* (Golden Gryphon, 2002).

Ford's short fiction has appeared in The *Magazine of Fantasy & Science Fiction*, *SciFiction*, *Black Gate*, *Lady Churchill's*, *Leviathan #3*, *The Green Man Anthology*, and *Year's Best Fantasy and Horror*, vols. 13 and 15. His stories have also been nominated for the Nebula and the World Fantasy Award.

Brian Stableford is a lecturer in Creative Writing at King Alfred's College, Winchester, where he teaches on an MA in "Writing for Children." The sixth and final volume of his future history series from Tor, *The Omega Expedition*, was published in December 2002. Novels scheduled for U.S. publication in 2003 are *Kiss the Goat: A Twenty-First Century Ghost Story* (Prime Press) and *Year Zero*.

David Prill has written novels, short stories, political humor, bowling columns and horoscopes. His other published novels are *Serial Killer Days* and *Second Coming Attractions*. His latest book, *Dating Secrets of the Dead*, is a collection of short fiction including a 20,000-word novella, "The Last Horror Show." It will soon be released in a limited edition from Subterranean Press. He lives in Dakota County, Minnesota.

James Patrick Kelly has had an eclectic writing career. He has written novels, short stories, essays, reviews, poetry, plays and planetarium shows. His books include *Strange But Not a Stranger*, *Think Like a Dinosaur and Other Stories*, *Wildlife*, and *Look into the Sun*. His fiction has been translated into fourteen languages. He has won the World Science Fiction Society's Hugo Award twice: in 1996, for his novelette "Think Like a Dinosaur" and in 2000, for his novelette, "Ten to the Sixteenth to One." He writes a column on the Internet for *Isaac Asimov's Science Fiction Magazine*, and his audio plays are a regular feature on Scifi.com's Seeing Ear Theater. He is currently one of fourteen councilors appointed to the New Hampshire State Council on the Arts. He bats right, thinks left and has too many hobbies.

Robert Reed is the author of nearly a dozen novels, including *Marrow* and the soon to be released *Sister Alice*, both published by Tor Books. He has also sold to most of the major magazines, including *Isaac Asimov's Science Fiction Magazine* and *The Magazine of Fantasy & Science Fiction*. A tiny portion of his short fiction has been collected in *The Dragons of Springplace*, published by Golden Gryphon Press. Reed lives in Lincoln, Nebraska, with his wife and daughter.

Paul Di Filippo is the author of hundreds of short stories, some of which have been collected in five widely-praised collections: *The Steampunk Trilogy*, *Ribofunk*, *Fractal Paisleys*, and *Lost Pages*—all from Four Wall Eight Windows—and *Strange Trades*, published by Golden Gryphon Press. Another collection, *Destroy All Brains*, was published by another small press, Pirate Writings, but is quite rare because of the extremely short print run (if you see one—buy it!). His long-awaited first novel, *Ciphers*, was published at the end of the 20th century, followed by his second novel, *Joe's Liver*, in February 2000, with a third, titled *Spondulix* on the way. Paul lives in Providence, Rhode Island.

John Langan is a Ph.D. candidate in English at the

CUNY Graduate Center. He is also an adjunct instructor at SUNY New Paltz. He lives with his wife in upstate New York.